Favorite Short Stories in Large Print

Also Available in Large Print

Favorite Poems in Large Print

Favorite Short Stories in Large Print

Edited by Virginia S. Reiser

G.K.HALL & CO.
Boston, Massachusetts
1982

Library of Congress Cataloging in Publication Data

Main entry under title:

Favorite short stories in large print.

Includes index.
1. Short stories, American. 2. Short stories, English. 3. Large type books. I. Reiser, Virginia S.
[PS648.S5F38 1982] 813'.01'08 82–18520
ISBN 0–8161–3434–0 (lg. print)

Set in 16 pt Times Roman

Acknowledgments

The editor gratefully acknowledges permission to reproduce copyright short stories in this book.

''Silent Snow, Secret Snow,'' Conrad Aiken, copyright 1932 by Conrad Aiken. Copyright renewed 1960 by Conrad Aiken. Reprinted by permission of Brandt & Brandt Literary Agents, Inc.

''The Devil and Daniel Webster,'' Stephen Vincent Benét, from *The Selected Works of Stephen Vincent Benét*. Copyright, 1936, by The Curtis Publishing Company. Copyright renewed 1964 by Thomas C. Benét, Stephanie B. Mahin, and Rachel B. Lewis. Reprinted by permission of Brandt & Brandt Literary Agents, Inc.

''A Rose for Emily,'' William Faulkner, copyright 1930 and renewed 1958 by William Faulkner. Reprinted from *Collected Stories of William Faulkner,* by permission of Random House, Inc.

''Winter Dreams,'' F. Scott Fitzgerald, (copyright 1922, Charles Scribner's Sons; copyright renewed) in *The Stories of F. Scott Fitzgerald,* selected by Malcolm Cowley. Copyright 1951 Charles Scribner's Sons; copyright renewed. Reprinted with the permission of Charles Scribner's Sons.

''The Killers,'' Ernest Hemingway, in *Men Without Women*. Copyright 1927, Charles Scribner's Sons; copyright renewed 1955 Ernest Hemingway. Reprinted with the permission of Charles Scribner's Sons.

''The Gift of the Magi,'' O. Henry, from *The Complete Works of O. Henry* by O. Henry. Reprinted by permission of Doubleday & Company, Inc.

''The Lottery,'' Shirley Jackson, reprinted by permission of Farrar, Straus and Giroux, Inc. ''The Lottery'' from *The Lottery* by Shirley Jackson. Copyright renewed 1976, 1977 by Laurence Hyman, Barry Hyman, Mrs. Sarah Webster, and Mrs. Joanne Schnurer. ''The Lottery'' originally appeared in *The New Yorker*.

“The Monkey’s Paw,” W. W. Jacobs, reprinted by permission of The Society of Authors as the literary representative of the Estate of W. W. Jacobs.

“The Man Who Would Be King,” Rudyard Kipling, from *Rudyard Kipling’s Verse: Definitive Edition*. Reprinted by permission of The National Trust and Doubleday & Company, Inc. Reprinted in Canada by permission of The National Trust and Macmillan London Limited.

“Haircut,” Ring Lardner, (copyright 1925 Ellis A. Lardner; copyright renewed) in *The Best Stories of Ring Lardner*. Copyright 1957 Charles Scribner’s Sons. Reprinted with the permission of Charles Scribner’s Sons.

“The Horse-Dealer’s Daughter,” D. H. Lawrence, from *The Complete Short Stories of D. H. Lawrence*. Copyright 1922 by Thomas Seltzer, Inc. Copyright renewed 1950 by Frieda Lawrence. Reprinted by permission of Viking Penguin Inc. Reprinted in Canada and the British Commonwealth by permission of Laurence Pollinger Ltd and The Estate of Frieda Lawrence Ravagli. Copyright 1974 by The Estate of Frieda Lawrence Ravagli from *The Collected Short Stories of D. H. Lawrence* by D. H. Lawrence published by William Heinemann Ltd.

“Life of Ma Parker,” Katherine Mansfield, copyright 1922 and renewed 1950 by John Middleton Murry. Reprinted from *The Short Stories of Katherine Mansfield,* by permission of Alfred A. Knopf, Inc.

“The Jilting of Granny Weatherall,” Katherine Anne Porter, copyright 1930, 1958 by Katherine Anne Porter. Reprinted from her volume *Flowering Judas and Other Stories,* by permission of Harcourt Brace Jovanovich, Inc.

“The Open Window” and “Tobermory,” Saki, from *The Complete Short Stories of Saki* (H. H. Munro). Copyright 1930 by The Viking Press, Inc. Copyright renewed 1958 by The Viking Press, Inc. Reprinted by permission of Viking Penguin Inc.

“The Secret Life of Walter Mitty,” James Thurber, copyright 1942 James Thurber. Copyright 1970 Helen Thurber. From *My World—and Welcome To It,* published by Harcourt Brace Jovanovich, Inc. Reprinted by permission of Helen Thurber.

“The Celebrated Jumping Frog of Calaveras County,” Mark Twain, from “The Jumping Frog” in *Sketches, New and Old* by Mark Twain, Harper & Row, Publishers, Inc. Reprinted by permission.

“Blackberry Winter,” Robert Penn Warren, from *The Circus in the Attic and Other Stories,* copyright 1947 by Robert Penn Warren. Reprinted by permission of Harcourt Brace Jovanovich, Inc.

For V.C.R.

Contents

A Note from the Editor

Compiling a collection of short stories in one volume is a formidable task. Which to include? Which to set aside in the hope of another collection in the future? In choosing the 29 stories in this anthology, I've tried to make a representative selection of stories past and present — stories with a moral and stories with a twist; tales of fun and tales of fear; stories to be shared and read aloud and stories to be contemplated. I hope the collection will bring back to the Large Print user the pleasure of rereading some of our most popular and remembered short stories.

No editor works alone and without the help of Prudence Schofield, Eliza Lewis, Pinky Chin, Amy Kessler, Cindy Schrom and Lynn Harmet, this anthology would not have been possible. My deepest thanks to each of you.

Virginia Reiser
Boston, Mass.

The Legend of Sleepy Hollow

Washington Irving

A pleasing land of drowsy head it was,
Of dreams that wave before the half-
shut eye;
And of gay castles in the clouds that
pass,
For ever flushing round a summer sky
CASTLE OF INDOLENCE

IN the bosom of one of the spacious coves which indent the eastern shore of the Hudson, at that broad expansion of the river denominated by the ancient Dutch navigators the Tappan Zee, and where they always prudently shortened sail, and implored the protection of St. Nicholas when they crossed, there lies a small market-town or rural port, which by some is called Greensburgh, but which is more generally and properly known by the name of Tarry Town. This name was given, we are told, in former days, by the good housewives of the adjacent country, from the inveterate propensity of their husbands to linger about the village tavern on market days. Be that as it may, I do not vouch for the fact, but merely advert to it, for the sake of being precise and authentic. Not far from this village, perhaps about two miles, there is a little valley, or rather lap of land, among high hills, which is one of the quietest places in the whole world. A small brook glides through it, with just murmur enough to lull one to repose; and the occasional whistle of a quail or tapping of a woodpecker, is almost the only sound that ever breaks in upon the uniform tranquillity.

I recollect that, when a stripling, my first exploit in squirrel-shooting was in a grove of tall walnut-trees that shades one side of the valley. I had wandered into it at noon time, when all nature is peculiarly quiet, and was startled by the roar of my own gun, as it broke the Sabbath stillness around, and was prolonged and reverberated by the angry echoes. If ever I should wish for a retreat, whither I might steal from the world and its distractions, and dream quietly away the remnant of a troubled life, I know of none more promising than this little valley.

From the listless repose of the place, and the peculiar character of its inhabitants, who are descendants from the original Dutch settlers, this sequestered glen has long been known by the name of SLEEPY HOLLOW, and its rustic lads are called the Sleepy Hollow Boys throughout all the neighboring country. A drowsy dreamy influence seems to hang over the land, and to pervade the very atmosphere. Some say that the place was bewitched by a high German doctor, during the early days of the settlement; others, that an old Indian chief, the prophet or wizard of his tribe, held his powwows there before the country was discovered by Master Hendrick Hudson. Certain it is, the place still continues under the sway of some witching power, that holds a spell over the minds of the good people, causing them to walk in a continual reverie. They are given to all kinds of marvelous beliefs; are subject to trances and visions; and frequently see strange sights, and hear music and voices in the air. The whole neighborhood abounds with local tales, haunted spots, and twilight superstitions; stars shoot and meteors glare oftener across the valley than in any other part of the country, and the nightmare, with her whole nine fold, seems to make it the favorite scene of her gambols.

The dominant spirit, however, that haunts this enchanted region, and seems to be commander-in-chief of all the powers of the air, is the apparition of a figure on horseback without a head. It is said by some to be the ghost of a Hessian trooper, whose head had been carried away by a cannon-ball, in some nameless battle during the Revolutionary War; and who is ever and anon seen by the country folk, hurrying along in the gloom of night, as if on the wings of the wind. His haunts are not confined to the valley, but extend at times to the adjacent roads, and especially to the vicinity of a church at no great distance. Indeed, certain of the most authentic historians of those parts, who have been careful in collecting and collating the floating facts concerning this specter, allege that the body of the trooper, having been buried in the churchyard, the ghost rides forth to the scene of battle in nightly quest of his head; and that the rushing speed with which he sometimes passes along the Hollow, like a midnight blast, is owing to his being belated, and in a hurry to get back to the churchyard before daybreak.

Such is the general purport of this legendary superstition, which has furnished materials for many a wild story in that region of shadows; and the specter is known at all the country firesides by the name of the Headless Horseman of Sleepy Hollow.

It is remarkable that the visionary propensity I have mentioned is not confined to the native inhabitants of the valley, but is unconsciously imbibed by everyone who resides there for a time. However wide awake they may have been before they entered that sleepy region, they are sure, in a little time, to inhale the witching influence of the air, and begin to grow imaginative — to dream dreams, and see apparitions.

I mention this peaceful spot with all possible laud; for it is in such little retired Dutch valleys, found here and there embosomed in the great state of New York, that population, manners, and customs remain fixed; while the great torrent of migration and improvement, which is making such incessant changes in other parts of this restless country, sweeps by them unobserved. They are like those little nooks of still water which border a rapid stream; where we may see the straw and bubble riding quietly at anchor, or slowly revolving in their mimic harbor, undisturbed by the rush of the passing current. Though many years have elapsed since I trod the drowsy shades of Sleepy Hollow, yet I question whether I should not still find the same trees and the same families vegetating in its sheltered bosom.

In this by-place of nature there abode, in a remote period of American history, that is to say, some thirty years since, a worthy wight of the name of Ichabod Crane; who sojourned, or, as he expressed it, "tarried," in Sleepy Hollow, for the purpose of instructing the children of the vicinity. He was a native of Connecticut; a state which supplies the Union with pioneers for the mind as well as for the forest, and sends forth yearly its legions of frontier woodmen and country schoolmasters. The cognomen of Crane was not inapplicable to his person. He was tall, but exceedingly lank, with narrow shoulders, long arms and legs, hands that dangled a mile out of his sleeves, feet that might have served for shovels, and his whole frame most loosely hung together. His head was small, and flat at top, with huge ears, large green glassy eyes, and a long snipe nose, so that it looked like a weather-cock, perched upon his spindle neck, to tell which way the wind blew. To see him striding along the profile of a hill on a windy day, with his clothes bagging and fluttering about him, one might have mistaken him for the genius of famine descending upon the earth, or some scarecrow eloped from a corn-field.

His school-house was a low building of one large room, rudely constructed of logs; the windows partly glazed, and partly patched with leaves of old copy-books. It was most ingeniously secured at vacant hours, by a withe twisted in the handle of the door, and stakes set against the window-shutters; so that, though a thief might get in with perfect ease, he would find some embarrassment in getting out; an idea most probably borrowed by the architect, Yost Van Houten, from the mystery of an eel-pot. The school-house stood in a rather lonely but pleasant situation, just at the foot of a woody hill, with a brook running close by, and a formidable birch-tree growing at one end of it. From hence the low murmur of his pupils' voices, conning over their lessons, might be heard in a drowsy summer's day, like the hum of a bee-hive; interrupted now and then by the authoritative voice of the master, in the tone of menace or command;

or, peradventure, by the appalling sound of the birch, as he urged some tardy loiterer along the flowery path of knowledge. Truth to say, he was a conscientious man, and ever bore in mind the golden maxim, "Spare the rod and spoil the child." Ichabod Crane's scholars certainly were not spoiled.

I would not have it imagined, however, that he was one of those cruel potentates of the school, who joy in the smart of their subjects; on the contrary, he administered justice with discrimination rather than severity; taking the burthen off the backs of the weak, and laying it on those of the strong. Your mere puny stripling, that winced at the least flourish of the rod, was passed by with indulgence; but the claims of justice were satisfied by inflicting a double portion on some little tough, wrong-headed, broad-skirted Dutch urchin, who sulked and swelled and grew dogged and sullen beneath the birch. All this he called "doing his duty by their parents"; and he never inflicted a chastisement without following it by the assurance, so consolatory to the smarting urchin, that "he would remember it and thank him for it the longest day he had to live."

When school-hours were over, he was even the companion and playmate of the larger boys; and on holiday afternoons would convoy some of the smaller ones home, who happened to have pretty sisters, or good housewives for mothers, noted for the comforts of the cupboard. Indeed, it behoved him to keep on good terms with his pupils. The revenue arising from his school was small, and would have been scarcely sufficient to furnish him with daily bread, for he was a huge feeder, and though lank, had the dilating powers of an anaconda; but to help out his maintenance, he was, according to country custom in those parts, boarded and lodged at the houses of the farmers, whose children he instructed. With these he lived successively a week at a time; thus going the rounds of the neighborhood, with all his worldly effects tied up in a cotton handkerchief.

That all this might not be too onerous on the purses of his rustic patrons, who are apt to consider the costs of schooling a grievous burden, and schoolmasters as mere drones, he had various ways of rendering himself both useful and agreeable. He assisted the farmers occasionally in the lighter labors of their farms; helped to make hay; mended the fences; took the horses to water; drove the cows from pasture; and cut wood for the winter fire. He laid aside, too, all the dominant dignity and absolute sway with which he lorded it in his little empire, the school, and became wonderfully gentle and ingratiating. He found favor in the eyes of the mothers by petting the children, particularly the youngest; and like the lion bold, which whilom so magnanimously the lamb did hold, he would sit with a child on one knee, and rock a cradle with his foot for whole hours together.

In addition to his other vocations, he was the singing-master of the neighborhood, and picked up many bright shillings by instructing the young folks in psalmody. It was a matter of no little vanity to him, on Sundays to take his station in front of the church gallery, with a band of chosen singers; where, in his own mind, he completely carried away the palm from the parson. Certain it is, his voice resounded far above all the rest of the congregation; and there are peculiar quavers still to be heard in that church, and which may even be heard half a mile off, quite to the opposite side of the mill-pond, on a still Sunday morning, which are said to be legitimately descended from the nose of Ichabod Crane. Thus, by divers little make-shifts, in that ingenious way which is commonly denominated "by hook and by crook," the worthy pedagogue got on tolerably enough, and was thought, by all who understand nothing of the labor of head-work, to have a wonderfully easy life of it.

The schoolmaster is generally a man of some importance in the female circle of a rural neighborhood; being considered a kind of idle gentleman-like personage, of vastly superior taste and accomplishments to the rough country swains, and, indeed, inferior in learning only to the parson. His appearance, therefore, is apt to occasion some little stir at the tea-table of a farm-house and the addition of a supernumerary dish of cakes or sweetmeats, or peradventure the parade of of a silver teapot. Our man of letters, therefore, was peculiarly happy in the smiles of all the country damsels. How he would figure among them in the churchyard between services on Sundays! gathering grapes for them from the wild vines that overran the surrounding trees; reciting for their amusement all the epitaphs on the tomb-stones; or sauntering with a whole bevy of them along the banks of the adjacent mill-pond; while the more bashful country bump-kins hung sheepishly back, envying his superior elegance and address.

From his half-itinerant life, also, he was a kind of traveling gazette, carrying the whole budget of local gossip from house to house; so that his appearance was always greeted with satisfaction. He was, moreover, esteemed by the women as a man of great erudition, for he had read several books quite through, and was a perfect master of Cotten Mather's *History of New England Witchcraft,* in which, by the way, he most firmly and potently believed.

He was, in fact, an odd mixture of small shrewdness and simple credulity. His appetite for the marvelous, and his powers of digesting it, were equally extraordinary; and both had been increased by his residence in this spell-bound region. No tale was too gross or monstrous for his capacious swallow. It was often his delight, after his school was dismissed in the afternoon, to stretch himself on the rich bed of clover, bordering the little brook that whimpered by his school-house, and there con over old Mather's direful tales, until the gathering dusk of the evening made the printed page a mere mist before his eyes. Then, as he wended his way by swamp and stream and awful woodland, to the farm-house where he happened to be quartered, every sound of nature, at that witching hour, fluttered his excited imagination: the moan of the whip-poor-will from the hill-side; the boding cry of the tree-toad, that harbinger of storm; the dreary hooting of the screech-owl, or the sudden rustling in the thicket of birds frightened from their roost. The fire-flies, too, which sparkled most vividly in the darkest places, now and then startled him, as one of uncommon brightness would stream across his path; and if by chance a huge blackhead of a beetle came winging his blundering flight against him, the poor varlet was ready to give up the ghost, with the idea that he was struck with a witch's token. His only resource on such occasions, either to drown thought or drive away evil spirits, was to sing psalm tunes; — and the good people of Sleepy Hollow, as they sat by their doors of an evening, were often filled with awe at hearing his nasal melody, "in linked sweetness long drawn out," floating from the distant hill, or along the dusky road.

Another of his sources of fearful pleasure was to pass long winter evenings with the old Dutch wives, as they sat spinning by the fire, with a row of apples roasting and spluttering along the hearth, and listen to their marvelous tales of ghosts and goblins, and haunted fields, and haunted brooks, and haunted bridges, and haunted houses, and particularly of the headless horseman, or Galloping Hessian of the Hollow, as they sometimes called him. He would delight them equally by his anecdotes of witchcraft, and of the direful omens and portentous sights and sounds in the air, which prevailed in the earlier times of Connecticut; and would frighten them woefully with speculations upon comets and shooting stars; and with the alarming fact that the world did absolutely turn round, and that they were half the time topsy-turvy!

But if there was a pleasure in all this, while snugly cuddling in the chimney-corner of a chamber that was all of a ruddy glow from the crackling wood fire, and where, of course, no specter dared to show its face, it was dearly purchased by the terrors of his subsequent walk homewards. What fearful shapes and shadows beset his path amidst the dim and ghastly glare of a snowy night! — With what wistful look did he eye every trembling ray of light streaming across the waste fields from some distant window! — How often was he appalled by some shrub covered with snow, which, like a sheeted specter, beset his very path!— How often did he shrink with curdling awe at the sound of his own steps on the frosty crust beneath his feet! and dread to look over his shoulder, lest he should behold some uncouth being tramping close behind him! — and how often was he thrown into complete dismay by some rushing blast, howling among the trees, in the idea that it was the Galloping Hessian on one of his nightly scourings!

All these, however, were mere terrors of the night, phantoms of the mind that walk in darkness; and though he had seen many specters in his time, and been more than once beset by Satan in divers shapes, in his lonely perambulations, yet daylight put an end to all these evils; and he would have passed a pleasant life of it, in despite of the devil and all his works, if his path had not been crossed by a being that causes more perplexity to mortal man than ghosts, goblins, and the whole race of witches put together, and that was — a woman.

Among the musical disciples who assembled one evening in each week to receive his instructions in psalmody, was Katrina Van Tassel, the daughter and only child of a substantial Dutch farmer. She was a blooming lass of fresh eighteen; plump as a partridge; ripe and melting and rosy-cheeked as one of her father's peaches, and universally famed, not merely for her beauty, but her vast expectations. She was, withal, a little of a coquette, as might be perceived even in her dress, which was a mixture of ancient and modern fashions, as most suited to set off her charms. She wore ornaments of pure yellow gold, which her great-great-grandmother had brought over from Saardam; the tempting stomacher of the olden time; and withal a provokingly short petticoat, to display the prettiest foot and ankle in the country round.

Ichabod Crane had a soft and foolish heart towards the sex, and it is not to be wondered at that so tempting a morsel soon found favor in his eyes, more especially after he had visited her paternal mansion. Old Baltus Van Tassel was a perfect picture of a thriving, contented, liberal-hearted farmer. He seldom, it is true, sent either his eyes or his thoughts beyond the boundaries of his own farm; but within those, everything was snug, happy, and well-conditioned. He was satisfied with his wealth, but not proud of it; and piqued himself upon the hearty abundance, rather than the style in which he lived. His stronghold was situated on the banks of the Hudson, in one of those green, sheltered, fertile nooks, in which the Dutch farmers are so fond of nestling. A great elm-tree spread its broad branches over it, at the foot of which bubbled up a spring of the softest and sweetest water, in a little well formed of a barrel, and then stole sparkling away through the grass to a neighboring brook that bubbled along among alders and drawf willows. Hard by the farm-house was a vast barn that might have served for a church, every window and crevice of which seemed bursting forth with the treasures of the farm; the flail was busily resounding within it from morning to night; swallows and martins skimmed twittering about the eaves; and rows of pigeons, some with one eye turned up, as if watching the weather, some with their heads under their wings, or buried in their bosoms, and others swelling, and cooing, and bowing about their dames, were enjoying the sunshine on the roof. Sleek unwieldy porkers were grunting in the repose and abundance of their pens, whence sallied forth now and then troops of sucking pigs, as if to snuff the air. A stately squadron of snowy geese were riding in an adjoining pond, convoying whole fleets of ducks; regiments of turkeys were gobbling through the farm-yard, and guinea-fowls fretting about it, like ill-tempered house-wives, with their peevish, discontented cry. Before the barn door strutted the gallant cock, that pattern of a husband, a warrior, and a fine gentleman, clapping his burnished wings, and crowing in the pride and gladness of his heart — sometimes tearing up the earth with his feet, and then generously calling his ever-hungry family of wives and children to enjoy the rich morsel which he had discovered.

The pedagogue's mouth watered as he

looked upon his sumptuous promise of luxurious winter fare. In his devouring mind's eye he pictured to himself every roasting-pig running about with a pudding in his belly, and an apple in his mouth; the pigeons were snugly put to bed in a comfortable pie, and tucked in with a coverlet of crust; the geese were swimming in their own gravy; and the ducks pairing cozily in dishes, like snug married couples, with a decent competency of onion sauce. In the porkers he saw carved out the future sleek side of bacon and juicy relishing ham; not a turkey but he beheld daintily trussed up, with its gizzard under its wing, and, peradventure, a necklace of savory sausages; and even bright chanticleer himself lay sprawling on his back in a side dish, with uplifted claws, as if craving that quarter which his chivalrous spirit disdained to ask while living.

As the enraptured Ichabod fancied all this, and as he rolled his great green eyes over the fat meadow-lands, the rich fields of wheat, of rye, of buckwheat, and Indian corn, and the orchards burthened with ruddy fruit, which surrounded the warm tenement of Van Tassel, his heart yearned after the damsel who was to inherit these domains, and his imagination expanded with the idea, how they might be readily turned into cash, and the money invested in immense tracts of wild land, and shingle palaces in the wilderness. Nay, his busy fancy already realized his hopes, and presented to him the blooming Katrina, with a whole family of children, mounted on the top of a wagon loaded with household trumpery, with pots and kettles dangling beneath; and he beheld himself bestriding a pacing mare, with a colt at her heels, setting out for Kentucky, Tennessee, or the Lord knows where.

When he entered the house, the conquest of his heart was complete. It was one of those spacious farm-houses, with high-ridged, but lowly sloping roofs, built in the style handed down from the first Dutch settlers; the low projecting eaves forming a piazza along the front, capable of being closed up in bad weather. Under this were hung flails, harness, various utensils of husbandry, and nets for fishing in the neighboring river. Benches were built along the sides for summer use; and a great spinning-wheel at one end, and a churn at the other, showed the various uses to which this important porch might be devoted. From this piazza the wondering Ichabod entered the hall, which formed the center of the mansion and the place of usual residence. Here rows of resplendent pewter, ranged on a long dresser, dazzled his eyes. In one corner stood a huge bag of wool ready to be spun; in another, a quantity of linsey-woolsey just from the loom; ears of Indian corn, and strings of fried apples and peaches, hung in gay festoons along the wall, mingled with the gaud of red peppers; and a door left ajar gave him a peep into the best parlor, where the claw-footed chairs and dark mahogany tables shone like mirrors; and irons, with their accompanying shovel and tongs, glistened from their covert of asparagus tops; mock oranges and conch-shells decorated the mantel-piece; strings of various colored birds' eggs were suspended above it; a great ostrich egg was hung from the center of the room, and a corner-cupboard, knowingly left open, displayed immense treasures of old silver and well-mended china.

From the moment Ichabod laid his eyes upon these regions of delight, the peace of his mind was at an end, and his only study was how to gain the affections of the peerless daughter of Van Tassel. In this enterprise, however, he had more real difficulties than generally fell to the lot of a knight-errant of yore, who seldom had anything but giants, enchanters, fiery dragons, and such like easily conquered adversaries, to contend with; and had to make his way merely through the gates of iron and brass, and walls of adamant, to the castle keep, where the lady of his heart was confined; all which he achieved as easily as a man would carve his way to the center of a Christmas pie, and then the lady gave him her hand as a matter of course. Ichabod, on the contrary, had to win his way to the heart of a country coquette, beset with a labyrinth of whims and caprices, which were forever presenting new difficulties and impediments; and he had to encounter a host of fearful adversaries of real flesh and blood, the numerous rustic admirers who beset every portal to her heart, keeping a watchful and angry eye upon each other, but ready to fly out in the common cause against any new competitor.

Among these the most formidable was a burly, roaring, roistering blade, of the name of Abraham, or, according to the Dutch abbreviation, Brom Van Brunt, the hero of the country round, which rang with his feats of strength and hardihood. He was broad-shouldered and double-jointed, with short curly black hair, and a bluff but not unpleasant countenance, having a mingled air of fun and arrogance. From her Herculean frame and great powers of limb, he had received the nickname of BROM BONES, by which he was universally known. He was famed for great knowledge and skill in horsemanship, being as dexterous on horseback as a Tartar. He was foremost at all races and cockfights, and, with the ascendency which bodily strength acquires in rustic life, was the umpire in all disputes, setting his hat on one side, and giving his decisions with an air and tone admitting of no gainsay, or appeal. He was always ready for either a fight or frolic, but had more mischief than ill-will in his composition; and, with all his overbearing roughness, there was a strong dash of waggish good humor at bottom. He had three or four boon companions, who regarded him as their model, and at the head of whom he scoured the country, attending every scene of feud or merriment for miles round. In cold weather he was distinguished by a fur cap, surmounted with a flaunting fox's tail; and when the folks at a country gathering descried this well-known crest at a distance, whisking about among a squad of hard riders, they always stood by for a squall. Sometimes his crew would be heard dashing along past the farm-houses at midnight, with hoop and halloo, like a troop of Don Cossacks, and the old dames, startled out of their sleep, would listen for a moment, till the hurry-scurry had clattered by, and then exclaim, "Ay, there goes BROM BONES and his gang!" The neighbors looked upon him with a mixture of awe, admiration, and good-will; and when any madcap prank or rustic brawl occurred in the vicinity, always shook their heads and warranted Brom Bones was at the bottom of it.

This rantipole hero had for some time singled out the blooming Katrina for the object of his uncouth gallantries, and though his amorous toyings were something like the gentle caresses and endearments of a bear, yet it was whispered that she did not altogether discourage his hopes. Certain it is, his advances were signals for rival candidates to retire, who felt no inclination to cross a lion in his amours; insomuch that when his horse was seen tied to Van Tassel's paling on a Sunday night, a sure sign that his master was courting, or, as it is termed, "sparking," within, all other suitors passed by in despair, and carried the war into other quarters.

Such was the formidable rival with whom Ichabod Crane had to contend, and, considering all things, a stouter man than he would have shrunk from the competition, and a wiser man would have despaired. He had, however, a happy mixture of pliability and perseverance in his nature; he was in form and spirit like a supple-jack, — yielding, but tough; though he bent, he never broke; and though he bowed beneath the slightest pressure, yet, the moment it was away — jerk! he was as erect, and carried his head as high as ever.

To have taken the field openly against his rival would have been madness; for he was not a man to be thwarted in his amours, any more than that stormy lover, Achilles. Ichabod, therefore, made his advances in a quiet and gently insinuating manner. Under cover of his character of singing-master, he made frequent visits at the farm-house; not that he had anything to apprehend from the meddlesome interference of parents, which is so often a stumbling-block in the path of lovers. Balt Van Tassel was an easy, indulgent soul; he loved his daughter better even than his pipe, and, like a reasonable man and an excellent father, let her have her way in everything. His notable little wife, too, had enough to do to attend to her housekeeping, and manage her poultry; for as she sagely observed, ducks and geese are foolish things, and must be looked after, but girls can take care of themselves. Thus, while the busy dame bustled about the house, or plied her spinning-wheel at one end of the piazza, honest Balt would sit smoking his evening pipe at the other, watching the achievements of a little wooden warrior, who, armed with a sword in each hand, was most valiantly fighting the wind on the pinnacle of the barn. In the meantime, Ichabod would carry on his suit with the daughter by the side of the spring under the great elm, or sauntering along in the twilight, that hour so favorable to the lover's eloquence.

I profess not to know how women's hearts are wooed and won. To me they have always been matters of riddle and admiration. Some seem to have but one vulnerable point, or door of access; while others have a thousand avenues, and may be captured in a thousand different ways. It is a great triumph of skill to gain the former, but a still greater proof of generalship to maintain possession of the latter, for a man must battle for his fortress at every door and window. He who wins a thousand common hearts is therefore entitled to some renown; but he who keeps undisputed sway over the heart of a coquette, is indeed a hero. Certain it is, this was not the case with the redoubtable Brom Bones; and from the moment Ichabod Crane made his advances, the interests of the former evidently declined; his horse was no longer seen tied at the palings on Sunday nights, and a deadly feud gradually arose between him and the preceptor of Sleepy Hollow.

Brom, who had a degree of rough chivalry in his nature, would fain have carried matters to open warfare, and have settled their pretensions to the lady, according to the mode of those most concise and simple reasoners, the knights-errant of yore — by single combat; but Ichabod was too conscious of the superior might of his adversary to enter the lists against him; he had overheard a boast of Bones, that he "would double the school-master up, and lay him on a shelf of his own school-house"; and he was too wary to give him an opportunity. There was something extremely provoking in this obstinately pacific system; it left Brom no alternative but to draw upon the funds of rustic waggery in his disposition, and to play off boorish practical jokes upon his rival. Ichabod became the object of whimsical persecution to Bones and his gang of rough riders. They harried his hitherto peaceful domains; smoked out his singing-school, by stopping up the chimney; broke into the school-house at night, in spite of his formidable fastenings of withe and window stakes, and turned everything topsy-turvy; so that the poor schoolmaster began to think all the witches in the country held their meetings there. But what was still more annoying, Brom took all opportunities of turning him into ridicule in the presence of his mistress, and had a scoundrel dog whom he taught to whine in the most ludicrous manner, and introduced as a rival of Ichabod's to instruct her in psalmody.

In this way matters went on for some time, without producing any material effect on the relative situation of the contending powers. On a fine autumnal afternoon, Ichabod, in pensive mood, sat enthroned on the lofty stool whence he usually watched all the concerns of his little literary realm. In his hand he swayed a ferule, that scepter of despotic power; the birch of justice reposed on three nails behind the throne, a constant terror to evil-doers; while on the desk before him might be seen sundry contraband articles and prohibited weapons, detected upon the persons of idle urchins; such as half-munched apples, pop-guns, whirligigs, fly-cages, and whole legions of rampant little paper game-cocks. Apparently there had been some appalling act of justice recently inflicted, for his scholars were all busily intent upon their books, or slyly whispering behind them with one eye kept upon the master; and a kind of buzzing stillness reigned throughout the school-room. It was suddenly interrupted by the appearance of a Negro, in tow-cloth jacket and trousers, a round-crowned fragment of a hat, like the cap of Mercury, and mounted on the back of a ragged, wild, half-broken colt, which he managed with a rope by the way of halter. He came clattering up to the school door with an invitation to Ichabod to attend a merry-making, or "quilting frolic," to be held that evening at Mynheer Van Tassel's; and having delivered his message with that air of importance and effort at fine language which a Negro is apt to display on petty embassies of the kind, he dashed over the brook, and was seen scampering away up the hollow, full of the importance and hurry of his mission.

All was now bustle and hubbub in the late quiet school-room. The scholars were hurried through their lessons without stopping at trifles; those who were nimble skipped over half with impunity, and those who were tardy had a smart application now and then in the rear, to quicken their speed, or help them over a tall word. Books were flung aside without being put away on the shelves; inkstands were overturned, benches thrown down, and the whole school was turned loose an hour before the usual time, bursting forth like a legion of young imps, yelping and racketing about the green in joy at their early emancipation.

The gallant Ichabod now spent at least an extra half-hour at his toilet, brushing and furbishing up his best, and indeed only suit of rusty black, and arranging his locks by a bit of broken looking-glass that hung up in the school-house. That he might make his appearance before his mistress in the true style of a cavalier, he borrowed a horse from the farmer with whom he was domiciliated, a choleric old Dutchman, of the name of Hans Van Ripper, and, thus gallantly mounted, issued forth like a knight-errant in quest of adventures. But it is meet I should, in the true spirit of romantic story, give some account of the looks and equipments of my hero and his steed. The animal he bestrode was a broken-down plough-horse that had outlived almost everything but his viciousness. He was gaunt and shagged, with a ewe neck and a head like a hammer; his rusty mane and tail were tangled and knotted with burrs; one eye had lost its pupil, and was glaring and spectral; but the other had the gleam of a genuine devil in it. Still he must have had fire and mettle in his day, if we may judge from the name he bore of Gunpowder. He had, in fact, been a favorite steed of his master's, the choleric Van Ripper, who was a furious rider, and had infused, very probably, some of his own spirit into the animal; for, old and broken-down as he looked, there was more of the lurking devil in him than in any young filly in the country.

Ichabod was a suitable figure for such a steed. He rode with short stirrups, which brought his knees nearly up to the pommel of the saddle; his sharp elbows stuck out like grasshoppers; he carried his whip perpendicularly in his hand, like a scepter, and, as his horse jogged on, the motion of his arms was not unlike the flapping of a pair of wings. A small wool hat rested on top of his nose, for so his scanty strip of forehead might be called; and the skirts of his black coat fluttered out almost to the horse's tail. Such was the appearance of Ichabod and his steed, as they shambled out of the gate of Hans Van Ripper, and it was altogether such an apparition as is seldom to be met in broad daylight.

It was, as I have said, a fine autumnal day, the sky was clear and serene, and nature wore that rich and golden livery which we always associate with the idea of abundance. The forests had put on their sober brown and yellow, while some trees of the tenderer kind had been nipped by the frosts into brilliant dyes of orange, purple, and scarlet. Streaming files of wild ducks began to make their appearance high in the air; the bark of the squirrel might be heard from the groves of beech and hickory nuts, and the pensive whistle of the quail at intervals from the neighboring stubble field.

The small birds were taking their farewell banquets. In the fulness of their revelry, they fluttered, chirping and frolicking, from bush to bush and tree to tree, capricious from the very profusion and variety around them. There was the honest cock-robin, the favorite game of stripling sportsmen, with its loud, querulous note; and the twittering blackbirds flying in sable clouds; and the golden-winged woodpecker, with his crimson crest, his broad black gorget, and splendid plumage; and the cedar-bird, with its red-tipt wings and yellow-tip tail, and its little monteiro cap of feathers; and the blue jay, that noisy coxcomb, in his gay light-blue coat and white underclothes; screaming and chattering, nodding and bobbing and bowing, and pretending to be on good terms with every songster of the grove.

As Ichabod jogged slowly on his way, his eye, ever open to every symptom of culinary abundance, ranged with delight over the treasures of jolly autumn. On all sides he beheld vast stores of apples; some hanging in oppressive opulence on the trees; some gathered into baskets and barrels for the market; others heaped up in rich piles for the cider-press. Further on he beheld great fields of Indian corn, with its golden ears peeping from their leafy coverts, and holding out the promise of cakes and hasty-pudding; and the yellow pumpkins lying beneath them, turning up their fair round bellies to the sun, and giving ample prospects of the most luxurious of pies; and anon he passed the fragrant buckwheat fields breathing the odor of the bee-hive, and as he beheld them, soft anticipations stole over his mind of dainty slapjacks, well buttered, and garnished with honey or treacle, by the delicate little dimpled hand of Katrina Van Tassel.

Thus feeding his mind with many sweet thoughts and "sugared suppositions," he journeyed along the sides of a range of hills which look out upon some of the goodliest scenes of the mighty Hudson. The sun gradually wheeled his broad disc down into the west. The wide bosom of the Tappan Zee lay motionless and glassy, except that here and there a gentle undulation waved and prolonged the blue shadow of the distant mountain. A few amber clouds floated in the sky, without a breath of air to move them. The horizon was of a fine golden tint, changing gradually into a pure apple-green, and from that into the deep blue of the mid-heaven. A slanting ray lingered on the woody crests of the precipices that overhung some parts of the river, giving greater depth to the dark-gray and purple of their rocky sides. A sloop was loitering in the distance, dropping slowly down with the tide, her sail hanging uselessly against the mast; and as the reflection of the sky gleamed along the still water, it seemed as if the vessel was suspended in the air.

It was towards evening that Ichabod arrived at the castle of the Heer Van Tassel, which he found thronged with the pride and flower of the adjacent country. Old farmers, a spare leathern-faced race, in homespun coats and breeches, blue stockings, huge shoes, and magnificent pewter buckles. Their brisk withered little dames, in close crimped caps, long-waisted short gowns, homespun petticoats, with scissors and pincushions, and gay calico pockets hanging on the outside. Buxom lasses, almost as antiquated as their mothers, excepting where a straw hat, a fine riband, or perhaps a white frock, gave symptoms of city innovation. The sons, in short square-skirted coats with rows of stupendous brass buttons, and their hair generally queued in the fashion of the times, especially if they could procure an eel-skin for the purpose, it being esteemed throughout the country as a potent nourisher and strengthener of the hair.

Brom Bones, however, was the hero of the scene, having come to the gathering on his favorite steed Daredevil, a creature like himself, full of mettle and mischief, and which no one but himself could manage. He was, in fact, noted for preferring vicious animals, given to all kinds of tricks, which kept the rider in constant risk of his neck, for he held a tractable, well-broken horse as unworthy of a lad of spirit.

Fain would I pause to dwell upon the world of charms that burst upon the enraptured gaze of my hero, as he entered the state parlor of Van Tassel's mansion. Not those of the bevy of buxom lasses, with their luxurious display of red and white; but the ample charms of a genuine Dutch country tea-table in the sumptuous time of autumn. Such heaped-up platters of cakes of various and almost indescribable kinds, known only to experienced Dutch housewives! There was the doughty doughnut, the tenderer oly koek, and the crisp and crumbling cruller; sweet-cakes and short-cakes, ginger-cakes and honey-cakes, and the whole family of cakes. And then there were apple-pies and peach-pies and pumpkin-pies; besides slices of ham and smoked beef; and, moreover, delectable dishes of preserved plums, and peaches, and pears, and quinces; not to mention broiled shad and roasted chickens; together with bowls of milk and cream, all mingled higgledy-piggledy, pretty much as I have enumerated them, with the motherly tea-pot sending up its clouds of vapor from the midst — Heaven bless the mark! I want breath and time to discuss this banquet as it deserves, and am too eager to get on with my story. Happily, Ichabod Crane was not in so great a hurry as his historian, but did ample justice to every dainty.

He was a kind and thankful creature, whose heart dilated in proportion as his skin was filled with good cheer; and whose spirits rose with eating as some men's do with drink. He could not help, too, rolling his large eyes round him as he ate, and chuckling with the possibility that he might one day be lord of all this scene of almost unimaginable luxury and splendor. Then he thought, how soon he'd turn his back upon the old school-house, snap his fingers in the face of Hans Van Ripper and every other niggardly patron, and kick any itinerant pedagogue out of doors that should dare to call him comrade!

Old Baltus Van Tassel moved about among his guests with a face dilated with content and good humor, round and jolly as the harvest moon. His hospitable attentions were brief, but expressive, being confined to a shake of the hand, a slap on the shoulder, a loud laugh, and a pressing invitation to "fall to, and help themselves."

And now the sound of the music from the common room or hall summoned to the dance. The musician was an old gray-headed Negro, who had been the itinerant orchestra of the neighborhood for more than half a century. His instrument was as old and battered as himself. The greater part of the time he scraped on two or three strings, accompanying every movement of the bow with a motion of the head; bowing almost to the ground, and stamping with his foot whenever a fresh couple were to start.

Ichabod prided himself upon his dancing as much as upon his vocal powers. Not a limb, not a fiber about him was idle; and to have seen his loosely hung frame in full motion, and clattering about the room, you would have thought Saint Vitus himself, that blessed patron of the dance, was figuring before you in person. He was the admiration of all the Negroes; who, having gathered, of all ages and sizes, from the farm and the neighborhood, stood forming a pyramid of shining black faces, at every door and window, gazing with delight at the scene, rolling their white eye-balls, and showing grinning rows of ivory from ear to ear. How could the flogger of urchins be otherwise than animated and joyous? the lady of his heart was his partner in the dance, and smiling graciously in reply to all his amorous oglings; while Brom Bones, sorely smitten with love and jealousy, sat brooding by himself in one corner.

When the dance was at an end, Ichabod was attracted to a knot of the sager folks, who, with old Van Tassel, sat smoking at one end of the piazza, gossiping over former times, and drawing out long stories about the war.

This neighborhood, at the time of which I am speaking, was one of those highly favored places which abound with chronicle and great men. The British and American line had run near it during the war; it had, therefore, been the scene of marauding, and infested with refugees, cow-boys, and all kinds of border chivalry. Just sufficient time had elapsed to enable each story-teller to dress up his tale with a little becoming fiction, and, in the indistinctness of his recollection, to make himself the hero of every exploit.

There was the story of Doffue Martling, a large bluebearded Dutchman, who had nearly taken a British frigate with an old iron nine-pounder from a mud breastwork, only that his gun burst at the sixth discharge. And there was an old gentleman who shall be nameless, being too rich a mynheer to be lightly mentioned, who, in the battle of White Plains, being an excellent master of defense, parried a musket-ball with a small sword, insomuch that he absolutely felt it whiz round the blade, and glance off at the hilt; in proof of which he was ready at any time to show the sword, with the hilt a little bent. There were several more that had been equally great in the field, not one of whom but was persuaded that he had a considerable hand in bringing the war to a happy termination.

But all these were nothing to the tales of ghosts and apparitions that succeeded. The neighborhood is rich in legendary treasures of the kind. Local tales and superstitions thrive best in these sheltered long-settled retreats; but are trampled under-foot by the shifting throng that forms the population of most of our country places. Besides, there is no encouragement for ghosts in most of our villages, for they have scarcely had time to finish their first nap, and turn themselves in their graves, before their surviving friends have traveled away from the neighborhood; so that when they turn out at night to walk their rounds, they have no acquaintance left to call upon. This is perhaps the reason why we so seldom hear of ghosts except in our long-established Dutch communities.

The immediate cause, however, of the prevalence of supernatural stories in these parts, was doubtless owing to the vicinity of Sleepy Hollow. There was a contagion in the very air that blew from that haunted region; it breathed forth an atmosphere of dreams and fancies infecting all the land. Several of the Sleepy Hollow people were present at Van Tassel's, and, as usual, were doling out their wild and wonderful legends. Many dismal tales were told about funeral trains, and mourning cries and wailings heard and seen about the great tree where the unfortunate Major André was taken, and which stood in the neighborhood. Some mention was made also of the woman in white, that haunted the dark glen at Raven Rock, and was often heard to shriek on winter nights before a storm, having perished there in the snow. The chief part of the stories, however, turned upon the favorite specter of Sleepy Hollow, the headless horseman, who had been heard several times of late, patrolling the country; and, it was said, tethered his horse nightly among the graves in the churchyard.

The sequestered situation of this church seems always to have made it a favorite haunt of troubled spirits. It stands on a knoll surrounded by locust-trees and lofty elms, from among which its decent white-washed walls shine modestly forth, like Christian purity, beaming through the shades of retirement. A gentle slope descends from it to a silver sheet of water, bordered by high trees, between which peeps may be caught at the blue hills of the Hudson. To look upon its grass-grown yard, where the sunbeams seem to sleep so quietly, one would think that there at least the dead might rest in peace. On one side of the church exends a wide woody dell, along which raves a large brook among broken rocks and trunks of fallen trees. Over a deep black part of the stream, not far from the church, was formerly thrown a wooden bridge; the road that led to it, and the bridge itself, were thickly shaded by overhanging trees, which cast a gloom about it, even in the daytime; but occasioned a fearful darkness at night. Such was one of the favorite haunts of the headless horseman, and the place where he was most frequently encountered. The tale was told of old Brouwer, a most heretical disbeliever in ghosts, how he met the horseman returning from his foray into Sleepy Hollow, and was obliged to get up behind him; how they galloped over bush and brake, over hill and swamp, until they reached the bridge; when the horseman suddenly turned into a skeleton, threw old Brouwer into the brook, and sprang away over the tree-tops with a clap of thunder.

This story was immediately matched by a thrice marvelous adventure of Brom Bones, who made light of the Galloping Hessian as an arrant jockey. He affirmed that, on returning one night from the neighboring village of Sing-Sing, he had been overtaken by this midnight trooper; that he had offered to race with him for a bowl of punch, and should have won it too, for Daredevil beat the goblin horse all hollow, but, just as they came to the church bridge, the Hessian bolted, and vanished in a flash of fire.

All these tales, told in that drowsy undertone with which men talk in the dark, the countenances of the listeners only now and then receiving a casual gleam from the glare of a pipe, sank deep in the mind of Ichabod. He repaid them in kind, with large extracts from his invaluable author, Cotton Mather, and added many marvelous events that had taken place in his native state of Connecticut, and fearful sights which he had seen in his nightly walks about Sleepy Hollow.

The revel now gradually broke up. The old farmers gathered together their families in their wagons, and were heard for some time rattling along the hollow roads, and over the distant hills. Some of the damsels mounted on pillions behind their favorite swains, and their light-hearted laughter, mingling with the clatter of hoofs, echoed along the silent woodlands, sounding fainter and fainter until they gradually died away — and the late scene of noise and frolic was all silent and deserted. Ichabod only lingered behind, according to the custom of country lovers, to have a *tête-à-tête* with the heiress, fully convinced that he was now on the high road to success. What passed at this interview I will not pretend to say, for in fact I do not know. Something, I fear me, must have gone wrong, for he certainly sallied forth, after no very great interval, with an air quite desolate and chop-fallen. Oh, these women! these women! Could that girl have been playing off any of her coquettish tricks? — Was her encouragement of the poor pedagogue all a mere sham to secure her conquest of his rival? — Heaven only knows, not I! — Let it suffice to say, Ichabod stole forth with the air of one who had been sacking a hen-roost, rather than a fair lady's heart. Without looking to the right or left to notice the scene of rural wealth on which he had so often gloated, he went straight to the stable, and with several hearty cuffs and kicks, roused his steed most uncourteously from the comfortable quarters in which he was soundly sleeping, dreaming of mountains of corn and oats, and whole valleys of timothy and clover.

It was the very witching time of night that Ichabod, heavy-hearted and crest-fallen, pursued his travels homewards, along the sides of the lofty hills which rise above Tarry Town, and which he had traversed so cheerily in the afternoon. The hour was as dismal as himself. Far below him the Tappan Zee spread its dusky and indistinct waste of waters, with here and there the tall mast of a sloop riding quietly at anchor under the land. In the dead hush of midnight he could even hear the barking of the watch-dog from the opposite shore of the Hudson; but it was so vague and faint as only to give an idea of his distance from this faithful companion of man. Now and then, too, the long-drawn crowing of a cock, accidentally awakened, would sound far, far off, from some farm-house away among the hills — but it was like a dreaming sound in his ear. No signs of life occurred near him, but occasionally the melancholy chirp of a cricket, or perhaps the gutteral twang of a bull-frog, from a neighboring marsh, as if sleeping uncomfortably, and turning suddenly in his bed.

All the stories of ghosts and goblins that he had heard in the afternoon now came crowding upon his recollection. The night grew darker and darker; the stars seemed to sink deeper in the sky, and driving clouds occasionally hid them from his sight. He had never felt so lonely and dismal. He was, moreover, approaching the very place where many of the scenes of the ghost-stories had been laid. In the center of the road stood an enormous tulip-tree, which towered like a giant above all the other trees of the neighborhood, and formed a kind of landmark. Its limbs were gnarled and fantastic, large enough to form trunks for ordinary trees, twisting down almost to the earth, and rising again into the air. It was connected with the tragical story of the unfortunate André, who had been taken prisoner hard by; and was universally known by the name of Major André's tree. The common people regarded it with a mixture of respect and superstition, partly from the tales of strange sights and doleful lamentations told concerning it.

As Ichabod approached this fearful tree, he began to whistle; he thought his whistle was answered; it was but a blast sweeping sharply through the dry branches. As he approached a little nearer, he thought he saw something white hanging in the midst of the tree — he paused and ceased whistling; but on looking more narrowly, perceived that it was a place where the tree had been scathed by lightning, and the white wood laid bare. Suddenly he heard a groan — his teeth chattered, and his knees smote against the saddle; it was but the rubbing of one huge bough upon another, as they were swayed about by the breeze. He passed the tree in safety, but new perils lay before him.

About two hundred yards from the tree a small brook crossed the road, and ran into a marshy and thickly wooded glen, known by the name of Wiley's Swamp. A few rough logs, laid side by side, served for a bridge over this stream. On that side of the road where the brook entered the wood, a group of oaks and chestnuts, matted thick with wild grapevines, threw a cavernous gloom over it. To pass this bridge was the severest trial. It was at this identical spot that the unfortunate André was captured, and under the covert of those chestnuts and vines were the sturdy yeomen concealed who surprised him. This has ever since been considered a haunted stream, and fearful are the feelings of the schoolboy who has to pass it alone after dark.

As he approached the stream, his heart began to thump; he summoned up, however, all his resolution, gave his horse half a score of kicks in the ribs, and attempted to dash briskly across the bridge; but instead of starting forward, the perverse old animal made a lateral movement, and ran broadside against the fence. Ichabod, whose fears increased with the delay, jerked the reins on the other side, and kicked lustily with the contrary foot: it was all in vain; his steed started, it is true, but it was only to plunge to the opposite side of the road into a thicket of brambles and alder-bushes. The schoolmaster now bestowed both whip and heel upon the starveling ribs of old Gunpowder, who dashed forward, snuffling and snorting, but came to a stand just by the bridge, with a suddenness that had nearly sent his rider sprawling over his head. Just at this moment a plashy tramp by the side of the bridge caught the sensitive ear of Ichabod. In the dark shadow of the grove, on the margin of the brook, he beheld something huge, mis-shapen, black and towering. It stirred not, but seemed gathered up in the gloom, like some gigantic monster ready to spring upon the traveler.

The hair of the affrighted pedagogue rose

upon his head with terror. What was to be done? To turn and fly was now too late; and besides, what chance was there of escaping ghost or goblin, if such it was, which could ride upon the wings of the wind? Summoning up, therefore, a show of courage, he demanded in stammering accents — "Who are you?" He received no reply. He repeated his demand in a still more agitated voice. Still there was no answer. Once more he cudgelled the sides of the inflexible Gunpowder, and, shutting his eys, broke forth with involuntary fervor into a psalm tune. Just then the shadowy object of alarm put itself in motion, and with a scramble and a bound, stood at once in the middle of the road. Though the night was dark and dismal, yet the form of the unknown might now in some degree be ascertained. He appeared to be a horseman of large dimensions, and mounted on a black horse of powerful frame. He made no offer of molestation or sociability, but kept aloof on one side of the road, jogging along on the blind side of old Gunpowder, who had now got over his fright and waywardness.

Ichabod, who had no relish for this strange midnight companion, and bethought himself of the adventure of Brom Bones with the Galloping Hessian, now quickened his steed, in hopes of leaving him behind. The stranger, however, quickened his horse to an equal pace. Ichabod pulled up, and fell into a walk, thinking to lag behind — the other did the same.

His heart began to sink within him; he endeavored to resume his psalm tune, but his parched tongue clove to the roof of his mouth, and he could not utter a stave. There was something in the moody and dogged silence of this pertinacious companion that was mysterious and appalling. It was soon fearfully accounted for. On mounting a rising ground, which brought the figure of his fellow-traveler in relief against the sky, gigantic in height, and muffled in a cloak, Ichabod was horror-struck on perceiving that he was headless! — but his horror was still more increased on observing that the head, which should have rested on his shoulders, was carried before him on the pommel of the saddle: his terror rose to desperation; he rained a shower of kicks and blows upon Gunpowder, hoping, by a sudden movement, to give his companion the slip — but the specter started full jump with him. Away then they dashed, through thick and thin; stones flying and sparks flashing at every bound. Ichabod's flimsy garments fluttered in the air, as he stretched his long lank body away over his horse's head, in the eagerness of his flight.

They had now reached the road which turns off to Sleepy Hollow, but Gunpowder, who seemed possessed with a demon, instead of keeping up it, made an opposite turn, and plunged headlong down the hill to the left. This road leads through a sandy hollow, shaded by trees for about a quarter of a mile, where it crosses the bridge famous in goblin story, and just beyond swells the green knoll on which stands the white-washed church.

As yet the panic of the steed had given his unskilful rider an apparent advantage in the chase; but just as he had got half way through the hollow, the girths of the saddle gave way, and he felt it slipping from under him. He seized it by the pommel, and endeavored to hold it firm, but in vain; and had just time to save himself by clasping old Gunpowder round the neck, when the saddle fell to the earth, and he heard it trampled under-foot by his pursuer. For a moment the terror of Hans Van Ripper's wrath passed across his mind — for it was his Sunday saddle; but this was no time for petty fears; the goblin was hard on his haunches; and (unskilful rider that he was!) he had much ado to maintain his seat; sometimes slipping on one side, sometimes on the other, and sometimes jolted on the high ridge of his horse's back-bone, with a violence that he verily feared would cleave him asunder.

An opening in the trees now cheered him with the hopes that the church bridge was at hand. The wavering reflection of a silver star in the bosom of the brook told him that he was not mistaken. He saw the walls of the church dimly glaring under the trees beyond. He recollected the place where Brom Bones' ghostly competitor had disappeared. "If I can but reach that bridge," thought Ichabod, "I am safe." Just then he heard the black steed panting and blowing close behind him; he even fancied that he felt his hot breath. Another convulsive kick in the ribs, and old Gunpowder sprang upon the bridge; he thundered over the resounding planks; he gained the opposite side; and now Ichabod cast a look behind to see if his pursuer should vanish, according to rule, in a flash of fire and brimstone. Just then he saw the goblin rising in his stirrups, and in the very act of hurling his head at him. Ichabod endeavored to dodge the horrible missile, but too late. It encountered his cranium with a tremendous crash — he was tumbled headlong into the dust, and Gunpowder, the black steed, and the goblin rider passed by like a whirlwind.

The next morning the old horse was found without his saddle and with the bridle under his feet, soberly cropping the grass at his master's gate. Ichabod did not make his appearance at breakfast — dinner-hour came, but no Ichabod. The boys assembled at the schoolhouse, and strolled idly about the banks of the brook; but no schoolmaster. Hans Van Ripper now began to feel some uneasiness about the fate of poor Ichabod and his saddle. An inquiry was set on foot, and after diligent investigation they came upon his traces. In one part of the road leading to the church was found the saddle trampled in the dirt; the tracks of horses' hoofs deeply dented in the road, and evidently at furious speed, were traced to the bridge, beyond which, on the bank of a broad part of the brook, where the water ran deep and black, was found the hat of the unfortunate Ichabod, and close beside it a shattered pumpkin.

The brook was searched, but the body of the schoolmaster was not to be discovered. Hans Van Ripper, as executor of his estate, examined the bundle, which contained all his worldly effects. They consisted of two shirts and a half; two stocks for the neck; a pair or two of worsted stockings; an old pair of corduroy small clothes; a rusty razor; a book of psalm tunes, full of dog's ears; and a broken pitch-pipe. As to the books and furniture of the school-house, they belonged to the community, excepting Cotton Mather's *History of Witchcraft,* a New England Almanac, and a book of dreams and fortune-telling; in which last was a sheet of foolscap much scribbled and blotted in several fruitless attempts to make a copy of verses in honor of the heiress of Van Tassel. These magic books and the poetic scrawl were forthwith consigned to the flames by Hans Van Ripper; who from that time forward determined to send his children no more to school, observing that he never knew any good come of this same reading and writing. Whatever money the schoolmaster possessed, and he had received his quarter's pay but a day or two before, he must have had about his person at the time of his disappearance.

The mysterious event caused much speculation at the church on the following Sunday. Knots of gazers and gossips were collected in the churchyard, at the bridge, and at the spot where the hat and pumpkin had been found. The stories of Brouwer, of Bones, and a whole budget of others, were called to mind; and when they had diligently considered them all, and compared them with the symptoms of the present case, they shook their heads, and came to the conclusion that Ichabod had been carried off by the Galloping Hessian. As he was a bachelor, and in nobody's debt, nobody troubled his head any more about him: the school was removed to a different quarter of the Hollow, and another pedagogue reigned in his stead.

It is true, an old farmer, who had been down to New York on a visit several years after, and from whom this account of the ghostly adventure was received, brought home the intelligence that Ichabod Crane was still alive; that he had left the neighborhood, partly through fear of the goblin and Hans Van Ripper, and partly in mortification at having been suddenly dismissed by the heiress; that he had changed his quarters to a distant part of the country; had kept school and studied law at the same time; he had been admitted to the bar, turned politician, electioneered, written for the newspapers, and finally had been made a justice of the Ten-pound Court. Brom Bones, too, who shortly after his rival's disappearance conducted the blooming Katrina in triumph to the altar, was observed to look exceedingly knowing whenever the story of Ichabod was related, and always burst into a hearty laugh at the mention of the pumpkin; which led some to suspect that he knew more about the matter than he chose to tell.

The old country wives, however, who are the best judges of these matters, maintain to this day that Ichabod was spirited away by supernatural means; and it is a favorite story often told about the neighborhood round the winter evening fire. The bridge became more than ever an object of superstitious awe, and that may be the reason why the road has been altered of late years, so as to approach the church by the border of the mill-pond. The school-house, being deserted, soon fell to decay, and was reported to be haunted by the ghost of the unfortunate pedagogue; and the plough-boy, loitering homeward of a still summer evening, has often fancied his voice at a distance, chanting a melancholy psalm tune among the tranquil solitudes of Sleepy Hollow.

Postscript

FOUND IN THE HANDWRITING OF MR. KNICKERBOCKER

The preceding tale is given, almost in the precise words in which I heard it related at a Corporation meeting of the ancient city of Manhattoes, at which were present many of its sagest and most illustrious burghers. The narrator was a pleasant, shabby, gentlemanly old fellow, in pepper-and-salt clothes, with a sadly humorous face; and one whom I strongly suspected of being poor — he made such efforts to be entertaining. When his story was concluded, there was much laughter and approbation, particularly from two or three deputy aldermen, who had been asleep the greater part of the time. There was, however, one tall, dry-looking old gentleman, with beetling eyebrows, who maintained a grave and rather a severe face throughout: now and then folding his arms, inclining his head, and looking down upon the floor, as if turning a doubt over in his mind. He was one of your wary men, who never laugh, but upon good grounds — when they have reason and the law on their side. When the mirth of the rest of the company had subsided, and silence was restored, he leaned one arm on the elbow of his chair, and sticking the other akimbo, demanded, with a slight but exceedingly sage motion of the head, and contraction of the brow, what was the moral of the story, and what it went to prove?

The story-teller, who was just putting a glass of wine to his lips, as a refreshment after his toils, paused for a moment, looked at his inquirer with an air of infinite deference, and, lowering the glass slowly to the table, observed that the story was intended most logically to prove: —

"That there is no situation in life but has its advantages and pleasures — provided we will but take a joke as we find it:

"That, therefore, he that runs races with goblin troopers is likely to have rough riding of it.

"Ergo, for a country schoolmaster to be refused the hand of a Dutch heiress is a certain step to high preferment in the state."

The cautious old gentleman knit his brows tenfold closer after this explanation, being sorely puzzled by the ratiocination of the syllogism: while, methought, the one in pepper-and-salt eyed him with something of a triumphant leer. At length he observed that all this was very well; but still he thought the story a little on the extravagant — there were one or two points on which he had his doubts.

"Faith sir," replied the story-teller, "as to that matter, I don't believe one half of it myself."

D. K.

Young Goodman Brown

Nathaniel Hawthorne

YOUNG Goodman Brown came forth at sunset into the street at Salem village; but put his head back, after crossing the threshold, to exchange a parting kiss with his young wife. And Faith, as the wife was aptly named, thrust her own pretty head into the street, letting the wind play with the pink ribbons of her cap while she called to Goodman Brown.

"Dearest heart," whispered she, softly and rather sadly, when her lips were close to his ear, "prithee put off your journey until sunrise and sleep in your own bed to-night. A lone woman is troubled with such dreams and such thoughts that she's afeared of herself sometimes. Pray tarry with me this night, dear husband, of all nights in the year."

"My love and my Faith," replied young Goodman Brown, "of all nights in the year, this one night must I tarry away from thee. My journey, as thou callest it, forth and back again, must needs be done 'twixt now and sunrise. What, my sweet, pretty wife, dost thou doubt me already, and we but three months married?"

"Then God bless you!" said Faith, with the pink ribbons; "and may you find all well when you come back."

"Amen!" cried Goodman Brown. "Say thy prayers, dear Faith, and go to bed at dusk, and no harm will come to thee."

So they parted; and the young man pursued his way until, being about to turn the corner by the meeting-house, he looked back and saw the head of Faith still peeping after him with a melancholy air, in spite of her pink ribbons.

"Poor little Faith!" thought he, for his heart smote him. "What a wretch am I to leave her on such an errand! She talks of dreams, too. Methought as she spoke there was trouble in her face, as if a dream had warned her what work is to be done to-night. But no, no; 'twould kill her to think it. Well, she's a blessed angel on earth; and after this one night I'll cling to her skirts and follow her to heaven."

With this excellent resolve for the future, Goodman Brown felt himself justified in making more haste on his present evil purpose. He had taken a dreary road, darkened by all the gloomiest trees of the forest, which barely stood aside to let the narrow path creep through, and closed immediately behind. It was all as lonely as could be; and there is this peculiarity in such a solitude, that the traveler knows not who may be concealed by the innumerable trunks and the thick boughs overhead; so that with lonely footsteps he may yet be passing through an unseen multitude.

"There may be a devilish Indian behind every tree," said Goodman Brown to himself; and he glanced fearfully behind him as he added. "What if the devil himself should be at my very elbow!"

His head being turned back, he passed a crook of the road, and, looking forward again, beheld the figure of a man, in grave and decent attire, seated at the foot of an old tree. He arose at Goodman Brown's approach and walked onward side by side with him.

"You are late, Goodman Brown," said he. "The clock of the Old South was striking as I came through Boston, and that is full fifteen minutes agone."

"Faith kept me back a while," replied the young man, with a tremor in his voice, caused by the sudden appearance of his companion, though not wholly unexpected.

It was now deep dusk in the forest, and deepest in that part of it where these two were journeying. As nearly as could be discerned, the second traveler was about fifty years old, apparently in the same rank of life as Goodman Brown, and bearing a considerable resemblance to him, though perhaps more in expression than features. Still they might have been taken for father and son. And yet, though the elder person was as simply clad as the younger, and as simple in manner too, he had an indescribable air of one who knew the world, and who would not have felt abashed at the governor's dinner table or in King William's court, were it possible that his affairs should call him thither. But the only thing about him that could be fixed upon as remarkable was his staff, which bore the likeness of a great black snake, so curiously wrought that it might almost be seen to twist and wriggle itself like a living serpent. This, of course, must have been an ocular deception, assisted by the uncertain light.

"Come, Goodman Brown," cried his fellow-traveler, "this is a dull pace for the beginning of a journey. Take my staff, if you are so soon weary."

"Friend," said the other, exchanging his slow pace for a full stop, "having kept covenant by meeting thee here, it is my purpose now to return whence I came. I have scruples touching the matter thou wot'st of."

"Sayest thou so?" replied he of the serpent, smiling apart. "Let us walk on, nevertheless, reasoning as we go; and if I convince thee not thou shalt turn back. We are but a little way in the forest yet."

"Too far! too far!" exclaimed the goodman, unconsciously resuming his walk. "My father never went into the woods on such an errand, nor his father before him. We have been a race of honest men and good Christians since the days of the martyrs; and shall I be the first of the name of Brown that ever took this path and kept'' —

''Such company, thou wouldst say,'' observed the elder person, interpreting his pause. ''Well said, Goodman Brown! I have been as well acquainted with your family as with ever a one among the Puritans; and that's no trifle to say. I helped your grandfather, the constable, when he lashed the Quaker woman so smartly through the streets of Salem; and it was I that brought your father a pitch-pine knot, kindled at my own hearth, to set fire to an Indian village, in King Philip's war. They were my good friends, both; and many a pleasant walk have we had along this path, and returned merrily after midnight. I would fain be friends with you for their sake.''

''If it be as thou sayest,'' replied Goodman Brown, ''I marvel they never spoke of these matters; or, verily, I marvel not, seeing that the least rumor of the sort would have driven them from New England. We are a people of prayer, and good works to boot, and abide no such wickedness.''

''Wickedness or not,'' said the traveler with the twisted staff, ''I have a very general acquaintance here in New England. The deacons of many a church have drunk the communion wine with me; the selectmen of divers towns make me their chairman; and a majority of the

Great and General Court are firm supporters of my interest. The governor and I, too — But these are state secrets."

"Can this be so?" cried Goodman Brown, with a stare of amazement at his undisturbed companion. "Howbeit, I have nothing to do with the governor and council; they have their own ways, and are no rule for a simple husbandman like me. But, were I to go on with thee, how should I meet the eye of that good old man, our minister, at Salem village? Oh, his voice would make me tremble both Sabbath day and lecture day."

Thus far the elder traveler had listened with due gravity; but now burst into a fit of irrepressible mirth, shaking himself so violently that his snake-like staff actually seemed to wriggle in sympathy.

"Ha! ha! ha!" shouted he again and again; then composing himself, "Well, go on, Goodman Brown, go on; but, prithee, don't kill me with laughing."

"Well, then, to end the matter at once," said Goodman Brown, considerably nettled. "there is my wife, Faith. It would break her dear little heart; and I'd rather break my own."

"Nay, if that be the case," answered the other, "e'en go thy ways, Goodman Brown. I would not for twenty old women like the one hobbling before us that Faith should come to any harm."

As he spoke he pointed his staff at a female

figure on the path, in whom Goodman Brown recognized a very pious and exemplary dame, who had taught him his catechism in youth, and was still his moral and spiritual adviser, jointly with the minister and Deacon Gookin.

"A marvel, truly, that Goody Cloyse should be so far in the wilderness at nightfall," said he. "But with your leave, friend, I shall take a cut through the woods until we have left this Christian woman behind. Being a stranger to you, she might ask whom I was consorting with and whither I was going."

"Be it so," said his fellow-traveler. "Betake you to the woods, and let me keep the path."

Accordingly the young man turned aside, but took care to watch his companion, who advanced softly along the road until he had come within a staff's length of the old dame. She, meanwhile, was making the best of her way, with singular speed for so aged a woman, and mumbling some indistinct words — a prayer, doubtless — as she went. The traveler put forth his staff and touched her withered neck with what seemed the serpent's tail.

"The devil!" screamed the pious old lady.

"Then Goody Cloyse knows her old friend?" observed the traveler, confronting her and leaning on his writhing stick.

"Ah, forsooth, and is it your worship indeed?" cried the good dame. "Yea, truly is it, and in the very image of my old gossip,

Goodman Brown, the grandfather of the silly fellow that now is. But — would your worship believe it? — my broomstick hath strangely disappeared, stolen, as I suspect, by that unhanged witch, Goody Cory, and that, too, when I was all anointed with the juice of smallage, and cinquefoil, and wolf's bane" —

"Mingled with fine wheat and the fat of a new-born babe," said the shape of old Goodman Brown.

"Ah, your worship knows the recipe," cried the old lady, cackling aloud. "So, as I was saying, being all ready for the meeting, and no horse to ride on, I made up my mind to foot it; for they tell me there is a nice young man to be taken into communion tonight. But now your good worship will lend me your arm, and we shall be there in a twinkling."

"That can hardly be," answered her friend. "I may not spare you my arm, Goody Cloyse; but here is my staff, if you will."

So saying, he threw it down at her feet, where, perhaps, it assumed life, being one of the rods which its owner had formerly lent to the Egyptian magi. Of this fact, however, Goodman Brown could not take cognizance. He had cast up his eyes in astonishment, and, looking down again, beheld neither Goody Cloyse nor the serpentine staff, but his fellow-traveler alone, who waited for him as calmly as if nothing had happened.

"That old woman taught me my catechism,'' said the young man; and there was a world of meaning in this simple comment.

They continued to walk onward, while the elder traveler exhorted his companion to make good speed and persevere in the path, discoursing so aptly that his arguments seemed rather to spring up in the bosom of his auditor than to be suggested by himself. As they went, he plucked a branch of maple to serve for a walking stick, and began to strip it of the twigs and little boughs, which were wet with evening dew. The moment his fingers touched them they became strangely withered and dried up as with a week's sunshine. Thus the pair proceeded, at a good free pace, until suddenly, in a gloomy hollow of the road, Goodman Brown sat himself down on the stump of a tree and refused to go any farther.

''Friend,'' said he, stubbornly, ''my mind is made up. Not another step will I budge on this errand. What if a wretched old woman do choose to go to the devil when I thought she was going to heaven: is that any reason why I should quit my dear Faith and go after her?''

''You will think better of this by and by,'' said his acquaintance, composedly. ''Sit here and rest yourself a while; and when you feel like moving again, there is my staff to help you along.''

Without more words, he threw his companion the maple stick, and was as speedily out of sight as if he had vanished into the deepening gloom. The young man sat a few moments by the roadside, applauding himself greatly, and thinking with how clear a conscience he should meet the minister in his morning walk, nor shrink from the eye of good old Deacon Gookin. And what calm sleep would be his that very night, which was to have been spent so wickedly, but so purely and sweetly now, in the arms of Faith! Amidst these pleasant and praiseworthy meditations, Goodman Brown heard the tramp of horses along the road, and deemed it advisable to conceal himself within the verge of the forest, conscious of the guilty purpose that had brought him thither, though now so happily turned from it.

On came the hoof tramps and the voices of the riders, two grave old voices, conversing soberly as they drew near. These mingled sounds appeared to pass along the road, within a few yards of the young man's hiding place; but, owing doubtless to the depth of the gloom at that particular spot, neither the travelers nor their steeds were visible. Though their figures brushed the small boughs by the wayside, it could not be seen that they intercepted, even for a moment, the faint gleam from the strip of bright sky athwart which they must have passed. Goodman Brown alternately crouched and stood on tiptoe, pulling aside the branches and thrusting forth his head as far as he durst without discerning so much as a shadow. It vexed him the more, because he could have sworn, were such a thing possible, that he recognized the voices of the minister and Deacon Gookin, jogging along quietly, as they were wont to do, when bound to some ordination or ecclesiastical council. While yet within hearing, one of the riders stopped to pluck a switch.

"Of the two, reverend sir," said the voice like the deacon's, "I had rather miss an ordination dinner than to-night's meeting. They tell me that some of our community are to be here from Falmouth and beyond, and others from Connecticut and Rhode Island, besides several of Indian powwows, who, after their fashion, know almost as much deviltry as the best of us. Moreover, there is a goodly young woman to be taken into communion."

"Mighty well, Deacon Gookin!" replied the solemn old tones of the minister. "Spur up, or we shall be late. Nothing can be done you know until I get on the ground."

The hoofs clattered again; and the voices, talking so strangely in the empty air, passed on through the forest, where no church had ever been gathered or solitary Christian prayed. Whither, then, could these holy men be journeying so deep into the heathen wilderness? Young Goodman Brown caught hold of a tree for support, being ready to sink down on the ground, faint and overburdened with the heavy sickness of his heart. He looked up to the sky, doubting whether there really was a heaven above him. Yet there was the blue arch, and the stars brightening in it.

"With heaven above and Faith below, I will yet stand firm against the devil!" cried Goodman Brown.

While he still gazed upward into the deep arch of the firmament and had lifted his hands to pray, a cloud, though no wind was stirring, hurried across the zenith and hid the brightening stars. The blue sky was still visible, except directly overhead, where this black mass of cloud was sweeping swiftly northward. Aloft in the air, as if from the depths of the cloud, came a confused and doubtful sound of voices. Once the listener fancied that he could distinguish the accents of towns-people of his own, men, and women, both pious and ungodly, many of whom he had met at the communion table, and had seen others rioting at the tavern. The next moment, so indistinct were the sounds, he doubted whether he had heard aught but the murmur of the old forest, whispering without a wind. Then came a stronger swell of those familiar tones, heard daily in the sunshine at Salem village, but never until now from a cloud of night. There was one voice of a young woman, uttering lamentations, yet with an uncertain sorrow, and entreating for some favor, which, perhaps, it would grieve her to obtain; and all the unseen multitude, both saints and sinners, seemed to encourage her onward.

"Faith!" shouted Goodman Brown, in a voice of agony and desperation; and the echoes of the forest mocked him, crying, "Faith! Faith!" as if bewildered wretches were seeking her all through the wilderness.

The cry of grief, rage, and terror was yet piercing the night, when the unhappy husband held his breath for a response. There was a scream, drowned immediately in a louder murmur of voices, fading into far-off laughter, as the dark cloud swept away, leaving the clear and silent sky above Goodman Brown. But something fluttered lightly down through the air and caught on the branch of a tree. The young man seized it, and beheld a pink ribbon.

"My Faith is gone!" cried he, after one stupefied moment. "There is no good on earth; and sin is but a name. Come, devil; for to thee is this world given."

And, maddened with despair, so that he laughed loud and long, did Goodman Brown grasp his staff and set forth again, at such a rate that he seemed to fly along the forest path rather than to walk or run. The road grew wilder and drearier and more faintly traced, and vanished at length, leaving him in the heart of the dark wilderness, still rushing onward with the instinct that guides mortal man to evil. The whole forest was peopled with frightful sounds — the creaking of the trees, the howling of wild beasts, and the yell of Indians; while sometimes the wind tolled like a distant church bell, and sometimes gave a broad roar around the traveler, as if all Nature were laughing him to scorn. But he was himself the chief horror of the scene, and shrank not from its other horrors.

"Ha! ha! ha!" roared Goodman Brown when the wind laughed at him. "Let us hear which will laugh loudest. Think not to frighten me with your deviltry. Come witch, come wizard, come Indian powwow, come devil himself, and here comes Goodman Brown. You may as well fear him as he fears you."

In truth, all through the haunted forest there could be nothing more frightful than the figure of Goodman Brown. On he flew among the black pines, brandishing his staff with frenzied gestures, now giving vent to an inspiration of horrid blasphemy, and now shouting forth such laughter as set all the echoes of the forest laughing like demons around him. The fiend in his own shape is less hideous than when he rages in the breast of man. Thus sped the demoniac on his course, until, quivering among the trees, he saw a red light before him, as when the felled trunks and branches of a clearing have been set on fire, and throw up their lurid blaze against the sky, at the hour of midnight. He paused, in a lull of the tempest that had driven him onward, and heard the swell of what seemed a hymn, rolling solemnly from a distance with the weight of many voices. He knew the tune; it was a familiar one in the choir of the village meeting-house. The verse died heavily away, and was lengthened by a chorus, not of human voices, but of all the sounds of the benighted wilderness pealing in awful harmony together. Goodman Brown cried out, and his cry was lost to his own ear by its unison with the cry of the desert.

In the interval of silence he stole forward until the light glared full upon his eyes. At one extremity of an open space, hemmed in by the dark wall of the forest, arose a rock, bearing some rude, natural resemblance either to an altar or a pulpit, and surrounded by four blazing pines, their tops aflame, their stems untouched, like candles at an evening meeting. The mass of foliage that had overgrown the summit of the rock was all on fire, blazing high into the night and fitfully illuminating the whole field. Each pendent twig and leafy festoon was in a blaze. As the red light arose and fell, a numerous congregation alternately shone forth, then disappeared in shadow, and again grew, as it were, out of the darkness, peopling the heart of the solitary woods at once.

"A grave and dark-clad company," quoth Goodman Brown.

In truth they were such. Among them, quivering to and fro between gloom and splendor, appeared faces that would be seen next day at the council board of the province, and others which, Sabbath after Sabbath, looked devoutly heavenward, and benignantly over the crowded pews, from the holiest pulpits in the land. Some affirm that the lady of the governor was there. At least there were high dames well known to her, and wives of honored husbands, and widows, a great multitude, and ancient maidens, all of excellent repute, and fair young girls, who trembled lest their mothers should espy them. Either the sudden gleams of light flashing over the obscure field bedazzled Goodman Brown, or he recognized a score of the church members of Salem village famous for their especial sanctity. Good old Deacon Gookin had arrived, and waited at the skirts of that venerable saint, his revered pastor. But, irreverently consorting with these grave, reputable, and pious people, these elders of the church, these chaste dames and dewy virgins, there were men of dissolute lives and women of spotted fame, wretches given over to all mean and filthy vice, and suspected even of horrid crimes. It was strange to see that the good shrank not from the wicked, nor were the sinners abashed by the saints. Scattered also among their pale-faced enemies were the Indian priests, or powwows, who had often scared their native forest with more hideous incantations than any known to English witchcraft.

"But where is Faith?" thought Goodman Brown; and, as hope came into his heart, he trembled.

Another verse of the hymn arose, a slow and mournful strain, such as the pious love, but joined to words which expressed all that our nature can conceive of sin, and darkly hinted at far more. Unfathomable to mere mortals is the lore of fiends. Verse after verse was sung; and still the chorus of the desert swelled between like the deepest tone of a mighty organ; and with the final peal of that dreadful anthem there came a sound, as if the roaring wind, the rushing streams, the howling beasts, and every other voice of the unconcerted wilderness were mingling and according with the voice of guilty man in homage to the prince of all. The four blazing pines threw up a loftier flame, and obscurely discovered shapes and visages of horror on the smoke wreaths above the impious assembly. At the same moment the fire on the rock shot redly forth and formed a glowing arch above its base, where now appeared a figure. With reverence be it spoken, the figure bore no slight similitude, both in garb and manner, to some grave divine of the New England churches.

"Bring forth the converts!" cried a voice that echoed through the field and rolled into the forest.

At the word, Goodman Brown stepped forth from the shadow of the trees and approached the congregation, with whom he felt a loathful brotherhood by the sympathy of all that was wicked in his heart. He could have well-nigh sworn that the shape of his own dead father beckoned him to advance, looking downward from a smoke wreath, while a woman, with dim features of despair, threw out her hand to warn him back. Was it his mother? But he had no power to retreat one step, nor to resist, even in thought, when the minister and good old Deacon Gookin seized his arms and led him to the blazing rock. Thither came also the slender form of a veiled female, led between Goody Cloyse, that pious teacher of the catechism, and Martha Carrier, who had received the devil's promise to be queen of hell. A rampant hag was she. And there stood the proselytes beneath the canopy of fire.

"Welcome, my children," said the dark figure, "to the communion of your race. Ye have found thus young your nature and your destiny. My children, look behind you!"

They turned; and flashing forth, as it were, in a sheet of flame, the fiend worshipers were seen; the smile of welcome gleamed darkly on every visage.

"There," resumed the sable form, "are all whom ye have reverenced from youth. Ye deemed them holier than yourselves, and shrank from your own sin, contrasting it with their lives of righteousness and prayerful aspirations heavenward. Yet here are they all in my worshiping assembly. This night it shall be granted you to know their secret deeds: how hoary-bearded elders of the church have whispered wanton words to the young maids of their households; how many a woman, eager for widows' weeds, has given her husband a drink at bedtime and let him sleep his last sleep in her bosom; how beardless youths have made haste to inherit their fathers' wealth; and how fair damsels — blush not, sweet ones — have dug little graves in the garden, and bidden me, the sole guest to an infant's funeral. By the sympathy of your human hearts for sin ye shall scent out all the places — whether in church, bedchamber, street, field, or forest — where crime has been committed, and shall exult to behold the whole earth one stain of guilt, one mighty blood spot. Far more than this. It shall be yours to penetrate, in every bosom, the deep mystery of sin, the fountain of all wicked arts, and which inexhaustibly supplies more evil impulses than human power — than my power at its utmost — can make manifest in deeds. And now, my children, look upon each other."

They did so; and, by the blaze of the hell-kindled torches, the wretched man beheld his Faith, and the wife her husband, trembling before that unhallowed altar.

"Lo, there ye stand, my children," said the figure, in a deep and solemn tone, almost sad with its despairing awfulness, as if his once angelic nature could yet mourn for our miserable race. "Depending upon one another's hearts, ye had still hoped that virtue were not all a dream. Now are ye undeceived. Evil is the nature of mankind. Evil must be your only happiness. Welcome again, my children, to the communion of your race."

"Welcome," repeated the fiend worshipers, in one cry of despair and triumph.

And there they stood, the only pair, as it seemed, who were yet hesitating on the verge of wickedness in this dark world. A basin was hollowed, naturally, in the rock. Did it contain water, reddened by the lurid light? or was it blood? or, perchance, a liquid flame? Herein did the shape of evil dip his hand and prepare to lay the mark of baptism upon their foreheads, that they might be partakers of the mystery of sin, more conscious of the secret guilt of others, both in deed and thought, than they could now be of their own. The husband cast one look at his pale wife, and Faith at him. What polluted wretches would the next glance show them to each other, shuddering alike at what they disclosed and what they saw!

"Faith! Faith!" cried the husband, "look up to heaven, and resist the wicked one."

Whether Faith obeyed he knew not. Hardly had he spoken when he found himself amid calm night and solitude, listening to a roar of the wind which died heavily away through the forest. He staggered against the rock, and felt it chill and damp; while a hanging twig, that had been all on fire, besprinkled his cheek with the coldest dew.

The next morning young Goodman Brown came slowly into the street of Salem village, staring around him like a bewildered man. The good old minister was taking a walk along the graveyard to get an appetite for breakfast and meditate his sermon, and bestowed a blessing, as he passed, on Goodman Brown. He shrank from the venerable saint as if to avoid an anathema. Old Deacon Gookin was at domestic worship, and the holy words of his prayer were heard through the open window. "What God doth the wizard pray to?" quoth Goodman Brown. Goody Cloyse, that excellent old Christian, stood in the early sunshine at her own lattice, catechizing a little girl who had brought her a pint of morning's milk. Goodman Brown snatched away the child as from the grasp of the fiend himself. Turning the corner by the meeting-house, he spied the head of Faith, with the pink ribbons, gazing anxiously forth, and bursting into such joy at sight of him that she skipped along the street and almost kissed her husband before the whole village. But Goodman Brown looked sternly and sadly into her face, and passed on without a greeting.

Had Goodman Brown fallen asleep in the forest and only dreamed a wild dream of a witch-meeting?

Be it so if you will; but, alas! it was a dream of evil omen for young Goodman Brown. A stern, a sad, a darkly meditative, a distrustful, if not a desperate man did he become from the night of that fearful dream. On the Sabbath day, when the congregation were singing a holy psalm, he could not listen because an anthem of sin rushed loudly upon his ear and drowned all the blessed strain. When the minister spoke from the pulpit with power and fervid eloquence, and, with his hand on the open Bible, of the sacred truths of our religion, and of saint-like lives and triumphant deaths, and of future bliss or misery unutterable, then did Goodman Brown turn pale, dreading lest the roof should thunder down upon the gray blasphemer and his hearers. Often, waking suddenly at midnight, he shrank from the bosom of Faith; and at morning or eventide, when the family knelt down at prayer, he scowled and muttered to himself, and gazed sternly at his wife, and turned away. And when he had lived long, and was borne to his grave a hoary corpse, followed by Faith, an aged woman, and children and grandchildren, a goodly procession besides neighbors not a few, they carved no hopeful verse upon his tombstone, for his dying hour was gloom.

The Birthmark

Nathaniel Hawthorne

IN the latter part of the last century there lived a man of science, an eminent proficient in every branch of natural philosophy, who not long before our story opens had made experience of a spiritual affinity more attractive than any chemical one. He had left his laboratory to the care of an assistant, cleared his fine countenance from the furnace smoke, washed the stain of acids from his fingers, and persuaded a beautiful woman to become his wife. In those days when the comparatively recent discovery of electricity and other kindred mysteries of Nature seemed to open paths into the region of miracle, it was not unusual for the love of science to rival the love of woman in its depth and absorbing energy. The higher intellect, the imagination, the spirit, and even the heart might all find their congenial aliment in pursuits which, as some of their ardent votaries believed, would ascend from one step of powerful intelligence to another, until the philosopher should lay his hand on the secret of creative force and perhaps make new worlds for himself. We know not whether Aylmer possessed this degree of faith in man's ultimate control over Nature. He had devoted himself, however, too unreservedly to scientific studies ever to be weaned from them by any second passion. His love for his young wife might prove the stronger of the two; but it could only be by intertwining itself with his love of science, and uniting the strength of the latter to his own.

Such a union accordingly took place, and was attended with truly remarkable consequences and a deeply impressive moral. One day, very soon after their marriage, Aylmer sat gazing at his wife with a trouble in his countenance that grew stronger until he spoke.

"Georgiana," said he, "has it never occurred to you that the mark upon your cheek might be removed?"

"No, indeed," said she, smiling; but perceiving the seriousness of his manner, she blushed deeply. "To tell you the truth it has been so often called a charm that I was simple enough to imagine it might be so."

"Ah, upon another face perhaps it might," replied her husband; "but never on yours. No, dearest Georgiana, you came so nearly perfect from the hand of Nature that this slightest possible defect, which we hesitate whether to term a defect or a beauty, shocks me, as being the visible mark of earthly imperfection."

"Shocks you, my husband!" cried Georgiana, deeply hurt; at first reddening with momentary anger, but then bursting into tears. "Then why did you take me from my mother's side? You cannot love what shocks you!"

To explain this conversation it must be mentioned that in the center of Georgiana's left cheek there was a singular mark, deeply interwoven, as it were, with the texture and substance of her face. In the usual state of her complexion — a healthy though delicate bloom — the mark wore a tint of deeper crimson, which imperfectly defined its shape amid the surrounding rosiness. When she blushed it gradually became more indistinct, and finally vanished amid the triumphant rush of blood that bathed the whole cheek with its brilliant glow. But if any shifting motion caused her to turn pale there was the mark again, a crimson stain upon the snow, in what Aylmer sometimes deemed an almost fearful distinctness. Its shape bore not a little similarity to the human hand, though of the smallest pygmy size. Georgiana's lovers were wont to say that some fairy at her birth hour had laid her tiny hand upon the infant's cheek, and left this impress there in token of the magic endowments that were to give her such sway over all hearts. Many a desperate swain would have risked life for the privilege of pressing his lips to the mysterious hand. It must not be concealed, however, that the impression wrought by this fairy sign manual varied exceedingly, according to the difference of temperament in the beholders. Some fastidious persons — but they were exclusively of her own sex — affirmed that the bloody hand, as they chose to call it, quite destroyed the effect of Georgiana's beauty, and rendered her countenance even hideous. But it would be as reasonable to say that one of those small blue stains which sometimes occur in the purest statuary marble would convert the Eve of Powers to a monster. Masculine observers, if the birthmark did not heighten their admiration, contented themselves with wishing it away, that the world might possess one living specimen of ideal loveliness without the semblance of a flaw. After his marriage, — for he thought little or nothing of the matter before, — Aylmer discovered that this was the case with himself.

Had she been less beautiful, — if Envy's self could have found aught else to sneer at, — he might have felt his affection heightened by the prettiness of this mimic hand, now vaguely portrayed, now lost, now stealing forth again and glimmering to and fro with every pulse of emotion that throbbed within her heart; but seeing her otherwise so perfect, he found this one defect grow more and more intolerable with every moment of their united lives. It was the fatal flaw of humanity which Nature, in one shape or another, stamps ineffaceably on all her productions, either to imply that they are temporary and finite, or that their perfection must be wrought by toil and pain. The crimson hand expressed the ineludible gripe in which mortality clutches the highest and purest of earthly mold, degrading them into kindred with the lowest, and even with the very brutes, like whom their visible frames return to dust. In this manner, selecting it as the symbol of his wife's liability to sin, sorrow, decay, and death, Aylmer's somber imagination was not long in rendering the birthmark a frightful object, causing him more trouble and horror than ever Georgiana's beauty, whether of soul or sense, had given him delight.

At all the seasons which should have been their happiest, he invariably and without intending it, nay, in spite of a purpose to the contrary, reverted to this one disastrous topic. Trifling as it at first appeared, it so connected itself with innumerable trains of thought and modes of feeling that it became the central point of all. With the morning twilight Aylmer opened his eyes upon his wife's face and recognized the symbol of imperfection; and when they sat together at the evening hearth his eyes wandered stealthily to her cheek, and beheld, flickering with the blaze of the wood fire, the spectral hand that wrote mortality where he would fain have worshiped. Georgiana soon learned to shudder at his gaze. It needed but a glance with the peculiar expression that his face often wore to change the roses of her cheek into a deathlike paleness, amid which the crimson hand was brought strongly out, like a bas-relief of ruby on the whitest marble.

Late one night when the lights were growing dim, so as hardly to betray the stain on the poor wife's cheek, she herself, for the first time, voluntarily took up the subject.

"Do you remember, my dear Aylmer," said she, with a feeble attempt at a smile, "have you any recollection of a dream last night about this odious hand?"

"None! none whatever!" replied Aylmer, starting; but then he added, in a dry, cold tone, affected for the sake of concealing the real depth of his emotion, "I might well dream of it; for before I fell asleep it had taken a pretty firm hold of my fancy."

"And you did dream of it?" continued Georgiana, hastily; for she dreaded lest a gush of tears should interrupt what she had to say. "A terrible dream! I wonder that you can forget it. Is it possible to forget this one expression? — 'It is in her heart now; we must have it out!' Reflect, my husband; for by all means I would have you recall that dream."

The mind is in a sad state when Sleep, the all-involving, cannot confine her specters within the dim region of her sway, but suffers them to break forth, affrighting this actual life with secrets that perchance belong to a deeper one. Aylmer now remembered his dream. He had fancied himself with his servant Aminadab, attempting an operation for the removal of the birthmark; but the deeper went the knife, the deeper sank the hand, until at length its tiny grasp appeared to have caught hold of Georgiana's heart; whence, however, her husband was inexorably resolved to cut or wrench it away.

When the dream had shaped itself perfectly in his memory, Aylmer sat in his wife's presence with a guilty feeling. Truth often finds its way to the mind close muffled in robes of sleep, and then speaks with uncompromising directness of matters in regard to which we practice an unconscious self-deception during our waking moments. Until now he had not been aware of the tyrannizing influence acquired by one idea over his mind, and of the lengths which he might find in his heart to go for the sake of giving himself peace.

"Aylmer," resumed Georgiana, solemnly, "I know not what may be the cost to both of us to rid me of this fatal birthmark. Perhaps its removal may cause cureless deformity; or it may be the stain goes as deep as life itself. Again: do we know that there is a possibility, on any terms, of unclasping the firm gripe of this little hand which was laid upon me before I came into the world?"

"Dearest Georgiana, I have spent much thought upon the subject," hastily interrupted

Aylmer. "I am convinced of the perfect practicability of its removal."

"If there be the remotest possibility of it," continued Georgiana, "let the attempt be made at whatever risk. Danger is nothing to me; for life, while this hateful mark makes me the object of your horror and disgust, — life is a burden which I would fling down with joy. Either remove this dreadful hand, or take my wretched life! You have deep science. All the world bears witness of it. You have achieved great wonders. Cannot you remove this little, little mark, which I cover with the tips of two small fingers? Is this beyond your power, for the sake of your own peace, and to save your poor wife from madness?"

"Noblest, dearest, tenderest wife," cried Aylmer, rapturously, "doubt not my power. I have already given this matter the deepest thought — thought which might almost have enlightened me to create a being less perfect than yourself. Georgiana, you have led deeper than ever into the heart of science. I feel myself fully competent to render this dear cheek as faultless as its fellow; and then, most beloved, what will be my triumph when I shall have corrected what Nature left imperfect in her fairest work! Even Pygmalion, when his sculptured woman assumed life, felt not greater ecstasy than mine will be."

"It is resolved, then," said Georgiana, faintly smiling. "And, Aylmer, spare me not, though you should find the birthmark take refuge in my heart at last.''

Her husband tenderly kissed her cheek — her right cheek — not that which bore the impress of the crimson hand.

The next day Aylmer apprised his wife of a plan that he had formed whereby he might have opportunity for the intense thought and constant watchfulness which the proposed operation would require; while Georgiana, likewise, would enjoy the perfect repose essential to its success. They were to seclude themselves in the extensive apartments occupied by Aylmer as a laboratory, and where, during his toilsome youth, he had made discoveries in the elemental powers of Nature that had roused the admiration of all the learned societies in Europe. Seated calmly in this laboratory, the pale philosopher had investigated the secrets of the highest cloud region and of the profoundest mines; he had satisfied himself of the causes that kindled and kept alive the fires of the volcano; and had explained the mystery of the fountains, and how it is that they gush forth, some so bright and pure, and others with such rich medicinal virtues, from the dark bosom of the earth. Here, too, at an earlier period, he had studied the wonders of the human frame, and attempted to fathom the very process by which Nature assimilates all her precious influences from earth and air, and from the spiritual world, to create and foster man, her masterpiece. The latter pursuit, however, Aylmer had long laid aside in unwilling recognition of the truth — against which all seekers sooner or later stumble — that our great creative Mother, while she amuses us with apparently working in the broadest sunshine, is yet severely careful to keep her own secrets, and, in spite of her pretended openness, shows us nothing but results. She permits us, indeed, to mar, but seldom to mend, and, like a jealous patentee, on no account to make. Now, however, Aylmer resumed these half-forgotten investigations; not, of course, with such hopes or wishes as first suggested them; but because they involved much physiological truth and lay in the path of his proposed scheme for the treatment of Georgiana.

As he led her over the threshold of the laboratory, Georgiana was cold and tremulous. Aylmer looked cheerfully into her face, with intent to reassure her, but was so startled with the intense glow of the birthmark upon the whiteness of her cheek that he could not restrain a strong convulsive shudder. His wife fainted.

"Aminadab! Aminadab!" shouted Aylmer, stamping violently on the floor.

Forthwith there issued from an inner apartment a man of low stature, but bulky frame, with shaggy hair hanging about his visage, which was grimed with the vapors of the furnace. This personage had been Aylmer's underworker during his whole scientific career, and was admirably fitted for that office by his great mechanical readiness, and the skill with which, while incapable of comprehending a single principle, he executed all the details of his master's experiments. With his vast strength, his shaggy hair, his smoky aspect, and the indescribable earthiness that incrusted him, he seemed to represent man's physical nature; while Aylmer's slender figure, and pale, intellectual face, were no less apt a type of the spiritual element.

"Throw open the door of the boudoir, Aminadab," said Aylmer, "and burn a pastil."

"Yes, master," answered Aminadab, looking intently at the lifeless form of Georgiana; and then he muttered to himself, "If she were my wife, I'd never part with that birthmark."

When Georgiana recoverd consciousness she found herself breathing an atmosphere of penetrating fragrance, the gentle potency of which had recalled her from her deathlike faintness. The scene around her looked like enchantment. Aylmer had converted those smoky, dingy, somber rooms, where he had spent his brightest years in recondite pursuits, into a series of beautiful apartments not unfit to be the secluded abode of a lovely woman. The walls were hung with gorgeous curtains, which imparted the combination of grandeur and grace that no other species of adornment can achieve; and as they fell from the ceiling to the floor, their rich and ponderous folds, concealing all angles and straight lines, appeared to shut in the scene from infinite space. For aught Georgiana knew, it might be a pavilion among the clouds. And Alymer, excluding the sunshine, which would have interfered with his chemical processes, had supplied its place with perfumed lamps, emitting flames of various hue, but all uniting in a soft, impurpled radiance. He now knelt by his wife's side, watching her earnestly, but without alarm; for he was confident in his science, and felt that he could draw a magic circle round her within which no evil might intrude.

"Where am I? Ah, I remember," said Georgiana, faintly; and she placed her hand over her cheek to hide the terrible mark from her husband's eyes.

"Fear not, dearest!" exclaimed he. "Do not shrink from me! Believe me, Georgiana, I even rejoice in this single imperfection, since it will be such a rapture to remove it."

"Oh, spare me!" sadly replied his wife. "Pray do not look at it again. I never can forget that convulsive shudder."

In order to soothe Georgiana, and, as it were, to release her mind from the burden of actual things, Aylmer now put in practice some of the light and playful secrets which science had taught him among its profounder lore. Airy figures, absolutely bodiless ideas, and forms of unsubstantial beauty came and danced before her, imprinting their momentary footsteps on beams of light. Though she had some indistinct idea of the method of these optical phenomena, still the illusion was almost perfect enough to warrant the belief that her husband possessed sway over the spiritual world. Then again, when she felt a wish to look forth from her seclusion, immediately, as if her thoughts were answered, the procession of external existence flitted across a screen. The scenery and the figures of actual life were perfectly represented, but with that bewitching, yet indescribable difference which always makes a picture, an image, or a shadow so much more attractive than the original. When wearied of this Aylmer bade her cast her eyes upon a vessel containing a quantity of earth. She did so, with little interest at first; but was soon startled to perceive the germ of a plant shooting upward from the soil. Then came the slender stalk; the leaves gradually unfolded themselves; and amid them was a perfect and lovely flower.

"It is magical!" cried Georgiana. "I dare not touch it."

"Nay, pluck it," answered Aylmer, — "pluck it, and inhale its brief perfume while you may. The flower will wither in a few moments and leave nothing save its brown seed vessels; but thence may be perpetuated a race as ephemeral as itself."

But Georgiana had no sooner touched the flower than the whole plant suffered a blight, its leaves turning coal-black as if by the agency of fire.

"There was too powerful a stimulus," said Aylmer, thoughtfully.

To make up for this abortive experiment, he proposed to take her portrait by a scientific process of his own invention. It was to be effected by rays of light striking upon a polished plate of metal. Georgiana assented; but, on looking at the result, was affrighted to find the features of the portrait blurred and indefinable; while the minute figure of a hand appeared where the cheek should have been. Aylmer snatched the metallic plate and threw it into a jar of corrosive acid.

Soon, however, he forgot these mortifying failures. In the intervals of study and chemical experiment he came to her flushed and exhausted, but seemed invigorated by her presence, and spoke in glowing language of the resources of his art. He gave a history of the long dynasty of the alchemists, who spent so many ages in quest of the universal solvent by which the golden principle might be elicited from all things vile and base. Aylmer appeared to believe that, by the plainest scientific logic, it was altogether within the limits of possibility to discover this long-sought medium; "but," he added, "a philosopher who should go deep enough to acquire the power would attain too lofty a wisdom to stoop to the exercise of it." Not less singular were his opinions in regard to the elixir vitae. He more than intimated that it was at his option to concoct a liquid that should prolong life for years, perhaps interminably; but that it would produce a discord in Nature which all the world, and chiefly the quaffer of the immortal nostrum, would find cause to curse.

"Aylmer, are you in earnest?" asked Georgiana, looking at him with amazement and fear. "It is terrible to possess such power, or even to dream of possessing it."

"Oh, do not tremble, my love," said her husband. "I would not wrong either you or myself by working such inharmonious effects upon our lives; but I would have you consider how trifling, in comparison, is the skill requisite to remove this little hand."

At the mention of the birthmark, Georgiana, as usual, shrank as if a redhot iron had touched her cheek.

Again Aylmer applied himself to his labors. She could hear his voice in the distant furnace room giving directions to Aminadab, whose harsh, uncouth, misshapen tones were audible in response, more like the grunt or growl of a brute than human speech. After hours of absence, Aylmer reappeared and proposed that she should now examine his cabinet of chemical products and natural treasures of the earth. Among the former he showed her a small vial, in which, he remarked, was contained a gentle yet most powerful fragrance, capable of impregnating all the breezes that blow across a kingdom. They were of inestimable value, the contents of that little vial; and, as he said so, he threw some of the perfume into the air and filled the room with piercing and invigorating delight.

"And what is this?" asked Georgiana, pointing to a small crystal globe containing a gold-colored liquid. "It is so beautiful to the eye that I could imagine it the elixir of life."

"In one sense it is," replied Aylmer; "or, rather, the elixir of immortality. It is the most precious poison that ever was concocted in this world. By its aid I could apportion the lifetime of any mortal at whom you might point your finger. The strength of the dose would determine whether he were to linger out years, or drop dead in the midst of a breath. No king on his guarded throne could keep his life if I, in my private station, should deem that the welfare of millions justified me in depriving him of it."

"Why do you keep such a terrific drug?" inquired Georgiana in horror.

"Do not mistrust me, dearest," said her husband, smiling; "its virtuous potency is yet greater than its harmful one. But see! here is a powerful cosmetic. With a few drops of this in a vase of water, freckles may be washed away as easily as the hands are cleansed. A stronger infusion would take the blood out of the cheek, and leave the rosiest beauty a pale ghost."

"Is it with this lotion that you intend to bathe my cheek?" asked Georgiana, anxiously.

"Oh, no," hastily replied her husband; "this is merely superficial. Your case demands a remedy that shall go deeper."

In his interviews with Georgiana, Aylmer generally made minute inquiries as to her sensations and whether the confinement of the rooms and the temperature of the atmosphere agreed with her. These questions had such a particular drift that Georgiana began to conjecture that she was already subjected to certain physical influences, either breathed in with the fragrant air or taken with her food. She fancied likewise, but it might be altogether fancy, that there was a stirring up of her system — a strange, indefinite sensation creeping through her veins, and tingling, half painfully, half pleasurably, at her heart. Still, whenever she dared to look into the mirror, there she beheld herself pale as a white rose and with the crimson birthmark stamped upon her cheek. Not even Aylmer now hated it so much as she.

To dispel the tedium of the hours which her husband found it necessary to devote to the processes of combination and analysis, Georgiana turned over the volumes of his scientific library. In many dark old tomes she met with chapters full of romance and poetry. They were the works of philosophers of the middle ages, such as Albertus Magnus, Cornelius Agrippa, Paracelsus, and the famous friar who created the prophetic Brazen Head. All these antique naturalists stood in advance of their centuries, yet were imbued with some of their credulity, and therefore were believed, and perhaps imagined themselves to have acquired from the investigation of Nature a power above Nature, and from physics a sway over the spiritual world. Hardly less curious and imaginative were the early volumes of the Transactions of the Royal Society, in which the members, knowing little of the limits of natural possibility, were continually recording wonders or proposing methods whereby wonders might be wrought.

But to Georgiana the most engrossing volume was a large folio from her husband's own hand, in which he had recorded every experiment of his scientific career, its original aim, the methods adopted for its development, and its final success or failure, with the circumstances to which either event was attributable. The book, in truth, was both the history and emblem of his ardent, ambitious, imaginative, yet practical and laborious life. He handled physical details as if there were nothing beyond them; yet spiritualized them all, and redeemed himself from materialism by his strong and eager aspiration towards the infinite. In his grasp the veriest clod of earth assumed a soul. Georgiana, as she read, reverenced Aylmer and loved him more profoundly than ever, but with a less entire dependence on his judgment than heretofore. Much as he had accomplished, she could not but observe that his most splendid successes were almost invariably failures, if compared with the ideal at which he aimed. His brightest diamonds were the merest pebbles, and felt to be so by himself, in comparison with the inestimable gems which lay hidden beyond his reach. The volume, rich with achievements that had won renown for its author, was yet as melancholy a record as ever mortal hand had penned. It was the sad confession and continual exemplification of the shortcomings of the composite man, the spirit burdened with clay and working in matter, and of the despair that assails the higher nature at finding itself so miserably thwarted by the earthly part. Perhaps every man of genius in whatever sphere might recognize the image of his own experience in Aylmer's journal.

So deeply did these reflections affect Georgiana that she laid her face upon the open volume and burst into tears. In this situation she was found by her husband.

"It is dangerous to read in a sorcerer's books," said he with a smile, though his countenance was uneasy and displeased. "Georgiana, there are pages in that volume which

I can scarcely glance over and keep my senses. Take heed lest it prove as detrimental to you."

"It has made me worship you more than ever," said she.

"Ah, wait for this one success," rejoined he, "then worship me if you will. I shall deem myself hardly unworthy of it. But come, I have sought you for the luxury of your voice. Sing to me, dearest."

So she poured out the liquid music of her voice to quench the thirst of his spirit. He then took his leave with a boyish exuberance of gaiety, assuring her that her seclusion would endure but a little longer, and that the result was already certain. Scarcely had he departed when Georgiana felt irresistibly impelled to follow him. She had forgotten to inform Aylmer of a symptom which for two or three hours past had begun to excite her attention. It was a sensation in the fatal birthmark, not painful, but which induced a restlessness throughout her system. Hastening after her husband, she intruded for the first time into the laboratory.

The first thing that struck her eye was the furnace, that hot and feverish worker, with the intense glow of its fire, which by the quantities of soot clustered above it seemed to have been burning for ages. There was a distilling apparatus in full operation. Around the room were retorts, tubes, cylinders, crucibles, and other apparatus of chemical research. An electrical machine stood ready for immediate use.

The atmosphere felt oppressively close, and was tainted with gaseous odors which had been tormented forth by the processes of science. The severe and homely simplicity of the apartment, with its naked walls and brick pavement, looked strange, accustomed as Georgiana had become to the fantastic elegance of her boudoir. But what chiefly, indeed almost solely, drew her attention, was the aspect of Aylmer himself.

He was pale as death, anxious and absorbed, and hung over the furnace as if it depended upon his utmost watchfulness whether the liquid which it was distilling should be the draught of immortal happiness or misery. How different from the sanguine and joyous mien that he had assumed for Georgiana's encouragement!

"Carefully now, Aminadab; carefully, thou human machine; carefully, thou man of clay!" muttered Aylmer, more to himself than his assistant. "Now if there be a thought too much or too little, it is all over."

"Ho! ho!" mumbled Aminadab. "Look, master! look!"

Aylmer raised his eyes hastily, and at first reddened, then grew paler than ever, on beholding Georgiana. He rushed towards her and seized her arm with a gripe that left the print of his fingers upon it.

"Why do you come hither? Have you no trust in your husband?" cried he, impetuously.

"Would you throw the blight of that fatal birthmark over my labors? It is not well done. Go, prying woman, go!"

"Nay, Aylmer," said Georgiana with the firmness of which she possessed no stinted endowment, "it is not you that have a right to complain. You mistrust your wife; you have concealed the anxiety with which you watch the development of this experiment. Think not so unworthily of me, my husband. Tell me all the risk we run, and fear not that I shall shrink; for my share in it is far less than your own."

"No, no, Georgiana!" said Aylmer, impatiently; "it must not be."

"I submit," replied she calmly. "And, Aylmer, I shall quaff whatever draught you bring me; but it will be on the same principle that would induce me to take a dose of poison if offered by your hand."

"My noble wife," said Aylmer, deeply moved, "I knew not the height and depth of your nature until now. Nothing shall be concealed. Know, then, that this crimson hand, superficial as it seems, has clutched its grasp into your being with a strength of which I had no previous conception. I have already administered agents powerful enough to do aught except to change your entire physical system. Only one thing remains to be tried. If that fail us we are ruined."

"Why did you hesitate to tell me this?" asked she.

"Because, Georgiana," said Aylmer, in a low voice, "there is danger."

"Danger? There is but one danger — that this horrible stigma shall be left upon my cheek!" cried Georgiana. "Remove it, remove it, whatever be the cost, or we shall both go mad!"

"Heaven knows your words are too true," said Aylmer, sadly. "And now, dearest, return to your boudoir. In a little while all will be tested."

He conducted her back and took leave of her with a solemn tenderness which spoke far more than his words how much was now at stake. After his departure, Georgiana became rapt in musings. She considered the character of Aylmer, and did it completer justice than at any previous moment. Her heart exulted, while it trembled, at his honorable love — so pure and lofty that it would accept nothing less than perfection nor miserably make itself contented with an earthlier nature than he had dreamed of. She felt how much more precious was such a sentiment than that meaner kind which would have borne with the imperfection for her sake, and have been guilty of treason to holy love by degrading its perfect idea to the level of the actual; and with her whole spirit she prayed that, for a single moment, she might satisfy his highest and deepest conception. Longer than one moment she well knew it could not be; for his spirit was ever on the march, ever ascending, and each instant required something that was beyond the scope of the instant before.

The sound of her husband's footsteps aroused her. He bore a crystal goblet containing a liquor colorless as water, but bright enough to be the draught of immortality. Aylmer was pale; but it seemed rather the consequence of a highly-wrought state of mind and tension of spirit than of fear or doubt.

"The concoction of the draught has been perfect," said he, in answer to Georgiana's look. "Unless all my science have deceived me, it cannot fail."

"Save on your account, my dearest Aylmer," observed his wife, "I might wish to put off this birthmark of mortality by relinquishing mortality itself in preference to any other mode. Life is but a sad possession to those who have attained precisely the degree of moral advancement at which I stand. Were I weaker and blinder it might be happiness. Were I stronger, it might be endured hopefully. But being what I find myself, methinks I am of all mortals the most fit to die."

"You are fit for heaven without tasting death!" replied her husband. "But why do we speak of dying? The draught cannot fail. Behold its effect upon this plant."

On the window seat there stood a geranium diseased with yellow blotches, which had overspread all its leaves. Aylmer poured a small quantity of the liquid upon the soil in which it grew. In a little time, when the roots of the plant had taken up the moisture, the unsightly blotches began to be extinguished in a living verdure.

"There needed no proof," said Georgiana, quietly. "Give me the goblet. I joyfully stake all upon your word."

"Drink, then, thou lofty creature!" exclaimed Aylmer, with fervid admiration. "There is no taint of imperfection on thy spirit. Thy sensible frame, too, shall soon be all perfect."

She quaffed the liquid and returned the goblet to his hand.

"It is grateful," said she with a placid smile. "Methinks it is like water from a heavenly fountain; for it contains I know not what of unobtrusive fragrance and deliciousness. It allays a feverish thirst that had parched me for many days. Now, dearest, let me sleep. My earthly senses are closing over my spirit like the leaves around the heart of a rose at sunset."

She spoke the last words with a gentle reluctance, as if it required almost more energy than she could command to pronounce the faint and lingering syllables. Scarcely had they loitered through her lips ere she was lost in slumber. Aylmer sat by her side, watching her aspect with the emotions proper to a man the whole value of whose existence was involved in the process now to be tested. Mingled with this mood, however, was the philosophic investigation characteristic of the man of science. Not the minutest symptom escaped him. A heightened flush of the cheek, a slight irregularity of breath, a quiver of the eyelid, a hardly perceptible tremor through the frame, — such were the details which, as the moments passed, he wrote down in his folio volume. Intense thought had set its stamp upon every previous page of that volume, but the thoughts of years were all concentrated upon the last.

While thus employed, he failed not to gaze often at the fatal hand, and not without a shudder. Yet once, by a strange and unaccountable impulse, he pressed it with his lips. His spirit recoiled, however, in the very act; and Georgiana, out of the midst of her deep sleep, moved uneasily and murmured as if in remonstrance. Again Aylmer resumed his watch. Nor was it without avail. The crimson hand, which at first had been strongly visible upon the marble paleness of Georgiana's cheek, now grew more faintly outlined. She remained not less pale than ever; but the birthmark, with every breath that came and went, lost somewhat of its former distinctness. Its presence had been awful; its departure was more awful still. Watch the stain of the rainbow fading out the sky, and you will know how that mysterious symbol passed away.

"By Heaven! it is well-nigh gone!" said Alymer to himself, in almost irrepressible ecstasy. "I can scarcely trace it now. Success! success! And now it is like the faintest rose color. The lightest flush of blood across her cheek would overcome it. But she is so pale!"

He drew aside the window curtain and suffered the light of natural day to fall into the room and rest upon her cheek. At the same time he heard a gross hoarse chuckle, which he had long known as his servant Aminadab's expression of delight.

"Ah, clod! ah, earthly mass!" cried Aylmer, laughing in a sort of frenzy, "you have served me well! Matter and spirit — earth and heaven — have both done their part in this! Laugh, thing of the senses! You have earned the right to laugh."

These exclamations broke Georgiana's sleep. She slowly unclosed her eyes and gazed into the mirror which her husband had arranged for that purpose. A faint smile flitted over her lips when she recognized how barely perceptible was now that crimson hand which had once blazed forth with such disastrous brilliancy as to scare away all their happiness. But then her eyes sought Aylmer's face with a trouble and anxiety that he could by no means account for.

"My poor Aylmer!" murmured she.

"Poor? Nay, richest, happiest, most favored!" exclaimed he. "My peerless bride, it is successful! You are perfect!"

"My poor Aylmer," she repeated, with a

more than human tenderness, "you have aimed loftily; you have done nobly. Do not repent that with so high and pure a feeling, you have rejected the best the earth could offer. Aylmer, dearest Aylmer, I am dying!"

Alas! it was too true! the fatal hand had grappled with the mystery of life, and was the bond by which an angelic spirit kept itself in union with a mortal frame. As the last crimson tint of the birthmark — that sole token of human imperfection — faded from her cheek, the parting breath of the now perfect woman passed into the atmosphere, and her soul, lingering a moment near her husband, took its heavenward flight. Then a hoarse, chuckling laugh was heard again! Thus ever does the gross fatality of earth exult in its invariable triumph over the immortal essence which, in this dim sphere of half development, demands the completeness of a higher state. Yet, had Aylmer reached a profounder wisdom, he need not thus have flung away the happiness which would have woven his mortal life of the selfsame texture with the celestial. The momentary circumstance was too strong for him; he failed to look beyond the shadowy scope of time, and, living once for all in eternity, to find the perfect future in the present.

The Murders in the Rue Morgue

Edgar Allan Poe

THE mental features discoursed of as the analytical, are, in themselves, but little susceptible of analysis. We appreciate them only in their effects. We know of them, among other things, that they are always to their possessor, when inordinately possessed, a source of the liveliest enjoyment. As the strong man exults in his physical ability, delighting in such exercises as call his muscles into action, so glories the analyst in that moral activity which *disentangles*. He derives pleasure from even the most trivial occupations bringing his talents into play. He is fond of enigmas, of conundrums, of hieroglyphics; exhibiting in his solutions of each a degree of *acumen* which appears to the ordinary apprehension preternatural. His results, brought about by the very soul and essence of method, have, in truth, the whole air of intuition. The faculty of re-solution is possibly much invigorated by mathematical study, and especially by that highest branch of it which, unjustly, and merely on account of its retrograde operations, has been called, as if *par excellence,* analysis. Yet to calculate is not in itself to analyze. A chess-player, for example, does the one without effort at the other. It follows that the game of chess, in its effects upon mental character, is greatly misunderstood. I am not now writing a treatise, but simply prefacing a somewhat peculiar narrative by observations very much at random; I will, therefore, take occasion to assert that the higher powers of the reflective intellect are more decidedly and more usefully tasked by the unostentatious game of draughts than by all the elaborate frivolity of chess. In this latter, where the pieces have different and *bizarre* motions, with various and variable values, what is only complex is mistaken (a not unusual error) for what is profound. The *attention* is here called powerfully into play. If it flag for an instant, an oversight is committed, resulting in injury or defeat. The possible moves being not only manifold but involute, the chances of such oversights are multiplied; and in nine cases out of ten it is the more concentrative rather than the more acute player who conquers. In draughts, on the contrary, where the moves are *unique* and have but little variation, the probabilities of inadvertence are diminished, and the mere attention being left comparatively unemployed, what advantages are obtained by either party are obtained by superior *acumen*. To be less abstract — Let us suppose a game of draughts where the pieces are reduced to four kings, and where, of course, no oversight is to be expected. It is obvious that here the victory can be decided (the players being at all equal) only by some *recherché* movement, the result of some strong exertion of the intellect. Deprived of ordinary resources, the analyst throws himself into the spirit of his opponent, identifies himself therewith, and not unfrequently sees thus, at a glance, the sole methods (sometimes indeed absurdly simple ones) by which he may seduce into error or hurry into miscalculation.

Whist has long been noted for its influence upon what is termed the calculating power; and men of the highest order of intellect have been known to take an apparently unaccountable delight in it, while eschewing chess as frivolous. Beyond doubt there is nothing of a similar nature so greatly tasking the faculty of analysis. The best chess-player in Christendom *may* be little more than the best player of chess; but proficiency in whist implies capacity for success in all these more important undertakings where mind struggles with mind. When I say proficiency, I mean that perfection in the game which includes a comprehension of *all* the sources whence legitimate advantage may be derived. These are not only manifold but multiform, and lie frequently among recesses of thought altogether inaccessible to the ordinary understanding. To observe attentively is to remember distinctly; and, so far, the concentrative chess-player will do very well at whist; while the rules of Hoyle (themselves based upon the mere mechanism of the game) are sufficiently and generally comprehensible. Thus to have a retentive memory, and to proceed by "the book," are points commonly regarded as the sum total of good playing. But it is in matters beyond the limits of mere rule that the skill of the analyst is evinced. He makes, in silence, a host of observations and inferences. So, perhaps, do his companions; and the difference in the extent of the information obtained, lies not so much in the validity of the inference as in the quality of the observation. The necessary knowledge is that of *what* to observe. Our player confines himself not at all; nor, because the game is the object, does he reject deductions from things external to the game. He examines the countenance of his partner, comparing it carefully with that of each of his opponents. He considers the mode of assorting the cards in each hand; often counting trump by trump, and honor by honor, through the glances bestowed by their holders upon each. He notes every variation of face as the play progresses, gathering a fund of thought from the differences in the expression of certainty, of surprise, of triumph, or chagrin. From the manner of gathering up a trick he judges whether the person taking it can make another in the suit. He recognizes what is played through feint, by the air with which it is thrown upon the table. A casual or inadvertent word; the accidental dropping or turning of a card, with the accompanying anxiety or carelessness in regard to its concealment; the counting of the tricks, with the order of their arrangement; embarrassment, hesitation, eagerness or trepidation — all afford, to his apparently intuitive perception, indications of the true state of affairs. The first two or three rounds having been played, he is in full possession of the contents of each hand, and thenceforward puts down his cards with as absolute a precision of purpose as if the rest of the party had turned outward the faces of their own.

The analytical power should not be confounded with simple ingenuity; for while the analyst is necessarily ingenious, the ingenious man is often remarkably incapable of analysis. The consecutive or combining power, by which ingenuity is usually manifested, and to which the phrenologists (I believe erroneously) have assigned a separate organ, supposing it a primitive faculty, has been so frequently seen in those whose intellect bordered otherwise upon idiocy, as to have attracted general observation among writers on morals. Between ingenuity and the analytic ability there exists a difference far greater, indeed, than that between the fancy and the imagination, but of a character very strictly analogous. It will be found, in fact, that the ingenious are always fanciful, and the *truly* imaginative never otherwise than analytic.

The narrative which follows will appear to the reader somewhat in the light of a commentary upon the propositions just advanced.

Residing in Paris during the spring and part of the summer of 18—, I there became acquainted with a Monsieur C. Auguste Dupin. This young gentleman was of an excellent — indeed of an illustrious family, but, by a variety of untoward events, had been reduced to such poverty that the energy of his character succumbed beneath it, and he ceased to bestir himself in the world, or to care for the retrieval of his fortunes. By courtesy of his creditors, there still remained in his possession a small remnant of his patrimony; and, upon the income arising from this, he managed, by means of a rigorous economy, to procure the necessaries of life, without troubling himself about its superfluities. Books, indeed, were his sole luxuries, and in Paris these are easily obtained.

Our first meeting was at an obscure library in the Rue Montmartre, where the accident of our both being in search of the same very rare and very remarkable volume brought us into closer communion. We saw each other again and again. I was deeply interested in the little family history which he detailed to me with all that candor which a Frenchman indulges whenever mere self is the theme. I was astonished, too, at the vast extent of his reading; and, above all, I felt my soul enkindled within me by the wild fervor, and the vivid freshness of his imagination. Seeking in Paris the objects I then sought, I felt that the society of such a man would be to me a treasure beyond price; and this feeling I frankly confided to him. It was at length arranged that we should live together during my stay in the city; and as my wordly circumstances were somewhat less embarrassed than his own, I was permitted to be at the expense of renting, and furnishing in a style which suited the rather fantastic gloom of our common temper, a time-eaten and grotesque mansion, long deserted through superstitions into which we did not inquire, and tottering to its fall in a retired and desolate portion of the Faubourg St. Germain.

Had the routine of our life at this place been known to the world, we should have been regarded as madmen — although, perhaps, as madmen of a harmless nature. Our seclusion was perfect. We admitted no visitors. Indeed the locality of our retirement had been carefully kept a secret from my own former associates; and it had been many years since Dupin had ceased to know or be known in Paris. We existed within ourselves alone.

It was a freak of fancy in my friend (for what else shall I call it?) to be enamored of the Night for her own sake; and into this *bizarrerie*, as into all his others, I quietly fell; giving myself up to his wild whims with a perfect *abandon*. The sable divinity would not herself dwell with us always; but we could counterfeit her presence. At the first dawn of the morning we closed all the massy shutters of our old building; lighted a couple of tapers which, strongly perfumed, threw out only the ghastliest and feeblest of rays. By the aid of these we then busied our souls in dreams — reading, writing, or conversing, until warned by the clock of the advent of the true Darkness. Then we sallied forth into the streets, arm and arm, continuing the topics of the day, or roaming far and wide until a late hour, seeking, amid the wild lights and shadows of the populous city, that infinity of mental excitement which quiet observation can afford.

At such times I could not help remarking and admiring (although from his rich ideality I had been prepared to expect it) a peculiar analytic ability in Dupin. He seemed, too, to take an eager delight in this exercise — if not exactly in its display — and did not hesitate to confess the pleasure thus derived. He boasted to me, with a low chuckling laugh, that most men, in respect to himself, wore windows in their bosoms, and was wont to follow up such assertions by direct and very startling proofs of his intimate knowledge of my own. His manner at these moments was frigid and abstract; his eyes were vacant in expression; while his voice, usually a rich tenor, rose into a treble which would have sounded petulantly but for the deliberateness and entire distinctness of the enunciation. Observing him in these moods, I often dwelt meditatively upon the old philosophy of the Bi-Part Soul, and amused myself with the fancy of a double Dupin — the creative and the resolvent.

let it not be supposed, from what I have just said, that I am detailing any mystery, or penning any romance. What I have described in the Frenchman was merely the result of an excited, or perhaps of a diseased, intelligence. But of the character of his remarks at the periods in question an example will best convey the idea.

We were strolling one night down a long dirty street, in the vicinity of the Palais Royal. Being both, apparently, occupied with thought, neither of us had spoken a syllable for fifteen minutes at least. All at once Dupin broke forth with these words:

"He is a very little fellow, that's true, and would do better for the *Théâtre des Variétés*."

"There can be no doubt of that," I replied unwittingly, and not at first observing (so much had I been absorbed in reflection) the extraordinary manner in which the speaker had chimed in with my meditations. In an instant afterwards I recollected myself, and my astonishment was profound.

"Dupin," said I, gravely, "this is beyond my comprehension. I do not hesitate to say that I am amazed, and can scarcely credit my senses. How was it possible you should know I was thinking of ——?" Here I paused, to ascertain beyond a doubt whether he really knew of whom I thought.—— "of Chantilly," said he, "why do you pause? You were remarking to yourself that his diminutive figure unfitted him for tragedy."

This was precisely what had formed the subject of my reflections. Chantilly was a *quondam* cobbler of the Rue St. Denis, who, becoming stage-mad, had attempted the *rôle* of Xerxes, in Crébillon's tragedy so called, and been notoriously Pasquinaded for his pains.

"Tell me, for Heaven's sake," I exclaimed, "the method — if method there is — by which you have enabled to fathom my soul in this matter." In fact I was even more startled than I would have been willing to express.

"It was the fruiterer," replied my friend, "who brought you to the conclusion that the mender of soles was not of sufficient height for Xerxes *et id genus omne*."

"The fruiterer! — you astonish me — I know no fruiterer whomsoever."

"The man who ran up against you as we entered the street — it may have been fifteen minutes ago."

I now remembered that, in fact, a fruiterer, carrying upon his head a large basket of apples, had nearly thrown me down, by accident, as we passed from the Rue C—— into the thoroughfare where we stood; but what this had to do with Chantilly I could not possibly understand.

There was not a particle of *charlatanerie* about Dupin. "I will explain," he said, "and that you may comprehend all clearly, we will first retrace the course of your meditations, from the moment in which I spoke to you until that of the *rencontre* with the fruiterer in question. The larger links of the chain run thus — Chantilly, Orion, Dr. Nichols, Epicurus, Stereotomy, the street stones, the fruiterer."

There are few persons who have not, at some period of their lives, amused themselves in retracing the steps by which particular conclusions of their own minds have been attained. The occupation is often full of interest; and he who attempts it for the first time is astonished by the apparently illimitable distance and incoherence between the starting-point and the goal. What, then, must have been my amazement when I heard the Frenchman speak what he had just spoken, and when I could not help acknowledging that he had spoken the truth. He continued:

"We had been talking of horses, if I remember aright, just before leaving the Rue C——. This was the last subject we discussed. As we crossed into this street, a fruiterer, with a large basket upon his head, brushing quickly past us, thrust you upon a pile of paving-stones collected at a spot where the causeway is undergoing repair. You stepped upon one of the loose fragments, slipped, slightly strained your ankle, appeared vexed or sulky, muttered a few words, turned to look at the pile, and then proceeded in silence. I was not particularly attentive to what you did; but observation has become with me, of late, a species of necessity.

"You kept your eyes upon the ground — glancing, with a petulant expression, at the holes and ruts in the pavement (so that I saw you were still thinking of the stones), until we reached the little alley called Lamartine, which has been paved, by way of experiment, with the overlapping and riveted blocks. Here your countenance brightened up, and, perceiving your lips move, I could not doubt that you murmured the word 'stereotomy,' a term very affectedly applied to this species of pavement. I knew that you could not say to yourself 'stereotomy' without being brought to think of atomies, and thus of the theories of Epicurus; and since, when we discussed this subject not very long ago, I mentioned to you how singularly, yet with how little notice, the vague guesses of that noble Greek had met with confirmation in the late nebular cosmogony, I felt that you could not avoid casting your eyes upwards to the great *nebula* in Orion, and I certainly expected that you would do so. You did look up; and I was now assured that I had correctly followed your steps. But in that bitter *tirade* upon Chantilly, which appeared in yesterday's *'Musée,'* the satirist, making some disgraceful allusions to the cobbler's change of name upon assuming the buskin, quoted a Latin line about which we have often conversed. I mean the line

Perdidit antiquum litera prima sonum

I had told you that this was in reference to Orion, formerly written Urion; and, from certain pungencies connected with this explanation, I was aware that you could not have forgotten it. It was clear, therefore, that you would not fail to combine the two ideas of Orion and Chantilly. That you did combine them I saw by the character of the smile which passed over your lips. You thought of the poor cobbler's immolation. So far, you had been stooping in your gait; but now I saw you draw yourself up to your full height. I was then sure that you reflected upon the diminutive figure of Chantilly. At this point I interrupted your meditations to remark that as, in fact, he *was* a very little fellow — that Chantilly — he would do better at the *Théâtre des Variétés.*''

Not long after this, we were looking over an evening edition of the ''Gazette des Tribunaux,'' when the following paragraphs arrested our attention.

"EXTRAORDINARY MURDERS. — This morning, about three o'clock, the inhabitants of the Quartier St. Roch were aroused from sleep by a succession of terrific shrieks, issuing, apparently, from the fourth story of a house in the Rue Morgue, known to be in the sole occupancy of one Madame L'Espanaye, and her daughter, Mademoiselle Camille L'Espanaye. After some delay, occasioned by a fruitless attempt to procure admission in the usual manner, the gateway was broken in with a crowbar, and eight or ten of the neighbors entered, accompanied by two *gendarmes*. By this time the cries had ceased; but, as the party rushed up the first flight of stairs, two or more rough voices, in angry contention, were distinguished, and seemed to proceed from the upper part of the house. As the second landing was reached, these sounds, also, had ceased, and everything remained perfectly quiet. The party spread themselves, and hurried from room to room. Upon arriving at a large back chamber in the fourth story (the door of which, being found locked, with the key inside, was forced open), a spectacle presented itself which struck every one present not less with horror than with astonishment.

"The apartment was in the wildest disorder — the furniture broken and thrown about in all directions. There was only one bedstead; and from this the bed had been removed, and thrown into the middle of the floor. On a chair lay a razor, besmeared with blood. On the hearth were two or three long and thick tresses of gray human hair, also dabbled in blood, and seeming to have been pulled out by the roots. Upon the floor were found four Napoleons, an earring of topaz, three large silver spoons, three smaller of *métal d' Alger*, and two bags, containing nearly four thousand francs in gold. The drawers of a *bureau*, which stood in one corner, were open, and had been, apparently, rifled, although many articles still remained in them. A small iron safe was discovered under the *bed* (not under the bedstead). It was open, with the key still in the door. It had no contents beyond a few old letters, and other papers of little consequence.

''Of Madame L'Espanaye no traces were here seen; but an unusual quantity of soot being observed in the fireplace, a search was made in the chimney, and (horrible to relate!) the corpse of the daughter, head downwards, was dragged therefrom; it having been thus forced up the narrow aperture for a considerable distance. The body was quite warm. Upon examining it, many excoriations were perceived, no doubt occasioned by the violence with which it had been thrust up and disengaged. Upon the face were many severe scratches, and, upon the throat, dark bruises, and deep indentations of finger-nails, as if the deceased had been throttled to death.

"After a thorough investigation of every portion of the house, without farther discovery, the party made its way into a small paved yard in the rear of the building, where lay the corpse of the old lady, with her throat so entirely cut that, upon an attempt to raise her, the head fell off. The body, as well as the head, was fearfully mutilated — the former so much so as scarcely to retain any semblance of humanity.

"To this horrible mystery there is not as yet, we believe, the slightest clue."

The next day's paper had these additional particulars.

"*The Tragedy in the Rue Morgue.* Many individuals have been examined in relation to this most extraordinary and frightful affair" (the word '*affaire*' has not yet, in France, that levity of import which it conveys with us), "but nothing whatever has transpired to throw light upon it. We give below all the material testimony elicited.

"*Pauline Dubourg,* laundress, deposes that she has known both the deceased for three years, having washed for them during that period. The old lady and her daughter seemed on good terms — very affectionate towards each other. They were excellent pay. Could not speak in regard to their mode or means of living. Believed that Madame L. told fortunes for a living. Was reputed to have money put by. Never met any persons in the house when she called for the clothes or took them home. Was sure that they had no servant in employ. There appeared to be no furniture in any part of the building except in the fourth story.

"*Pierre Moreau,* tobacconist, deposes that he has been in the habit of selling small quantities of tobacco and snuff to Madame L'Espanaye for nearly four years. Was born in the neighborhood, and has always resided there. The deceased and her daughter had occupied the house in which the corpses were found, for more than six years. It was formerly occupied by a jeweler, who under-let the upper rooms to various persons. The house was the property of Madame L. She became dissatisfied with the abuse of the premises by her tenant, and moved into them herself, refusing to let any portion. The old lady was childish. Witness had seen the daughter some five or six times during the six years. The two lived an exceedingly retired life — were reputed to have money. Had heard it said among the neighbors that Madame L. told fortunes — did not believe it. Had never seen any person enter the door except the old lady and her daughter, a porter once or twice, and a physician some eight or ten times.

"Many other persons, neighbors, gave evidence to the same effect. No one was spoken of as frequenting the house. It was not known whether there were any living connections of Madame L. and her daughter. The shutters of the front windows were seldom opened. Those in the rear were always closed, with the exception of the large back room, fourth story. The house was a good house — not very old.

"*Isidore Musèt, gendarme,* deposes that he was called to the house about three o'clock in the morning, and found some twenty or thirty persons at the gateway, endeavoring to gain admittance. Forced it open, at length, with a bayonet — not with a crowbar. Had but little difficulty in getting it open, on account of its being a double or folding gate, and bolted neither at bottom nor top. The shrieks were continued until the gate was forced — and then suddenly ceased. They seemed to be screams of some person (or persons) in great agony — were loud and drawn out, not short and quick. Witness led the way upstairs. Upon reaching the first landing, heard two voices in loud and angry contention — the one a gruff voice, the other much shriller — a very strange voice. Could distinguish some words of the former, which was that of a Frenchman. Was positive that it was not a woman's voice. Could distinguish the words '*sacré*' and '*diable*.' The shrill voice was that of a foreigner. Could not be sure whether it was the voice of a man or of a woman. Could not make out what was said, but believed the language to be Spanish. The state of the room and of the bodies was described by this witness as we described them yesterday.

"*Henri Duval,* a neighbor, and by trade a silversmith, deposes that he was one of the party who first entered the house. Corroborates the testimony of Musèt in general. As soon as they forced an entrance, they reclosed the door, to keep out the crowd, which collected very fast, notwithstanding the lateness of the hour. The shrill voice, the witness thinks, was that of an Italian. Was certain it was not French. Could not be sure it was a man's voice. It might have been a woman's. Was not acquainted with the Italian language. Could not distinguish the words, but was convinced by the intonation that the speaker was an Italian. Knew Madame L. and her daughter. Had conversed with both frequently. Was sure that the shrill voice was not that of either of the deceased.

"——— *Odenheimer restaurateur.* This witness volunteered his testimony. Not speaking French, was examined through an interpreter. Is a native of Amsterdam. Was passing the house at the time of the shrieks. They lasted for several minutes — probably ten. They were long and loud — very awful and distressing. Was one of those who entered the building. Corroborated the previous evidence in every respect but one. Was sure that the shrill voice was that of a man — of a Frenchman. Could not distinguish the words uttered. They were loud and quick — unequal — spoken apparently in fear as well as in anger. The voice was harsh — not so much shrill as harsh. Could not call it a shrill voice. The gruff voice said repeatedly *'sacré,' 'diable'* and once *'mon Dieu.'*

"*Jules Mignaud,* banker, of the firm of Mignaud et Fils, Rue Deloraine. Is the elder Mignaud. Madame L'Espanaye had some property. Had opened an account with his banking house in the spring of the year —— (eight years previously). Made frequent deposits in small sums. Had checked for nothing until the third day before her death, when she took out in person the sum of 4000 francs. This sum was paid in gold, and a clerk sent home with the money.

"*Adolphe Le Bon,* clerk to Mignaud et Fils, deposes that on the day in question, about noon, he accompanied Madame L'Espanaye to her residence with the 4000 francs, put up in two bags. Upon the door being opened, Mademoiselle L. appeared and took from his hands one of the bags, while the old lady relieved him of the other. He then bowed and departed. Did not see any person in the street at the time. It is a bye-street — very lonely.

"*William Bird,* tailor, deposes that he was one of the party who entered the house. Is an Englishman. Has lived in Paris two years. Was one of the first to ascend the stairs. Heard the voices in contention. The gruff voice was that of a Frenchman. Could make out several words, but cannot now remember all. Heard distinctly '*sacré*' and '*mon Dieu*.' There was a sound at the moment as if of several persons struggling — a scraping and scuffling sound. The shrill voice was very loud — louder than the gruff one. Is sure that it was not the voice of an Englishman. Appeared to be that of a German. Might have been a woman's voice. Does not understand German.

"Four of the above-named witnesses, being recalled, deposed that the door of the chamber in which was found the body of Mademoiselle L. was locked on the inside when the party reached it. Everything was perfectly silent — no groans or noises of any kind. Upon forcing the door no person was seen. The windows, both of the back and front room, were down and firmly fastened from within. A door between the two rooms was closed, but not locked. The door leading from the front room into the passage was locked, with the key on the inside. A small room in the front of the house, on the fourth story, at the head of the passage, was open, the door being ajar. This room was crowded with old beds, boxes, and so forth. These were carefully removed and searched. There was not an inch of any portion of the house which was not carefully searched. Sweeps were sent up and down the chimneys. The house was a four-story one, with garrets (*mansardes*). A trap-door on the roof was nailed down very securely — did not appear to have been opened for years. The time elapsing between the hearing of the voices in contention and the breaking open of the room door, was variously stated by the witnesses. Some made it as short as three minutes — some as long as five. The door was opened with difficulty.

"*Alfonzo Garcio,* undertaker, deposes that he resides in the Rue Morgue. Is a native of Spain. Was one of the party who entered the house. Did not proceed upstairs. Is nervous, and was apprehensive of the consequences of agitation. Heard the voices in contention. The gruff voice was that of a Frenchman. Could not distinguish what was said. The shrill voice was that of an Englishman — is sure of this. Does not understand the English language, but judges by the intonation.

"*Alberto Montani,* confectioner, deposes that he was among the first to ascend the stairs. Heard the voices in question. The gruff voice was that of a Frenchman. Distinguished several words. The speaker appeared to be expostulating. Could not make out the words of the shrill voice. Spoke quickly and unevenly. Thinks it the voice of a Russian. Corroborates the general testimony. Is an Italian. Never conversed with a native of Russia.

"Several witnesses, recalled, here testified that the chimneys of all the rooms on the fourth story were too narrow to admit the passage of a human being. By 'sweeps' were meant cylindrical sweeping-brushes, such as are employed by those who clean chimneys. These brushes were passed up and down every flue in the house. There is no back passage by which any one could have descended while the party proceeded up stairs. The body of Mademoiselle L'Espanaye was so firmly wedged in the chimney that it could not be got down until four or five of the party united their strength.

"*Paul Dumas,* physician, deposes that he was called to view the bodies about daybreak. They were both then lying on the sacking of the bedstead in the chamber where Mademoiselle L. was found. The corpse of the young lady was much bruised and excoriated. The fact that it had been thrust up the chimney would sufficiently account for these appearances. The throat was greatly chafed. There were several deep scratches just below the chin, together with a series of livid spots which were evidently the impression of fingers. The face was fearfully discolored, and the eyeballs protruded. The tongue had been partially bitten through. A large bruise was discovered upon the pit of the stomach, produced, apparently, by the pressure of a knee. In the opinion of M. Dumas, Mademoiselle L'Espanaye had been throttled to death by some person or persons unknown. The corpse of the mother was horribly mutilated. All the bones of the right leg and arm were more or less shattered. The left *tibia* much splintered, as well as all the ribs of the left side. Whole body dreadfully bruised and discolored. It was not possible to say how the injuries had been inflicted. A heavy club of wood, or a broad bar of iron — a chair — any large, heavy, and obtuse weapon would have produced such results, if wielded by the hands of a very powerful man. No woman could have inflicted the blows with any weapon. The head of the deceased, when seen by witness, was entirely separated from the body, and was also greatly shattered. The throat had evidently been cut with some very sharp instrument — probably with a razor.

"*Alexandre Etienne*, surgeon, was called with M. Dumas to view the bodies. Corroborated the testimony, and the opinions of M. Dumas.

"Nothing farther of importance was elicited, although several other persons were examined. A murder so mysterious, and so perplexing in all its particulars, was never before committed in Paris — if indeed a murder has been committed at all. The police are entirely at fault — an unusual occurrence in affairs of this nature. There is not, however, the shadow of a clue apparent."

The evening edition of the paper stated that the greatest excitement still continued in the Quartier St. Roch — that the premises in question had been carefully re-searched, and fresh examinations of witnesses instituted, but all to no purpose. A postscript, however, mentioned that Adolphe Le Bon had been arrested and imprisoned — although nothing appeared to criminate him, beyond the facts already detailed.

Dupin seemed singularly interested in the progress of this affair — at least so I judged from his manner, for he made no comments. It was only after the announcement that Le Bon had been imprisoned, that he asked me my opinion respecting the murders.

I could merely agree with all Paris in considering them an insoluble mystery. I saw no means by which it would be possible to trace the murderer.

"We must not judge of the means," said Dupin, "by this shell of an examination. The Parisian police, so much extolled for *acumen,* are cunning, but no more. There is no method in their proceedings, beyond the method of the moment. They make a vast parade of measures; but, not unfrequently, these are so ill adapted to the objects proposed, as to put us in mind of Monsieur Jourdain's calling for his *robe-de-chambre — pour mieux entendre la musique*. The results attained by them are not unfrequently surprising, but, for the most part, are brought about by simple diligence and activity. When these qualities are unavailing, their schemes fail, Vidocq, for example, was a good guesser, and a persevering man. But, without educated thought, he erred continually by the very intensity of his investigations. He impaired his vision by holding the object too close. He might see, perhaps, one or two points with unusual clearness, but in so doing he, necessarily, lost sight of the matter as a whole. Thus there is such a thing as being too profound. Truth is not always in a well. In fact, as regards the more important knowledge, I do believe that she is invariably superficial. The depth lies in the valleys where we seek her, and not upon the mountain-tops where she is found. The modes and sources of this kind of error are well typified in the contemplation of the heavenly bodies. To look at a star by glances — to view it in a side-long way, by turning towards it the exterior portions of the *retina* (more susceptible of feeble impressions of light than the interior), is to behold the star distinctly — is to have the best appreciation of its luster — a luster which grows dim just in proportion as we turn our vision *fully* upon it. A greater number of rays actually fall upon the eye in the latter case, but, in the former, there is the more refined capacity for comprehension. By undue profundity we perplex and enfeeble thought; and it is possible to make even Venus herself vanish from the firmament by a scrutiny too sustained, too concentrated, or too direct.

"As for these murders, let us enter into some examinations for ourselves, before we make up an opinion respecting them. An inquiry will afford us amusement" (I thought this an odd term, so applied, but said nothing), "and, besides, Le Bon once rendered me a service for which I am not ungrateful. We will go and see the premises with our own eyes. I know G——, the Prefect of Police, and shall have no difficulty in obtaining the necessary permission."

The permission was obtained, and we proceeded at once to the Rue Morgue. This is one of those miserable thoroughfares, which intervene between the Rue Richelieu and the Rue St. Roch. It was late in the afternoon when we reached it; as this quarter is at a great distance from that in which we resided. The house was readily found; for there were still many persons gazing up at the closed shutters, with an objectless curiosity, from the opposite side of the way. It was an ordinary Parisian house, with a gateway, on one side of which was a glazed watch-box, with a sliding panel in the window, indicating a *loge de concierge*. Before going in we walked up the street, turned down an alley, and then, again turning, passed in the rear of the building — Dupin, meanwhile, examining the whole neighborhood, as well as the house, with a minuteness of attention for which I could see no possible object.

Retracing our steps, we came again to the front of the dwelling, rang, and, having shown our credentials, were admitted by the agents in charge. We went upstairs — into the chamber where the body of Mademoiselle

L'Espanaye had been found, and where both the deceased still lay. The disorders of the room had, as usual, been suffered to exist. I saw nothing beyond what had been stated in the "Gazette des Tribunaux." Dupin scrutinized everything — not excepting the bodies of the victims. We then went into the other rooms, and into the yard: a *gendarme* accompanying us throughout. The examination occupied us until dark, when we took our departure. On our way home my companion stopped in for a moment at the office of the daily papers.

I have said that the whims of my friend were manifold, and that *Je les ménageais*: — for this phrase there is no English equivalent. It was his humor, now, to decline all conversation on the subject of the murder, until about noon the next day. He then asked me, suddenly, if I had observed anything *peculiar* at the scene of the atrocity.

There was something in his manner of emphasizing the word "peculiar," which caused me to shudder, without knowing why.

"No, nothing *peculiar,*" I said; "nothing more, at least, than we both saw stated in the paper."

"The 'Gazette,' " he replied, "has not entered, I fear, into the unusual horror of the thing. But dismiss the idle opinions of this print. It appears to me that this mystery is considered insoluble, for the very reason which should cause it to be regarded as easy of solution — I mean for the *outré* character of its features. The police are confounded by the seeming absence of motive — not for the murder itself — but for the atrocity of the murder. They are puzzled, too, by the seeming impossibility of reconciling the voices heard in contention, with the facts that no one was discovered upstairs but the assassinated Mademoiselle L'Espanaye, and that there were no means of egress without the notice of the party ascending. The wild disorder of the room; the corpse thrust, with the head downwards, up the chimney; the frightful mutilation of the body of the old lady; these considerations, with those just mentioned, and others which I need not mention, have sufficed to paralyze the powers, by putting completely at fault the boasted *acumen,* of the government agents. They have fallen into the gross but common error of confounding the unusual with the abstruse. But is is by these deviations from the plane of the ordinary, that reason feels its way, if at all, in its search for the true. In investigations such as we are now pursuing, it should not be so much asked 'what has occurred,' as 'what has occurred that has never occurred before.' In fact, the facility with which I shall arrive, or have arrived, at the solution of this mystery, is in the direct ratio of its apparent insolubility in the eyes of the police."

I stared at the speaker in mute astonishment.

"I am now awaiting," continued he, looking towards the door of our apartment — "I am now awaiting a person who, although perhaps not the perpetrator of these butcheries, must have been in some measure implicated in their perpetration. Of the worst portion of the crimes committed, it is probable that he is innocent. I hope that I am right in this supposition; for upon it I build my expectation of reading the entire riddle. I look for the man here — in this room — every moment. It is true that he may not arrive; but the probability is that he will. Should he come, it will be necessary to detain him. Here are pistols; and we both know how to use them when occasion demands their use."

I took the pistols, scarcely knowing what I did, or believing what I heard, while Dupin went on, very much as if in a soliloquy. I have already spoken of his abstract manner at such times. His discourse was addressed to myself; but his voice, although by no means loud, had that intonation which is commonly employed in speaking to some one at a great distance. His eyes, vacant in expression, regarded only the wall.

"That the voices heard in contention," he said, "by the party upon the stairs, were not the voices of the women themselves, was fully proved by the evidence. This relieves us of all doubt upon the question whether the old lady could have first destroyed the daughter, and afterward have committed suicide. I speak of this point chiefly for the sake of method; for the strength of Madame L'Espanaye would have been utterly unequal to the task of thrusting her daughter's corpse up the chimney as it was found; and the nature of the wounds upon her own person entirely preclude the idea of self-destruction. Murder, then, has been committed by some third party; and the voices of this third party were those heard in contention. Let me now advert — not to the whole testimony respecting these voices — but to what was *peculiar* in that testimony. Did you observe anything peculiar about it?"

I remarked that, while all the witnesses agreed in supposing the gruff voice to be that of a Frenchman, there was much disagreement in regard to the shrill, or, as one individual termed it, the harsh voice.

"That was the evidence itself," said Dupin, "but it was not the peculiarity of the evidence. You have observed nothing distinctive. Yet there *was* something to be observed. The witnesses, as you remark, agreed about the gruff voice; they were here unanimous. But in regard to the shrill voice, the peculiarity is — not that they disagreed — but that, while an Italian, an Englishman, a Spaniard, a Hollander, and a Frenchman attempted to describe it, each one spoke of it as that *of a foreigner*. Each is sure that it was not the voice of one of his own countrymen. Each likens it — not to the voice of an individual of any nation with whose language he is conversant — but the converse. The Frenchman supposes it the voice of a Spaniard, and 'might have distinguished some words *had he been acquainted with the Spanish.'* The Dutchman maintains it to have been that of a Frenchman; but we find it stated that *'not understanding French this witness was examined through an interpreter.'* The Englishman thinks it the voice of a German, and *'does not understand German.'* The Spaniard 'is sure' that it was that of an Englishman, but 'judges by the intonation' altogether, *'as he has no knowledge of the English.'* The Italian believes it the voice of a Russian, but *'has never conversed with a native of Russia.'* A second Frenchman differs, moreover, with the first, and is positive that the voice was that of an Italian; but, *not being cognizant of that tongue,* is, like the Spaniard, 'convinced by the intonation.' Now, how strangely unusual must that voice have really been, about which such testimony as this *could* have been elicited! — in whose *tones,* even, denizens of the five great divisions of Europe could recognize nothing familiar! You will say that it might have been the voice of an Asiatic — of an African. Neither Asiatics nor Africans abound in Paris; but, without denying the inference, I will now merely call your attention to three points. The voice is termed by one witness 'harsh rather than shrill.' It is represented by two others to have been 'quick and *unequal*.' No words — no sound resembling words — were by any witness mentioned as distinguishable.

"I know not," continued Dupin, "what impression I may have made, so far, upon your own understanding; but I do not hesitate to say that legitimate deductions even from this portion of the testimony — the portion respecting the gruff and shrill voices — are in themselves sufficient to engender a suspicion which should give direction to all farther progress in the investigation of the mystery. I said 'legitimate deductions'; but my meaning is not thus fully expressed. I designed to imply that the deductions are the *sole* proper ones, and that the suspicion arises *inevitably* from them as the single result. What the suspicion is, however, I will not say just yet. I merely wish you to bear in mind that, with myself, it was sufficiently forcible to give a definite form — a certain tendency — to my inquiries in the chamber.

"Let us now transport ourselves, in fancy, to this chamber. What shall we first seek here? The means of egress employed by the murderers. It is not too much to say that neither of us believe in præternatural events. Madame and Mademoiselle L'Espanaye were not destroyed by spirits. The doers of the deed were material, and escaped materially. Then how?

Fortunately, there is but one mode of reasoning upon the point, and that mode *must* lead us to a definite decision. — Let us examine, each by each, the possible means of egress. It is clear that the assassins were in the room where Mademoiselle L'Espanaye was found, or at least in the room adjoining, when the party ascended the stairs. It is then only from these two apartments that we have to seek issues. The police have laid bare the floors, the ceilings, and the masonry of the walls, in every direction. No *secret* issues could have escaped their vigilance. But not trusting to *their* eyes, I examined with my own. There were, then, *no* secret issues. Both doors leading from the rooms into the passage were securely locked, with the keys inside. Let us turn to the chimneys. These, although of ordinary width for some eight or ten feet above the hearths, will not admit, throughout their extent, the body of a large cat. The impossibility of egress, by means already stated, being thus absolute, we are reduced to the windows. Through those of the front room no one could have escaped without notice from the crowd in the street. The murderers *must* have passed, then, through those of the back room. Now, brought to this conclusion is so unequivocal a manner as we are, it is not our part, as reasoners, to reject it on account of apparent impossibilities. It is only left for us to prove that these apparent 'impossibilities' are, in reality, not such.

"There are two windows in the chamber. One of them is unobstructed by furniture, and is wholly visible. The lower portion of the other is hidden from view by the head of the unwieldy bedstead which is thrust close up against it. The former was found securely fastened from within. It resisted the utmost force of those who endeavored to raise it. A large gimlet-hole had been pierced in its frame to the left, and a very stout nail was found fitted therein, nearly to the head. Upon examining the other window, a similar nail was seen similarly fitted in it; and a vigorous attempt to raise this sash, failed also. The police were now entirely satisfied that egress had not been in these directions. And, *therefore,* it was thought a matter of supererogation to withdraw the nails and open the windows.

"My own examination was somewhat more particular, and was so for the reason I have just given — because here it was, I knew, that all apparent impossibilities *must* be proved to be not such in reality.

"I proceeded to think thus — *à posteriori*. The murderers *did* escape from one of these windows. This being so, they could not have refastened the sashes from the inside, as they were found fastened; — the consideration which put a stop, through its obviousness, to the scrutiny of the police in this quarter. Yet the sashes *were* fastened. They *must,* then, have the power of fastening themselves. There was no escape from this conclusion. I stepped to the unobstructed casement, withdrew the nail with some difficulty, and attempted to raise the sash. It resisted all my efforts, as I had anticipated. A concealed spring must, I now knew, exist; and this corroboration of my idea convinced me that my premises, at least, were correct, however mysterious still appeared the circumstances attending the nails. A careful search soon brought to light the hidden spring. I pressed it, and, satisfied with the discovery, forbore to upraise the sash.

"I now replaced the nail and regarded it attentively. A person passing out through this window might have reclosed it, and the spring would have caught — but the nail could not have been replaced. The conclusion was plain, and again narrowed in the field of my investigations. The assassins *must* have escaped through the other window. Supposing, then, the springs upon each sash to be the same, as was probable, there *must* be found a difference between the nails, or at least between the modes of their fixture. Getting upon the sacking of the bedstead, I looked over the headboard minutely at the second casement. Passing my hand down behind the board, I readily discovered and pressed the spring, which was, as I had supposed, identical in character with its neighbor. I now looked at the nail. It was as stout as the other, and apparently fitted in the same manner — driven in nearly up to the head.

"You will say that I was puzzled; but, if you think so, you must have misunderstood the nature of the inductions. To use a sporting phrase, I had not been once 'at fault.' The scent had never for an instant been lost. There was no flaw in any link of the chain. I had traced the secret to its ultimate result, — and that result was *the nail*. It had, I say, in every respect, the appearance of its fellow in the other window; but this fact was an absolute nullity (conclusive as it might seem to be) when compared with the consideration that here, at this point, terminated the clue. 'There *must* be something wrong,' I said, 'about the nail.' I touched it; and the head, with about a quarter of an inch of the shank, came off in my fingers. The rest of the shank was in the gimlet-hole, where it had been broken off. The fracture was an old one (for its edges were incrusted with rust), and had apparently been accomplished by the blow of a hammer, which had partially imbedded, in the top of the bottom sash, the head portion of the nail. I now carefully replaced this head portion in the indentation whence I had taken it, and the resemblance to a perfect nail was complete — the fissure was invisible. Pressing the spring, I gently raised the sash for a few inches; the head went up with it, remaining firm in its bed. I closed the window, and the semblance of the whole nail was again perfect.

"The riddle, so far, was now unriddled. The assassin had escaped through the window which looked upon the bed. Dropping of its own accord upon his exit (or perhaps purposely closed), it had become fastened by the spring; and it was the retention of this spring which had been mistaken by the police for that of the nail, — farther inquiry being thus considered unnecessary.

"The next question is that of the mode of descent. Upon this point I had been satisfied in my walk with you around the building. About five feet and a half from the casement in question there runs a lightning-rod. From this rod it would have been impossible for any one to reach the window itself, to say nothing of entering it. I observed, however, that the shutters of the fourth story were of the peculiar kind called by Parisian carpenters *ferrades* — a kind rarely employed at the present day, but frequently seen upon very old mansions at Lyons and Bordeaux. They are in the form of an ordinary door (a single, not a folding door), except that the upper half is latticed or worked in open trellis — thus affording an excellent hold for the hands. In the present instance these shutters are fully three feet and a half broad. When we saw them from the rear of the house, they were both about half open — that is to say, they stood off at right angles from the wall. It is probable that the police, as well as myself, examined the back of the tenement; but, if so, in looking at these *ferrades* in the line of their breadth (as they must have done), they did not perceive this great breadth itself, or, at all events, failed to take it into due consideration. In fact, having once satisfied themselves that no egress could have been made in this quarter, they would naturally bestow here a very cursory examination. It was clear to me, however, that the shutter belonging to the window at the head of the bed, would, if swung fully back to the wall, reach to within two feet of the lightning-rod. It was also evident that by exertion of a very unusual degree of activity and courage, an entrance into the window, from the rod, might have been thus effected. — By reaching to the distance of two feet and a half (we now suppose the shutter open to its whole extent) a robber might have taken a firm grasp upon the trellis-work. Letting go, then, his hold upon the rod, placing his feet securely against the wall, and springing boldly from it, he might have swung the shutter so as to close it, and, if we imagine the window open at the time, might even have swung himself into the room.

"I wish you to bear especially in mind that I have spoken of a *very* unusual degree of activity as requisite to success in so hazardous and so difficult a feat. It is my design to show you, first, that the thing might possibly have been accomplished: — but, secondly and *chiefly*, I wish to impress upon your understanding the *very extraordinary* — the almost præternatural character of that agility which could have accomplished it.

"You will say, no doubt, using the language of the law, that 'to make out my case' I should rather undervalue, than insist upon a full estimation of the activity required in this matter. This may be the practice in law, but it is not the usage of reason. My ultimate object is only the truth. My immediate purpose is to lead you to place in juxtaposition that *very unusual* activity of which I have just spoken, with that *very peculiar* shrill (or harsh) and *unequal* voice, about whose nationality no two persons could be found to agree, and in whose utterance no syllabification could be detected."

At these words a vague and half-formed conception of the meaning of Dupin flitted over my mind. I seemed to be upon the verge of comprehension, without power to comprehend — as men, at times, find themselves upon the brink of remembrance, without being able, in the end, to remember. My friend went on with his discourse.

"You will see," he said, "that I have shifted the question from the mode of egress to that of ingress. It was my design to suggest that both were effected in the same manner, at the same point. Let us now revert to the interior of the room. Let us survey the appearances here. The drawers of the bureau, it is said, had been rifled, although many articles of apparel still remained within them. The conclusion here is absurd. It is a mere guess — a very silly one — and no more. How are we to know that the articles found in the drawers were not all these drawers had originally contained? Madame L'Espanaye and her daughter lived an exceedingly retired life — saw no company — seldom went out — had little use for numerous changes of habiliment. Those found were at least of as good quality as any likely to be possessed by these ladies. If a thief had taken any, why did he not take the best — why did he not take all? In a word, why did he abandon four thousand francs in gold to encumber himself with a bundle of linen? The gold *was* abandoned. Nearly the whole sum mentioned by Monsieur Mignaud, the banker, was discovered, in bags, upon the floor. I wish you, therefore, to discard from your thoughts the blundering idea of *motive*, engendered in the brains of the police by that portion of the evidence which speaks of money delivered at the door of the house. Coincidences ten times as remarkable as this (the delivery of the money, and murder committed within three days upon the party receiving it), happen to all of us every hour of our lives, without attracting even momentary notice. Coincidences, in general, are great stumbling-blocks in the way of that class of thinkers who have been educated to know nothing of the theory of probabilities — that theory to which the most glorious objects of human research are indebted for the most glorious of illustration. In the present instance, had the gold been gone, the fact of its delivery three days before would have formed something more than a coincidence. It would have been corroborative of this idea of motive. But, under the real circumstances of the case, if we are to suppose gold the motive of this outrage, we must also imagine the perpetrator so vacillating an idiot as to have abandoned his gold and his motive together.

"Keeping now steadily in mind the points to which I have drawn your attention — that peculiar voice, that unusual agility, and that startling absence of motive in a murder so singularly atrocious as this — let us glance at the butchery itself. Here is a woman strangled to death by manual strength, and thrust up a chimney, head downwards. Ordinary assassins employ no such modes of murder as this. Least of all, do they thus dispose of the murdered. In the manner of thrusting the corpse up the chimney, you will admit that there was something *excessively outré* — something altogether irreconcilable with our common notions of human action, even when we suppose the actors the most depraved of men. Think, too, how great must have been that strength which could have thrust the body *up* such an aperture so forcibly that the united vigor of several persons was found barely sufficient to drag it *down!*

"Turn, now, to other indications of the employment of a vigor most marvelous. On the hearth were thick tresses — very thick tresses — of gray human hair. These had been torn out by the roots. You are aware of the great force necessary in tearing thus from the head even twenty or thirty hairs together. You saw the locks in question as well as myself. Their roots (a hideous sight!) were clotted with fragments of the flesh of the scalp — sure token of the prodigious power which had been exerted in uprooting perhaps half a million of hairs at a time. The throat of the old lady was not merely cut, but the head absolutely severed from the body: the instrument was a mere razor. I wish you also to look at the *brutal* ferocity of these deeds. Of the bruises upon the body of Madame L'Espanaye I do not speak. Monsieur Dumas, and his worthy coadjutor Monsieur Etienne, have pronounced that they were inflicted by some obtuse instrument; and so far these gentlemen are very correct. The obtuse instrument was clearly the stone pavement in the yard, upon which the victim had fallen from the window which looked in upon the bed. This idea, however simple it may now seem, escaped the police for the same reason that the breadth of the shutters escaped them — because, by the affair of the nails, their perceptions had been hermetically sealed against the possibility of the windows having ever been opened at all.

"If now, in addition to all these things, you have properly reflected upon the odd disorder of the chamber, we have gone so far as to combine the ideas of an agility astounding, a strength superhuman, a ferocity brutal, a butchery without motive, a *grotesquerie* in horror absolutely alien from humanity, and a voice foreign in tone to the ears of men of many nations, and devoid of all distinct or intelligible syllabification. What result, then, has ensued? What impression have I made upon your fancy?"

I felt a creeping of the flesh as Dupin asked me the question. "A madman," I said, "has done this deed — some raving maniac, escaped from a neighboring *Maison de Santé*."

"In some respects," he replied, "your idea is not irrelevant. But the voices of madmen, even in their wildest paroxysms, are never found to tally with that peculiar voice heard upon the stairs. Madmen are of some nation, and their language, however incoherent in its words, has always the coherence of syllabification. Besides, the hair of a madman is not such as I now hold in my hand. I disentangled this little tuft from the rigidly clutched fingers of Madame L'Espanaye. Tell me what you can make of it."

"Dupin!" I said, completely unnerved; "this hair is most unusual — this is no *human* hair."

"I have not asserted that it is," said he; "but, before we decide this point, I wish you to glance at the little sketch I have here traced upon this paper. It is a *facsimile* drawing of what has been described in one portion of the testimony as 'dark bruises, and deep indentations of fingernails,' upon the throat of Mademoiselle L'Espanaye, and in another (by Messrs. Dumas and Etienne), as a 'series of livid spots, evidently the impression of fingers.'

"You will perceive," continued my friend, spreading out the paper upon the table before us, "that this drawing gives the idea of a firm and fixed hold. There is no *slipping* apparent. Each finger has retained — possibly until the death of the victim — the fearful grasp by which it originally imbedded itself. Attempt, now, to place all your fingers, at the same time, in the respective impressions as you see them."

I made the attempt in vain.

"We are possibly not giving this matter a fair trial," he said. "The paper is spread out upon a plane surface; but the human throat is cylindrical. Here is a billet of wood, the circumference of which is about that of the throat. Wrap the drawing around it, and try the experiment again."

I did so; but the difficulty was even more obvious than before.

"This," I said, "is the mark of no human

hand.''

''Read now,'' replied Dupin, ''this passage from Cuvier.''

It was a minute anatomical and generally descriptive account of the large fulvous Orang-Outang of the East Indian Islands. The gigantic stature, the prodigious strength and activity, the wild ferocity, and the imitative propensities of these mammalia are sufficiently well known to all. I understood the full horrors of the murder at once.

''The description of the digits,'' said I, as I made an end of reading, ''is in exact accordance with this drawing. I see that no animal but an Orang-Outang, of the species here mentioned, could have impressed the indentations as you have traced them. This tuft of tawny hair, too, is identical in character with that of the beast of Cuvier. But I cannot possibly comprehend the particulars of this frightful mystery. Besides, there were *two* voices heard in contention, and one of them was unquestionably the voice of a Frenchman.''

''True; and you will remember an expression attributed almost unanimously, by the evidence, to this voice, — the expression, '*mon Dieu!*' This, under the circumstances, has been justly characterized by one of the witnesses (Montani, the confectioner), as an expression of remonstrance or expostulation. Upon these two words, therefore, I have mainly built my hopes of a full solution of the riddle. A Frenchman was cognizant of the murder. It is possible — indeed it is far more than probable — that he was innocent of all participation in the bloody transactions which took place. The Orang-Outang may have escaped from him. He may have traced it to the chamber; but, under the agitating circumstances which ensued, he could never have recaptured it. It is still at large. I will not pursue these guesses — for I have no right to call them more — since the shades of reflection upon which they are based are scarcely of sufficient depth to be appreciable by my own intellect, and since I could not pretend to make them intelligible to the understanding of another. We will call them guesses then, and speak of them as such. If the Frenchman in question is indeed, as I suppose, innocent of this atrocity, this advertisement, which I left last night, upon our return home, at the office of 'Le Monde' (a paper devoted to the shipping interest, and much sought by sailors), will bring him to our residence.''

He handed me a paper, and I read thus:

CAUGHT — *In the Bois de Boulogne, early in the morning of the — inst.* (the morning of the murder), *a very large, tawny Orang-Outang of the Bornese species. The owner (who is ascertained to be a sailor, belonging to a Maltese vessel), may have the animal again, upon identifying it satisfactorily, and paying a few charges arising from its capture and keeping. Call at No. —, Rue —, Faubourg St. Germain — au troisième.*

"How was it possible," I asked, "that you should know the man to be a sailor, and belonging to a Maltese vessel?"

"I do *not* know it," said Dupin. "I am not *sure* of it. Here, however, is a small piece of ribbon, which from its form, and from its greasy appearance, has evidently been used in tying the hair in one of those long *queues* of which sailors are so fond. Moreover, this knot is one which few besides sailors can tie, and is peculiar to the Maltese. I picked the ribbon up at the foot of the lightning-rod. It could not have belonged to either of the deceased. Now if, after all, I am wrong in my induction from this ribbon, that the Frenchman was a sailor belonging to a Maltese vessel, still I can have done no harm in saying what I did in the advertisement. If I am in error, he will merely suppose that I have been misled by some circumstance into which he will not take the trouble to inquire. But if I am right, a great point is gained. Cognizant although innocent of the murder, the Frenchman will naturally hesitate about replying to the advertisement — about demanding the Orang-Outang. He will reason thus: — 'I am innocent; I am poor; my Orang-Outang is of great value — to one in my circumstances a fortune of itself — why should

I lose it through idle apprehensions of danger? Here it is, within my grasp. It was found in the Bois de Boulogne — at a vast distance from the scene of that butchery. How can it ever be suspected that a brute beast should have done the deed? The police are at fault — they have failed to procure the slightest clue. Should they even trace the animal, it would be impossible to prove me cognizant of the murder, or to implicate me in guilt on account of that cognizance. Above all, *I am known*. The advertiser designates me as the possessor of the beast. I am not sure to what limit his knowledge may extend. Should I avoid claiming a property of so great value, which it is known that I possess, I will render the animal, at least, liable to suspicion. It is not my policy to attract attention either to myself or to the beast. I will answer the advertisement, get the Orang-Outang, and keep it close until this matter has blown over.' "

At this moment we heard a step upon the stairs.

"Be ready," said Dupin, "with your pistols, but neither use them nor show them until a signal from myself."

The front door of the house had been left open, and the visitor had entered, without ringing, and advanced several steps upon the staircase. Now, however, he seemed to hesitate. Presently we heard him descending. Dupin was moving quickly to the door, when we again heard him coming up. He did not turn back a second time, but stepped up with decision and rapped at the door of our chamber.

"Come in," said Dupin, in a cheerful and hearty tone.

A man entered. He was a sailor, evidently, — a tall, stout, and muscular-looking person, with a certain dare-devil expression of countenance, not altogether unprepossessing. His face, greatly sunburnt, was more than half hidden by whisker and *mustachio*. He had with him a huge oaken cudgel, but appeared to be otherwise unarmed. He bowed awkwardly, and bade us "good evening," in French accents, which, although somewhat Neufchatel-ish, were still sufficiently indicative of a Parisian origin.

"Sit down, my friend," said Dupin, "I suppose you have called about the Orang-Outang. Upon my word, I almost envy you the possession of him; a remarkably fine, and no doubt a very valuable animal. How old do you suppose him to be?"

The sailor drew a long breath, with the air of a man relieved of some intolerable burthen, and then replied, in an assured tone:

"I have no way of telling — but he can't be more than four or five years old. Have you got him here?"

"Oh no; we had no conveniences for keeping him here. He is at a livery stable in the Rue Dubourg, just by. You can get him in the morning. Of course you are prepared to identify the property?"

"To be sure I am, sir."

"I shall be sorry to part with him," said Dupin.

"I don't mean that you should be at all this trouble for nothing, sir," said the man. "Couldn't expect it. Am very willing to pay a reward for the finding of the animal — that is to say, anything in reason."

"Well," replied my friend, "that is all very fair, to be sure. Let me think! — what should I have? Oh! I will tell you. My reward shall be this. You shall give me all the information in your power about these murders in the Rue Morgue."

Dupin said the last words in a very low tone, and very quietly. Just as quietly, too, he walked towards the door, locked it, and put the key in his pocket. He then drew a pistol from his bosom and placed it, without the least flurry, upon the table.

The sailor's face flushed up as if he were struggling with suffocation. He started to his feet and grasped his cudgel; but the next moment he fell back into his seat, trembling violently, and with the countenance of death itself. He spoke not a word. I pitied him from the bottom of my heart.

"My friend," said Dupin, in a kind tone, "you are alarming yourself unnecessarily — you are indeed. We mean you no harm whatever. I pledge you the honor of a gentleman, and of a Frenchman, that we intend you no injury. I perfectly well know that you are innocent of the atrocities in the Rue Morgue. It will not do, however, to deny that you are in some measure implicated in them. From what I have already said, you must know that I have had means of information about this matter — means of which you could never have dreamed. Now the thing stands thus. You have done nothing which you could have avoided — nothing, certainly, which renders you culpable. You were not even guilty of robbery, when you might have robbed with impunity. You have nothing to conceal. You have no reason for concealment. On the other hand, you are bound by every principle of honor to confess all you know. An innocent man is now imprisoned, charged with that crime of which you can point out the perpetrator.''

The sailor had recovered his presence of mind, in a great measure, while Dupin uttered these words; but his original boldness of bearing was all gone.

``So help me, God,'' said he, after a brief pause, ``I *will* tell you all I know about this affair; — but I do not expect you to believe one half I say — I would be a fool indeed if I did. Still, I *am* innocent, and I will make a clean breast if I die for it.''

What he stated was, in substance, this. He had lately made a voyage to the Indian Archipelago. A party, of which he formed one, landed at Borneo, and passed into the interior on an excursion of pleasure. Himself and a companion had captured the Orang-Outang. This companion dying, the animal fell into his own exclusive possession. After great trouble, occasioned by the intractible ferocity of his captive during the home voyage, he at length succeeded in lodging it safely at his own residence in Paris, where, not to attract towards himself the unpleasant curiosity of his neighbors, he kept it carefully secluded, until such time as it should recover from a wound in the foot, received from a splinter on board ship. His ultimate design was to sell it.

Returning home from some sailors' frolic on the night, or rather in the morning of the murder, he found the beast occupying his own bedroom, into which it had broken from a closet adjoining, where it had been, as was thought, securely confined. Razor in hand, and fully lathered, it was sitting before a looking-glass, attempting the operation of shaving, in which it had no doubt previously watched its master through the keyhole of the closet. Terrified at the sight of so dangerous a weapon in the possession of an animal so ferocious, and so well able to use it, the man, for some moments, was at a loss what to do. He had been accustomed, however, to quiet the creature, even in its fiercest moods, by the use of a whip, and to this he now resorted. Upon sight of it, the Orang-Outang sprang at once through the door of the chamber, down the stairs, and thence, through a window, unfortunately open, into the street.

The Frenchman followed in despair; the ape, razor still in hand, occasionally stopped to look back and gesticulate at its pursuer, until the latter had nearly come up with it. It then again made off. In this manner the chase continued for a long time. The streets were profoundly quiet, as it was nearly three o'clock in the morning. In passing down an alley in the rear of the Rue Morgue, the fugitive's attention was arrested by a light gleaming from the open window of Madame L'Espanaye's chamber, in the fourth story of her house. Rushing to the building, it perceived the lightning-rod, clambered up with inconceivable agility, grasped the shutter, which was thrown fully back against the wall, and, by its means, swung itself directly upon the headboard of the bed. The whole feat did not occupy a minute. The shutter was kicked open again by the Orang-Outang as it entered the room.

The sailor, in the meantime, was both rejoiced and perplexed. He had strong hopes of now recapturing the brute, as it could scarcely escape from the trap into which it had ventured, except by the rod, where it might be intercepted as it came down. On the other hand, there was much cause for anxiety as to what it might do in the house. This latter reflection urged the man still to follow the fugitive. A lightning-rod is ascended without difficulty, especially by a sailor; but, when he had arrived as high as the window, which lay far to his left, his career was stopped; the most that he could accomplish was to reach over so as to obtain a glimpse of the interior of the room. At this glimpse he nearly fell from his hold through excess of horror. Now it was that those hideous shrieks arose upon the night, which had startled from slumber the inmates of the Rue Morgue. Madame L'Espanaye and her daughter, habited in their night clothes, had apparently been arranging some papers in the iron chest already mentioned, which had been wheeled into the middle of the room. It was open, and its contents lay beside it on the floor. The victims must have been sitting with their backs toward the window; and, from the time elapsing between the ingress of the beast and the screams, it seems probable that it was not immediately perceived. The flapping-to of the shutter would naturally have been attributed to the wind.

As the sailor looked in, the gigantic animal had seized Madame L'Espanaye by the hair (which was loose, as she had been combing it), and was flourishing the razor about her face, in imitation of the motions of a barber. The daughter lay prostrate and motionless; she had swooned. The screams and struggle of the old lady (during which the hair was torn from her head) had the effect of changing the probably pacific purposes of the Orang-Outang into those of wrath. With one determined sweep of its muscular arm it nearly severed her head from her body. The sight of blood inflamed its anger into frenzy. Gnashing its teeth, and flashing fire from its eyes, it flew upon the body of the girl, and imbedded its fearful talons in her throat, retaining its grasp until she expired. Its wandering and wild glances fell at this moment upon the head of the bed, over which the face of its master, rigid with horror, was just discernible. The fury of the beast, who no doubt bore still in mind the dreaded whip, was instantly converted into fear. Conscious of having deserved punishment, it seemed desirous of concealing its bloody deeds, and skipped about the chamber in an agony of nervous agitation; throwing down and breaking the furniture as it moved, and dragging the bed from the bedstead. In conclusion, it seized first the corpse of the daughter, and thrust it up the chimney, as it was found; then that of the old lady, which it immediately hurled through the window headlong.

As the ape approached the casement with its mutilated burthen, the sailor shrank aghast to the rod, and, rather gliding than clambering down it, hurried at once home — dreading the consequences of the butchery, and gladly abandoning, in his terror, all solicitude about the fate of the Orang-Outang. The words heard by the party upon the staircase were the Frenchman's exclamations of horror and affright, co-mingled with the fiendish jabberings of the brute.

I have scarcely anything to add. The Orang-Outang must have escaped from the chamber, by the rod, just before the breaking of the door. It must have closed the window as it passed through it. It was subsequently caught by the owner himself, who obtained for it a very large sum at the *Jardin des Plantes*. Le Bon was instantly released, upon our narration of the circumstances (with some comments from Dupin) at the *bureau* of the Prefect of Police. This functionary, however well disposed to my friend, could not altogether conceal his chagrin at the turn which affairs had taken, and was fain to indulge in a sarcasm or two, about the propriety of every person minding his own business.

"Let them talk," said Dupin, who had not thought it necessary to reply. "Let him discourse; it will ease his conscience. I am satisfied with having defeated him in his own castle. Nevertheless, that he failed in the solution of this mystery, is by no means that matter for wonder which he supposes it; for, in truth, our friend the Prefect is somewhat too cunning to be profound. In his wisdom is no *stamen*. It is all head and no body, like the pictures of the Goddess Laverna, — or, at best, all head and shoulders, like a codfish. But he is a good creature after all. I like him especially for one master stoke of cant, by which he has attained his reputation for ingenuity. I mean the way he has *'de nier ce qui est, et d'expliquer ce qui n'est pas.'* "

The Purloined Letter

Edgar Allan Poe

Nil sapientiæ odiosius acumine nimio.

SENECA

AT Paris, just after dark one gusty evening in the autumn of 18—, I was enjoying the twofold luxury of meditation and a meerschaum, in company with my friend C. Auguste Dupin, in his little back library, or book-closet, *au troisième, No.* 33, *Rue Dunôt, Faubourg St. Germain*. For one hour at least we had maintained a profound silence; while each, to any casual observer, might have seemed intently and exclusively occupied with the curling eddies of smoke that oppressed the atmosphere of the chamber. For myself, however, I was mentally discussing certain topics which had formed matter for conversation between us at an earlier period of the evening. I mean the affair of the Rue Morgue, and the mystery attending the murder of Marie Rogêt. I looked upon it, therefore, as something of a coincidence, when the door of our apartment was thrown open and admitted our old acquaintance, Monsieur G——, the Prefect of the Parisian police.

We gave him a hearty welcome; for there was nearly half as much of the entertaining as of the contemptible about the man, and we had not seen him for several years. We had been sitting in the dark, and Dupin now arose for the purpose of lighting a lamp, but sat down again, without doing so, upon G——'s saying that he had called to consult us, or rather to ask the opinion of my friend, about some official business which had occasioned a great deal of trouble.

"If it is any point requiring reflection," observed Dupin, as he forebore to enkindle the wick, "we shall examine it to better purpose in the dark."

"That is another of your odd notions," said the Prefect, who had a fashion of calling everything "odd" that was beyond his comprehension, and thus lived amid an absolute legion of "oddities."

"Very true," said Dupin, as he supplied his visitor with a pipe, and rolled towards him a comfortable chair.

"And what is the difficulty now?" I asked. "Nothing more in the assassination way, I hope?"

"Oh no; nothing of that nature. The fact is, the business is *very* simple indeed, and I make no doubt that we can manage it sufficiently well ourselves; but then I thought Dupin would like to hear the details of it, because it is so excessively *odd.*''

''Simple and odd,'' said Dupin.

''Why, yes; and not exactly that, either. The fact is, we have all been a good deal puzzled because the affair *is* so simple, and yet baffles us altogether.''

''Perhaps it is the very simplicity of the thing which puts you at fault,'' said my friend.

''What nonsense you *do* talk!'' replied the Prefect, laughing heartily.

''Perhaps the mystery is a little *too* plain,'' said Dupin.

''Oh, good heavens! who ever heard of such an idea?''

''A little *too* self-evident.''

''Ha! ha! ha! — ha! ha! ha! — ho! ho! ho!'' — roared our visitor, profoundly amused, ''oh Dupin, you will be the death of me yet!''

''And what, after all, *is* the matter on hand?'' I asked.

''Why, I will tell you,'' replied the Prefect, as he gave a long, steady, and contemplative puff, and settled himself in his chair. ''I will tell you in a few words; but, before I begin, let me caution you that this is an affair demanding the greatest secrecy, and that I should most probably lose the position I now hold, were it known that I confided it to any one.''

''Proceed,'' said I.

"Or not," said Dupin.

"Well, then; I have received personal information, from a very high quarter, that a certain document of the last importance, has been purloined from the royal apartments. The individual who purloined it is known; this beyond a doubt; he was seen to take it. It is known, also, that it still remains in his possession."

"How is this known?" asked Dupin.

"It is clearly inferred," replied the Prefect, "from the nature of the document, and from the non-appearance of certain results which would at once arise from its passing *out* of the robber's possession; — that is to say, from his employing it as he must design in the end to employ it."

"Be a little more explicit," I said.

"Well, I may venture so far as to say that the paper gives its holder a certain power in a certain quarter where such power is immensely valuable." The Prefect was fond of the cant of diplomacy.

"Still I do not quite understand," said Dupin.

"No? Well; the disclosure of the document to a third person, who shall be nameless, would bring in question the honor of a personage of most exalted station; and this fact gives the holder of the document an ascendancy over the illustrious personage whose honor and peace are so jeopardized."

"But this ascendancy," I interposed, "would depend upon the robber's knowledge of the loser's knowledge of the robber. Who would dare —"

"The thief," said G——, "is the Minister D——, who dares all things, those unbecoming as well as those becoming a man. The method of the theft was not less ingenious than bold. The document in question — a letter, to be frank — has been received by the personage robbed while alone in the royal *boudoir*. During its perusal she was suddenly interrupted by the entrance of the other exalted personage from whom especially it was her wish to conceal it. After a hurried and vain endeavor to thrust it in a drawer, she was forced to place it, open as it was, upon a table. The address, however, was uppermost, and, the contents thus unexposed, the letter escaped notice. At this juncture enters the Minister D——. His lynx eye immediately perceives the paper, recognizes the handwriting of the address, observes the confusion of the personage addressed, and fathoms her secret. After some business transactions, hurried through in his ordinary manner, he produces a letter somewhat similar to the one in question, opens it, pretends to read it, and then places it in close juxtaposition to the other. Again he converses, for some fifteen minutes, upon the public affairs. At length, in taking leave, he takes also from the table the letter to which he had no claim. Its rightful owner saw, but, of course, dared not call attention to the act, in the presence of the third personage who stood at her elbow. The minister decamped; leaving his own letter — one of no importance — upon the table."

"Here, then," said Dupin to me, "you have precisely what you demand to make the ascendancy complete — the robber's knowledge of the loser's knowledge of the robber."

"Yes," replied the Prefect; "and the power thus attained has, for some months past, been wielded, for political purposes, to a very dangerous extent. The personage robbed is more thoroughly convinced, every day, of the necessity of reclaiming her letter. But this, of course, cannot be done openly. In fine, driven to despair, she has committed the matter to me."

"Than whom," said Dupin, amid a perfect whirlwind of smoke, "no more sagacious agent could, I suppose, be desired, or even imagined."

"You flatter me," replied the Prefect; "but it is possible that some such opinion may have been entertained."

"It is clear," said I, "as you observe, that the letter is still in possession of the minister; since it is this possession, and not any employment of the letter, which bestows the power. With the employment the power departs."

“True,” said G——; “and upon this conviction I proceeded. My first care was to make thorough search of the minister’s hotel; and here my chief embarrassment lay in the necessity of searching without his knowledge. Beyond all things, I have been warned of the danger which would result from giving him reason to suspect our design.”

“But,” said I, “you are quite *au fait* in these investigations. The Parisian police have done this thing often before.”

“Oh, yes; and for this reason I did not despair. The habits of the minister gave me, too, a great advantage. He is frequently absent from home all night. His servants are by no means numerous. They sleep at a distance from their master’s apartment, and, being chiefly Neapolitans, are readily made drunk. I have keys, as you know, with which I can open any chamber or cabinet in Paris. For three months a night has not passed, during the greater part of which I have not been engaged, personally, in ransacking the D—— hotel. My honor is interested, and, to mention a great secret, the reward is enormous. So I did not abandon the search until I had become fully satisfied that the thief is a more astute man than myself. I fancy that I have investigated every nook and corner of the premises in which it is possible that the paper can be concealed.”

“But is it not possible,” I suggested, “that although the letter may be in possession of the minister, as it unquestionably is, he may have concealed it elsewhere than upon his own premises?''

"This is barely possible," said Dupin. "The present peculiar condition of affairs at court, and especially of those intrigues in which D—— is known to be involved, would render the instant availability of the document — its susceptibility of being produced at a moment's notice — a point of nearly equal importance with its possession."

"Its susceptibility of being produced?" said I.

"That is to say, of being *destroyed,*" said Dupin.

"True," I observed; "the paper is clearly then upon the premises. As for its being upon the person of the minister, we may consider that as out of the question."

"Entirely," said the Prefect. "He has been twice waylaid, as if by footpads, and his person rigorously searched under my own inspection."

"You might have spared yourself this trouble," said Dupin. "D——, I presume, is not altogether a fool, and, if not, must have anticipated these waylayings, as a matter of course."

"Not *altogether* a fool," said G——, "but then he's a poet, which I take to be only one remove from a fool."

"True," said Dupin, after a long and

thoughtful whiff from his meerschaum, "although I have been guilty of certain doggerel myself."

"Suppose you detail," said I, "the particulars of your search."

"Why, the fact is, we took our time, and we searched *everywhere*. I have had long experience in these affairs. I took the entire building, room by room; devoting the nights of a whole week to each. We examined, first, the furniture of each apartment. We opened every possible drawer; and I presume you know that, to a properly trained police agent, such a thing as a *secret* drawer is impossible. Any man is a dolt who permits a 'secret' drawer to escape him in a search of this kind. The thing is *so* plain. There is a certain amount of bulk — of space — to be accounted for in every cabinet. Then we have accurate rules. The fiftieth part of a line could not escape us. After the cabinets we took the chairs. The cushions we probed with the fine long needles you have seen me employ. From the tables we removed the tops."

"Why so?"

"Sometimes the top of a table, or other similarly arranged piece of furniture, is removed by the person wishing to conceal an article; then the leg is excavated, the article deposited within the cavity, and the top replaced. The bottoms and tops of bed posts are employed in the same way."

"But could not the cavity be detected by sounding?" I asked.

"By no means, if, when the article is deposited, a sufficient wadding of cotton be placed around it. Besides, in our case, we were obliged to proceed without noise."

"But you could not have removed — you could not have taken to pieces *all* articles of furniture in which it would have been possible to make a deposit in the manner you mention. A letter may be compressed into a thin spiral roll, not differing much in shape or bulk from a large knitting-needle, and in this form it might be inserted into the rung of a chair, for example. You did not take to pieces all the chairs?"

"Certainly not; but we did better — we examined the rungs of every chair in the hotel, and, indeed, the jointings of every description of furniture, by the aid of a most powerful microscope. Had there been any traces of recent disturbance we should not have failed to detect it instantly. A single grain of gimlet-dust, for example, would have been as obvious as an apple. Any disorder in the gluing — any unusual gaping in the joints — would have sufficed to insure detection."

"I presume you looked to the mirrors, between the boards and the plates, and you probed the beds and the bedclothes, as well as the curtains and carpets."

"That of course; and when we had absolutely completed every particle of the furniture in this way, then we examined the house itself. We divided its entire surface into compartments, which we numbered, so that none might be missed; then we scrutinized each individual square inch throughout the premises, including the two houses immediately adjoining, with the microscope, as before."

"The two houses adjoining!" I exclaimed; "you must have had a great deal of trouble."

"We had; but the reward offered is prodigious."

"You include the *grounds* about the houses?"

"All the grounds are paved with brick. They gave us comparatively little trouble. We examined the moss between the bricks, and found it undisturbed."

"You looked among D——'s papers, of course, and into the books of the library?"

"Certainly; we opened every package and parcel; we not only opened every book, but we turned over every leaf in each volume, not contenting ourselves with a mere shake, according to the fashion of some of our police officers. We also measured the thickness of every book-*cover*, with the most accurate admeasurement, and applied to each the most jealous scrutiny of the microscope. Had any of the bindings been recently meddled with, it would have been utterly impossible that the fact should have escaped observation. Some five or six volumes, just from the hands of the binder, we carefully probed, longitudinally, with the needles.''

''You explored the floors beneath the carpets?''

''Beyond doubt. We removed every carpet, and examined the boards with the microscope.''

''And the paper on the walls?''

''Yes.''

''You looked into the cellars?''

''We did.''

''Then,'' I said, ''you have been making a miscalculation, and the letter is *not* upon the premises, as you suppose.''

''I fear you are right there,'' said the Prefect. ''And now, Dupin, what would you advise me to do?''

''To make a thorough research of the premises.''

''That is absolutely needless,'' replied G——. ''I am not sure that I breathe than I am that the letter is not at the hotel.''

''I have no better advice to give you,'' said Dupin. ''You have, of course, an accurate description of the letter?''

''Oh yes!'' — And here the Prefect, producing a memorandum book, proceeded to read aloud a minute account of the internal, and especially of the external appearance of the missing document. Soon after finishing the perusal of this description, he took his departure, more entirely depressed in spirits than I had ever known the good gentleman before.

In about a month afterwards he paid us another visit, and found us occupied very nearly as before. He took a pipe and a chair and entered into some ordinary conversation. At length I said:

"Well, but G——, what of the purloined letter? I presume you have at last made up your mind that there is no such thing as overreaching the minister?"

"Confound him, say I — yes; I made the re-examination, however, as Dupin suggested — but it was all labor lost, as I knew it would be."

"How much was the reward offered, did you say?" asked Dupin.

"Why, a very great deal — a *very* liberal reward — I don't like to say how much, precisely; but one thing I *will* say, that I wouldn't mind giving my individual check for fifty thousand francs to any one who could obtain me that letter. The fact is, it is becoming of more and more importance every day; and the reward has been lately doubled. If it were trebled, however, I could do no more than I have done."

"Why, yes," said Dupin, drawlingly, between the whiffs of his meerschaum, "I really — think, G——, you have not exerted yourself — to the utmost in this matter. You might — do a little more, I think, eh?"

"How? — in what way?"

"Why — puff, puff — you might — puff, puff — employ counsel in the matter, eh? — puff, puff, puff. Do you remember the story they tell of Abernethy?"

"No; hang Abernethy!"

"To be sure! hang him and welcome. But, once upon a time, a certain rich miser conceived the design of sponging upon this Abernethy for a medical opinion. Getting up, for this purpose, an ordinary conversation in a private company, he insinuated his case to the physician, as that of an imaginary individual.

" 'We will suppose,' said the miser, 'that his symptoms are such and such; now, doctor, what would *you* have directed him to take?'

" 'Take!' said Abernethy, 'why, take *advice,* to be sure.' "

"But," said the Prefect, a little discomposed, "I am *perfectly* willing to take advice, and to pay for it. I would *really* give fifty thousand francs to any one who would aid me in the matter."

"In that case," replied Dupin, opening a drawer, and producing a check-book, "you may as well fill me up a check for the amount mentioned. When you have signed it, I will hand you the letter."

I was astounded. The Prefect appeared absolutely thunder-stricken. For some minutes he remained speechless and motionless, looking incredulously at my friend with open mouth, and eyes that seemed starting from their sockets; then, apparently recovering himself in some measure, he seized a pen, and after several pauses and vacant stares, finally filled up and signed a check for fifty thousand francs, and handed it across the table to Dupin. The latter examined it carefully and deposited it in his pocketbook; then, unlocking an *escritoire,* took thence a letter and gave it to the Prefect. This functionary grasped it in a perfect agony of joy, opened it with a trembling hand, cast a rapid glance at its contents, and then, scrambling and struggling to the door, rushed at length unceremoniously from the room and from the house, without having uttered a syllable since Dupin had requested him to fill up the check.

When he had gone, my friend entered into some explanations.

"The Parisian police," he said, "are exceedingly able in their way. They are persevering, ingenious, cunning, and thoroughly versed in the knowledge which their duties seem chiefly to demand. Thus, when G—— detailed to us his mode of searching the premises at the Hôtel D——, I felt entire confidence in his having made a satisfactory investigation — so far as his labors extended."

"So far as his labors extended?" said I.

"Yes," said Dupin. "The measures adopted were not only the best of their kind, but carried out to absolute perfection. Had the letter been deposited within the range of their search, these fellows would, beyond a question, have found it."

I merely laughed — but he seemed quite serious in all that he said.

"The measures, then," he continued, "were good in their kind, and well executed; their defect lay in their being inapplicable to the case, and to the man. A certain set of highly ingenious resources are, with the Prefect, a sort of Procrustean bed, to which he forcibly adapts his designs. But he perpetually errs by being too deep or too shallow for the matter in hand; and many a schoolboy is a better reasoner than he. I knew one about eight years of age whose success at guessing in the game of 'even and odd' attracted universal admiration. This game is simple, and is played with marbles. One player holds in his hand a number of these toys, and demands of another whether that number is even or odd. If the guess is right, the guesser wins one; if wrong, he loses one. The boy to whom I allude won all the marbles of the school. Of course he had some principle of guessing; and this lay in mere observation and admeasurement of the astuteness of his opponents. For example, an arrant simpleton is his opponent, and, holding up his closed hand, asks, 'Are they even or odd?' Our schoolboy replies, 'odd' and loses; but upon the second trial he wins, for he then says to himself, 'the simpleton had them even upon the first trial, and his amount of cunning is just sufficient to make him have them odd upon the second; I will therefore guess odd'; — he guesses odd, and wins. Now, with a simpleton a degree above the first, he would have reasoned thus: 'This fellow finds that in the first instance I guessed odd, and, in the second, he will propose to himself upon the first impulse, a simple variation from even to odd, as did the first simpleton; but then a second thought will suggest that this is too simple a variation, and finally he will decide upon putting it even as before. I will therefore guess even'; — he guesses even, and wins. Now this mode of reasoning in the schoolboy, whom his fellows termed 'lucky,' — what, in its last analysis, is it?"

"It is merely," I said, "an identification of the reasoner's intellect with that of his opponent."

"It is," said Dupin; "and, upon inquiring of the boy by what means he effected the *thorough* identification in which his success consisted, I received answer as follows: 'When I wish to find out how wise, or how stupid, or how good, or how wicked is any one, or what are his thoughts at the moment, I fashion the expression of my face, as accurately as possible, in accordance with the expression of his, and then wait to see what thoughts or sentiments arise in my mind or heart, as if to match or correspond with the expression.' This response of the schoolboy lies at the bottom of all the spurious profundity which has been attributed to Rochefoucauld, to La Bougive, to Machiavelli, and to Campanella.''

''And the identification,'' I said, ''of the reasoner's intellect with that of his opponent, depends, if I understand you aright, upon the accuracy with which the opponent's intellect is admeasured.''

''For its practical value it depends upon this,'' replied Dupin; ''and the Prefect and his cohort fail so frequently, first, by default of this identification, and, secondly, by ill-admeasurement, or rather through non-admeasurement, of the intellect with which they are engaged. They consider only their *own* ideas of ingenuity; and, in searching for anything hidden, advert only to the modes in which *they* would have hidden it. They are right in this much — that their own ingenuity is a faithful representative of that of *the mass;* but when the cunning of the individual felon is diverse in character from their own, the felon foils them, of course. This always happens when it is above their own, and very usually when it is below. They have no variation of principle in their investigations; at best, when urged by some unusual emergency — by some extraordinary reward — they extend or exaggerate their old modes of *practice*, without touching their principles. What, for example, in this case of D——, has been done to vary the principle of action? What is all this boring, and probing, and sounding, and scrutinizing with the microscope, and dividing the surface of the building into registered square inches — what is it all but an exaggeration *of the application* of the one principle or set of principles of search, which are based upon the one set of notions regarding human ingenuity, to which the Prefect, in the long routine of his duty, has been accustomed? Do you not see he has taken it for granted that *all* men proceed to conceal a letter, — not exactly in a gimlet-hole bored in a chair-leg — but,at least, in *some* out-of-the-way hole or corner suggested by the same tenor of thought which would urge a man to secrete a letter in a gimlet-hole bored in a chair-leg? And do you not see also, that such *recherchés* nooks for concealment are adapted only for ordinary occasions, and would be adopted only by ordinary intellects; for, in all cases of concealment, a disposal of the article concealed — a disposal of it in this *recherché* manner, — is, in the very first instance, presumable and presumed; and thus its discovery depends, not at all upon the acumen, but altogether upon the mere care, patience, and determination of the seekers; and where the case is of importance — or, what amounts to the same thing in the political eyes, when the reward is of magnitude, — the qualities in question have *never* been known to fail. You will now understand what I mean in suggesting that, had the purloined letter been hidden anywhere within the limits of the Prefect's examination — in other words, had the principle of its concealment been comprehended within the principles of the Prefect — its discovery would have been a matter altogether beyond question. This functionary, however, has been thoroughly mystified; and the remote source of his defeat lies in the supposition that the minister is a fool, because he has acquired renown as a poet. All fools are poets; this the Prefect *feels;* and he is merely guilty of a *non distributio medii* in thence inferring that all poets are fools."

"But is this really the poet?" I asked. "There are two brothers, I know; and both have attained reputation in letters. The minister I believe has written learnedly on Differential Calculus. He is a mathematician, and no poet."

"You are mistaken; I know him well; he is both. As poet *and* mathematician, he would reason well; as mere mathematician, he could not have reasoned at all, and thus would have been at the mercy of the Prefect."

"You surprise me," I said, "by these opinions, which have been contradicted by the voice of the world. You do not mean to set at naught the well-digested idea of centuries. The mathematical reason has long been regarded as *the* reason *par excellence.*"

" *'Il y a à parier,'* " replied Dupin, quoting

from Chamfort, " '*que toute idée publique, toute convention reçue, est une sottise, car elle a convenu au plus grand nombre.*' The mathematicians, I grant you, have done their best to promulgate the popular error to which you allude, and which is none the less an error for its promulgation as truth. With an art worthy a better cause, for example, they have insinuated the term 'analysis' into application to algebra. The French are the originators of this particular deception; but if a term is of any importance — if words derive any value from applicability — then 'analysis' conveys 'algebra' about as much as, in Latin, '*ambitus*' implies 'ambition,' '*religio*' 'religion,' or '*homines honesti,*' a set of *honorable* men."

"You have a quarrel on hand, I see," said I, "with some of the algebraists of Paris; but proceed."

"I dispute the availability, and thus the value, of that reason which is cultivated in any special form other than the abstractly logical. I dispute, in particular, the reason educed by mathematical study. The mathematics are the science of form and quantity; mathematical reasoning is merely logic applied to observation upon form and quantity. The great error lies in supposing that even the truths of what is called *pure* algebra, are abstract or general truths. And this error is so egregious that I am confounded at the universality with which it has been received. Mathematical axioms are *not* axioms of general truth. What is true of *relation* — of form and quantity — is often grossly false in regard to morals, for example. In this latter science it is very usually *un*true that the aggregated parts are equal to the whole. In chemistry also the axiom fails. In the consideration of motive it fails; for two motives, each of a given value, have not, necessarily, a value when united, equal to the sum of their values apart. There are numerous other mathematical truths which are only truths within the limits of *relation*. But the mathematician argues, from his *finite truths*, through habit, as if they were of an absolutely general applicability — as the world indeed imagines them to be. Bryant, in his very learned 'Mythology,' mentions an analogous source of error, when he says that 'although the Pagan fables are not believed, yet we forget ourselves continually, and make inferences from them as existing realities.' With the algebraists, however, who are Pagans themselves, the 'Pagan fables' *are* believed, and the inferences are made, not so much through lapse of memory, as through an unaccountable addling of the brains. In short, I never yet encountered the mere mathematician who could be trusted out of equal roots, or one who did not clandestinely hold it as a point of his faith that $x^2 + px$ was absolutely and unconditionally equal to q. Say to one of these gentlemen, by way of experiment, if you please, that you believe occasions may occur where $x^2 + px$ is *not* altogether equal to q, and, having made him understand what you mean, get out of his reach as speedily as convenient, for, beyond a doubt, he will endeavor to knock you down.

"I mean to say," continued Dupin, while I merely laughed at his last observations, "that if the minister had been no more than a mathematician, the Prefect would have been under no necessity of giving me this check. I knew him, however, as both mathematician and poet, and my measures were adapted to his capacity, with reference to the circumstances by which he was surrounded. I knew him as a courtier, too, and as a bold *intrigant*. Such a man, I considered, could not fail to be aware of the ordinary policial modes of action. He could not have failed to anticipate — and events have proved that he did not fail to anticipate — the waylayings to which he was subjected. He must have foreseen, I reflected, the secret investigations of his premises. His frequent absences from home at night, which were hailed by the Prefect as certain aids to his success, I regarded only as *ruses*, to afford oportunity for thorough search to the police, and thus the sooner to impress them with the conviction to which G——, in fact, did finally arrive — the conviction that the letter was not upon the premises. I felt, also that the whole train of thought, which I was at some pains in detailing to you just now, concerning the invariable principle of policial action in searches for articles concealed — I felt that this whole train of thought would necessarily pass through the mind of the minister. It would imperatively lead him to despise all the ordinary *nooks* of concealment. *He* could not, I reflected, be so weak as not to see that the most intricate and remote recess of his hotel would be as open as his commonest closets to the eyes, to the probes, to the gimlets, and to the microscopes of the Prefect. I saw, in fine, that he would be driven, as a matter of course to *simplicity,* if not deliberately induced to it as a matter of choice. You will remember, perhaps, how desperately the Prefect laughed when I suggested, upon our first interview, that it was just possible this mystery troubled him so much on account of its being so *very* self-evident."

"Yes," said I, "I remember his merriment well. I really thought he would have fallen into convulsions."

"The material world," continued Dupin, "abounds with very strict analogies to the immaterial; and thus some color of truth has been given to the rhetorical dogma, that metaphor, or simile, may be made to strengthen an argument, as well as to embellish a description. The principle of the *vis inertiæ,* for example, seems to be identical in physics and metaphysics. It is not more true in the former, that a large body is with more difficulty set in motion than a smaller one, and that its subsequent *momentum* is commensurate with this difficulty, than it is, in the latter, that intellects of the vaster capacity, while more forcible, more constant, and more eventful in their movements than those of inferior grade, are yet the less readily moved, and more embarrassed and full of hesitation in the first few steps of their progress. Again: have you ever noticed which of the street signs, over the shop doors, are the most attractive of attention?''

''I have never given the matter a thought,'' I said.

''There is a game of puzzles,'' he resumed, ''which is played upon a map. One party playing requires another to find a given word — the name of town, river, state or empire — any word, in short, upon the motley and perplexed surface of the chart. A novice in the game generally seeks to embarrass his opponents by giving them the most minutely-lettered names; but the adept selects such words as stretch, in large characters, from one end of the chart to the other. These, like the over-largely lettered signs and placards of the street, escape observation by dint of being excessively obvious; and here the physical oversight is precisely analogous with the moral inapprehension by which the intellect suffers to pass unnoticed those considerations which are too obtrusively and too palpably self-evident. But this is a point, it appears, somewhat above or beneath the understanding of the Prefect. He never once thought it probable, or possible, that the minister had deposited the letter immediately beneath the nose of the whole world, by way of best preventing any portion of that world from perceiving it.

"But the more I reflected upon the daring, dashing, and discriminating ingenuity of D——; upon the fact that the document must always have been *at hand*, if he intended to use it to good purpose; and upon the decisive evidence, obtained by the Prefect, that it was not hidden within the limits of that dignitary's ordinary search — the more satisfied I became that, to conceal this letter, the minister had resorted to the comprehensive and sagacious expedient of not attempting to conceal it at all.

"Full of these ideas, I prepared myself with a pair of green spectacles, and called one fine morning, quite by accident, at the ministerial hotel. I found D—— at home, yawning, lounging, and dawdling, as usual, and pretending to be in the last extremity of *ennui*. He is, perhaps, the most really energetic human being now alive — but that is only when nobody sees him.

"To be even with him, I complained of my weak eyes, and lamented the necessity of the spectacles, under cover of which I cautiously and thoroughly surveyed the apartment, while seemingly intent only upon the conversation of my host.

"I paid special attention to a large writing-table near which he sat, and upon which lay confusedly, some miscellaneous letters and other papers, with one or two musical instruments and a few books. Here, however, after a long and very deliberate scrutiny, I saw nothing to excite particular suspicion.

"At length my eyes, in going the circuit of the room, fell upon a trumpery filigree card-rack of pasteboard, that hung dangling by a dirty blue ribbon, from a little brass knob just beneath the middle of the mantelpiece. In this rack, which had three or four compartments, were five or six visiting cards and a solitary letter. This last was much soiled and crumpled. It was torn nearly in two, across the middle — as if a design, in the first instance, to tear it entirely up as worthless, had been altered, or stayed, in the second. It had a large black seal, bearing the D—— cipher *very* conspicuously, and was addressed, in a diminutive female hand, to D——, the minister, himself. It was thrust carelessly, and even, as it seemed, contemptuously, into one of the upper divisions of the rack.

"No sooner had I glanced at this letter, than I concluded it to be that of which I was in search. To be sure, it was, to all appearance, radically different from the one of which the Prefect had read us so minute a description. Here the seal was large and black, with the D—— cipher; there it was small and red, with the ducal arms of the S—— family. Here, the address, to the minister, was diminutive and feminine; there the superscription, to a certain royal personage, was markedly bold and decided; the size alone formed a point of correspondence. But, then, the *radicalness* of these differences, which was excessive; the dirt; the soiled and torn condition of the paper, so inconsistent with the *true* methodical habits of D——, and so suggestive of a design to delude the beholder into an idea of the worthlessness of the document; these things, together with the hyperobtrusive situation of this document, full in the view of every visitor, and thus exactly in accordance with the conclusions to which I had previously arrived; these things, I say, were strongly corroborative of suspicion, in one who came with the intention to suspect.

"I protracted my visit as long as possible, and, while I maintained a most animated discussion with the minister, on a topic which I knew well had never failed to interest and excite him, I kept my attention really riveted upon the letter. In this examination, I committed to memory its external appearance and arrangement in the rack; and also fell, at length, upon a discovery which set at rest whatever trivial doubt I might have entertained. In scrutinizing the edges of the paper, I observed them to be more *chafed* than seemed necessary. They presented the *broken* appearance which is manifested when a stiff paper, having been once folded and pressed with a folder, is refolded in a reversed direction, in the same creases or edges which had formed the original fold. This discovery was sufficient. It was clear to me that the letter had been turned, as a glove, inside out, redirected, and resealed. I bade the minister good morning, and took my departure at once, leaving a gold snuff-box upon the table.

"The next morning I called for the snuff-box, when we resumed, quite eagerly, the conversation of the preceding day. While thus engaged, however, a loud report, as if of a pistol, was heard immediately beneath the windows of the hotel, and was succeeded by a series of fearful screams, and the shouting of a mob. D—— rushed to a casement, threw it open, and looked out. In the meantime, I stepped to the card-rack, took the letter, put it in my pocket, and replaced it by a *facsimile* (so far as regards externals), which I had carefully prepared at my lodgings; imitating the D—— cipher, very readily, by means of a seal formed of bread.

"The disturbance in the street had been occasioned by the frantic behavior of a man with a musket. He had fired it among a crowd of women and children. It proved, however, to have been without ball, and the fellow was suffered to go his way as a lunatic or a drunkard. When he had gone, D—— came from the window, whither I had followed him immediately upon securing the object in view. Soon afterwards I bade him farewell. The pretended lunatic was a man in my own pay."

"But what purpose had you," I asked, "in replacing the letter by a *facsimile?* Would it not have been better, at the first visit, to have seized it openly, and departed?"

"D——," replied Dupin, "is a desperate man, and a man of nerve. His hotel, too, is not without attendants devoted to his interests. Had I made the wild attempt you suggest, I might never have left the ministerial presence alive. The good people of Paris might have heard of me no more. But I had an object apart from these considerations. You know my political prepossessions. In this matter, I act as a partisan of the lady concerned. For eighteen months the minister has had her in his power. She has now him in hers; since, being unaware that the letter is not in his possession, he will proceed with his exactions as if it was. Thus will he inevitably commit himself, at once, to his political destruction. His downfall, too, will not be more precipitate than awkward. It is all very well to talk about the *facilis descensus Averni;* but in all kinds of climbing, as Catalani said of singing, it is far more easy to get up than to come down. In the present instance I have no sympathy — at least no pity — for him who descends. He is that *monstrum horrendum,* an unprincipled man of genius. I confess, however, that I should like very well to know the precise character of his thoughts, when, being defied by her whom the Prefect terms 'a certain personage,' he is reduced to opening the letter which I left for him in the card-rack."

"How? Did you put anything particular in it?"

"Why — it did not seem altogether right to leave the interior blank — that would have been insulting. D——, at Vienna once, did me an evil turn, which I told him, quite good-humoredly, that I should remember. So, as I knew he would feel some curiosity in regard to the identity of the person who had outwitted him, I thought it a pity not to give him a clue. He is well acquainted with my MS., and I just copied into the middle of the blank sheet the words —

'——Un dessein si funeste,
S'il n'est digne d'Atrée, est digne de Thyeste.'

They are to be found in Crébillon's 'Atrée.' "

A Christmas Carol

Charles Dickens

STAVE ONE: MARLEY'S GHOST

MARLEY was dead, to begin with. There is no doubt whatever about that. The register of his burial was signed by the clergyman, the clerk, the undertaker, and the chief mourner. Scrooge signed it. And Scrooge's name was good upon 'Change for anything he chose to put his hand to.

Old Marley was as dead as a doornail.

Scrooge knew he was dead? Of course he did. How could it be otherwise? Scrooge and he were partners for I don't know how many years. Scrooge was his sole executor, his sole administrator, his sole assign, his sole residuary legatee, his sole friend, his sole mourner.

Scrooge never painted out old Marley's name, however. There it yet stood, years afterward, above the warehouse door — Scrooge and Marley. The firm was known as Scrooge and Marley. Sometimes people new to the business called Scrooge Scrooge, and sometimes Marley. He answered to both names. It was all the same to him.

Oh! But he was a tight-fisted hand at the grindstone, was Scrooge! a squeezing, wrenching, grasping, scraping, clutching, covetous old sinner! External heat and cold had little influence on him. No warmth could warm, no cold could chill him. No wind that blew was bitterer than he, no falling snow was more intent upon its purpose, no pelting rain less open to entreaty. Foul weather didn't know where to have him. The heaviest rain and snow and hail and sleet could boast of the advantage over him in only one respect — they often "came down" handsomely, and Scrooge never did.

Nobody ever stopped him in the street to say, with gladsome looks, "My dear Scrooge, how are you? When will you come to see me?" No beggars implored him to bestow a trifle, no children asked him what it was o'clock, no man or woman ever once in all his life inquired the way to such and such a place of Scrooge. Even the blind men's dogs appeared to know him; and when they saw him coming on, would tug their owners into doorways and up courts; and then would wag their tails as though they said, "No eye at all is better than evil eye, dark master!"

But what did Scrooge care! It was the very thing he liked. To edge his way along the crowded paths of life, warning all human sympathy to keep its distance, was what the knowing ones call "nuts" to Scrooge.

Once upon a time — of all the good days in the year, upon a Christmas eve — old Scrooge sat busy in his counting-house. It was cold, bleak, biting, foggy weather; and the city clocks had only just gone three, but it was quite dark already.

The door of Scrooge's counting-house was open, that he might keep his eye upon his clerk, who, in a dismal little cell beyond, a sort of tank, was copying letters. Scrooge had a very small fire, but the clerk's fire was so very much smaller that it looked like one coal. But he couldn't replenish it, for Scrooge kept the coal-box in his own room; and so surely as the clerk came in with the shovel the master predicted that it would be necessary for them to part. Wherefore the clerk put on his white comforter, and tried to warm himself at the candle; in which effort, not being a man of a strong imagination, he failed.

"A merry Christmas, uncle! God save you!" cried a cheerful voice. It was the voice of Scrooge's nephew, who came upon him so quickly that this was the first intimation Scrooge had of his approach.

"Bah!" said Scrooge; "humbug!"

"Christmas a humbug, uncle! You don't mean that, I am sure?"

"I do. Out upon merry Christmas! What's Christmas-time to you but a time for paying bills without money; a time for finding yourself a year older, and not an hour richer; a time for balancing your books and having every item in 'em through a round dozen of months presented dead against you? If I had my will, every idiot who goes about with 'Merry Christmas' on his lips should be boiled with his own pudding, and buried with a stake of holly through his heart! He should!"

"Uncle!"

"Nephew, keep Christmas in your own way, and let me keep it in mine."

"Keep it! But you don't keep it."

"Let me leave it alone, then. Much good may it do you! Much good it has ever done you!"

"There are many things from which I might have derived good, by which I have not profited, I dare say, Christmas among the rest. But I am sure I have always thought of Christmas-time, when it has come round — apart from the veneration due to its sacred origin, if anything belonging to it *can* be apart from that — as a good time; a kind, forgiving, charitable, pleasant time; the only time I know of, in the long calendar of the year, when men and women seem by one consent to open their shut-up hearts freely, and to think of people below them as if they really were fellow travelers to the grave, and not another race of creatures bound on other journeys. And therefore, uncle, though it has never put a scrap of gold or silver in my pocket, I believe that it *has* done me good, and *will* do me good; and I say, God bless it!"

The clerk in the tank involuntarily applauded.

"Let me hear another sound from *you,*" said Scrooge, "and you'll keep your Christmas by losing your situation! You're quite a powerful speaker, sir," he added, turning to his nephew. "I wonder you don't go into Parliament."

"Don't be angry, uncle. Come! Dine with us to-morrow."

Scrooge said that he would see him — yes, indeed he did. He went the whole length of the expression, and said that he would see him in that extremity first.

"But why?" cried Scrooge's nephew. "Why?"

"Why did you get married?"

"Because I fell in love."

"Because you fell in love!" growled Scrooge, as if that were the only one thing in the world more ridiculous than a merry Christmas. "Good afternoon!"

"Nay, uncle, but you never came to see me before that happened. Why give it as a reason for not coming now?"

"Good afternoon."

"I want nothing from you; I ask nothing of you; why cannot we be friends?"

"Good afternoon."

"I am sorry, with all my heart, to find you so resolute. We have never had any quarrel, to which I have been a party. But I have made the trial in homage to Christmas, and I'll keep my Christmas humor to the last. So A Merry Christmas, uncle!"

"Good afternoon!"

"And A Happy New Year!"

"Good afternoon!"

His nephew left the room without an angry word, notwithstanding. The clerk, in letting Scrooge's nephew out, had let two other people in. They were portly gentlemen, pleasant to behold, and now stood, with their hats off, in Scrooge's office. They had books and papers in their hands, and bowed to him.

"Scrooge and Marley's, I believe?" said one of the gentlemen, referring to his list. "Have I the pleasure of addressing Mr. Scrooge, or Mr. Marley?"

"Mr. Marley has been dead these seven years. He died seven years ago, this very night."

"At this festive season of the year, Mr. Scrooge," said the gentleman, taking up a pen, "it is more than usually desirable that we should make some slight provision for the poor and destitute, who suffer greatly at the present time. Many thousands are in want of common necessaries; hundreds of thousands are in want of common comforts, sir."

"Are there no prisons?"

"Plenty of prisons. But under the impression that they scarcely furnish Christian cheer of mind or body to the unoffending multitude, a few of us are endeavoring to raise a fund to buy the poor some meat and drink, and means of warmth. We choose this time, because it is a time of all others when Want is keenly felt and Abundance rejoices. What shall I put you down for?"

"Nothing!"

"You wish to be anonymous?"

"I wish to be left alone. Since you ask me what I wish gentlemen, that is my answer. I don't make merry myself at Christmas, and I can't afford to make idle people merry. I help to support the prisons and the workhouses — they cost enough — and those who are badly off must go there."

"Many can't go there; and many would rather die."

"If they would rather die, they had better do it, and decrease the surplus population."

At length the hour of shutting up the counting-house arrived. With an ill will Scrooge, dismounting from his stool, tacitly admitted the fact to the expectant clerk in the Tank, who instantly snuffed his candle out, and put on his hat.

"You'll want all day to-morrow, I suppose?"

"If quite convenient, sir."

"It's not convenient, and it's not fair. If I

was to stop half a crown for it, you'd think yourself mightily ill-used, I'll be bound?"

"Yes, sir."

"And yet you don't think *me* ill-used, when I pay a day's wages for no work."

"It's only once a year, sir."

"A poor excuse for picking a man's pocket every twenty-fifth of December! But I suppose you must have the whole day. Be here all the earlier *next* morning."

The clerk promised that he would; and Scrooge walked out with a growl. The office was closed in a twinkling, and the clerk, with the long ends of his white comforter dangling below his waist (for he boasted no great-coat), went down a slide, at the end of a lane of boys, twenty times, in honor of its being Christmas eve, and then ran home as hard as he could pelt, to play at blind man's buff.

Scrooge took his melancholy dinner in his usual melancholy tavern; and having read all the newspapers, and beguiled the rest of the evening with his banker's book, went home to bed. He lived in chambers which had once belonged to his deceased partner. They were a gloomy suite of rooms, in a lowering pile of building up a yard. The building was old enough now, and dreary enough; for nobody lived in it but Scrooge, the other rooms being all let out as offices.

Now it is a fact, that there was nothing at all particular about the knocker on the door of this house, except that it was very large; also, that Scrooge had seen it, night and morning, during his whole residence in that place; also, that Scrooge had as little of what is called fancy about him as any man in the city of London. And yet Scrooge, having his key in the lock of the door, saw in the knocker, without its undergoing any intermediate process of change, not a knocker, but Marley's face.

Marley's face, with a dismal light about it, like a bad lobster in a dark cellar. It was not angry or ferocious, but it looked at Scrooge as Marley used to look — with ghostly spectacles turned up upon its ghostly forehead.

As Scrooge looked fixedly at this phenomenon, it was a knocker again. He said, "Pooh, pooh!" and closed the door with a bang.

The sound resounded through the house like thunder. Every room above, and every cask in the wine-merchant's cellars below, appeared to have a separate peal of echoes of its own. Scrooge was not a man to be frightened by echoes. He fastened the door, and walked across the hall, and up the stairs. Slowly, too, trimming his candle as he went.

Up Scrooge went, not caring a button for its being very dark. Darkness is cheap, and Scrooge liked it. But before he shut his heavy door, he walked through his rooms to see that all was right. He had just enough recollection of the face to desire to do that.

Sitting-room, bedroom, lumber-room, all as

they should be. Nobody under the table, nobody under the sofa; a small fire in the grate; spoon and basin ready; and the little saucepan of gruel (Scrooge had a cold in his head) upon the hob. Nobody under the bed; nobody in the closet; nobody in his dressing-gown, which was hanging up in a suspicious attitude against the wall. Lumber-room as usual. Old fire-guard, old shoes, two fish-baskets, washing-stand on three legs, and a poker.

Quite satisfied, he closed his door, and locked himself in; double-locked himself in, which was not his custom. Thus secured against surprise, he took off his cravat, put on his dressing-gown and slippers and his night-cap, and sat down before the very low fire to take his gruel.

As he threw his head back in the chair, his glance happened to rest upon a bell, a disused bell, that hung in the room, and communicated, for some purpose now forgotten, with a chamber in the highest story of the building. It was with great astonishment, and with a strange, inexplicable dread, that, as he looked, he saw this bell begin to swing. Soon it rang out loudly, and so did every bell in the house.

This was succeeded by a clanking noise, deep down below, as if some person were dragging a heavy chain over the casks in the wine-merchant's cellar.

Then he heard the noise much louder, on the floors below; then coming up the stairs; then coming straight toward his door.

It came on through the heavy door, and a specter passed into the room before his eyes. And upon its coming in, the dying flame leaped up, as though it cried, "I know him! Marley's ghost!"

The same face, the very same. Marley in his pigtail, usual waistcoat, tights, and boots. His body was transparent; so that Scrooge, observing him, and looking through his waistcoat, could see the two buttons on his coat behind.

Scrooge had often heard it said that Marley had no bowels, but he had never believed it until now.

No, nor did he believe it even now. Though he looked the fantom through and through, and saw it standing before him — though he felt the chilling influence of its death-cold eyes, and noticed the very texture of the folded kerchief bound about its head and chin — he was still incredulous.

"How now!" said Scrooge, caustic and cold as ever. "What do you want with me?"

"Much!" — Marley's voice, no doubt about it.

"Who are you!"

"Ask me who I *was*."

"Who *were* you, then?"

"In life I was your partner, Jacob Marley."

"Can you — can you sit down?'

"I can."

"Do it, then."

Scrooge asked the question because he didn't know whether a ghost so transparent might find himself in a condition to take a chair; and felt that, in the event of its being impossible, it might involve the necessity of an embarrassing explanation. But the ghost sat down on the opposite side of the fireplace, as if he were quite used to it.

"You don't believe in me."

"I don't."

"What evidence would you have of my reality beyond that of your senses?"

"I don't know."

"Why do you doubt your senses?"

"Because a little thing affects them. A slight disorder of the stomach makes them cheats. You may be an undigested bit of beef, a blot of mustard, a crumb of cheese, a fragment of an underdone potato. There's more of gravy than of grave about you, whatever you are!"

Scrooge was not much in the habit of cracking jokes, nor did he feel in his heart by any means waggish then. The truth is, that he tried to be smart, as a means of distracting his own attention, and keeping down his horror.

But how much greater was his horror when, the fantom taking off the bandage round his head, as if it were too warm to wear indoors, its lower jaw dropped down upon its breast!

"Mercy! Dreadful apparition, why do you trouble me? Why do spirits walk the earth, and why do they come to me?''

''It is required of every man, that the spirit within him should walk abroad among his fellow men, and travel far and wide; and if that spirit goes not forth in life, it is condemned to do so after death. I cannot tell you all I would. A very little more is permitted to me. I cannot rest, I cannot stay, I cannot linger anywhere. My spirit never walked beyond our counting-house — mark me! — in life my spirit never roved beyond the narrow limits of our money-changing hole; and weary journeys lie before me!''

''Seven years dead. And traveling all the time? You travel fast?''

''On the wings of the wind.''

''You might have got over a great quantity of ground in seven years.''

''O blind man, blind man! not to know that ages of incessant labor by immortal creatures for this earth must pass into eternity before the good of which it is susceptible is all developed. Not to know that any Christian spirit working kindly in its little sphere, whatever it may be, will find its mortal life too short for its vast means of usefulness. Not to know that no space of regret can make amends for one life's opportunities misused! Yet I was like this man; I once was like this man!''

''But you were always a good man of business, Jacob,'' faltered Scrooge, who now began to apply this to himself.

"Business!" cried the Ghost, wringing his hands again. "Mankind was my business. The common welfare was my business; charity, mercy, forbearance, benevolence, were all my business. The dealings of my trade were but a drop of water in the comprehensive ocean of my business."

Scrooge was very much dismayed to hear the specter going on at this rate, and began to quake exceedingly.

"Hear me! My time is nearly gone."

"I will. But don't be hard upon me! Don't be flowery, Jacob! Pray!"

"I am here to-night to warn you that you have yet a chance and hope of escaping my fate. A chance and a hope of my procuring, Ebenezer."

"You were always a good friend to me. Thank'ee!"

"You will be haunted by Three Spirits."

"Is that the chance and hope you mentioned, Jacob? I — I think I'd rather not."

"Without their visits you cannot hope to shun the path I tread. Expect the first to-morrow night, when the bell tolls One. Expect the second on the next night at the same hour. The third, upon the next night, when the last stroke of Twelve has ceased to vibrate. Look to see me no more; and look that, for your own sake, you remember what has passed between us!"

It walked backward from him; and at every

step it took, the window raised itself a little, so that, when the apparition reached it, it was wide open.

Scrooge closed the window, and examined the door by which the Ghost had entered. It was double-locked, as he had locked it with his own hands, and the bolts were undisturbed. Scrooge tried to say "Humbug!" but stopped at the first syllable. And being, from the emotion he had undergone, or the fatigues of the day, or his glimpse of the invisible world, or the dull conversation of the Ghost, or the lateness of the hour, much in need of repose, he went straight to bed, without undressing, and fell asleep on the instant.

STAVE TWO: THE FIRST OF THE THREE SPIRITS

When Scrooge awoke it was so dark that, looking out of bed, he could scarcely distinguish the transparent window from the opaque walls of his chamber, until suddenly the church clock tolled a deep, dull, hollow, melancholy ONE.

Light flashed up in the room upon the instant, and the curtains of his bed were drawn aside by a strange figure — like a child: yet not so like a child as like an old man, viewed through some supernatural medium, which gave him the appearance of having receded from the view, and being diminished to a child's proportions. Its hair, which hung about its neck and down its back, was white as if with age; and yet the face had not a wrinkle in it, and the tenderest bloom was on the skin. It held a branch of fresh green holly in its hand; and, in singular contradiction of that wintry emblem, had its dress trimmed with summer flowers. But the strangest thing about it was, that from the crown of its head there sprung a bright clear jet of light, by which all this was visible; and which was doubtless the occasion of its using, in its duller moments, a great extinguisher for a cap, which it now held under its arm.

"Are you the Spirit, sir, whose coming was foretold to me?"

"I am!"

"Who and what are you?"

"I am the Ghost of Christmas Past."

"Long past?"

"No. Your past. The things that you will see with me are shadows of the things that have been; they will have no consciousness of us."

Scrooge then made bold to inquire what business brought him there.

"Your welfare. Rise, and walk with me!"

It would have been in vain for Scrooge to plead that the weather and the hour were not adapted to pedestrian purposes; that the bed was warm, and the thermometer a long way below freezing; that he was clad but only lightly in his slippers, dressing-gown, and nightcap; and that he had a cold upon him at that time. The grasp, though gentle as a woman's hand, was not to be resisted. He rose; but, finding that the Spirit made toward the window, clasped its robe in supplication.

"I am a mortal, and liable to fall."

"Bear but a touch of my hand *there,*" said the Spirit, laying it upon his heart, "and you shall be upheld in more than this!"

As the words were spoken, they passed through the wall, and stood in the busy thoroughfares of a city. It was made plain enough by the dressing of the shops that here, too, it was Christmas-time.

The Ghost stopped at a certain warehouse door, and asked Scrooge if he knew it.

"Know it? Was I apprenticed here!"

They went in. At sight of an old gentleman in a Welsh wig, sitting behind such a high desk that, if he had been two inches taller, he must have knocked his head against the ceiling, Scrooge cried in great excitement, "Why it's old Fezziwig! Bless his heart, it's Fezziwig, alive again!"

Old Fezziwig laid down his pen, and looked up at the clock, which pointed to the hour of seven. He rubbed his hands; adjusted his capacious waistcoat; laughed all over himself, from his shoes to his organ of benevolence; and called out in a comfortable, oily, rich, fat, jovial voice, "Yo ho, there! Ebenezer! Dick!"

A living and moving picture of Scrooge's

former self, a young man, came briskly in, accompanied by his fellow 'prentice.

"Dick Wilkins, to be sure!" said Scrooge to the Ghost. "My old fellow 'prentice, bless me, yes. There he is. He was very much attached to me, was Dick. Poor Dick! Dear, dear!"

"Yo ho, my boys!" said Fezziwig. "No more work to-night. Christmas eve, Dick. Christmas, Ebenezer! Let's have the shutters up before a man can say Jack Robinson! Clear away, my lads, and let's have lots of room here!"

Clear away! There was nothing they wouldn't have cleared away, or couldn't have cleared away, with old Fezziwig looking on. It was done in a minute. Every movable was packed off, as if it were dismissed from public life forevermore; the floor was swept and watered, the lamps were trimmed, fuel was heaped upon the fire; and the warehouse was as snug and warm and dry and bright a ballroom as you would desire to see upon a winter's night.

In came a fiddler with a music-book, and went up to the lofty desk, and made an orchestra of it, and tuned like fifty stomachaches. In came Mrs. Fezziwig, one vast substantial smile. In came the three Miss Fezziwigs, beaming and lovable. In came the six young followers whose hearts they broke. In came all the young men and women employed in the business. In came the housemaid, with her cousin the baker. In came the cook, with her brother's particular friend the milkman.

In they all came one after another; some shyly, some boldly, some gracefully, some awkwardly, some pushing, some pulling; in they all came, anyhow and everyhow. Away they all went, twenty couples at once; hands half round and back again the other way; down the middle and up again; round and round in various stages of affectionate grouping; old top couple always turning up in the wrong place; new top couple starting off again, as soon as they got there; all top couples at last, and not a bottom one to help them. When this result was brought about, old Fezziwig, clapping his hands to stop the dance, cried out, "Well done!" and the fiddler plunged his hot face into a pot of porter especially provided for that purpose.

There were more dances, and there were forfeits, and more dances, and there was cake, and there was negus, and there was a great piece of Cold Roast, and there was a great piece of Cold Boiled, and there were mince-pies and plenty of beer. But the great effect of the evening came after the Roast and Boiled, when the fiddler struck up "Sir Roger de Coverley." Then old Fezziwig stood out to dance with Mrs. Fezziwig. Top couple, too; with a good stiff piece of work cut out for them; three or four and twenty pairs of partners; people who were not to be trifled with; people who *would* dance, and had no notion of walking.

But if they had been twice as many — four times — old Fezziwig would have been a match for them, and so would Mrs. Fezziwig. As to *her,* she was worthy to be his partner in every sense of the term. A positive light appeared to issue from Fezziwig's calves. They shone in every part of the dance. You couldn't have predicted, at any given time, what would become of 'em next. And when old Fezziwig and Mrs. Fezziwig had gone all through the dance — advance and retire, turn your partner, bow and courtesy, corkscrew, thread the needle, and back again to your place — Fezziwig "cut" — cut so deftly, that he appeared to wink with his legs.

When the clock struck eleven this domestic ball broke up. Mr. And Mrs. Fezziwig took their stations, one on either side of the door, and shaking hands with every person individually as he or she went out, wished him or her a Merry Christmas. When everybody had retired but the two 'prentices, they did the same to them; and thus the cheerful voices died away, and the lads were left to their beds, which were under a counter in the back shop.

"A small matter," said the Ghost, "to make these silly folks so full of gratitude. He has spent but a few pounds of your mortal money — three or four perhaps. Is that so much that he deserves this praise?"

"It isn't that," said Scrooge, heated by the remark, and speaking unconsciously like his former, not his latter self — "it isn't that, Spirit. He has the power to render us happy or unhappy; to make our service light or burdensome, a pleasure or a toil. Say that his power lies in words and looks; in things so slight and insignificant that it is impossible to add and count 'em up: what then? The happiness he gives is quite as great as if it cost a fortune."

He felt the Spirit's glance, and stopped.

"What is the matter?"

"Nothing particular."

"Something, I think?"

"No, no. I should like to be able to say a word or two to my clerk just now. That's all."

"My time grows short," observed the Spirit. "Quick!"

This was not addressed to Scrooge, or to any one whom he could see, but it produced an immediate effect. For again he saw himself. He was older now; a man in the prime of life.

He was not alone, but sat by the side of a fair young girl in a black dress, in whose eyes there were tears.

"It matters little," she said softly to Scrooge's former self. "To you, very little. Another idol has displaced me; and if it can comfort you in time to come, as I would have tried to do, I have no just cause to grieve."

"What Idol has displaced you?"

"A golden one. You fear the world too much. I have seen your nobler aspirations fall off one by one, until the master-passion, Gain, engrosses you. Have I not?"

"What then? Even if I have grown so much wiser, what then? I am not changed toward you. Have I ever sought release from our engagement?"

"In words, no. Never."

"In what, then?"

"In a changed nature; in an altered spirit; in another atmosphere of life; another Hope as its great end. If you were free to-day, to-morrow, yesterday, can even I believe that you would choose a dowerless girl; or, choosing her, do I not know that your repentance and regret would surely follow? I do; and I release you. With a full heart, for the love of him you once were."

"Spirit! remove me from this place."

"I told you these were shadows of the things that have been," said the Ghost. "That they are what they are, do not blame me!"

"Remove me!" Scrooge exclaimed. "I cannot bear it! Leave me! Take me back. Haunt me no longer!"

As he struggled with the Spirit he was conscious of being exhausted, and overcome by an irresistible drowsiness; and, further, of being in his own bedroom. He had barely time to reel to bed before he sank into a heavy sleep.

Scrooge awoke in his own bedroom. There was no doubt about that. But it and his own adjoining sitting-room, into which he shuffled in his slippers, attracted by a great light there, had undergone a surprising transformation. The walls and ceiling were so hung with living green, that it looked a perfect grove. The leaves of holly, mistletoe, and ivy reflected back the light, as if so many little mirrors had been scattered there; and such a mighty blaze went roaring up the chimney, as that petrifaction of a hearth had never known in Scrooge's time, or Marley's, or for many and many a winter season gone.

Heaped upon the floor, to form a kind of throne, were turkeys, geese, game, brawn, great joints of meat, sucking-pigs, long wreaths of sausages, mince-pies, plum-puddings, barrels of oysters, red-hot chestnuts, cherry-cheeked apples, juicy oranges, luscious pears, immense twelfth-cakes, and great bowls of punch. In easy state upon this couch there sat a Giant glorious to see; who bore a glowing torch, in shape not unlike Plenty's horn, and who raised it high to shed its light on Scrooge as he came peeping round the door.

"Come in; come in! and know me better, man! I am the Ghost of Christmas Present. Look upon me! You have never seen the like of me before!''

''Never.''

''Have never walked forth with the younger members of my family; meaning (for I am very young) my elder brothers born in these later years?'' pursued the Fantom.

''I don't think I have, I am afraid I have not. Have you had many brothers, Spirit?''

''More than eighteen hundred.''

''A tremendous family to provide for! Spirit, conduct me where you will. I went forth last night on compulsion, and I learned a lesson which is working now. To-night, if you have aught to teach me, let me profit by it.''

''Touch my robe!''

Scrooge did as he was told, and held it fast.

The room and its contents all vanished instantly, and they stood in the city streets upon a snowy Christmas morning.

Scrooge and the Ghost passed on, invisible, straight to Scrooge's clerk's; and on the threshold of the door the Spirit smiled, and stopped to bless Bob Cratchit's dwelling with the sprinklings of his torch. Think of that! Bob had but fifteen ''Bob'' a week himself; he pocketed on Saturdays but fifteen copies of his Christian name; and yet the Ghost of Christmas Present blessed his four-roomed house!

Then up rose Mrs. Cratchit, Cratchit's wife, dressed out but poorly in a twice-turned gown, but brave in ribbons, which are cheap and make a goodly show for sixpence; and she laid the cloth, assisted by Belinda Cratchit, second of her daughters, also brave in ribbon; while Master Peter Cratchit plunged a fork into the saucepan of potatoes, and, getting the corners of his monstrous shirt-collar (Bob's private property, conferred upon his son and heir in honor of the day) into his mouth, rejoiced to find himself so gallantly attired, and yearned to show his linen in the fashionable Parks.

And now two smaller Cratchits, boy and girl, came tearing in, screaming that outside the baker's they had smelled the goose, and known it for their own; and, basking in luxurious thoughts of sage and onion, these young Cratchits danced about the table, and exalted Master Peter Cratchit to the skies, while he (not proud, although his collars nearly choked him) blew the fire, until the slow potatoes, bubbling up, knocked loudly at the saucepan-lid to be let out and peeled.

"What has ever got your precious father, then?" said Mrs. Cratchit. "And your brother Tiny Tim? And Martha warn't as late last Christmas day by half an hour!"

"Here's Martha, mother!" said a girl, appearing as she spoke.

"Here's Martha, mother!" cried the two young Cratchits. "Hurrah! There's *such* a goose, Martha!"

"Why, bless your heart alive, my dear, how late you are!" said Mrs. Cratchit, kissing her a dozen times, and taking off her shawl and bonnet for her.

"We'd a deal of work to finish up last night," replied the girl, "and had to clear away this morning, mother!"

"Well! Never mind so long as you are come," said Mrs. Cratchit. "Sit ye down before the fire, my dear, and have a warm, Lord bless ye!"

"No, no! There's father coming," cried the two young Cratchits, who were everywhere at once. "Hide, Martha, hide!"

So Martha hid herself, and in came little Bob, the father, with at least three feet of comforter, exclusive of the fringe, hanging down before him; and his threadbare clothes darned up and brushed, to look seasonable; and Tiny Tim upon his shoulder. Alas for Tiny Tim, he bore a little crutch, and had his limbs supported by an iron frame!

"Why, where's our Martha?" cried Bob Cratchit, looking round.

"Not coming," said Mrs. Cratchit.

"Not coming?" said Bob, with a sudden declension in his high spirits; for he had been Tim's blood-horse all the way from the church, and had come home rampant — "not coming upon Christmas day?"

Martha didn't like to see him disappointed, if it were only in joke; so she came out prematurely from behind the closet door, and ran into his arms, while the two young Cratchits hustled Tiny Tim, and bore him off into the wash-house that he might hear the pudding singing in the copper.

"And how did little Tim behave?" asked Mrs. Cratchit, when she had rallied Bob on his credulity, and Bob had hugged his daughter to his heart's content.

"As good as gold," said Bob, "and better. Somehow he gets thoughtful, sitting by himself so much, and thinks the strangest things you ever heard. He told me, coming home, that he hoped the people saw him in the church, because he was a cripple, and it might be pleasant to them to remember, upon Christmas day, who made lame beggars walk and blind men see."

Bob's voice was tremulous when he told them this, and trembled more when he said that Tiny Tim was growing strong and hearty.

His active little crutch was heard upon the floor, and back came Tiny Tim before another word was spoken, escorted by his brother and sister to his stool beside the fire; and while Bob, turning up his cuffs — as if, poor fellow, they were capable of being made more shabby — compounded some hot mixture in a jug with gin and lemons, and stirred it round and round and put it on the hob to simmer, Master Peter and the two ubiquitous young Cratchits went to fetch the goose, with which they soon returned in high procession.

Mrs. Cratchit made the gravy (ready beforehand in a little saucepan) hissing hot; Master Peter mashed the potatoes with incredible vigor; Miss Belinda sweetened up the apple-sauce; Martha dusted the hot plates; Bob took Tiny Tim beside him in a tiny corner at the table; the two young Cratchits set chairs for everybody, not forgetting themselves, and mounting guard upon their posts, crammed spoons into their mouths, lest they should shriek for goose before their turn came to be helped.

At last the dishes were set on, and grace was said. It was succeeded by a breathless pause, as Mrs. Cratchit, looking slowly all along the carving-knife, prepared to plunge it in the breast; but when she did and when the long-expected gush of stuffing issued forth, one murmur of delight arose all round the board, and even Tiny Tim, excited by the two young Cratchits, beat on the table with the handle of his knife, and feebly cried, Hurrah!

There never was such a goose. Bob said he didn't believe there ever was such a goose cooked. Its tenderness and flavor, size and cheapness, were the themes of universal admiration. Eked out by apple-sauce and mashed potatoes, it was a sufficient dinner for the whole family; indeed, as Mrs. Cratchit said with great delight (surveying one small atom of a bone upon the dish), they hadn't ate it all at last!

Yet every one had had enough, and the youngest Cratchits in particular were steeped in sage and onion to the eyebrows! But now, the plates being changed by Miss Belinda, Mrs. Cratchit left the room alone — too nervous to bear witnesses — to take the pudding up, and bring it in.

Suppose it should not be done enough! Suppose it should break in turning out! Suppose somebody should have got over the wall of the back yard, and stolen it, while they were merry with the goose — a supposition at which the two young Cratchits became livid! All sorts of horrors were supposed.

Hallo! A great deal of steam! The pudding was out of the copper. A smell like a washing-day! That was the cloth. A smell like an eating-house and a pastry-cook's next door to each other, with a laundress's next door to that! That was the pudding! In half a minute Mrs. Cratchit entered — flushed but smiling proudly — with the pudding, like a speckled cannon-ball, so hard and firm, blazing in half of half a quartern of ignited brandy, and bedight with Christmas holly stuck into the top.

Oh, a wonderful pudding! Bob Cratchit said, and calmly, too, that he regarded it as the greatest success achieved by Mrs. Cratchit since their marriage. Mrs. Cratchit said that now the weight was off her mind, she would confess she had had her doubts about the quantity of flour. Everybody had something to say about it, but nobody said or thought it was at all a small pudding for a large family. Any

Cratchit would have blushed to hint at such a thing.

At last the dinner was all done, the cloth was cleared, the hearth swept, and the fire made up. The compound in the jug being tasted and considered perfect, apples and oranges were put upon the table, and a shovelful of chestnuts on the fire.

Then all the Cratchit family drew round the hearth, in what Bob Cratchit called a circle, and at Bob Cratchit's elbow stood the family display of glass — two tumblers, and a custard-cup without a handle.

These held the hot stuff from the jug, however, as well as golden goblets would have done; and Bob served it out with beaming looks, while the chestnuts on the fire sputtered and crackled noisily. Then Bob proposed:

"A merry Christmas to us all, my dears. God bless us!"

Which all the family reechoed.

"God bless us every one!" said Tiny Tim, the last of all.

He sat very close to his father's side, upon his little stool. Bob held his withered little hand in his, as if he loved the child, and wished to keep him by his side, and dreaded that he might be taken from him.

Scrooge raised his head speedily, on hearing his own name.

"Mr. Scrooge!" said Bob; "I'll give you Mr. Scrooge, the Founder of the Feast!"

"The Founder of the Feast, indeed!" cried Mrs. Cratchit, reddening. "I wish I had him here. I'd give him a piece of my mind to feast upon, and I hope he'd have a good appetite for it."

"My dear," said Bob, "the children! Christmas day."

"It should be Christmas day, I am sure," said she, "on which one drinks the health of such an odious, stingy, hard, unfeeling man as Mr. Scrooge. You know he is, Robert! Nobody knows it better than you do, poor fellow!"

"My dear," was Bob's mild answer, "Christmas day."

"I'll drink his health for your sake and the day's," said Mrs. Cratchit, "not for his. Long life to him! A merry Christmas and a happy New Year! He'll be very merry and very happy, I have no doubt!"

The children drank the toast after her. It was the first of their proceedings which had no heartiness in it. Tiny Tim drank it last of all, but he didn't care twopence for it. Scrooge was the Ogre of the family. The mention of his name cast a dark shadow on the party, which was not dispelled for full five minutes.

After it had passed away, they were ten times merrier than before, from the mere relief of Scrooge the Baleful being done with. Bob Cratchit told them how he had a situation in his eye for Master Peter, which would bring in, if obtained, full five and sixpence weekly. The two young Cratchits laughed tremendously at the idea of Peter's being a man of business; and Peter himself looked thoughtfully at the fire from between his collars, as if he were deliberating what particular investments he should favor when he came into the receipt of that bewildering income.

Martha, who was a poor apprentice at a milliner's then told them what kind of work she had to do, and how many hours she worked at a stretch, and how she meant to lie abed tomorrow morning for a good long rest; tomorrow being a holiday she passed at home. Also how she had seen a countess and a lord some days before, and how the lord "was much about as tall as Peter"; at which Peter pulled up his collars so high that you couldn't have seen his head if you had been there. All this time the chestnuts and the jug went round and round; and by and by they had a song, about a lost child traveling in the snow, from Tiny Tim, who had a plaintive little voice, and sang it very well indeed.

There was nothing of high mark in this. They were not a handsome family; they were not well dressed; their shoes were far from being water-proof; their clothes were scanty; and Peter might have known, and very likely did, the inside of a pawnbroker's. But they were happy, grateful, pleased with one another, and contented with the time; and when they faded, and looked happier yet in the bright sprinklings of the Spirit's torch at parting, Scrooge had his eye upon them, and especially on Tiny Tim, until the last.

It was a great surprise to Scrooge, as this scene vanished, to hear a hearty laugh. It was a much greater surprise to Scrooge to recognize it as his own nephew's, and to find himself in a bright, dry, gleaming room, with the Spirit standing smiling by his side, and looking at that same nephew.

It is a fair, even-handed, noble adjustment of things, that while there is infection in disease and sorrow, there is nothing in the world so irresistibly contagious as laughter and good-humor. When Scrooge's nephew laughed, Scrooge's niece by marriage laughed as heartily as he. And their assembled friends, being not a bit behindhand, laughed out lustily.

"He said that Christmas was a humbug, as I live!" cried Scrooge's nephew. "He believed it, too!"

"More shame for him, Fred!" said Scrooge's niece, indignantly. Bless those women! they never do anything by halves. They are always in earnest.

She was very pretty, exceedingly pretty. With a dimpled, surprised-looking, capital face; a ripe little mouth that seemed made to be kissed — as no doubt it was; all kinds of good little dots about her chin, that melted into one another when she laughed; and the sunniest pair of eyes you ever saw in any little creature's head. Altogether she was what you would have called provoking, but satisfactory, too. Oh, perfectly satisfactory!

"He's a comical old fellow," said Scrooge's nephew, "that's the truth; and not so pleasant as he might be. However, his offenses carry their own punishment, and I have nothing to say against him. Who suffers by his ill whims? Himself, always. Here he takes it into his head to dislike us, and he won't come and dine with us. What's the consequence? He doesn't lose much of a dinner."

"Indeed, I think he loses a very good dinner," interrupted Scrooge's niece. Everybody else said the same, and they must be allowed to have been competent judges, because they had just had dinner; and, with the dessert upon the table, were clustered round the fire, by lamplight.

"Well, I am very glad to hear it," said Scrooge's nephew, "because I haven't any great faith in these young housekeepers. What do *you* say, Topper?"

Topper clearly had his eye on one of Scrooge's niece's sisters, for he answered that a bachelor was a wretched outcast, who had no right to express an opinion on the subject. Whereat Scrooge's niece's sister — the plump one with the lace tucker, not the one with the roses — blushed.

After tea they had some music. For they

were a musical family, and knew what they were about, when they sung a Glee or Catch, I can assure you — especially Topper, who could growl away in the bass like a good one, and never swell the large veins in his forehead, or get red in the face over it.

But they didn't devote the whole evening to music. After a while they played at forfeits; for it is good to be children sometimes, and never better than at Christmas, when its mighty Founder was a child himself. There was first a game at blind man's buff, though. And I no more believe Topper was really blinded than I believe he had eyes in his boots. Because the way in which he went after that plump sister in the lace tucker was an outrage on the credulity of human nature. Knocking down the fire-irons, tumbling over the chairs, bumping up against the piano, smothering himself among the curtains, wherever she went there went he!

He always knew where the plump sister was. He wouldn't catch anybody else. If you had fallen up against him, as some of them did, and stood there, he would have made a feint of endeavoring to seize you, which would have been an affront to your understanding, and would instantly have sidled off in the direction of the plump sister.

"Here is a new game," said Scrooge. "One half-hour, Spirit, only one!"

It was a Game called Yes and No, where

Scrooge's nephew had to think of something, and the rest must find out what; he only answering to their questions yes or no, as the case was. The fire of questioning to which he was exposed elicited from him that he was thinking of an animal, a live animal, rather a disagreeable animal, a savage animal, an animal that growled and grunted sometimes, and talked sometimes, and lived in London, and walked about the streets, and wasn't made a show of, and wasn't led by anybody, and didn't live in a menagerie, and was never killed in a market, and was not a horse, or an ass, or a cow, or a bull, or a tiger, or a dog, or a pig, or a cat, or a bear.

At every new question put to him, this nephew burst into a fresh roar of laughter; and was so inexpressibly tickled, that he was obliged to get up off the sofa and stamp. At last the plump sister cried out:

"I have found it out! I know what it is, Fred! I know what it is!"

"What is it?" cried Fred.

"It's your uncle Scro-o-o-o-oge!"

Which it certainly was. Admiration was the universal sentiment, though some objected that the reply to "Is it a bear?' ought to have been "Yes."

Uncle Scrooge had imperceptibly become so gay and light of heart, that he would have drank to the unconscious company in an inaudible speech. But the whole scene passed off in the breath of the last word spoken by his nephew; and he and the Spirit were again upon their travels.

Much they saw, and far they went, and many homes they visited, but always with a happy end. The Spirit stood beside sick-beds, and they were cheerful; on foreign lands, and they were close at home; by struggling men, and they were patient in their greater hope; by poverty, and it was rich. In almshouse, hospital, and jail, in misery's every refuge, where vain man in his little brief authority had not made fast the door, and barred the Spirit out, he left his blessing, and taught Scrooge his precepts. Suddenly, as they stood together in an open place, the bell struck twelve.

Scrooge looked about him for the Ghost, and saw it no more. As the last stroke ceased to vibrate, he remembered the prediction of old Jacob Marley, and, lifting up his eyes, beheld a solemn Fantom, draped and hooded, coming like a mist along the ground toward him.

STAVE FOUR: THE LAST OF THE SPIRITS

The Fantom slowly, gravely, silently approached. When it came near him, Scrooge bent down upon his knee; for in the air through which this Spirit moved it seemed to scatter gloom and mystery.

It was shrouded in a deep black garment,

which concealed its head, its face, its form, and left nothing of it visible save one outstretched hand. He knew no more, for the Spirit neither spoke nor moved.

"I am in the presence of the Ghost of Christmas Yet to Come? Ghost of the Future! I fear you more than any specter I have seen. But as I know your purpose is to do me good, and as I hope to live to be another man from what I was, I am prepared to bear you company, and to do it with a thankful heart. Will you not speak to me?"

It gave him no reply. The hand was pointed straight before them.

"Lead on! Lead on! The night is waning fast, and it is precious time to me, I know. Lead on, Spirit!"

They scarcely seemed to enter the city; for the city rather seemed to spring up about them. But there they were in the heart of it; on 'Change, among the merchants.

The Spirit stopped beside one little knot of business men. Observing that the hand was pointed to them, Scrooge advanced to listen to their talk.

"No," said a great fat man with a monstrous chin, "I don't know much about it either way. I only know he's dead."

"When did he die?" inquired another.

"Last night, I believe."

"Why, what was the matter with him? I thought he'd never die."

"God knows," said the first, with a yawn.

"What has he done with his money?" asked a red-faced gentleman.

"I haven't heard," said the man with the large chin. "Company, perhaps. He hasn't left it to me. That's all I know. By, by!"

Scrooge was at first inclined to be surprised that the Spirit should attach importance to conversation apparently so trivial; but feeling assured that it must have some hidden purpose, he set himself to consider what it was likely to be. It could scarcely be supposed to have any bearing on the death of Jacob, his old partner, for that was Past, and this Ghost's province was the Future.

He looked about in that very place for his own image; but another man stood in his accustomed corner, and though the clock pointed to his usual time of day for being there, he saw no likeness of himself among the multitudes that poured in through the Porch. It gave him little surprise, however; for he had been revolving in his mind a change of life, and he thought and hoped he saw his new-born resolutions carried out in this.

They left this busy scene, and went into an obscure part of the town, to a low shop where iron, old rags, bottles, bones, and greasy offal were bought. A gray-haired rascal, of great age, sat smoking his pipe.

Scrooge and the Fantom came into the presence of this man, just as a woman with a heavy bundle slunk into the shop. But she had scarcely entered, when another woman, similarly laden, came in, too; and she was closely followed by a man in faded black. After a short period of blank astonishment, in which the old man with the pipe had joined them, they all three burst into a laugh.

"Let the charwoman alone to be the first!" cried she who had entered first. "Let the laundress alone to be the second; and let the undertaker's man alone to be the third. Look here, old Joe, here's a chance! If we haven't all three met here without meaning it!"

"You couldn't have met in a better place. You were made free of it long ago, you know; and the other two ain't strangers. What have you got to sell?"

"Half a minute's patience, Joe, and you shall see."

"What odds, then! What odds, Mrs. Dilber?" said the woman. "Every person has a right to take care of themselves. *He* always did! Who's the worse for the loss of a few things like these? Not a dead man, I suppose."

Mrs. Dilber, whose manner was remarkable for general propitiation, said, "No, indeed, ma'am."

"If he wanted to keep 'em after he was dead, a wicked old screw, why wasn't he natural in his lifetime? If he had been, he'd have had somebody to look after him when he was struck with Death, instead of lying gasping out his last there, alone by himself."

"It's the truest word that ever was spoke; it's a judgment on him."

"I wish it was a little heavier judgment, and it should have been, you may depend upon it, if I could have laid my hands on anything else. Open that bundle, old Joe, and let me know the value of it. Speak out plain. I'm not afraid to be the first, not afraid for them to see it."

Joe went down on his knees for the greater convenience of opening the bundle, and dragged out a large and heavy roll of some dark stuff.

"What do you call this? Bed-curtains!"

"Ah! Bed-curtains! Don't drop that oil upon the blankets, now."

"*His* blankets?"

"Whose else's, do you think? He isn't likely to take cold without 'em, I dare say. Ah! You may look through that shirt till your eyes ache; but you won't find a hole in it, nor a threadbare place. It's the best he had, and a fine one, too. They'd have wasted it by dressing him up in it, if it hadn't been for me."

Scrooge listened to this dialogue in horror.

"Spirit! I see, I see. The case of this unhappy man might be my own. My life tends that way now. Merciful Heaven, what is this?"

The scene had changed, and now he almost touched a bare, uncurtained bed. A pale light, rising in the outer air, fell straight upon this bed; and on it, unwatched, unwept, uncared for, was the body of this plundered unknown man.

"Spirit, let me see some tenderness connected with a death, or this dark chamber, Spirit, will be forever present to me."

The Ghost conducted him to poor Bob Cratchit's house — the dwelling he had visited before — and found the mother and the children seated round the fire.

Quiet. Very quiet. The noisy little Cratchits were as still as statues in one corner, and sat looking up at Peter, who had a book before him. The mother and her daughters were engaged in needlework. But surely they were very quiet!

" 'And He took a child, and set him in the midst of them.' "

Where had Scrooge heard those words? He had not dreamed them. The boy must have read them out, as he and the Spirit crossed the threshold. Why did he not go on?

The mother laid her work upon the table, and put her hand up to her face.

"The color hurts my eyes," she said.

The color? Ah, poor Tiny Tim!

"They're better now again. It makes them weak by candle-light; and I wouldn't show weak eyes to your father when he comes home, for the world. It must be near his time."

"Past it, rather," Peter answered, shutting up his book. "But I think he has walked a little slower than he used, these few last evenings, mother.''

''I have known him walk with — I have known him walk with Tiny Tim upon his shoulder, very fast indeed.''

''And so have I,'' cried Peter. ''Often.''

''And so have I,'' exclaimed another. So had all.

''But he was very light to carry, and his father loved him so, that it was no trouble — no trouble. And there is your father at the door!''

She hurried out to meet him; and little Bob in his comforter — he had need of it, poor fellow — came in. His tea was ready for him on the hob, and they all tried who should help him to it most. Then the two young Cratchits got upon his knees and laid, each child, a little cheek against his face, as if they said, ''Don't mind it, father. Don't be grieved!''

Bob was very cheerful with them, and spoke pleasantly to all the family. He looked at the work upon the table, and praised the industry and speed of Mrs. Cratchit and the girls. They would be done long before Sunday, he said.

''Sunday! You went to-day, then, Robert?''

''Yes, my dear,'' returned Bob. ''I wish you could have gone. It would have done you good to see how green a place it is. But you'll see it often. I promised him that I would walk there on a Sunday. My little, little child! My little child!''

He broke down all at once. He couldn't help

it. If he could have helped it, he and his child would have been farther apart, perhaps, than they were.

"Specter," said Scrooge, "something informs me that our parting moment is at hand. I know it, but I know not how. Tell me what man that was, with the covered face, whom we saw lying dead?"

The Ghost of Christmas Yet To Come conveyed him to a dismal, wretched, ruinous churchyard.

The Spirit stood among the graves, and pointed down to One.

"Before I draw nearer to that stone to which you point, answer me one question. Are these the shadows of the things that Will be, or are they shadows of the things that May be only?"

Still the Ghost pointed downward to the grave by which it stood.

"Men's courses will foreshadow certain ends, to which, if persevered in, they must lead. But if the courses be departed from, the ends will change. Say it is thus with what you show me!"

The Spirit was immovable as ever.

Scrooge crept toward it, trembling as he went; and, following the finger, read upon the stone of the neglected grave his own name — EBENEZER SCROOGE.

"Am *I* that man who lay upon the bed? No, Spirit! Oh, no, no! Spirit! hear me! I am not the man I was. I will not be the man I must have been but for this intercourse. Why show me this, if I am past all hope? Assure me that I yet may change these shadows you have shown me by an altered life.''

For the first time the kind hand faltered.

''I will honor Christmas in my heart, and try to keep it all the year. I will live in the Past, the Present, and the Future. The Spirits of all three shall strive within me. I will not shut out the lessons that they teach. Oh, tell me I may sponge away the writing on this stone!''

Holding up his hands in one last prayer to have his fate reversed, he saw an alteration in the Fantom's hood and dress. It shrunk, collapsed, and dwindled down into a bedpost.

Yes, and the bedpost was his own. The bed was his own, the room was his own. Best and happiest of all, the Time before him was his own, to make amends in!

He was checked in his transports by the churches ringing out the lustiest peals he had ever heard.

Running to the window, he opened it, and put out his head. No fog, no mist, no night; clear, bright, stirring, golden day.

''What's to-day?'' cried Scrooge, calling downward to a boy in Sunday clothes, who perhaps had loitered in to look about him.

''EH?''

''What's to-day, my fine fellow?''

''To-day! Why, CHRISTMAS DAY.''

"It's Christmas day! I haven't missed it. Hallo, my fine fellow!"

"Hallo!"

"Do you know the Poulterer's, in the next street but one, at the corner?"

"I should hope I did."

"An intelligent boy! A remarkable boy! Do you know whether they've sold the prize Turkey that was hanging up there? Not the little prize Turkey — the big one?"

"What, the one as big as me?"

"What a delightful boy! It's a pleasure to talk to him. Yes, my buck!"

"It's hanging there now."

"Is it? Go and buy it."

"Walk-ER!" exclaimed the boy.

"No, no, I am in earnest. Go and buy it, and tell 'em to bring it here, that I may give them the direction where to take it. Come back with the man, and I'll give you a shilling. Come back with him in less than five minutes, and I'll give you half a crown!"

The boy was off like a shot.

"I'll send it to Bob Cratchit's! He sha'n't know who sends it. It's twice the size of Tiny Tim. Joe Miller never made such a joke as sending it to Bob's will be!"

The hand in which he wrote the address was not a steady one; but write it he did, somehow, and went down-stairs to open the street door, ready for the coming of the poulterer's man.

It *was* a Turkey! He never could have stood

upon his legs, that bird. He would have snapped 'em short off in a minute, like sticks of sealing-wax.

Scrooge dressed himself "all in his best," and at last got out into the streets. The people were by this time pouring forth, as he had seen them with the Ghost of Christmas Present; and, walking with his hands behind him, Scrooge regarded every one with a delighted smile. He looked so irresistibly pleasant, in a word, that three or four good-humored fellows said, "Good morning, sir! A merry Christmas to you!" And Scrooge said often afterward, that, of all the blithe sounds he had ever heard, those were the blithest in his ears.

In the afternoon, he turned his steps toward his nephew's house.

He passed the door a dozen times, before he had the courage to go up and knock. But he made a dash, and did it.

"Is your master at home, my dear?" said Scrooge to the girl. Nice girl! Very.

"Yes, sir."

"Where is he, my love?"

"He's in the dining-room, sir, along with mistress."

"He knows me," said Scrooge, with his hand already on the dining-room lock. "I'll go in here, my dear."

"Fred!"

"Why, bless my soul!" cried Fred, "who's that?"

"It's I. Your Uncle Scrooge. I have come to dinner. Will you let me in, Fred?"

Let him in! It is a mercy he didn't shake his arm off. He was at home in five minutes. Nothing could be heartier. His niece looked just the same. So did Topper when *he* came. So did the plump sister when *she* came. So did every one when *they* came. Wonderful party, wonderful games, wonderful unanimity, won-derful happiness!

But he was early at the office next morning. Oh, he was early there! If he could only be there first, and catch Bob Cratchit coming late! That was the thing he had set his heart upon.

And he did it. The clock struck nine. No Bob. A quarter past. No Bob. Bob was full eighteen minutes and a half behind his time. Scrooge sat with his door wide open, that he might see him come into the Tank.

Bob's hat was off before he opened the door; his comforter, too. He was on his stool in a jiffy; driving away with his pen, as if he were trying to overtake nine o'clock.

"Hallo!" growled Scrooge in his accustomed voice, as near as he could feign it. "What do you mean by coming here at this time of day?"

"I am very sorry, sir. I *am* behind my time."

"You are? Yes. I think you are. Step this way, if you please."

"It's only once a year, sir. It shall not be

repeated. I was making rather merry yesterday, sir."

"Now, I'll tell you what, my friend. I am not going to stand this sort of thing any longer. And therefore," Scrooge continued, leaping from his stool, and giving Bob such a dig in the waistcoat that he staggered back into the Tank again — "and therefore I am about to raise your salary!"

Bob trembled, and got a little nearer to the ruler.

"A merry Christmas, Bob!" said Scrooge, with an earnestness that could not be mistaken, as he clapped him on the back. "A merrier Christmas, Bob, my good fellow, than I have given you for many a year! I'll raise your salary, and endeavor to assist your struggling family, and we will discuss your affairs this very afternoon, over a Christmas bowl of smoking bishop, Bob! Make up the fires, and buy a second coal-scuttle before you dot another i, Bob Cratchit!"

Scrooge was better than his word. He did it all, and infinitely more; and to Tiny Tim, who did NOT die, he was a second father. He became as good a friend, as good a master, and as good a man as the good old city knew, or any other good old city, town, or borough in the good old world. Some people laughed to see the alteration in him; but his own heart laughed, and that was quite enough for him.

He had no further intercourse with spirits,

but lived in that respect upon the total-abstinence principle ever afterward; and it was always said of him, that he knew how to keep Christmas well, if any man alive possessed the knowledge. May that be truly said of us, and all of us! And so, as Tiny Tim observed, God bless us, every one!

The Necklace

Guy de Maupassant

SHE was one of those pretty, charming young ladies, born, as if through an error of destiny, into a family of clerks. She had no dowry, no hopes, no means of becoming known, appreciated, loved, and married by a man either rich or distinguished; and she allowed herself to marry a petty clerk in the office of the Board of Education.

She was simple, not being able to adorn herself; but she was unhappy, as one out of her class; for women belong to no caste, no race; their grace, their beauty, and their charm serving them in the place of birth and family. Their inborn finesse, their instinctive elegance, their suppleness of wit are their only aristocracy, making some daughters of the people the equal of great ladies.

She suffered incessantly, feeling herself born for all delicacies and luxuries. She suffered from the poverty of her apartment, the shabby walls, the worn chairs, and the faded stuffs. All these things, which another woman of her station would not have noticed, tortured and angered her. The sight of the little Breton, who made this humble home, awoke in her sad regrets and desperate dreams. She thought of quiet antechambers, with their Oriental hangings, lighted by high, bronze torches, and of the two great footmen in short trousers who sleep in the large armchairs, made sleepy by the heavy air from the heating apparatus. She thought of large drawing-rooms, hung in old silks, of graceful pieces of furniture carrying bric-à-brac of inestimable value, and of the little perfumed coquettish apartments, made for five o'clock chats with most intimate friends, men known and sought after, whose attention all women envied and desired.

When she seated herself for dinner, before the round table where the tablecloth had been used three days, opposite her husband who uncovered the tureen with a delighted air, saying: "Oh! the good potpie! I know nothing better than that —" she would think of the elegant dinners, of the shining silver, of the tapestries peopling the walls with ancient personages and rare birds in the midst of fairy forests; she thought of the exquisite food served on marvelous dishes, of the whispered gallantries, listened to with the smile of the sphinx, while eating the rose-colored flesh of the trout or a chicken's wing.

She had neither frocks nor jewels, nothing. And she loved only those things. She felt that she was made for them. She had such a desire to please, to be sought after, to be clever, and courted.

She had a rich friend, a schoolmate at the convent, whom she did not like to visit, she suffered so much when she returned. And she wept for whole days from chagrin, from regret, from despair, and disappointment.

One evening her husband returned elated, bearing in his hand a large envelope.

"Here," said he, "here is something for you."

She quickly tore open the wrapper and drew out a printed card on which were inscribed these words:

> "The Minister of Public Instruction and Madame George Ramponneau ask the honor of Mr. and Mrs. Loisel's company Monday evening, January 18, at the Minister's residence."

Instead of being delighted, as her husband had hoped, she threw the invitation spitefully upon the table murmuring:

"What do you suppose I want with that?"

"But, my dearie, I thought it would make you happy. You never go out, and this is an occasion, and a fine one! I had a great deal of trouble to get it. Everybody wishes one, and it is very select; not many are given to employees. You will see the whole official world there.''

She looked at him with an irritated eye and declared impatiently:

''What do you suppose I have to wear to such a thing as that?''

He had not thought of that; he stammered:

''Why, the dress you wear when we go to the theater. It seems very pretty to me —''

He was silent, stupefied, in dismay, at the sight of his wife weeping. Two great tears fell slowly from the corners of his eyes toward the corners of his mouth; he stammered:

''What is the matter? What is the matter?''

By a violent effort, she had controlled her vexation and responded in a calm voice, wiping her moist cheeks:

''Nothing. Only I have no dress and consequently I cannot go to this affair. Give your card to some colleague whose wife is better fitted out than I.''

He was grieved, but answered:

''Let us see, Matilda. How much would a suitable costume cost, something that would serve for other occasions, something very simple?''

She reflected for some seconds, making estimates and thinking of a sum that she could ask for without bringing with it an immediate refusal and a frightened exclamation from the economical clerk.

Finally she said, in a hesitating voice:

"I cannot tell exactly, but it seems to me that four hundred francs ought to cover it."

He turned a little pale, for he had saved just this sum to buy a gun that he might be able to join some hunting parties the next summer, on the plains at Nanterre, with some friends who went to shoot larks up there on Sunday. Nevertheless, he answered:

"Very well. I will give you four hundred francs. But try to have a pretty dress."

The day of the ball approached and Mrs. Loisel seemed sad, disturbed, anxious. Nevertheless, her dress was nearly ready. Her husband said to her one evening:

"What is the matter with you? You have acted strangely for two or three days."

And she responded: "I am vexed not to have a jewel, not one stone, nothing to adorn myself with. I shall have such a poverty-laden look. I would prefer not to go to this party."

He replied: "You can wear some natural flowers. At this season they look very *chic*. For ten francs you can have two or three magnificent roses."

She was not convinced. "No," she replied, "there is nothing more humiliating than to have a shabby air in the midst of rich women."

Then her husband cried out: "How stupid we are! Go and find your friend Mrs. Forestier and ask her to lend you her jewels. You are well enough acquainted with her to do this."

She uttered a cry of joy: "It is true!" she said. "I had not thought of that."

The next day she took herself to her friend's house and related her story of distress. Mrs. Forestier went to her closet with the glass doors, took out a large jewel-case, brought it, opened it, and said: "Choose, my dear."

She saw at first some bracelets, then a collar of pearls, then a Venetian cross of gold and jewels and of admirable workmanship. She tried the jewels before the glass, hesitated, but could neither decide to take them nor leave them. Then she asked:

"Have you nothing more?"

"Why, yes. Look for yourself. I do not know what will please you."

Suddenly she discovered, in a black satin box, a supurb necklace of diamonds, and her heart beat fast with an immoderate desire. Her hands trembled as she took them up. She placed them about her throat against her dress, and remained in ecstasy before them. Then she asked, in a hesitating voice, full of anxiety:

"Could you lend me this? Only this?"

"Why, yes, certainly."

She fell upon the neck of her friend, embraced her with passion, then went away with her treasure.

The day of the ball arrived. Mrs. Loisel was a great success. She was the prettiest of all, elegant, gracious, smiling, and full of joy. All the men noticed her, asked her name, and wanted to be presented. All the members of the Cabinet wished to waltz with her. The Minister of Education paid her some attention.

She danced with enthusiasm, with passion, intoxicated with pleasure, thinking of nothing, in the triumph of her beauty, in the glory of her success, in a kind of cloud of happiness that came of all this homage, and all this admiration, of all these awakened desires, and this victory so complete and sweet to the heart of woman.

She went home toward four o'clock in the morning. Her husband had been half asleep in one of the little salons since midnight, with three other gentlemen whose wives were enjoying themselves very much.

He threw around her shoulders the wraps they had carried for the coming home, modest garments of everyday wear, whose poverty clashed with the elegance of the ball costume. She felt this and wished to hurry away in order not to be noticed by the other women who were wrapping themselves in rich furs.

Loisel retained her: "Wait," said he. "You will catch cold out there. I am going to call a cab."

But she would not listen and descended the steps rapidly. When they were in the street, they found no carriage; and they began to seek one, hailing the coachmen whom they saw at a distance.

They walked along toward the Seine, hopeless and shivering. Finally they found on the dock one of those old, nocturnal *coupés* that one sees in Paris after nightfall, as if they were ashamed of their misery by day.

It took them as far as their door in Martyr street, and they went wearily up to their apartment. It was all over for her. And on his part, he remembered that he would have to be at the office by ten o'clock.

She removed the wraps from her shoulders before the glass, for a final view of herself in her glory. Suddenly she uttered a cry. Her necklace was not around her neck.

Her husband, already half undressed, asked: "What is the matter?"

She turned toward him excitedly:

"I have — I have — I no longer have Mrs. Forestier's necklace."

He arose in dismay: "What! How is that? It is not possible."

And they looked in the folds of the dress, in the folds of the mantle, in the pockets, everywhere. They could not find it.

He asked: "You are sure you still had it when we left the house?"

"Yes, I felt it in the vestibule as we came out."

"But if you had lost it in the street, we should have heard it fall. It must be in the cab."

"Yes. It is probable. Did you take the

number?"

"No. And you, did you notice what it was?"

"No."

They looked at each other utterly cast down. Finally, Loisel dressed himself again.

"I am going," said he, "over the track where we went on foot, to see if I can find it."

And he went. She remained in her evening gown, not having the force to go to bed, stretched upon a chair, without ambition or thoughts.

Toward seven o'clock her husband returned. He had found nothing.

He went to the police and to the cab offices, and put an advertisement in the newspapers, offering a reward; he did everything that afforded them a suspicion of hope.

She waited all day in a state of bewilderment before this frightful disaster. Loisel returned at evening with his face harrowed and pale; he had discovered nothing.

"It will be necessary," said he, "to write to your friend that you have broken the clasp of the necklace and that you will have it repaired. That will give us time to turn around."

She wrote as he dictated.

At the end of a week, they had lost all hope. And Loisel, older by five years, declared:

"We must take measures to replace this jewel."

The next day they took the box which had inclosed it, to the jeweler whose name was on the inside. He consulted his books:

"It is not I, Madame," said he, "who sold this necklace; I only furnished the casket."

Then they went from jeweler to jeweler seeking a necklace like the other one, consulting their memories, and ill, both of them, with chagrin and anxiety.

In a shop of the Palais-Royal, they found a chaplet of diamonds which seemed to them exactly like the one they had lost. It was valued at forty thousand francs. They could get it for thirty-six thousand.

They begged the jeweler not to sell it for three days. And they made an arrangement by which they might return it for thirty-four thousand francs if they found the other one before the end of February.

Loisel possessed eighteen thousand francs which his father had left him. He borrowed the rest.

He borrowed it, asking for a thousand francs of one, five hundred of another, five louis of this one, and three louis of that one. He gave notes, made ruinous promises, took money of usurers and the whole race of lenders. He compromised his whole existence, in fact, risked his signature, without even knowing whether he could make it good or not, and, harassed by anxiety for the future, by the black misery which surrounded him, and by the prospect of all physical privations and moral torture, he went to get the new necklace, depositing on the merchant's counter thirty-six thousand francs.

When Mrs. Loisel took back the jewels to Mrs. Forestier, the latter said to her in a frigid tone:

"You should have returned them to me sooner, for I might have needed them."

She did open the jewel-box as her friend feared she would. If she should perceive the substitution, what would she think? What should she say? Would she take her for a robber?

Mrs. Loisel now knew the horrible life of necessity. She did her part, however, completely, heroically. It was necessary to pay this frightful debt. She would pay it. They sent away the maid; they changed their lodgings; they rented some rooms under a mansard roof.

She learned the heavy cares of a household, the odious work of a kitchen. She washed the dishes, using her rosy nails upon the greasy pots and the bottoms of the stewpans. She washed the soiled linen, the chemises and dishcloths, which she hung on the line to dry; she took down the refuse to the street each morning and brought up the water, stopping at each landing to breathe. And, clothed like a woman of the people, she went to the grocer's, the butcher's, and the fruiterer's, with her basket on her arm, shopping, haggling, defending to the last sou her miserable money.

Every month it was necessary to renew some notes, thus obtaining time, and to pay others.

The husband worked evenings, putting the books of some merchants in order, and nights he often did copying at five sous a page.

And this life lasted for ten years.

At the end of ten years, they had restored all, all, with interest of the usurer, and accumulated interest besides.

Mrs. Loisel seemed old now. She had become a strong, hard woman, the crude woman of the poor household. Her hair badly dressed, her skirts awry, her hands red, she spoke in a loud tone, and washed the floors in large pails of water. But sometimes, when her husband was at the office, she would seat herself before the window and think of that evening party of former times, of that ball where she was so beautiful and so flattered.

How would it have been if she had not lost that necklace? Who knows? Who knows? How singular is life, and how full of changes! How small a thing will ruin or save one!

One Sunday, as she was taking a walk in the Champs-Elysées to rid herself of the cares of the week, she suddenly perceived a woman walking with a child. It was Mrs. Forestier, still young, still pretty, still attractive. Mrs. Loisel was affected. Should she speak to her?

Yes, certainly. And now that she had paid, she would tell her all. Why not?

She approached her. "Good morning, Jeanne."

Her friend did not recognize her and was astonished to be so familiarly addressed by this common personage. She stammered:

"But, Madame — I do not know — You must be mistaken —"

"No, I am Matilda Loisel."

Her friend uttered a cry of astonishment: "Oh! my poor Matilda! How you have changed —"

"Yes, I have had some hard days since I saw you; and some miserable ones — and all because of you —"

"Because of me? How is that?"

"You recall the diamond necklace that you loaned me to wear to the Commissioner's ball?"

"Yes, very well."

"Well, I lost it."

"How is that, since you returned it to me?"

"I returned another to you exactly like it. And it has taken us ten years to pay for it. You can understand that it was not easy for us who have nothing. But it is finished and I am decently content."

Madame Forestier stopped short. She said:

"You say that you bought a diamond necklace to replace mine?"

"Yes. You did not perceive it then? They

were just alike.''

And she smiled with a proud and simple joy. Madame Forestier was touched and took both her hands as she replied:

''Oh! my poor Matilda! Mine were false. They were not worth over five hundred francs!''

The Lady or the Tiger?

Frank R. Stockton

IN the very olden time, there lived a semi-barbaric king, whose ideas, though somewhat polished and sharpened by the progressiveness of distant Latin neighbors, were still large, florid, and untrammelled, as became the half of him which was barbaric. He was a man of exuberant fancy, and, withal, of an authority so irrestistible that, at his will, he turned his varied fancies into facts. He was greatly given to self-communing; and, when he and himself agreed upon anything, the thing was done. When every member of his domestic and political systems moved smoothly in its appointed course, his nature was bland and genial; but whenever there was a little hitch, and some of his orbs got out of their orbits, he was blander and more genial still, for nothing pleased him so much as to make the crooked straight, and crush down uneven places.

Among the borrowed notions by which his barbarism had become semified was that of the public arena, in which, by exhibitions of manly and beastly valor, the minds of his subjects were refined and cultured.

But even here the exuberant and barbaric fancy asserted itself. The arena of the king was built, not to give the people an opportunity of hearing the rhapsodies of dying gladiators, nor to enable them to view the inevitable conclusion of a conflict between religious opinions and hungry jaws, but for purposes far better adapted to widen and develop the mental energies of the people. This vast amphitheater, with its encircling galleries, its mysterious vaults, and its unseen passages, was an agent of poetic justice, in which crime was punished, or virtue rewarded, by the decrees of an impartial and incorruptible chance.

When a subject was accused of a crime of sufficient importance to interest the king, public notice was given that on an appointed day the fate of the accused person would be decided in the king's arena, — a structure which well deserved its name; for, although its form and plan were borrowed from afar, its purpose emanated solely from the brain of this man, who, every barleycorn a king, knew no tradition to which he owed more allegiance than pleased his fancy, and who ingrafted on every adopted form of human thought and action the rich growth of his barbaric idealism.

When all the people had assembled in the galleries, and the king, surrounded by his court, sat high up on his throne of royal state on one side of the arena, he gave a signal, a door beneath him opened, and the accused subject stepped out into the amphitheater. Directly opposite him, on the other side of the enclosed space, were two doors, exactly alike and side by side. It was the duty and the privilege of the person on trial, to walk directly to these doors and open one of them. He could open either door he pleased: he was subject to no guidance or influence but that of the aforementioned impartial and incorruptible chance. If he opened the one, there came out of it a hungry tiger, the fiercest and most cruel that could be procured, which immediately sprang upon him, and tore him to pieces, as a punishment for his guilt. The moment that the case of the criminal was thus decided, doleful iron bells were clanged, great wails went up from the hired mourners posted on the outer rim of the arena, and the vast audience, with bowed heads and downcast hearts, wended slowly their homeward way, mourning greatly that one so young and fair, or so old and respected, should have merited so dire a fate.

But, if the accused person opened the other door, there came forth from it a lady, the most suitable to his years and station that his majesty could select among his fair subjects; and to this lady he was immediately married, as a reward of his innocence. It mattered not that he might already possess a wife and family, or that his affections might be engaged upon an object of his own selection: the king allowed no such subordinate arrangements to interfere with his great scheme of retribution and reward. The exercises, as in the other instance, took place immediately, and in the arena. Another door opened beneath the king, and a priest, followed by a band of choristers, and dancing maidens blowing joyous airs on golden horns and treading an epithalamic measure, advanced to where the pair stood, side by side; and the wedding was promptly and cheerily solemnized. Then the gay brass bells rang forth their merry peals, the people shouted glad hurrahs, and the innocent man, preceded by children strewing flowers on his path, led his bride to his home.

This was the king's semi-barbaric method of administering justice. Its perfect fairness is obvious. The criminal could not know out of which door would come the lady: he opened either he pleased, without having the slightest idea whether, in the next instant, he was to be devoured or married. On some occasions the tiger came out of one door, and on some out of the other. The decisions of this tribunal were not only fair, they were positively determinate: the accused person was instantly punished if he found himself guilty; and, if innocent, he was rewarded on the spot, whether he liked it or not. There was no escape from the judgments of the king's arena.

The institution was a very popular one. When the people gathered together on one of the great trial days, they never knew whether they were to witness a bloody slaughter or a hilarious wedding. This element of uncertainty lent an interest to the occasion which it could not otherwise have attained. Thus, the masses were entertained and pleased, and the thinking part of the community could bring no charge of unfairness against this plan; for did not the accused person have the whole matter in his own hands?

This semi-barbaric king had a daughter as blooming as his most florid fancies, and with a soul as fervent and imperious as his own. As is usual in such cases, she was the apple of his eye, and was loved by him above all humanity. Among his courtiers was a young man of that fineness of blood and lowness of station common to the conventional heroes of romance who love royal maidens. This royal maiden was well satisfied with her lover, for he was handsome and brave to a degree unsurpassed in all this kingdom; and she loved him with an ardor that had enough of barbarism in it to make it exceedingly warm and strong. This love affair moved on happily for many months, until one day the king happened to discover its existence. He did not hesitate nor waver in regard to his duty in the premises. The youth was immediately cast into prison, and a day was appointed for his trial in the king's arena.

This, of course, was an especially important occasion; and his majesty, as well as all the people, was greatly interested in the workings and development of this trial. Never before had such a case occurred; never before had a subject dared to love the daughter of a king. In after-years such things became commonplace enough; but then they were, in no slight degree, novel and startling.

The tiger-cages of the kingdom were searched for the most savage and relentless beasts, from which the fiercest monster might be selected for the arena; and the ranks of maiden youth and beauty throughout the land were carefully surveyed by competent judges, in order that the young man might have a fitting bride in case fate did not determine for him a different destiny. Of course, everybody knew that the deed with which the accused was charged had been done. He had loved the princess, and neither he, she, nor any one else thought of denying the fact; but the king would not think of allowing any fact of this kind to interfere with the workings of the tribunal, in which he took such great delight and satisfaction. No matter how the affair turned out, the youth would be disposed of; and the king would take an aesthetic pleasure in watching the course of events, which would determine whether or not the young man had done wrong in allowing himself to love the princess.

The appointed day arrived. From far and

near the people gathered, and thronged the great galleries of the arena; and the crowds, unable to gain admittance, massed themselves against its outside walls. The king and his court were in their places, opposite the twin doors, — those fateful portals, so terrible in their similarity.

All was ready. The signal was given. A door beneath the royal party opened, and the lover of the princess walked into the arena. Tall, beautiful, fair, his appearance was greeted with a low hum of admiration and anxiety. Half the audience had not known so grand a youth had lived among them. No wonder the princess loved him! What a terrible thing for him to be there!

As the youth advanced into the arena, he turned, as the custom was, to bow to the king: but he did not think at all of that royal personage; his eyes were fixed upon the princess, who sat to the right of her father. Had it not been for the moiety of barbarism in her nature, it is probable that lady would not have been there; but her intense and fervid soul would not allow her to be absent on an occasion in which she was so terribly interested. From the moment that the decree had gone forth, that her lover should decide his fate in the king's arena, she had thought of nothing, night or day, but this great event and the various subjects connected with it. Possessed of more power, influence, and force of character than any one who had ever before been interested in such a case, she had done what no other person had done, — she had possessed herself of the secret of the doors. She knew in which of the two rooms, that lay behind those doors, stood the cage of the tiger, with its open front, and in which waited the lady. Through these thick doors, heavily curtained with skins on the inside, it was impossible that any noise or suggestion should come from within to the person who should approach to raise the latch of one of them; but gold, and the power of a woman's will, had brought the secret to the princess.

And not only did she know in which room stood the lady ready to emerge, all blushing and radiant, should her door be opened, but she knew who the lady was. It was one of the fairest and loveliest of the damsels of the court who had been selected as the reward of the accused youth, should he be proved innocent of the crime of aspiring to one so far above him; and the princess hated her. Often she had seen, or imagined that she had seen, this fair creature throwing glances of admiration upon the person of her lover, and sometimes she thought these glances were perceived and even returned. Now and then she had seen them talking together; it was but for a moment or two, but much can be said in a brief space; it may have been on most unimportant topics, but how could she know that? The girl was lovely, but she had dared to raise her eyes to the loved one of the princess; and, with all the intensity of the savage blood transmitted to her through long lines of wholly barbaric ancestors, she hated the woman who blushed and trembled behind that silent door.

When her lover turned and looked at her, and his eye met hers as she sat there paler and whiter than any one in the vast ocean of anxious faces about her, he saw, by that power of quick perception which is given to those whose souls are one, that she knew behind which door crouched the tiger, and behind which stood the lady. He had expected her to know it. He understood her nature, and his soul was assured that she would never rest until she had made plain to herself this thing, hidden to all other lookers-on, even to the king. The only hope for the youth in which there was any element of certainty was based upon the success of the princess in discovering this mystery; and the moment he looked upon her, he saw she had succeeded, as in his soul he knew she would succeed.

Then it was that his quick and anxious glance asked the question: "Which?" It was as plain to her as if he shouted it from where he stood. There was not an instant to be lost. The question was asked in a flash; it must be answered in another.

Her right arm lay on the cushioned parapet before her. She raised her hand, and made a slight, quick movement toward the right. No one but her lover saw her. Every eye but his was fixed on the man in the arena.

He turned, and with a firm and rapid step he walked across the empty space. Every heart stopped beating, every breath was held, every eye was fixed immovably upon that man. Without the slightest hesitation, he went to the door on the right, and opened it.

Now, the point of the story is this: Did the tiger come out of that door, or did the lady?

The more we reflect upon this question, the harder it is to answer. It involves a study of the human heart which leads us through devious mazes of passion, out of which it is difficult to find our way. Think of it, fair reader, not as if the decision of the question depended upon yourself, but upon that hot-blooded, semi-barbaric princess, her soul at a white heat beneath the combined fires of despair and jealousy. She had lost him, but who should have him?

How often, in her waking hours and in her dreams, had she started in wild horror, and covered her face with her hands as she thought of her lover opening the door on the other side of which waited the cruel fangs of the tiger!

But how much oftener had she seen him at the other door! How in her grievous reveries had she gnashed her teeth, and torn her hair, when she saw his start of rapturous delight as he opened the door of the lady! How her soul had burned in agony when she had seen him rush to meet that woman, with her flushing cheek and sparkling eye of triumph; when she had seen him lead her forth, his whole frame kindled with the joy of recovered life; when she had heard the glad shouts from the multitude, and the wild ringing of the happy bells; when she had seen the priest, with his joyous followers, advance to the couple, and make them man and wife before her very eyes; and when she had seen them walk away together upon their path of flowers, followed by the tremendous shouts of the hilarious multitude, in which her one despairing shriek was lost and drowned!

Would it not be better for him to die at once, and go to wait for her in the blessed regions of semi-barbaric futurity?

And yet, that awful tiger, those shrieks, that blood!

Her decision had been indicated in an instant, but it had been made after days and nights of anguished deliberation. She had known she would be asked, she had decided what she would answer, and, without the slightest hesitation, she had moved her hand to the right.

The question of her decision is one not to be lightly considered, and it is not for me to presume to set myself up as the one person able to answer it. And so I leave it with all of you: Which came out of the opened door, — the lady, or the tiger?

The Celebrated Jumping Frog of Calaveras County

Mark Twain

In compliance with the request of a friend of mine, who wrote me from the East, I called on good-natured, garrulous old Simon Wheeler, and inquired after my friend's friend, *Leonidas W.* Smiley, as requested to do, and I hereunto append the result. I have a lurking suspicion that *Leonidas W.* Smiley is a myth; that my friend never knew such a personage; and that he only conjectured that, if I asked old Wheeler about him, it would remind him of his infamous *Jim* Smiley, and he would go to work and bore me nearly to death with some infernal reminiscence of him as long and tedious as it should be useless to me. If that was the design, it certainly succeeded.

I found Simon Wheeler dozing comfortably by the barroom stove of the old, dilapidated tavern in the ancient mining camp of Angel's, and I noticed that he was fat and bald-headed, and had an expression of winning gentleness and simplicity upon his tranquil countenance. He roused up and gave me good-day. I told him a friend of mine had commissioned me to make some inquiries about a cherished companion of his boyhood named *Leonidas W.* Smiley — *Rev. Leonidas W.* Smiley — a young minister of the Gospel, who he had heard was at one time a resident of Angel's Camp. I added, that, if Mr. Wheeler could tell me anything about this Rev. Leonidas W. Smiley, I would feel under many obligations to him.

Simon Wheeler backed me into a corner and blockaded me there with his chair, and then sat me down and reeled off the monotonous narrative which follows this paragraph. He never smiled, he never frowned, he never changed his voice from the gentle-flowing key to which he tuned the initial sentence, he never betrayed the slightest suspicion of enthusiasm; but all through the interminable narrative there ran a vein of impressive earnestness and sincerity, which showed me plainly that, so far from his imagining that there was anything ridiculous or funny about his story, he regarded it as a really important matter, and admitted its two heroes as men of transcendent genius in *finesse*. To me, the spectacle of a man drifting serenely along through such a queer yarn without ever smiling, was exquisitely absurd. As I said before, I asked him to tell me what he knew of Rev. Leonidas W. Smiley, and he replied as follows. I let him go on in his own way, and never interrupted him once:

There was a feller here once by the name of *Jim* Smiley, in the winter of '49 — or maybe it was the spring of '50 — I don't recollect exactly, somehow, though what makes me think it was one or the other is because I remember the big flume wasn't finished when he first came to the camp; but anyway, he was the curiousest man about always betting on anything that turned up you ever see, if he could get anybody to bet on the other side; and if he couldn't, he'd change sides. Any way what suited the other man would suit him — any way just so's he got a bet, *he* was satisfied. But still he was lucky, uncommon lucky — he most always come out winner. He was always ready and laying for a chance; there couldn't be no solit'ry thing mentioned but that feller'd offer to bet on it, and take any side you please, as I was just telling you. If there was a horse-race, you'd find him flush, or you'd find him busted at the end of it; if there was a dog-fight, he'd bet on it; if there was a cat-fight, he'd bet on it; if there was a chicken-fight, he'd bet on it; why, if there was two birds setting on a fence, he would bet you which one would fly first; or if there was a camp meeting, he would be there reg'lar, to bet on Parson Walker, which he judged to be the best exhorter about here, and so he was, too, and a good man. If he even seen a straddle-bug start to go anywheres, he would bet you how long it would take him to get wherever he was going to, and if you took him up, he would foller that straddle-bug to Mexico but what he would find out where he was bound for and how long he was on the road. Lots of the boys here has seen that Smiley, and can tell you about him. Why, it never made no difference to *him* — he would bet on *any*thing — the dangdest feller. Parson Walker's wife laid very sick once, for a good while, and it seemed as if they warn't going to save her; but one morning he came in, and Smiley asked how she was, and he said she was considerable better — thank the Lord for his inf'nit mercy — and coming on so smart that, with the blessing of Prov'dence, she'd get well yet; and Smiley, before he thought says, "Well, I'll risk two-and-a-half that she don't, anyway."

Thish-yer Smiley had a mare — the boys called her the fifteen-minute nag, but that was only in fun, you know, because, of course, she was faster than that — and he used to win money on that horse, for all she was so slow and always had the asthma, or the distemper, or the consumption, or something of that kind. They used to give her two or three hundred yards start, and then pass her under way; but always at the fag-end of the race she'd get excited and desperate-like, and come cavorting and straddling up, and scattering her legs around limber, sometimes in the air, and sometimes out to one side amongst the fences, and kicking up m-o-r-e dust, and raising m-o-r-e racket with her coughing and sneezing and blowing her nose — and always fetch up at the stand just about a neck ahead, as near as you could cipher it down.

And he had a little small bull pup, that to look at him you'd think he wan't worth a cent but to set around and look ornery and lay for a chance to steal something. But as soon as money was up on him, he was a different dog; his under-jaw'd begin to stick out like the fo'castle of a steamboat, and his teeth would uncover, and shine savage like the furnaces. And a dog might tackle him, and bullyrag him, and bite him, and throw him over his shoulder two or three times, and Andrew Jackson — which was the name of the pup — Andrew Jackson would never let on but what *he* was satisfied, and hadn't expected nothing else — and the bets being doubled and doubled on the other side all the time, till the money was all up; and then all of a sudden he would grab that other dog jest by the j'int of his hind leg and freeze to it — not claw, you understand, but only jest grip and hang on till they throwed up the sponge, if it was a year. Smiley always come out winner on that pup, till he harnessed a dog once that didn't have no hind legs, because they'd been sawed off by a circular saw, and when the thing had gone along far enough, and the money was all up, and he come to make a snatch for his pet holt, he saw in a minute how he'd been imposed on, and how the other dog had him in the door, so to speak, and he 'peared surprised, and then he looked sorter discouraged-like, and didn't try no more to win the fight, and so he got shucked out bad. He give Smiley a look, as much to say his heart was broke and it was *his* fault for putting up a dog that hadn't no hind legs for him to take holt of, which was his main dependence in a fight, and then he limped off a piece and laid down and died. It was a good pup, was that Andrew Jackson, and would have made a name for hisself if he'd lived, for the stuff was in him, and he had genius — I know it, because he hadn't no opportunities to speak of, and it don't stand to reason that a dog could make such a fight as he could under them circumstances, if he hadn't no talent. It always makes me feel sorry when I think of that last fight of his'n, and the way it turned out.

Well, thish-yer Smiley had rat-tarriers, and chicken-cocks, and tomcats, and all them kind of things, till you couldn't rest, and you couldn't fetch nothing for him to bet on but he'd match you. He ketched a frog one day, and took him home, and said he cal'klated to edercate him; and so he never done nothing for these three months but set in his back yard and learn that frog to jump. And you bet you he *did* learn him, too. He'd give him a little punch behind, and the next minute you'd see that frog whirling in the air like a doughnut — see him turn one summerset, or maybe a couple, if he got a good start, and come down flat-footed and all right, like a cat. He got him up so in the matter of catching flies, and kept him in practice so constant, that he'd nail a fly every time as far as he could see him. Smiley said all a frog wanted was education, and he could do most anything — and I believe him. Why, I've seen him set Dan'l Webster down here on this floor — Dan'l Webster was the name of the frog — and sing out, "Flies, Dan'l, flies!" and quicker'n you could wink, he'd spring straight up, and snake a fly off'n the counter there, and flop down on the floor again as solid as a gob of mud, and fall to scratching the side of his head with his hind foot as indifferent as if he hadn't no idea he's been doin' any more'n any frog might do. You never see a frog so modest and straight-for'ard as he was, for all he was so gifted. And when it come to fair and square jumping on the dead level, he could get over more ground at one straddle than any animal of his breed you ever see. Jumping on a dead level was his strong suit, you understand; and when it came to that, Smiley would ante up money on him as long as he had a red. Smiley was monstrous proud of his frog, and well he might be, for fellers that had traveled and been everywhere all said he laid over any frog that ever *they* see.

Well, Smiley kept the beast in a little lattice

box, and he used to fetch him downtown sometimes and lay for a bet. One day a feller — a stranger in the camp, he was — come across him with his box, and says:

"What might it be that you've got in that box?"

And Smiley says, sorter indifferent like, "It might be a parrot, or it might be a canary, maybe, but it ain't — it's only just a frog."

An' the feller took it, and looked at it careful, and turned it round this way and that, and says, "H'm — so 'tis. Well, what's *he* good for?"

"Well," Smiley says, easy and careless, "he's good enough for *one* thing, I should judge — he can outjump any frog in Calaveras county."

The feller took the box again, and took another long, particular look, and give it back to Smiley, and says, very deliberate, "Well, I don't see no p'ints about that frog that's any better'n any other frog."

"Maybe you don't," Smiley says. "Maybe you understand frogs, and maybe you don't understand 'em; maybe you've had experience, and maybe you ain't only a amature, as it were. Anyways, I've got *my* opinion and I'll risk forty dollars that he can outjump any frog in Calaveras county."

And the feller studied a minute, and then says, kinder sad like, "Well, I'm only a stranger here, and I ain't got no frog; but if

I had a frog, I'd bet you."

And then Smiley says, "That's all right — that's all right — if you'll hold my box a minute, I'll go and get you a frog." And so the feller took the box, and put up his forty dollars along with Smiley's, and set down to wait.

So he set there a good while thinking and thinking to hisself, and then he got the frog out and pried his mouth open and took a teaspoon and filled him full of quail shot — filled him pretty near up to his chin — and set him on the floor. Smiley he went to the swamp and slopped around in the mud for a long time, and finally he ketched a frog, and fetched him in, and give him to this feller, and says:

"Now, if you're ready, set him alongside of Dan'l, with his forepaws just even with Dan'l, and I'll give the word."Then he says. "One — two — three — jump!" and him and the feller touched up the frogs from behind, and the new frog hopped off, but Dan'l give a heave, and hysted up his shoulders — so — like a Frenchman, but it wasn't no use — he couldn't budge; he was planted as solid as an anvil, and he couldn't no more stir than if he was anchored out. Smiley was a good deal surprised, and he was disgusted too, but he didn't have no idea what the matter was, of course.

The feller took the money and started away; and when he was going out at the door, he sorter jerked his thumb over his shoulder — this way — at Dan'l, and says again, very deliberate, "Well, *I* don't see no p'ints about that frog that's any better'n any other frog."

Smiley he stood scratching his head and looking down at Dan'l a long time, and at last he says, "I do wonder what in the nation that frog throw'd off for — I wonder if there ain't something the matter with him — he 'pears to look mighty baggy, somehow." And he ketched Dan'l by the nap of the neck, and lifted him up and says, "Why, blame my cats, if he don't weigh five pounds!" and turned him upside down, and he belched out a double handful of shot. And then he see how it was, and he was the maddest man — he set the frog down and took out after that feller, but he never ketched him. And —

(Here Simon Wheeler heard his name called from the front yard, and got up to see what was wanted.) And turning to me as he moved away, he said: "Just set where you are, stranger, and rest easy — I ain't going to be gone a second."

But, by your leave, I did not think that a continuation of the history of the enterprising vagabond *Jim* Smiley would be likely to afford me much information concerning the Rev. *Leonidas W*. Smiley, and so I started away.

At the door I met the sociable Wheeler returning, and he buttonholed me and recommenced:

"Well thish-yer Smiley had a yeller one-eyed cow that didn't have no tail, only jest a short stump like a bannanner, and —"

"Oh, hang Smiley and his afflicted cow!" I muttered, good-naturedly, and bidding the old gentleman good-day, I departed.

The Adventure of the Speckled Band

Arthur Conan Doyle

In glancing over my notes of the seventy-odd cases in which I have during the last eight years studied the methods of my friend Sherlock Holmes, I find many tragic, some comic, a large number merely strange, but none commonplace; for, working as he did rather for the love of his art than for the acquirement of wealth, he refused to associate himself with any investigation which did not tend toward the unusual, and even the fantastic. Of all these varied cases, however, I cannot recall any which presented more singular features than that which was associated with the well-known Surrey family of the Roylotts of Stoke Moran. The events in question occurred in the early days of my association with Holmes, when we were sharing rooms as bachelors in Baker Street. It is possible that I might have placed them upon record before, but a promise of secrecy was made at the time, from which I have only been freed during the last month by the untimely death of the lady to whom the pledge was given. It is perhaps as well that the facts should now come to light, for I have reasons to know that there are wide-spread rumors as to the death of Dr. Grimesby Roylott which tend to make the matter even more terrible than the truth.

It was early in April in the year '83 that I woke one morning to find Sherlock Holmes standing, fully dressed, by the side of my bed. He was a late riser as a rule, and as the clock on the mantel-piece showed me that it was only a quarter past seven, I blinked up at him in some surprise, and perhaps just a little resentment, for I was myself regular in my habits.

"Very sorry to knock you up, Watson," said he, "but it's the common lot this morning. Mrs. Hudson has been knocked up, she retorted upon me, and I on you."

"What is it, then — a fire?"

"No; a client. It seems that a young lady has arrived in a considerable state of excitement, who insists upon seeing me. She is waiting now in the sitting-room. Now, when young ladies wander about the metropolis at this hour of the morning, and knock sleepy people up out of their beds, I presume that it is something very pressing which they have to communicate. Should it prove to be an interesting case, you would, I am sure, wish to follow it from the outset. I thought, at any rate, that I should call you and give you the chance."

"My dear fellow, I would not miss it for anything."

I had no keener pleasure than in following Holmes in his professional investigations, and in admiring the rapid deductions, as swift as intuitions, and yet always founded on a logical basis, with which he unravelled the problems which were submitted to him. I rapidly threw on my clothes, and was ready in a few minutes to accompany my friend down to the sitting-room. A lady dressed in black and heavily veiled, who had been sitting in the window, rose as we entered.

"Good-morning, madam," said Holmes, cheerily. "My name is Sherlock Holmes. This is my intimate friend and associate, Dr. Watson, before whom you can speak as freely as before myself. Ha! I am glad to see that Mrs. Hudson has had the good sense to light the fire. Pray draw up to it, and I shall order you a cup of hot coffee, for I observe that you are shivering."

"It is not cold which makes me shiver," said the woman, in a low voice, changing her seat as requested.

"What, then?"

"It is fear, Mr. Holmes. It is terror." She raised her veil as she spoke, and we could see that she was indeed in a pitiable state of agitation, her face all drawn and gray, with restless, frightened eyes, like those of some hunted animal. Her features and figure were those of a woman of thirty, but her hair was shot with premature gray, and her expression was weary and haggard. Sherlock Holmes ran her over with one of his quick, all-comprehensive glances.

"You must not fear," said he, soothingly, bending forward and patting her forearm. "We shall soon set matters right, I have no doubt. You have come in by train this morning, I see."

"You know me, then?"

"No, but I observe the second half of a return ticket in the palm of your left glove. You must have started early, and yet you had a good drive in a dog-cart, along heavy roads, before you reached the station."

The lady gave a violent start and stared in bewilderment at my companion.

"There is no mystery, my dear madam," said he, smiling. "The left arm of your jacket is spattered with mud in no less than seven places. The marks are perfectly fresh. There is no vehicle save a dog-cart which throws up mud in that way, and then only when you sit on the left-hand side of the driver."

"Whatever your reasons may be, you are perfectly correct," said she. "I started from home before six, reached Leatherhead at twenty past, and came in by the first train to Waterloo. Sir, I can stand this strain no longer; I shall go mad if it continues. I have no one to turn to — none, save only one, who cares for me, and he, poor fellow, can be of little aid. I have heard of you, Mr. Holmes; I have heard of you from Mrs. Farintosh, whom you helped in the hour of her sore need. It was from her that I had your address. Oh, sir, do you not think that you could help me, too, and at least throw a little light through the dense darkness which surrounds me? At present it is out of my power to reward you for your services, but in a month or six weeks I shall be married, with the control of my own income, and then at least you shall not find me ungrateful.''

Holmes turned to his desk, and unlocking it, drew out a small casebook, which he consulted.

''Farintosh,'' said he. ''Ah yes, I recall the case; it was concerned with an opal tiara. I think it was before your time, Watson. I can only say, madam, that I shall be happy to devote the same care to your case as I did to that of your friend. As to reward, my profession is its own reward; but you are at liberty to defray whatever expenses I may be put to, at the time which suits you best. And now I beg that you will lay before us everything that may help us in forming an opinion upon the matter.''

''Alas!'' replied our visitor, ''the very horror of my situation lies in the fact that my fears are so vague, and my suspicions depend so entirely upon small points, which might seem trivial to another, that even he to whom of all others I have a right to look for help and advice looks upon all that I tell him about it as the fancies of a nervous woman. He does not say so, but I can read it from his soothing answers and averted eyes. But I have heard, Mr. Holmes, that you can see deeply into the manifold wickedness of the human heart. You may advise me how to walk amid the dangers which encompass me."

"I am all attention, madam."

"My name is Helen Stoner, and I am living with my step-father, who is the last survivor of one of the oldest Saxon families in England, the Roylotts of Stoke Moran, on the western border of Surrey."

Holmes nodded his head. "The name is familiar to me," said he.

"The family was at one time among the richest in England, and the estates extended over the borders into Berkshire in the north and Hampshire in the west. In the last century, however, four successive heirs were of a dissolute and wasteful disposition, and the family ruin was eventually completed by a gambler in the days of the Regency. Nothing was left save a few acres of ground, and the two-hundred-year-old house, which is itself crushed under a heavy mortgage. The last squire dragged out his existence there, living the horrible life of an aristocratic pauper; but his only son, my step-father, seeing that he must adapt himself to the new conditions, obtained an advance from a relative, which enabled him to take a medical degree, and went out to Calcutta, where, by his professional skill and his force of character, he established a large practice. In a fit of anger, however, caused by some robberies which had been perpetrated in the house, he beat his native butler to death, and narrowly escaped a capital sentence. As it was, he suffered a long term of imprisonment, and afterward returned to England a morose and disappointed man.

"When Dr. Roylott was in India he married my mother, Mrs. Stoner, the young widow of Major-General Stoner, of the Bengal Artillery. My sister Julia and I were twins, and we were only two years old at the time of my mother's remarriage. She had a considerable sum of money — not less than £1000 a year — and this she bequeathed to Dr. Roylott entirely while we resided with him, with a provision that a certain annual sum should be allowed to each of us in the event of our marriage. Shortly after our return to England my mother died — she was killed eight years ago in a railway accident near Crewe. Dr. Roylott then abandoned his attempts to establish himself in practice in London, and took us to live with him in the old ancestral house at Stoke Moran. The money which my mother had left was enough for all our wants, and there seemed to be no obstacle to our happiness.

"But a terrible change came over our step-father about this time. Instead of making friends and exchanging visits with our neighbors, who had at first been overjoyed to see a Roylott of Stoke Moran back in the old family seat, he shut himself up in his house, and seldom came out save to indulge in ferocious quarrels with whoever might cross his path. Violence of temper approaching to mania has been hereditary in the men of the family, and in my step-father's case it had, I believe, been intensified by his long residence in the tropics. A series of disgraceful brawls took place, two of which ended in the police-court, until at last he became the terror of the village, and the folks would fly at his approach, for he is a man of immense strength, and absolutely uncontrollable in his anger.

"Last week he hurled the local blacksmith over a parapet into a stream, and it was only by paying over all the money which I could gather together that I was able to avert another public exposure. He had no friends at all save the wandering gypsies, and he would give these vagabonds leave to encamp upon the few acres of bramble-covered land which represent the family estate, and would accept in return the hospitality of their tents, wandering away with them sometimes for weeks on end. He has a passion also for Indian animals, which are sent over to him by a correspondent, and he has at this moment a cheetah and a baboon, which wander freely over his grounds, and are feared by the villagers almost as much as their master.

"You can imagine from what I say that my poor sister Julia and I had no great pleasure in our lives. No servant would stay with us, and for a long time we did all the work of the house. She was but thirty at the time of her death, and yet her hair had already begun to whiten, even as mine has."

"Your sister is dead, then?"

"She died just two years ago, and it is of her death that I wish to speak to you. You can understand that, living the life which I have described, we were little likely to see any one of our own age and position. We had, however, an aunt, my mother's maiden sister, Miss Honoria Westphail, who lives near Harrow, and we were occasionally allowed to pay short visits at this lady's house. Julia went there at Christmas two years ago, and met there a half-pay major of marines, to whom she became engaged. My step-father learned of the engagement when my sister returned, and offered no objection to the marriage; but within a fortnight of the day which had been fixed for the wedding, the terrible event occurred which has deprived me of my only companion."

Sherlock Holmes had been leaning back in his chair with his eyes closed and his head sunk in a cushion, but he half opened his lids now and glanced across at his visitor.

"Pray be precise as to details," said he.

"It is easy for me to be so, for every event of that dreadful time is seared into my memory. The manor-house is, as I have already said, very old, and only one wing is now inhabited. The bedrooms in this wing are on the ground floor, the sitting-rooms being in the central block of the buildings. Of these bedrooms the first is Dr. Roylott's, the second my sister's, and the third my own. There is no communication between them, but they all open out into the same corridor. Do I make myself plain?"

"Perfectly so."

"The windows of the three rooms open out upon the lawn. That fatal night Dr. Roylott had gone to his room early, though we knew that he had not retired to rest, for my sister was troubled by the smell of the strong Indian cigars which it was his custom to smoke. She left her room, therefore, and came into mine, where she sat for some time, chatting about her approaching wedding. At eleven o'clock she rose to leave me, but she paused at the door and looked back.

" 'Tell me, Helen,' said she, 'have you ever heard any one whistle in the dead of the night?'

" 'Never,' said I.

" 'I suppose that you could not possibly whistle, yourself, in your sleep?'

" 'Certainly not. But why?'

" 'Because during the last few nights I have always, about three in the morning, heard a low, clear whistle. I am a light sleeper, and it has awakened me. I cannot tell where it came from — perhaps from the next room, perhaps from the lawn. I thought that I would just ask you whether you had heard it.'

" 'No, I have not. It must be those wretched gypsies in the plantation.'

" 'Very likely. And yet if it were on the lawn, I wonder that you did not hear it also.'

" 'Ah, but I sleep more heavily than you.'

" 'Well, it is of no great consequence, at any rate.' She smiled back at me, closed my door, and a few moments later I heard her key turn in the lock."

"Indeed," said Holmes. "Was it your custom always to lock yourselves in at night?"

"Always."

"And why?"

"I think that I mentioned to you that the doctor kept a cheetah and a baboon. We had no feeling of security unless our doors were locked."

"Quite so. Pray proceed with your statement."

"I could not sleep that night. A vague feeling of impending misfortune impressed me. My sister and I, you will recollect, were twins, and you know how subtle are the links which bind two souls which are so closely allied. It was a wild night. The wind was howling outside, and the rain was beating and splashing against the windows. Suddenly, amid all the hubbub of the gale, there burst forth the wild scream of a terrified woman. I knew that it was my sister's voice. I sprang from my bed, wrapped a shawl around me, and rushed into the corridor. As I opened my door I seemed to hear a low whistle, such as my sister described, and a few moments later a clanging sound, as if a mass of metal had fallen. As I ran down the passage my sister's door was unlocked, and revolved slowly upon its hinges. I stared at it horror-stricken, not knowing what was about to issue from it. By the light of the corridor-lamp I saw my sister appear at the opening, her face blanched with terror, her hands groping for help, her whole figure swaying to and fro like that of a drunkard. I ran to her and threw my arms round her, but at that moment her knees seemed to give way and she fell to the ground. She writhed as one who is in terrible pain, and her limbs were dreadfully convulsed. At first I thought that she had not recognized me, but as I bent over her she suddenly shrieked out, in a voice which I shall never forget: 'Oh, my God! Helen! It was the band! The speckled band!' There was something else which she would fain have said, and she stabbed with her finger into the air in the direction of the doctor's room, but a fresh convulsion seized her and choked her words. I rushed out, calling loudly for my step-father, and I met him hastening from his room in his dressing-gown. When he reached my sister's side she was unconscious, and though he poured brandy down her throat and sent for medical aid from the village, all efforts were in vain, for she slowly sank and died without having recovered her consciousness. Such was the dreadful end of my beloved sister."

"One moment," said Holmes; "are you sure about this whistle and metallic sound? Could you swear to it?"

"That was what the county coroner asked me at the inquiry. It is my strong impression that I heard it, and yet, among the crash of the gale and the creaking of an old house, I may possibly have been deceived."

"Was your sister dressed?"

"No, she was in her night-dress. In her right hand was found the charred stump of a match, and in her left a match-box."

"Showing that she had struck a light and looked about her when the alarm took place. That is important. And what conclusions did the coroner come to?"

"He investigated the case with great care, for Dr. Roylott's conduct had long been notorious in the county, but he was unable to find any satisfactory cause of death. My evidence showed that the door had been fastened upon the inner side, and the windows were blocked by old-fashioned shutters with broad iron bars, which were secured every night. The walls were carefully sounded, and were shown to be quite solid all round, and the flooring was also thoroughly examined, with the same result. The chimney is wide, but is barred up by four large staples. It is certain, therefore, that my sister was quite alone when she met her end. Besides, there were no marks of any violence upon her."

"How about poison?"

"The doctors examined her for it, but without success."

"What do you think that this unfortunate lady died of, then?"

"It is my belief that she died of pure fear and nervous shock, though what it was that frightened her I cannot imagine."

"Were there gypsies in the plantation at the time?"

"Yes, there are nearly always some there."

"Ah, and what did you gather from this allusion to a band — a speckled band?"

"Sometimes I have thought that it was merely the wild talk of delirium, sometimes that it may have referred to some band of people, perhaps to these very gypsies in the plantation. I do not know whether the spotted handkerchiefs which so many of them wear over their heads might have suggested the strange adjective which she used."

Holmes shook his head like a man who is far from being satisfied.

"These are very deep waters," said he; "pray go on with your narrative."

"Two years have passed since then, and my life has been until lately lonelier than ever. A month ago, however, a dear friend, whom I have known for many years, has done me the honor to ask my hand in marriage. His name is Armitage — Percy Armitage — the second son of Mr. Armitage, of Crane Water, near Reading. My step-father has offered no opposition to the match, and we are to be married in the course of the spring. Two days ago some repairs were started in the west wing of the building, and my bedroom wall has been pierced, so that I have had to move into the chamber in which my sister died, and to sleep in the very bed in which she slept. Imagine, then, my thrill of terror when last night, as I lay awake, thinking over her terrible fate, I suddenly heard in the silence of the night the low whistle which had been the herald of her own death. I sprang up and lit the lamp, but nothing was to be seen in the room. I was too shaken to go to bed again, however, so I dressed, and as soon as it was daylight I slipped down, got a dog-cart at the 'Crown-Inn,' which is opposite, and drove to Leatherhead, from whence I have come on this morning with the one object of seeing you and asking your advice."

"You have done wisely," said my friend. "But have you told me all?"

"Yes, all."

"Miss Roylott, you have not. You are

screening your step-father.''

''Why, what do you mean?''

For answer Holmes pushed back the frill of black lace which fringed the hand that lay upon our visitor's knee. Five little livid spots, the marks of four fingers and a thumb, were printed upon the white wrist.

''You have been cruelly used,'' said Holmes.

The lady colored deeply and covered over her injured wrist. ''He is a hard man,'' she said, ''and perhaps he hardly knows his own strength.''

There was a long silence, during which Holmes leaned his chin upon his hands and stared into the crackling fire.

''This is a very deep business,'' he said, at last. ''There are a thousand details which I should desire to know before I decide upon our course of action. Yet we have not a moment to lose. If we were to come to Stoke Moran to-day, would it be possible for us to see over these rooms without the knowledge of your step-father?''

''As it happens, he spoke of coming into town to-day upon some most important business. It is probable that he will be away all day, and that there would be nothing to disturb you. We have a housekeeper now, but she is old and foolish, and I could easily get her out of the way.''

''Excellent. You are not averse to this trip,

Watson?"

"By no mean."

"Then we shall both come. What are you going to do yourself?"

"I have one or two things which I would wish to do now that I am in town. But I shall return by the twelve-o'clock train, so as to be there in time for your coming."

"And you may expect us early in the afternoon. I have myself some small business matters to attend to. Will you not wait and breakfast?"

"No, I must go. My heart is lightened already since I have confided my trouble to you. I shall look forward to seeing you again this afternoon." She dropped her thick black veil over her face and glided from the room.

"And what do you think of it all, Watson?" asked Sherlock Holmes, leaning back in his chair.

"It seems to me to be a most dark and sinister business."

"Dark enough and sinister enough."

"Yet if the lady is correct in saying that the flooring and walls are sound, and that the door, window, and chimney are impassible, then her sister must have been undoubtedly alone when she met her mysterious end."

"What becomes, then, of these nocturnal whistles, and what of the very peculiar words of the dying woman?"

"I cannot think."

"When you combine the ideas of whistles at night, the presence of a band of gypsies who are on intimate terms with this old doctor, the fact that we have every reason to believe that the doctor has an interest in preventing his step-daughter's marriage, the dying allusion to a band, and, finally, the fact that Miss Helen Stoner heard a metallic clang, which might have been caused by one of those metal bars which secured the shutters falling back into its place, I think that there is good ground to think that the mystery may be cleared along those lines."

"But what, then, did the gypsies do?"

"I cannot imagine."

"I see many objections to any such theory."

"And so do I. It is precisely for that reason that we are going to Stoke Moran this day. I want to see whether the objections are fatal, or if they may be explained away. But what in the name of the devil!"

The ejaculation had been drawn from my companion by the fact that our door had been suddenly dashed open, and that a huge man had framed himself in the aperture. His costume was a peculiar mixture of the professional and of the agricultural, having a black top-hat, a long frock-coat, and a pair of high gaiters, with a hunting-crop swinging in his hand. So tall was he that his hat actually brushed the cross-bar of the doorway, and his breadth seemed to span it across from side to side. A large face, seared with a thousand wrinkles, burned yellow with the sun, and marked with every evil passion, was turned from one to the other of us, while his deep-set, bile-shot eyes, and his high, thin, fleshless nose, gave him somewhat the resemblance to a fierce old bird of prey.

"Which of you is Holmes?" asked this apparition.

"My name, sir; but you have the advantage of me," said my companion, quietly.

"I am Dr. Grimesby Roylott, of Stoke Moran."

"Indeed, doctor," said Holmes, blandly. "Pray take a seat."

"I will do nothing of the kind. My step-daughter has been here. I have traced her. What has she been saying to you?"

"It is a little cold for the time of the year," said Holmes.

"What has she been saying to you?" screamed the old man, furiously.

"But I have heard that the crocuses promise well," continued my companion, imperturbably.

"Ha! You put me off, do you?" said our new visitor, taking a step forward and shaking his hunting-crop. "I know you, you scoundrel! I have heard of you before. You are Holmes, the meddler."

My friend smiled.

"Holmes, the busybody!"

His smile broadened.

"Holmes, the Scotland-yard Jack-in-office!"

Holmes chuckled heartily. "Your conversation is most entertaining," said he. "When you go out close the door, for there is a decided draught."

"I will go when I have said my say. Don't you dare to meddle with my affairs. I know that Miss Stoner has been here. I traced her! I am a dangerous man to fall foul of! See here." He stepped swiftly forward, seized the poker, and bent it into a curve with his huge brown hands.

"See that you keep yourself out of my grip," he snarled; and hurling the twisted poker into the fireplace, he strode out of the room.

"He seems a very amiable person," said Holmes, laughing. "I am not quite so bulky, but if he had remained I might have shown him that my grip was not much more feeble than his own." As he spoke he picked up the steel poker, and with a sudden effort straightened it out again.

"Fancy his having the insolence to confound me with the official detective force! This incident gives zest to our investigation, however, and I only trust that our little friend will not suffer from her imprudence in allowing this brute to trace her. And now, Watson, we shall order breakfast, and afterward I shall walk down to Doctors' Commons, where I hope to get some data which may help us in this matter."

It was nearly one o'clock when Sherlock Holmes returned from his excursion. He held in his hand a sheet of blue paper, scrawled over with notes and figures.

"I have seen the will of the deceased wife," said he. "To determine its exact meaning I have been obliged to work out the present prices of the investments with which it is concerned. The total income, which at the time of the wife's death was little short of £1100, is now, through the fall in agricultural prices, not more than £750. Each daughter can claim an income of £250, in case of marriage. It is evident, therefore, that if both girls had married, this beauty would have had a mere pittance, while even one of them would cripple him to a very serious extent. My morning's work has not been wasted, since it has proved that he has the very strongest motives for standing in the way of anything of the sort. And now, Watson, this is too serious for dawdling, especially as the old man is aware that we are interesting ourselves in his affairs; so if you are ready, we shall call a cab and drive to Waterloo. I should be very much obliged if you would slip your revolver into your pocket. An Eley's No. 2 is an excellent argument with gentlemen who can twist steel pokers into knots. That and a tooth-brush are, I think all that we need."

At Waterloo we were fortunate in catching a train for Leatherhead, where we hired a trap at the station inn, and drove for four or five miles through the lovely Surrey lanes. It was a perfect day, with a bright sun and a few fleecy clouds in the heavens. The trees and wayside hedges were just throwing out their first green shoots, and the air was full of the pleasant smell of the moist earth. To me at least there was a strange contrast between the sweet promise of the spring and this sinister quest upon which we were engaged. My companion sat in front of the trap, his arms folded, his hat pulled down over his eyes, and his chin sunk upon his breast, buried in the deepest thought. Suddenly, however, he started, tapped me on the shoulder, and pointed over the meadows.

"Look there!" said he.

A heavily timbered park stretched up in a gentle slope, thickening into a grove at the highest point. From amid the branches there jutted out the gray gables and high roof-tree of a very old mansion.

"Stoke Moran?" said he.

"Yes, sir, that be the house of Dr. Grimesby Roylott," remarked the driver.

"There is some building going on there," said Holmes; "that is where we are going."

"There's the village," said the driver,

pointing to a cluster of roofs some distance to the left; "but if you want to get to the house, you'll find it shorter to get over this stile, and so by the foot-path over the fields. There it is, where the lady is walking."

"And the lady, I fancy, is Miss Stoner," observed Holmes, shading his eyes. "Yes, I think we had better do as you suggest."

We got off, paid our fare, and the trap rattled back on its way to Leatherhead.

"I thought it as well," said Holmes, as we climbed the stile, "that this fellow should think we had come here as architects or on some definite business. It may stop his gossip. Good-afternoon, Miss Stoner. You see that we have been as good as our word."

Our client of the morning had hurried forward to meet us with a face which spoke her joy. "I have been waiting so eagerly for you!" she cried, shaking hands with us warmly. "All has turned out splendidly. Dr. Roylott has gone to town, and it is unlikely that he will be back before evening."

"We have had the pleasure of making the doctor's acquaintance," said Holmes, and in a few words he sketched out what had occurred. Miss Stoner turned white to the lips as she listened.

"Good heavens!" she cried, "he has followed me, then."

"So it appears."

"He is so cunning that I never know when

I am safe from him. What will he say when he returns?''

"He must guard himself, for he may find that there is some one more cunning than himself upon his track. You must lock yourself up from him to-night. If he is violent, we shall take you away to your aunt's at Harrow. Now, we must make the best use of our time, so kindly take us at once to the rooms which we are to examine."

The building was of gray, lichen-blotched stone, with a high central portion, and two curving wings, like the claws of a crab, thrown out on each side. In one of these wings the windows were broken, and blocked with wooden boards, while the roof was partly caved in, a picture of ruin. The central portion was in little better repair, but the right-hand block was comparatively modern, and the blinds in the windows, with the blue smoke curling up from the chimneys, showed that this was where the family resided. Some scaffolding had been erected against the end wall, and the stone-work had been broken into, but there were no signs of any workmen at the moment of our visit. Holmes walked slowly up and down the ill-trimmed lawn, and examined with deep attention the outsides of the windows.

"This, I take it, belongs to the room in which you used to sleep, the centre one to your sister's, and the one next to the main building to Dr. Roylott's chamber?"

"Exactly so. But I am now sleeping in the middle one."

"Pending the alterations, as I understand. By-the-way, there does not seem to be any very pressing need for repairs at that end wall."

"There were none. I believe that it was an excuse to move me from my room."

"Ah! that is suggestive. Now, on the other side of this narrow wing runs the corridor from which these three rooms open. There are windows in it, of course?"

"Yes, but very small ones. Too narrow for any one to pass through."

"As you both locked your doors at night, your rooms were unapproachable from that side. Now, would you have the kindness to go into your room and bar your shutters."

Miss Stoner did so, and Holmes, after a careful examination through the open window, endeavored in every way to force the shutter open, but without success. There was no slit through which a knife could be passed to raise the bar. Then with his lens he tested the hinges, but they were of solid iron, built firmly into the massive masonry. "Hum!" said he, scratching his chin in some perplexity; "my theory certainly presents some difficulties. No one could pass these shutters if they were bolted. Well, we shall see if the inside throws any light upon the matter."

A small side door led into the whitewashed

corridor from which the three bedrooms opened. Holmes refused to examine the third chamber, so we passed at once to the second, that in which Miss Stoner was now sleeping, and in which her sister had met with her fate. It was a homely little room, with a low ceiling and a gaping fireplace, after the fashion of old country-houses. A brown chest of drawers stood in one corner, a narrow white-counter-paned bed in another, and a dressing-table on the left-hand side of the window. These articles, with two small wicker-work chairs, made up all the furniture in the room, save for a square of Wilton carpet in the centre. The boards round and the panelling of the walls were of brown, worm-eaten oak, so old and discolored that it may have dated from the original building of the house. Holmes drew one of the chairs into a corner and sat silent, while his eyes travelled round and round and up and down, taking in every detail of the apartment.

"Where does that bell communicate with?" he asked, at last, pointing to a thick bell-rope which hung down beside the bed, the tassel actually lying upon the pillow.

"It goes to the housekeeper's room."

"It looks newer than the other things?"

"Yes, it was only put there a couple of years ago."

"Your sister asked for it, I suppose?"

"No, I never heard of her using it. We used

always to get what we wanted for ourselves.''

"Indeed, it seemed unnecessary to put so nice a bell-pull there. You will excuse me for a few minutes while I satisfy myself as to this floor." He threw himself down upon his face with his lens in his hand, and crawled swiftly backward and forward, examining minutely the cracks between the boards. Then he did the same with the woodwork with which the chamber was panelled. Finally he walked over to the bed, and spent some time in staring at it, and in running his eye up and down the wall. Finally he took the bell-rope in his hand and gave it a brisk tug.

"Why, it's a dummy," said he.

"Won't it ring?"

"No, it is not even attached to a wire. This is very interesting. You can see now that it is fastened to a hook just above where the little opening for the ventilator is."

"How very absurd! I never noticed that before."

"Very strange!" muttered Holmes, pulling at the rope. "There are one or two very singular points about this room. For example, what a fool a builder must be to open a ventilator into another room, when, with the same trouble, he might have communicated with the outside air!"

"That is also quite modern," said the lady.

"Done about the same time as the bell-rope?" remarked Holmes.

"Yes, there were several little changes carried out about that time."

"They seem to have been of a most interesting character — dummy bell-ropes, and ventilators which do not ventilate. With your permission, Miss Stoner, we shall now carry our researches into the inner apartment."

Dr. Grimesby Roylott's chamber was larger than that of his step-daughter, but was as plainly furnished. A camp-bed, a small wooden shelf full of books, mostly of a technical character, an arm-chair beside the bed, a plain wooden chair against the wall, a round table, and a large iron safe were the principal things which met the eye. Holmes walked slowly round and examined each and all of them with the keenest interest.

"What's in here?" he asked, tapping the safe.

"My step-father's business papers."

"Oh! you have seen inside, then?"

"Only once, some years ago. I remember that it was full of papers."

"There isn't a cat in it, for example?"

"No. What a strange idea!"

"Well, look at this!" He took up a small saucer of milk which stood on the top of it."

"No; we don't keep a cat. But there is a cheetah and a baboon."

"Ah, yes, of course! Well, a cheetah is just a big cat, and yet a saucer of milk does not go very far in satisfying its wants, I dare say.

There is one point which I should wish to determine." He squatted down in front of the wooden chair, and examined the seat of it with the greatest attention.

"Thank you. That is quite settled," said he, rising and putting his lens in his pocket. "Hello! Here is something interesting!"

The object which had caught his eye was a small dog-lash hung on one corner of the bed. The lash, however, was curled upon itself, and tied so as to make a loop of whip-cord.

"What do you make of that, Watson?"

"It's a common enough lash. But I don't know why it should be tied."

"That is not quite so common, is it? Ah, me! it's a wicked world, and when a clever man turns his brains to crime it is the worst of all. I think that I have seen enough now, Miss Stoner, and with your permission we shall walk out upon the lawn."

I had never seen my friend's face so grim or his brow so dark as it was when we turned from the scene of this investigation. We had walked several times up and down the lawn, neither Miss Stoner nor myself liking to break in upon his thoughts before he roused himself from his reverie.

"It is very essential, Miss Stoner," said he, "that you should absolutely follow my advice in every respect."

"I shall most certainly do so."

"The matter is too serious for any hesitation. Your life may depend upon your compliance."

"I assure you that I am in your hands."

"In the first place, both my friend and I must spend the night in your room."

Both Miss Stoner and I gazed at him in astonishment.

"Yes, it must be so. Let me explain. I believe that that is the village inn over there?"

"Yes, that is the 'Crown.' "

"Very good. Your windows would be visible from there?"

"Certainly."

"You must confine yourself to your room, on pretence of a headache, when your stepfather comes back. Then when you hear him retire for the night, you must open the shutters of your window, undo the hasp, put your lamp there as a signal to us, and then withdraw quietly with everything which you are likely to want into the room which you used to occupy. I have no doubt that, in spite of the repairs, you could manage there for one night."

"Oh yes, easily."

"The rest you will leave in our hands."

"But what will you do?"

"We shall spend the night in your room, and we shall investigate the cause of this noise which has disturbed you."

"I believe, Mr. Holmes, that you have already made up your mind," said Miss Stoner, laying her hand upon my companion's sleeve.

"Perhaps I have."

"Then, for pity's sake, tell me what was the cause of my sister's death."

"I should prefer to have clearer proofs before I speak."

"You can at least tell me whether my own thought is correct, and if she died from some sudden fright."

"No, I do not think so. I think that there was probably some more tangible cause. And now, Miss Stoner, we must leave you, for if Dr. Roylott returned and saw us, our journey would be in vain. Good-bye, and be brave, for if you will do what I have told you, you may rest assured that we shall soon drive away the dangers that threaten you."

Sherlock Holmes and I had no difficulty in engaging a bedroom and sitting-room at the "Crown Inn." They were on the upper floor, and from our window we could command a view of the avenue gate, and of the inhabited wing of Stoke Moran Manor-House. At dusk we saw Dr. Grimesby Roylott drive past, his huge form looming up beside the little figure of the lad who drove him. The boy had some slight difficulty in undoing the heavy iron gates, and we heard the hoarse roar of the doctor's voice, and saw the fury with which he shook his clinched fists at him. The trap drove on, and a few minutes later we saw a sudden light spring up among the trees as the lamp was lit in one of the sitting-rooms.

"Do you know, Watson," said Holmes, as we sat together in the gathering darkness, "I have really some scruples as to taking you tonight. There is a distinct element of danger."

"Can I be of assistance?"

"Your presence might be invaluable."

"Then I shall certainly come."

"It is very kind of you."

"You speak of danger. You have evidently seen more in these rooms than was visible to me."

"No, but I fancy that I may have deduced a little more. I imagine that you saw all that I did."

"I saw nothing remarkable save the bell-rope, and what purpose that could answer I confess is more than I can imagine."

"You saw the ventilator, too?"

"Yes, but I do not think that it is such a very unusual thing to have a small opening between two rooms. It was so small that a rat could hardly pass through."

"I knew that we should find a ventilator before ever we came to Stoke Moran."

"My dear Holmes!"

"Oh yes, I did. You remember in her statement she said that her sister could smell Dr. Roylott's cigar. Now, of course that suggested at once that there must be a communication between the two rooms. It could only be a small one, or it would have been remarked upon at the coroner's inquiry. I deduced a ventilator."

"But what harm can there be in that?"

"Well, there is at least a curious coincidence of dates. A ventilator is made, a cord is hung, and a lady who sleeps in the bed dies. Does not that strike you?"

"I cannot as yet see any connection."

"Did you observe anything very peculiar about that bed?"

"No."

"It was clamped to the floor. Did you ever see a bed fastened like that before?"

"I cannot say that I have."

"The lady could not move her bed. It must always be in the same relative position to the ventilator and to the rope — for so we may call it, since it was clearly never meant for a bell-pull."

"Holmes," I cried, "I seem to see dimly what you are hinting at! We are only just in time to prevent some subtle and horrible crime."

"Subtle enough and horrible enough. When a doctor does go wrong, he is the first of criminals. He has nerve and he has knowledge. Palmer and Pritchard were among the heads of their profession. This man strikes even deeper; but I think, Watson, that we shall be able to strike deeper still. But we shall have horrors enough before the night is over; for goodness' sake let us have a quiet pipe, and turn our minds for a few hours to something more cheerful."

About nine o'clock the light among the trees was extinguished, and all was dark in the direction of the Manor-House. Two hours passed slowly away, and then, suddenly, just at the stroke of eleven, a single bright light shone out in front of us.

"That is our signal," said Holmes, springing to his feet; "it comes from the middle window."

As we passed out he exchanged a few words with the landlord, explaining that we were going on a late visit to an acquaintance, and that it was possible that we might spend the night there. A moment later we were out on the dark road, a chill wind blowing in our faces, and one yellow light twinkling in front of us through the gloom to guide us on our sombre errand.

There was little difficulty in entering the grounds, for unrepaired breaches gaped in the old park wall. Making our way among the trees, we reached the lawn, crossed it, and were about to enter through the window, when out from a clump of laurel-bushes there darted what seemed to be a hideous and distorted child, who threw itself upon the grass with writhing limbs, and then ran swiftly across the lawn into the darkness.

"My God!" I whispered; "did you see it?"

Holmes was for the moment as startled as

I. His hand closed like a vise upon my wrist in his agitation. Then he broke into a low laugh, and put his lips to my ear.

"It is a nice household," he murmured. "That is the baboon."

I had forgotten the strange pets which the doctor affected. There was a cheetah, too; perhaps we might find it upon our shoulders at any moment. I confess that I felt easier in my mind when, after following Holmes's example and slipping off my shoes, I found myself inside the bedroom. My companion noiselessly closed the shutters, moved the lamp onto the table, and cast his eyes round the room. All was as we had seen it in the daytime. Then creeping up to me and making a trumpet of his hand, he whispered into my ear again so gently that it was all that I could do to distinguish the words:

"The least sound would be fatal to our plans."

I nodded to show that I had heard.

"We must sit without light. He would see it through the ventilator."

I nodded again.

"Do not go asleep; your very life may depend upon it. Have your pistol ready in case we should need it. I will sit on the side of the bed, and you in that chair."

I took out my revolver and laid it on the corner of the table.

Holmes had brought up a long, thin cane,

and this he placed upon the bed beside him. By it he laid the box of matches and the stump of a candle. Then he turned down the lamp, and we were left in darkness.

How shall I ever forget that dreadful vigil? I could not hear a sound, not even the drawing of a breath, and yet I knew that my companion sat open-eyed, within a few feet of me, in the same state of nervous tension in which I was myself. The shutters cut off the least ray of light, and we waited in absolute darkness. From outside came the occasional cry of a night-bird, and once at our very window a long-drawn, cat-like whine, which told us that the cheetah was indeed at liberty. Far away we could hear the deep tones of the parish clock, which boomed out every quarter of an hour. How long they seemed, those quarters! Twelve struck, and one and two and three, and still we sat waiting silently for whatever might befall.

Suddenly there was the momentary gleam of a light up in the direction of the ventilator, which vanished immediately, but was succeeded by a strong smell of burning oil and heated metal. Some one in the next room had lit a dark-lantern. I heard a gentle sound of movement, and then all was silent once more, though the smell grew stronger. For half an hour I sat with straining ears. Then suddenly another sound became audible — a very gentle, soothing sound, like that of a small jet of steam escaping continually from a kettle. The instant that we heard it, Holmes sprang from the bed, struck a match, and lashed furiously with his cane at the bell-pull.

"You see it, Watson?" he yelled. "You see it?"

But I saw nothing. At the moment when Holmes struck the light I heard a low, clear whistle, but the sudden glare flashing into my weary eyes made it impossible for me to tell what it was at which my friend lashed so savagely. I could, however, see that his face was deadly pale, and filled with horror and loathing.

He had ceased to strike, and was gazing up at the ventilator, when suddenly there broke from the silence of the night the most horrible cry to which I have ever listened. It swelled up louder and louder, a hoarse yell of pain and fear and anger all mingled in the one dreadful shriek. They say that away down in the village, and even in the distant parsonage, that cry raised the sleepers from their beds. It struck cold to our hearts, and I stood gazing at Holmes, and he at me, until the last echoes of it had died away into the silence from which it rose.

"What can it mean?" I gasped.

"It means that it is all over," Holmes answered. "And perhaps, after all, it is for the best. Take your pistol, and we will enter Dr. Roylott's room."

With a grave face he lit the lamp and led the way down the corridor. Twice he struck at the chamber door without any reply from within. Then he turned the handle and entered, I at his heels, with the cocked pistol in my hand.

It was a singular sight which met our eyes. On the table stood a dark-lantern with the shutter half open, throwing a brilliant beam of light upon the iron safe, the door of which was ajar. Beside this table, on the wooden chair, sat Dr. Grimesby Roylott, clad in a long gray dressing-gown, his bare ankles protruding beneath, and his feet thrust into red heelless Turkish slippers. Across his lap lay the short stock with the long lash which we had noticed during the day. His chin was cocked upward and his eyes were fixed in a dreadful, rigid stare at the corner of the ceiling. Round his brow he had a peculiar yellow band, with brownish speckles, which seemed to be bound tightly round his head. As we entered he made neither sound nor motion.

"The band! the speckled band!" whispered Holmes.

I took a step forward. In an instant his strange head-gear began to move, and there reared itself from among his hair the squat diamond-shaped head and puffed neck of a loathsome serpent.

"It is a swamp adder!" cried Holmes; "the deadliest snake in India. He has died within ten seconds of being bitten. Violence does, in truth, recoil upon the violent, and the schemer falls into the pit which he digs for another. Let us thrust this creature back into its den, and we can then remove Miss Stoner to some place of shelter, and let the county police know what has happened."

As he spoke he drew the dog-whip swiftly from the dead man's lap, and throwing the noose round the reptile's neck, he drew it from its horrid perch, and carrying it at arm's-length, threw it into the iron safe, which he closed upon it.

Such are the facts of the death of Dr. Grimesby Roylott, of Stoke Moran. It is not necessary that I should prolong a narrative which has already run to too great a length, by telling how we broke the sad news to the terrified girl, how we conveyed her by the morning train to the care of her good aunt at Harrow, of how the slow process of official inquiry came to the conclusion that the doctor met his fate while indiscreetly playing with a dangerous pet. The little which I had yet to learn of the case was told me by Sherlock Holmes as we travelled back next day.

"I had," said he, "come to an entirely erroneous conclusion, which shows, my dear Watson, how dangerous it always is to reason from insufficient data. The presence of the gypsies, and the use of the word 'band,' which was used by the poor girl, no doubt to explain the appearance which she had caught a hurried glimpse of by the light of her match, were sufficient to put me upon an entirely wrong scent. I can only claim the merit that I instantly reconsidered my position when, however, it became clear to me that whatever danger threatened an occupant of the room could not come either from the window or the door. My attention was speedily drawn, as I have already remarked to you, to this ventilator, and to the bell-rope which hung down to the bed. The discovery that this was a dummy, and that the bed was clamped to the floor, instantly gave rise to the suspicion that the rope was there as bridge for something passing through the hole and coming to the bed. The idea of a snake instantly occurred to me, and when I coupled it with my knowledge that the doctor was furnished with a supply of creatures from India, I felt that I was probably on the right track. The idea of using a form of poison which could not possibly be discovered by any chemical test was just such a one as would occur to a clever and ruthless man who had had an Eastern training. The rapidity with which such a poison would take effect would also, from his point of view, be an advantage. It would be a sharp-eyed coroner, indeed, who could distinguish the two little dark punctures which would show where the poison fangs had done their work. Then I thought of the whistle. Of course he must recall the snake before the morning light revealed it to the victim. He had trained it, probably by the use of the milk which we saw, to return to him when summoned. He would put it through this ventilator at the hour that he thought best, with the certainty that it would crawl down the rope and land on the bed. It might or might not bite the occupant, perhaps she might escape every night for a week, but sooner or later she must fall a victim.

"I had come to these conclusions before ever I had entered his room. An inspection of his chair showed me that he had been in the habit of standing on it, which of course would be necessary in order that he should reach the ventilator. The sight of the safe, the saucer of milk, and the loop of whip-cord were enough to finally dispel any doubts which may have remained. The metallic clang heard by Miss Stoner was obviously caused by her step-father hastily closing the door of his safe upon its terrible occupant. Having once made up my mind, you know the steps which I took in order to put the matter to the proof. I heard the creature hiss, as I have no doubt that you did also, and I instantly lit the light and attacked it."

"With the result of driving it through the ventilator."

"And also with the result of causing it to turn upon its master at the other side. Some of the blows of my cane came home, and roused its snakish temper, so that it flew upon the first person it saw. In this way I am no doubt indirectly responsible for Dr. Grimesby Roylott's death, and I cannot say that it is likely to weigh very heavily upon my conscience."

The Red-Headed League

Arthur Conan Doyle

I HAD called upon my friend, Mr. Sherlock Holmes, one day in the autumn of last year and found him in deep conversation with a very stout, florid-faced, elderly gentleman with fiery red hair. With an apology for my intrusion. I was about to withdraw when Holmes pulled me abruptly into the room and closed the door behind me.

"You could not possibly have come at a better time, my dear Watson," he said cordially.

"I was afraid that you were engaged."

"So I am. Very much so."

"Then I can wait in the next room."

"Not at all. This gentleman, Mr. Wilson, has been my partner and helper in many of my most successful cases, and I have no doubt that he will be of the utmost use to me in yours also."

The stout gentleman half rose from his chair and gave a bob of greeting, with a quick little questioning glance from his small, fat-encircled eyes.

"Try the settee," said Holmes, relapsing into his armchair and putting his finger-tips together, as was his custom when in judicial moods. "I know, my dear Watson, that you share my love of all that is bizarre and outside the conventions and humdrum routine of everyday life. You have shown your relish for it by the enthusiasm which has prompted you to chronicle, and, if you will excuse my saying so, somewhat to embellish so many of my own little adventures."

"Your cases have indeed been of the greatest interest to me," I observed.

"You will remember that I remarked the other day, just before we went into the very simple problem presented by Miss Mary Sutherland, that for strange effects and extraordinary combinations we must go to life itself, which is always far more daring than any effort of the imagination."

"A proposition which I took the liberty of doubting."

"You did, Doctor, but none the less you must come round to my view, for otherwise I shall keep on piling fact upon fact on you until your reason breaks down under them and acknowledges me to be right. Now, Mr. Jabez Wilson here has been good enough to call upon me this morning, and to begin a narrative which promises to be one of the most singular which I have listened to for some time. You have heard me remark that the strangest and most unique things are very often connected not with the larger but with the smaller crimes, and occasionally, indeed, where there is room for doubt whether any positive crime has been committed. As far as I have heard it is impossible for me to say whether the present case is an instance of crime or not, but the course of events is certainly among the most singular that I have ever listened to. Perhaps, Mr. Wilson, you would have the great kindness to recommence your narrative. I ask you not merely because my friend Dr. Watson has not heard the opening part but also because the peculiar nature of the story makes me anxious to have every possible detail from your lips. As a rule, when I have heard some slight indication of the course of events, I am able to guide myself by the thousands of other similar cases which occur to my memory. In the present instance I am forced to admit that the facts are, to the best of my belief, unique."

The portly client puffed out his chest with an appearance of some little pride and pulled a dirty and wrinkled newspaper from the inside of his great-coat. As he glanced down the advertisement column, with his head thrust forward and the paper flattened out upon his knee, I took a good look at the man and endeavoured, after the fashion of my companion, to read the indications which might be presented by his dress or appearance.

I did not gain very much, however, by my inspection. Our visitor bore every mark of being an average commonplace British tradesman, obese, pompous, and slow. He wore rather baggy gray shepherd's check trousers, a not over-clean black frock-coat, unbuttoned in the front, and a drab waistcoat with a heavy brassy Albert chain, and a square pierced bit of metal dangling down as an ornament. A frayed top-hat and a faded brown overcoat with a wrinkled velvet collar lay upon a chair beside him. Altogether, look as I would, there was nothing remarkable about the man save his blazing red head, and the expression of extreme chagrin and discontent upon his features.

Sherlock Holmes's quick eye took in my occupation, and he shook his head with a smile as he noticed my questioning glances. "Beyond the obvious facts that he has at some time done manual labour, that he takes snuff, that he is a Freemason, that he has been in China, and that he has done a considerable amount of writing lately, I can deduce nothing else."

Mr. Jabez Wilson started up in his chair, with his forefinger upon the paper, but his eyes upon my companion.

"How, in the name of good-fortune, did you know all that, Mr. Holmes?" he asked. "How did you know, for example, that I did manual labour? It's as true as gospel, for I began as a ship's carpenter."

"Your hands, my dear sir. Your right hand is quite a size larger than your left. You have worked with it, and the muscles are more developed."

"Well, the snuff, then, and the Freemasonry?"

"I won't insult your intelligence by telling you how I read that, especially as, rather against the strict rules of your order, you use an arc-and-compass breastpin."

"Ah, of course, I forgot that. But the writing?"

"What else can be indicated by that right cuff so very shiny for five inches, and the left one with the smooth patch near the elbow where you rest it upon the desk?"

"Well, but China?"

"The fish that you have tattooed immediately above your right wrist could only have been done in China. I have made a small study of tattoo marks and have even contributed to the literature of the subject. That trick of staining the fishes' scales a delicate pink is quite peculiar to China. When, in addition, I see a Chinese coin hanging from your watch-chain, the matter becomes even more simple."

Mr. Jabez Wilson laughed heavily. "Well, I never!" said he. "I thought at first that you had done something clever, but I see that there was nothing in it, after all."

"I begin to think, Watson," said Holmes, "that I make a mistake in explaining. *'Omne ignotum pro magnifico,'* you know, and my poor little reputation, such as it is, will suffer shipwreck if I am so candid. Can you not find the advertisement, Mr. Wilson?"

"Yes, I have got it now," he answered with his thick red finger planted halfway down the column. "Here it is. This is what began it all. You just read it for yourself, sir."

I took the paper from him and read as follows:

> TO THE RED-HEADED LEAGUE:
>
> On account of the bequest of the late Ezekiah Hopkins, of Lebanon, Pennsylvania, U.S.A., there is now another vacancy open which entitles a member of the League to a salary of £4 a week for purely nominal services. All red-headed men who are sound in body and mind, and above the age of twenty-one years, are eligible. Apply in person on Monday, at eleven o'clock, to Duncan Ross, at the offices of the League, 7 Pope's Court, Fleet Street.

"What on earth does this mean?" I ejaculated after I had twice read over the extraordinary announcement.

Holmes chuckled and wriggled in his chair, as was his habit when in high spirits. "It is a little off the beaten track, isn't it?" said he. "And now, Mr. Wilson, off you go at scratch and tell us all about yourself, your household, and the effect which this advertisement had upon your fortunes. You will first make a note, Doctor, of the paper and the date."

"It is *The Morning Chronicle* of April 27, 1890. Just two months ago."

"Very good. Now, Mr. Wilson?"

"Well, it is just as I have been telling you, Mr. Sherlock Holmes," said Jabez Wilson, mopping his forehead; "I have a small pawnbroker's business at Coburg Square, near the City. It's not a very large affair, and of late years it has not done more than just give me a living. I used to be able to keep two assistants, but now I only keep one; and I would have a job to pay him but that he is willing to come for half wages so as to learn the business."

"What is the name of this obliging youth?" asked Sherlock Holmes.

"His name is Vincent Spaulding, and he's not such a youth, either. It's hard to say his age. I should not wish a smarter assistant, Mr. Holmes; and I know very well that he could better himself and earn twice what I am able to give him. But, after all, if he is satisfied, why should I put ideas in his head?"

"Why, indeed? You seem most fortunate in having an employee who comes under the full market price. It is not a common experience among employers in this age. I don't know that your assistant is not as remarkable as your advertisement."

"Oh, he has his faults, too," said Mr. Wilson. "Never was such a fellow for photography. Snapping away with a camera when he ought to be improving his mind, and then diving down into the cellar like a rabbit into its hole to develop his pictures. That is his main fault, but on the whole he's a good worker. There's no vice in him."

"He is still with you, I presume?"

"Yes, sir. He and a girl of fourteen, who does a bit of simple cooking and keeps the place clean — that's all I have in the house, for I am a widower and never had any family. We live very quietly, sir, the three of us; and we keep a roof over our heads and pay our debts, if we do nothing more.

"The first thing that put us out was that advertisement. Spaulding, he came down into the office just this day eight weeks, with this very paper in his hand, and he says:

" 'I wish to the Lord, Mr. Wilson, that I was a red-headed man.'

" 'Why that?' I asks.

" 'Why,' says he, 'here's another vacancy on the League of the Red-headed Men. It's worth quite a little fortune to any man who gets it, and I understand that there are more vacancies than there are men, so that the trustees are at their wits' end what to do with the money. If my hair would only change colour, here's a nice little crib all ready for me to step into.'

" 'Why, what is it, then?' I asked. You see, Mr. Holmes, I am a very stay-at-home man, and as my business came to me instead of my having to go to it, I was often weeks on end without putting my foot over the door-mat. In that way I didn't know much of what was going on outside, and I was always glad of a bit of news.

" 'Have you never heard of the League of the Red-headed men?' he asked with his eyes open.

" 'Never.'

" 'Why, I wonder at that, for you are eligible yourself for one of the vacancies.'

" 'And what are they worth?' I asked.

" 'Oh, merely a couple of hundred a year, but the work is slight, and it need not interfere very much with one's other occupations.'

"Well, you can easily think that that made me prick up my ears, for the business has not been over-good for some years, and an extra couple of hundred would have been very handy.

" 'Tell me all about it,' said I.

" 'Well,' said he, showing me the advertisement, 'you can see for yourself that the League has a vacancy, and there is the address where you should apply for particulars. As far as I can make out, the League was founded by an American millionaire, Ezekiah Hopkins, who was very peculiar in his ways. He was himself red-headed, and he had a great sympathy for all red-headed men; so when he died it was found that he had left his enormous fortune in the hands of trustees, with instructions to apply the interest to the providing of easy berths to men whose hair is of that colour. From all I hear it is splendid pay and very little to do.'

"'But,' said I, 'there would be millions of red-headed men who would apply.'

"'Not so many as you might think,' he answered. 'You see it is really confined to Londoners, and to grown men. This American had started from London when he was young, and he wanted to do the old town a good turn. Then, again, I have heard it is no use your applying if your hair is light red, or dark red, or anything but real bright, blazing, fiery red. Now, if you cared to apply, Mr. Wilson, you would just walk in; but perhaps it would hardly be worth your while to put yourself out of the way for the sake of a few hundred pounds.'

"Now, it is a fact, gentlemen, as you may see for yourselves, that my hair is of a very full and rich tint, so that it seemed to me that if there was to be any competition in the matter I stood as good a chance as any man that I had ever met. Vincent Spaulding seemed to know so much about it that I thought he might prove useful, so I just ordered him to put up the shutters for the day and to come right away with me. He was very willing to have a holiday, so we shut the business up and started off for the address that was given us in the advertisement.

"I never hope to see such a sight as that again, Mr. Holmes. From north, south, east, and west every man who had a shade of red in his hair had tramped into the city to answer the advertisement. Fleet Street was choked with red-headed folk, and Pope's Court looked like a coster's orange barrow. I should not have thought there were so many in the whole country as were brought together by that single advertisement. Every shade of colour they were — straw, lemon, orange, brick, Irish-setter, liver, clay; but, as Spaulding said, there were not many who had the real vivid flame-coloured tint. When I saw how many were waiting, I would have given it up in despair; but Spaulding would not hear of it. How he did it I could not imagine, but he pushed and pulled and butted until he got me through the crowd, and right up to the steps which led to the office. There was a double stream upon the stair, some going up in hope, and some coming back dejected; but we wedged in as well as we could and soon found ourselves in the office."

"Your experience has been a most entertaining one," remarked Holmes as his client paused and refreshed his memory with a huge pinch of snuff. "Pray continue your very interesting statement."

"There was nothing in the office but a couple of wooden chairs and a deal table, behind which sat a small man with a head that was even redder than mine. He said a few words to each candidate as he came up, and then he always managed to find some fault in them which would disqualify them. Getting a vacancy did not seem to be such a very easy matter, after all. However, when our turn came the little man was much more favourable to me than to any of the others, and he closed the door as we entered, so that he might have a private word with us.

" 'This is Mr. Jabez Wilson,' said my assistant, 'and he is willing to fill a vacancy in the League.'

" 'And he is admirably suited for it,' the other answered. 'He has every requirement. I cannot recall when I have seen anything so fine.' He took a step backward, cocked his head on one side, and gazed at my hair until I felt quite bashful. Then suddenly he plunged forward, wrung my hand, and congratulated me warmly on my success.

" 'It would be injustice to hesitate,' said he. 'You will, however, I am sure, excuse me for taking an obvious precaution.' With that he seized my hair in both his hands, and tugged until I yelled with the pain. 'There is water in your eyes,' said he as he released me. 'I perceive that all is as it should be. But we have to be careful, for we have twice been deceived by wigs and once by paint. I could tell you tales of cobbler's wax which would disgust you with human nature.' He stepped over to the window and shouted through it at the top of his voice that the vacancy was filled. A groan of disappointment came up from below, and the folk all trooped away in different directions until there was not a red head to be seen except my own and that of the manager.

" 'My name, said he, 'is Mr. Duncan Ross, and I am myself one of the pensioners upon the fund left by our noble benefactor. Are you a married man, Mr. Wilson? Have you a family?'

"I answered that I had not.

"His face fell immediately.

" 'Dear me!' he said gravely, 'that is very serious indeed! I am sorry to hear you say that. The fund was, of course, for the propagation and spread of the red-heads as well as for their maintenance. It is exceedingly unfortunate that you should be a bachelor.'

"My face lengthened at this, Mr. Holmes, for I thought that I was not to have the vacancy after all; but after thinking it over for a few minutes he said that it would be all right.

" 'In the case of another,' said he, 'the objection might be fatal, but we must stretch a point in favour of a man with such a head of hair as yours. When shall you be able to enter upon your new duties?'

" 'Well, it is a little awkward, for I have a business already,' said I.

" 'Oh, never mind about that, Mr. Wilson!'

said Vincent Spaulding. 'I should be able to look after that for you.'

"'What would be the hours?' I asked.

"'Ten to two.'

"Now a pawnbroker's business is mostly done of an evening, Mr. Holmes, especially Thursday and Friday evening, which is just before pay-day; so it would suit me very well to earn a little in the mornings. Besides, I knew that my assistant was a good man, and that he would see to anything that turned up.

"'That would suit me very well,' said I. 'And the pay?'

"'Is £4 a week.'

"'And the work?'

"'Is purely nominal.'

"'What do you call purely nominal?'

"'Well, you have to be in the office, or at least in the building, the whole time. If you leave, you forfeit your whole position forever. The will is very clear upon that point. You don't comply with the conditions if you budge from the office during that time.'

"'It's only four hours a day, and I should not think of leaving,' said I.

"'No excuse will avail,' said Mr. Duncan Ross; 'neither sickness nor business nor anything else. There you must stay, or you lose your billet.'

"'And the work?'

"'Is to copy out the Encyclopædia Britannica. There is the first volume of it in that press. You must find your own ink, pens, and blotting-paper, but we provide this table and chair. Will you be ready tomorrow?'

" 'Certainly,' I answered.

" 'Then, good-bye, Mr. Jabez Wilson, and let me congratulate you once more on the important position which you have been fortunate enough to gain.' He bowed me out of the room, and I went home with my assistant, hardly knowing what to say or do, I was so pleased at my own good fortune.

"Well, I thought over the matter all day, and by evening I was in low spirits again; for I had quite persuaded myself that the whole affair must be some great hoax or fraud, though what its object might be I could not imagine. It seemed altogether past belief that anyone could make such a will, or that they would pay such a sum for doing anything so simple as copying out the Encyclopædia Britannica. Vincent Spaulding did what he could to cheer me up, but by bedtime I had reasoned myself out of the whole thing. However, in the morning I determined to have a look at it anyhow, so I bought a penny bottle of ink, and with a quill-pen, and seven sheets of foolscap paper, I started off for Pope's Court.

"Well, to my surprise and delight, everything was as right as possible. The table was set out ready for me, and Mr. Duncan Ross was there to see that I got fairly to work. He started me off upon the letter A, and then he left me; but he would drop in from time to time to see that all was right with me. At two o'clock he bade me good-day, complimented me upon the amount that I had written, and locked the door of the office after me.

"This went on day after day, Mr. Holmes, and on Saturday the manager came in and planked down four golden sovereigns for my week's work. It was the same next week, and the same the week after. Every morning I was there at ten, and every afternoon I left at two. By degrees Mr. Duncan Ross took to coming in only once of a morning, and then, after a time, he did not come in at all. Still, of course, I never dared to leave the room for an instant, for I was not sure when he might come, and the billet was such a good one, and suited me so well, that I would not risk the loss of it.

"Eight weeks passed away like this, and I had written about Abbots and Archery and Armour and Architecture and Attica, and hoped with diligence that I might get to the B's before very long. It cost me something in foolscap, and I had pretty nearly filled a shelf with my writings. And then suddenly the whole business came to an end."

"To an end?"

"Yes, sir. And no later than this morning. I went to my work as usual at ten o'clock, but the door was shut and locked, with a little square of card-board hammered on to the middle of the panel with a tack. Here it is, and you can read for yourself.''

He held up a piece of white card-board about the size of a sheet of note-paper. It read in this fashion:

THE RED-HEADED LEAGUE
IS
DISSOLVED.
OCTOBER 9, 1890.

Sherlock Holmes and I surveyed this curt announcement and the rueful face behind it, until the comical side of the affair was so completely overtopped every other consideration that we both burst out into a roar of laughter.

''I cannot see that there is anything very funny,'' cried our client, flushing up to the roots of his flaming head. ''If you can do nothing better than laugh at me, I can go elsewhere.''

''No, no,'' cried Holmes, shoving him back into the chair from which he had half risen. ''I really wouldn't miss your case for the world. It is most refreshingly unusual. But there is, if you will excuse my saying so, something just a little funny about it. Pray what steps did you take when you found the card upon the door?''

''I was staggered, sir. I did not know what to do. Then I called at the offices round, but none of them seemed to know anything about it. Finally, I went to the landlord, who is an accountant living on the ground-floor, and I asked him if he could tell me what had become of the Red-headed League. He said that he had never heard of any such body. Then I asked him who Mr. Duncan Ross was. He answered that the name was new to him.

" 'Well,' said I, 'the gentlemen at No. 4.'

" 'What, the red-headed man?'

" 'Yes.'

" 'Oh,' said he, 'his name was William Morris. He was a solicitor and was using my room as a temporary convenience until his new premises were ready. He moved out yesterday.'

" 'Where could I find him?'

" 'Oh, at his new offices. He did tell me the address. Yes, 17 King Edward Street, near St. Paul's.'

"I started off, Mr. Holmes, but when I got to that address it was a manufactory of artificial knee-caps, and no one in it had every heard of either Mr. William Morris or Mr. Duncan Ross."

"And what did you do then?" asked Holmes.

"I went home to Saxe-Coburg Square, and I took the advice of my assistant. But he could not help me in any way. He could only say that if I waited I should hear by post. But that was not quite good enough, Mr. Holmes. I did not wish to lose such a place without a struggle, so, as I had heard that you were good enough to give advice to poor folk who were in need of it, I came right away to you."

"And you did very wisely," said Holmes. "Your case is an exceedingly remarkable one, and I shall be happy to look into it. From what you have told me I think that it is possible that graver issues hang from it than might at first sight appear."

"Grave enough!" said Mr. Jabez Wilson. "Why, I have lost four pounds a week."

"As far as you are personally concerned," remarked Holmes, "I do not see that you have any grievance against this extraordinary league. On the contrary, you are, as I understand, richer by some £30, to say nothing of the minute knowledge which you have gained on every subject which comes under the letter A. You have lost nothing by them."

"No, sir. But I want to find out about them, and who they are, and what their object was in playing this prank — if it was a prank — upon me. It was a pretty expensive joke for them, for it cost them two and thirty pounds."

"We shall endeavour to clear up these points for you. And, first, one or two questions, Mr. Wilson. This assistant of yours who first called your attention to the advertisement — how long had he been with you?"

"About a month then."

"How did he come?"

"In answer to an advertisement."

"Was he the only applicant?"

"No, I had a dozen."

"Why did you pick him?"

"Because he was handy and would come cheap."

"At half-wages, in fact."

"Yes."

"What is he like, this Vincent Spaulding?"

"Small, stout-built, very quick in his ways, no hair on his face, though he's not short of thirty. Has a white splash of acid upon his forehead."

Holmes sat up in his chair in considerable excitement. "I thought as much," said he. "Have you ever observed that his ears are pierced for earrings?"

"Yes, sir. He told me that a gypsy had done it for him when he was a lad."

"Hum!" said Holmes, sinking back in deep thought. "He is still with you?"

"Oh, yes, sir; I have only just left him."

"And has your business been attended to in your absence?"

"Nothing to complain of, sir. There's never very much to do of a morning."

"That will do, Mr. Wilson. I shall be happy to give you an opinion upon the subject in the course of a day or two. Today is Saturday, and I hope that by Monday we may come to a conclusion."

"Well, Watson," said Holmes when our visitor had left us, "what do you make of it all?"

"I make nothing of it," I answered frankly. "It is a most mysterious business."

"As a rule," said Holmes, "the more bizarre a thing is the less mysterious it proves to be. It is your commonplace, featureless crimes which are really puzzling, just as a commonplace face is the most difficult to identify. But I must be prompt over this matter."

"What are you going to do, then?" I asked.

"To smoke," he answered. "It is quite a three-pipe problem, and I beg that you won't speak to me for fifty minutes." He curled himself up in his chair, with his thin knees drawn up to his hawk-like nose, and there he sat with his eyes closed and his black clay pipe thrusting out like the bill of some strange bird. I had come to the conclusion that he had dropped asleep, and indeed was nodding myself, when he suddenly sprang out of his chair with the gesture of a man who has made up his mind and put his pipe down upon the mantelpiece.

"Sarasate plays at the St. James's Hall this afternoon," he remarked.

"What do you think, Watson? Could your patients spare you for a few hours?"

"I have nothing to do today. My practice is never very absorbing."

"Then put on your hat and come. I am going through the City first, and we can have some lunch on the way. I observe that there is a good deal of German music on the programme, which is rather more to my taste than Italian or French. It is introspective, and I want to introspect. Come along!"

We travelled by the Underground as far as Aldersgate; and a short walk took us to Saxe-Coburg Square, the scene of a singular story which we had listened to in the morning. It was a poky, little, shabby-genteel place, where four lines of dingy two-storied brick houses looked out into a small railed-in enclosure, where a lawn of weedy grass and a few clumps of faded laurel-bushes made a hard fight against a smoke-laden and uncongenial atmosphere. Three gilt balls and a brown board with "JABEZ WILSON" in white letters, upon a corner house, announced the place where our red-headed client carried on his business. Sherlock Holmes stopped in front of it with his head on one side and looked it all over, with his eyes shining brightly between puckered lids. Then he walked slowly up the street, and then down again to the corner, still looking keenly at the houses. Finally he returned to the pawnbroker's, and, having thumped vigorously upon the pavement with his stick two or three times, he went up to the door and knocked. It was instantly opened by a bright-looking, clean-shaven young fellow, who asked him to step in.

"Thank you," said Holmes, "I only wished to ask you how you would go from here to the Strand."

"Third right, fourth left," answered the

assistant promptly, closing the door.

"Smart fellow, that," observed Holmes as we walked away. "He is, in my judgment, the fourth smartest man in London, and for daring I am not sure that he has not a claim to be third. I have known something of him before."

"Evidently," said I, "Mr. Wilson's assistant counts for a good deal in this mystery of the Red-headed League. I am sure that you inquired your way merely in order that you might see him."

"Not him."

"What then?"

"The knees of his trousers."

"And what did you see?"

"What I expected to see."

"Why did you beat the pavement?"

"My dear doctor, this is a time for observation, not for talk. We are spies in an enemy's country. We know something of Saxe-Coburg Square. Let us now explore the parts which lie behind it."

The road in which we found ourselves as we turned round the corner from the retired Saxe-Coburg Square presented as great a contrast to it as the front of a picture does to the back. It was one of the main arteries which conveyed the traffic of the City to the north and west. The roadway was blocked with the immense stream of commerce flowing in a double tide inward and outward, while the foot-paths were black with the hurrying swarm of pedestrians.

It was difficult to realize as we looked at the line of fine shops and stately business premises that they really abutted on the other side upon the faded and stagnant square which we had just quitted.

"Let me see," said Holmes, standing at the corner and glancing along the line, "I should like just to remember the order of the houses here. It is a hobby of mine to have an exact knowledge of London. There is Mortimer's, the tobacconist, the little newspaper shop, the Coburg branch of the City and Suburban Bank, the Vegetarian Restaurant, and McFarlane's carriage-building depot. That carries us right on to the other block. And now, Doctor, we've done our work, so it's time we had some play. A sandwich and a cup of coffee, and then off to violin-land, where all is sweetness and delicacy and harmony, and there are no red-headed clients to vex us with their conundrums."

My friend was an enthusiastic musician, being himself not only a very capable performer but a composer of no ordinary merit. All the afternoon he sat in the stalls wrapped in the most perfect happiness, gently waving his long, thin fingers in time to the music, while his gently smiling face and his languid, dreamy eyes were as unlike those of Holmes, the sleuth-hound, Holmes the relentless, keen-witted, ready-handed criminal agent, as it was possible to conceive. In his singular character the dual nature alternately assserted itself, and his extreme exactness and astuteness represented, as I have often thought, the reaction against the poetic and contemplative mood which occasionally predominated in him. The swing of his nature took him from extreme languor to devouring energy; and, as I knew well, he was never so truly formidable as when, for days on end, he had been lounging in his armchair amid his improvisations and his black-letter editions. Then it was that the lust of the chase would suddenly come upon him, and that his brilliant reasoning power would rise to the level of intuition, until those who were unacquainted with his methods would look askance at him as on a man whose knowledge was not that of other mortals. When I saw him that afternoon so enwrapped in the music at St. James's Hall I felt that an evil time might be coming upon those whom he had set himself to hunt down.

"You want to go home, no doubt, Doctor," he remarked as we emerged.

"Yes, it would be as well."

"And I have some business to do which will take some hours. This business at Coburg Square is serious."

"Why serious?"

"A considerable crime is in contemplation. I have every reason to believe that we shall be in time to stop it. But today being Saturday rather complicates matters. I shall want your help tonight."

"At what time?"

"Ten will be early enough."

"I shall be at Baker Street at ten."

"Very well. And, I say, Doctor, there may be some little danger, so kindly put your army revolver in your pocket." He waved his hand, turned on his heel, and disappeared in an instant among the crowd.

I trust that I am not more dense than my neighbours, but I was always oppressed with a sense of my own stupidity in my dealings with Sherlock Holmes. Here I had heard what he had heard, I had seen what he had seen, and yet from his words it was evident that he saw clearly not only what had happened but what was about to happen, while to me the whole business was still confused and grotesque. As I drove home to my house in Kensington I thought over it all, from the extraordinary story of the red-headed copier of the Encyclopædia down to the visit to Saxe-Coburg Square, and the ominous words with which he had parted from me. What was this nocturnal expedition, and why should I go armed? Where were we going, and what were we to do? I had the hint from Holmes that this smooth-faced pawnbroker's assistant was a formidable man — a man who might play a deep game. I tried to puzzle it out, but gave it up in despair and set the matter aside until night should bring an explanation.

It was a quarter-past nine when I started from home and made my way across the Park, and so through Oxford Street to Baker Street. Two hansoms were standing at the door, and as I entered the passage I heard the sound of voices from above. On entering his room I found Holmes in animated conversation with two men, one of whom I recognized as Peter Jones, the official police agent, while the other was a long, thin, sad-faced man, with a very shiny hat and oppressively respectable frock-coat.

"Ha! our party is complete," said Holmes, buttoning up his pea-jacket and taking his heavy hunting crop from the rack. "Watson, I think you know Mr. Jones, of Scotland Yard? Let me introduce you to Mr. Merryweather, who is to be our companion in tonight's adventure."

"We're hunting in couples again, Doctor, you see," said Jones in his consequential way. "Our friend here is a wonderful man for starting a chase. All he wants is an old dog to help him to do the running down."

"I hope a wild goose may not prove to be the end of our chase," observed Mr. Merryweather gloomily.

"You may place considerable confidence in Mr. Holmes, sir," said the police agent loftily. "He has his own little methods, which are, if he won't mind my saying so, just a little too theoretical and fantastic, but he has the makings of a detective in him. It is not too much to say that once or twice, as in that business of the Sholto murder and the Agra treasure, he has been more nearly correct than the official force.''

''Oh, if you say so, Mr. Jones, it is all right,'' said the stranger with deference. ''Still, I confess that I miss my rubber. It is the first Sunday night for seven-and-twenty years that I have not had my rubber.''

''I think you will find,'' said Sherlock Holmes, ''that you will play for a higher stake tonight than you have ever done yet, and that the play will be more exciting. For you, Mr. Merryweather, the stake will be some £30,000; and for you, Jones, it will be the man upon whom you wish to lay your hands.''

''John Clay, the murderer, thief, smasher, and forger. He's a young man, Mr. Merryweather, but he is at the head of his profession, and I would rather have my bracelets on him than on any criminal in London. He's a remarkable man, is young John Clay. His grandfather was a royal duke, and he himself has been to Eton and Oxford. His brain is as cunning as his fingers, and though we meet signs of him at every turn, we never know where to find the man himself. He'll crack a crib in Scotland one week, and be raising money to build an orphanage in Cornwall the next. I've been on his track for years and have never set eyes on him yet.''

"I hope that I may have the pleasure of introducing you tonight. I've had one or two little turns also with Mr. John Clay, and I agree with you that he is at the head of his profession. It is past ten, however, and quite time that we started. If you two will take the first hansom, Watson and I will follow in the second."

Sherlock Holmes was not very communicative during the long drive and lay back in the cab humming the tunes which he had heard in the afternoon. We rattled through an endless labyrinth of gas-lit streets until we emerged into Farringdon Street.

"We are close there now," my friend remarked. "This fellow Merryweather is a bank director, and personally interested in the matter. I thought it as well to have Jones with us also. He is not a bad fellow, though an absolute imbecile in his profession. He has one positive virtue. He is as brave as a bulldog and as tenacious as a lobster if he gets his claws upon anyone. Here we are, and they are waiting for us."

We had reached the same crowded thoroughfare in which we had found ourselves in the morning. Our cabs were dismissed, and, following the guidance of Mr. Merryweather, we passed down a narrow passage and through a side door, which he opened for us. Within there was a small corridor, which ended in a very massive iron gate. This also was opened, and led down a flight of winding stone steps, which terminated at another formidable gate. Mr. Merryweather stopped to light a lantern, and then conducted us down a dark, earth-smelling passage, and so, after opening a third door, into a huge vault or cellar, which was piled all round with crates and massive boxes.

"You are not very vulnerable from above," Holmes remarked as he held up the lantern and gazed about him.

"Nor from below," said Mr. Merryweather, striking his stick upon the flags which lined the floor. "Why, dear me, it sounds quite hollow!" he remarked, looking up in surprise.

"I must really ask you to be a little more quiet!" said Holmes severely. "You have already imperilled the whole success of our expedition. Might I beg that you would have the goodness to sit down upon one of those boxes, and not to interfere?"

The solemn Mr. Merryweather perched himself upon a crate, with a very injured expression upon his face, while Holmes fell upon his knees upon the floor and, with the lantern and a magnifying lens, began to examine minutely the cracks between the stones. A few seconds sufficed to satisfy him, for he sprang to his feet again and put his glass in his pocket.

"We have at least an hour before us," he remarked, "for they can hardly take any steps until the good pawnbroker is safely in bed. Then they will not lose a minute, for the sooner they do their work the longer time they will have for their escape. We are at present, Doctor — as no doubt you have divined — in the cellar of the City branch of one of the principal London banks. Mr. Merryweather is the chairman of directors, and he will explain to you that there are reasons why the more daring criminals of London should take a considerable interest in this cellar at present."

"It is our French gold," whispered the director. "We have had several warnings that an attempt might be made upon it."

"Your French gold?"

"Yes. We had occasion some months ago to strengthen our resources, and borrowed for that purpose 30,000 napoleons from the Bank of France. It has become known that we have never had occasion to unpack the money, and that it is still lying in our cellar. The crate upon which I sit contains 2,000 napoleons packed between layers of lead foil. Our reserve of bullion is much larger at present than is usually kept in a single branch office, and the directors have had misgivings upon the subject."

"Which were very well justified," observed Holmes. "And now it is time we arranged our little plans. I expect that within an hour matters will come to a head. In the meantime, Mr. Merryweather, we must put the screen over that dark lantern."

"And sit in the dark?"

"I am afraid so. I had brought a pack of cards in my pocket, and I thought that, as we were a *partie carrée,* you might have your rubber after all. But I see that the enemy's preparations have gone so far that we cannot risk the presence of a light. And, first of all, we must choose our positions. These are daring men, and though we shall take them at a disadvantage, they may do us harm unless we are careful. I shall stand behind this crate, and do you conceal yourselves behind those. Then, when I flash a light upon them, close in swiftly. If they fire, Watson, have no compunction about shooting them down."

I placed my revolver, cocked, upon the top of the wooden case behind which I crouched. Holmes shot the slide across the front of his lantern and left us in pitch darkness — such an absolute darkness as I have never before experienced. The smell of hot metal remained to assure us that the light was still there, ready to flash out at a moment's notice. To me, with my nerves worked up to a pitch of expectancy, there was something depressing and subduing in the sudden gloom, and in the cold dank air of the vault.

"They have but one retreat," whispered Holmes. "That is back through the house into Saxe-Coburg Square. I hope that you have done what I asked you, Jones?"

"I have an inspector and two officers waiting at the front door."

"Then we have stopped all the holes. And now we must be silent and wait."

What a time it seemed! From comparing notes afterwards it was but an hour and a quarter, yet it appeared to me that the night must have almost gone, and the dawn be breaking above us. My limbs were weary and stiff, for I feared to change my position; yet my nerves were worked up to the highest pitch of tension, and my hearing was so acute that I could not only hear the gentle breathing of my companions, but I could distinguish the deeper, heavier in-breath of the bulky Jones from the thin, sighing note of the bank director. From my position I could look over the case in the direction of the floor. Suddenly my eyes caught the glint of a light.

At first it was but a lurid spark upon the stone pavement. Then it lengthened out until it became a yellow line, and then, without any warning or sound, a gash seemed to open and a hand appeared; a white, almost womanly hand, which felt about in the centre of the little area of light. For a minute or more the hand, with its writhing fingers, protruded out of the floor. Then it was withdrawn as suddenly as it appeared, and all was dark again save the single lurid spark which marked a chink between the stones.

Its disappearance, however, was but momentary. With a rending, tearing sound, one of the broad, white stones turned over upon its side and left a square, gaping hole, through which streamed the light of a lantern. Over the edge there peeped a clean-cut, boyish face, which looked keenly about it, and then, with a hand on either side of the aperture, drew itself shoulder-high and waist-high, until one knee rested upon the edge. In another instant he stood at the side of the hole and was hauling after him a companion, lithe and small like himself, with a pale face and a shock of very red hair.

"It's all clear," he whispered. "Have you the chisel and the bags? Great Scott! Jump, Archie, jump, and I'll swing for it!"

Sherlock Holmes had sprung out and seized the intruder by the collar. The other dived down the hole, and I heard the sound of rending cloth as Jones clutched at his skirts. The light flashed upon the barrel of a revolver, but Holmes's hunting crop came down on the man's wrist, and the pistol clinked upon the stone floor.

"It's no use, John Clay," said Holmes blandly. "You have no chance at all."

"So I see," the other answered with the utmost coolness. "I fancy that my pal is all right, though I see you have got his coat-tails."

"There are three men waiting for him at the door," said Holmes.

"Oh, indeed! You seem to have done the thing very completely. I must compliment you."

"And I you," Holmes answered. "Your

red-headed idea was very new and effective.''

''You'll see your pal again presently,'' said Jones. ''He's quicker at climbing down holes than I am. Just hold out while I fix the derbies.''

''I beg that you will not touch me with your filthy hands,'' remarked our prisoner as the handcuffs clattered upon his wrists. ''You may not be aware that I have royal blood in my veins. Have the goodness, also, when you address me always to say 'sir' and 'please.' ''

''All right,'' said Jones with a stare and a snigger. ''Well, would you please, sir, march upstairs, where we can get a cab to carry your Highness to the police-station?''

''That is better,'' said John Clay serenely. He made a sweeping bow to the three of us and walked quietly off in the custody of the detective.

''Really, Mr. Holmes,'' said Mr. Merryweather as we followed them from the cellar, ''I do not know how the bank can thank you or repay you. There is no doubt that you have detected and defeated in the most complete manner one of the most determined attempts at bank robbery that have every come within my experience.''

''I have had one or two little scores of my own to settle with Mr. John Clay,'' said Holmes. ''I have been at some small expense over this matter, which I shall expect the bank to refund, but beyond that I am amply repaid by having had an experience which is in many ways unique, and by hearing the very remarkable narrative of the Red-headed League.''

"You see, Watson,'' he explained in the early hours of the morning as we sat over a glass of whisky and soda in Baker Street, "it was perfectly obvious from the first that the only possible object of this rather fantastic business of the advertisement of the League, and the copying of the Encyclopædia, must be to get this not over-bright pawnbroker out of the way for a number of hours every day. It was a curious way of managing it, but, really, it would be difficult to suggest a better. The method was no doubt suggested to Clay's ingenious mind by the colour of his accomplice's hair. The £4 a week was a lure which must draw him, and what was it to them, who were playing for thousands? They put in the advertisement, one rogue has the temporary office, the other rogue incites the man to apply for it, and together they manage to secure his absence every morning in the week. From the time that I heard of the assistant having come for half wages, it was obvious to me that he had some strong motive for securing the situation.''

"But how could you guess what the motive was?''

"Had there been women in the house, I should have suspected a mere vulgar intrigue. That, however, was out of the question. The man's business was a small one, and there was nothing in his house which could account for such elaborate preparations, and such an expenditure as they were at. It must, then, be something out of the house. What could it be? I thought of the assistant's fondness for photography, and his trick of vanishing into the cellar. The cellar! There was the end of this tangled clue. Then I made inquiries as to this mysterious assistant and found that I had to deal with one of the coolest and most daring criminals in London. He was doing something in the cellar — something which took many hours a day for months on end. What could it be, once more? I could think of nothing save that he was running a tunnel to some other building.

"So far I had got when we went to visit the scene of action. I surprised you by beating upon the pavement with my stick. I was ascertaining whether the cellar stretched out in front or behind. It was not in front. Then I rang the bell, and, as I hoped, the assistant answered it. We have had some skirmishes, but we had never set eyes upon each other before. I hardly looked at his face. His knees were what I wished to see. You must yourself have remarked how worn, wrinkled, and stained they were. They spoke of those hours of burrowing. The only remaining point was what they were burrowing for. I walked round the corner, saw that the City and Suburban

Bank abutted on our friend's premises, and felt that I had solved my problem. When you drove home after the concert I called upon Scotland Yard and upon the chairman of the bank directors, with the result that you have seen."

"And how could you tell that they would make their attempt tonight?" I asked.

"Well, when they closed their League offices that was a sign that they cared no longer about Mr. Jabez Wilson's presence — in other words, that they had completed their tunnel. But it was essential that they should use it soon, as it might be discovered, or the bullion might be removed. Saturday would suit them better than any other day, as it would give them two days for their escape. For all these reasons I expected them to come tonight."

"You reasoned it out beautifully," I exclaimed in unfeigned admiration. "It is so long a chain, and yet every link rings true."

"It saved me from ennui," he answered, yawning. "Alas! I already feel it closing in upon me. My life is spent in one long effort to escape from the commonplaces of existence. These little problems help me to do so."

"And you are a benefactor of the race," said I.

He shrugged his shoulders. "Well, perhaps, after all, it is of some little use. *'L'homme c'est rien — l'œuvre c'est tout,'* as Gustave Flaubert wrote to George Sand."

The Monkey's Paw

W. W. Jacobs

WITHOUT, the night was cold and wet, but in the small parlor of Lakesnam Villa the blinds were drawn and the fire burned brightly. Father and son were at chess, the former, who possessed ideas about the game involving radical changes, putting his king into such sharp and unnecessary perils that it even provoked comment from the white-haired old lady knitting placidly by the fire.

"Hark at the wind," said Mr. White, who, having seen a fatal mistake after it was too late, was amiably desirous of preventing his son from seeing it.

"I'm listening," said the latter, grimly surveying the board as he stretched out his hand, "Check."

"I should hardly think that he'd come tonight," said his father, with his hand poised over the board.

"Mate," replied the son.

"That's the worst of living so far out," bawled Mr. White, with sudden and unlooked-for violence; "of all the beastly, slushy, out-of-the-way places to live in, this is the worst. Pathway's a bog, and the road's a torrent. I don't know what people are thinking about. I suppose because only two houses on the road are let, they think it doesn't matter."

"Never mind, dear," said his wife soothingly; "perhaps you'll win the next one."

Mr. White looked up sharply, just in time to intercept a knowing glance between mother and son. The words died away on his lips, and he hid a guilty grin in his thin gray beard.

"There he is," said Herbert White, as the gate banged to loudly and heavy footsteps came toward the door.

The old man rose with hospitable haste, and opening the door, was heard condoling with the new arrival. The new arrival also condoled with himself, so that Mrs. White said, "Tut, tut!" and coughed gently as her husband entered the room, followed by a tall burly man, beady of eye and rubicund of visage.

"Sergeant-Major Morris," he said, introducing him.

The sergeant-major shook hands, and taking the proffered seat by the fire, watched contentedly while his host got out whisky and tumblers and stood a small copper kettle on the fire.

At the third glass his eyes got brighter, and he began to talk, the little family circle regarding with eager interest this visitor from distant parts, as he squared his broad shoulders in the chair and spoke of strange scenes and doughty deeds, of wars and plagues and strange peoples.

"Twenty-one years of it," said Mr. White, nodding at his wife and son. "When he went away he was a slip of a youth in the warehouse. Now look at him."

"He don't look to have taken much harm," said Mrs. White politely.

"I'd like to go to India myself," said the old man, "just to look round a bit, you know."

"Better where you are," said the sergeant-major, shaking his head. He put down the empty glass and, sighing softly, shook it again.

"I should like to see those old temples and fakirs and jugglers," said the old man. "What was that you started telling me the other day about a monkey's paw or something, Morris?"

"Nothing," said the soldier hastily. "Leastways, nothing worth hearing."

"Monkey's paw?" said Mrs. White curiously.

"Well, it's just a bit of what you might call magic, perhaps," said the sergeant-major offhandedly.

His three listeners leaned forward eagerly. The visitor absent-mindedly put his empty glass to his lips and then set it down again. His host filled it for him.

"To look at," said the sergeant-major, fumbling in his pocket, "it's just an ordinary little paw, dried to a mummy.''

He took something out of his pocket and proffered it. Mrs. White drew back with a grimace, but her son, taking it, examined it curiously.

''And what is there special about it?'' inquired Mr. White, as he took it from his son and, having examined it, placed it upon the table.

''It had a spell put on it by an old fakir,'' said the sergeant-major, ''a very holy man. He wanted to show that fate ruled people's lives, and that those who interfered with it did so to their sorrow. He put a spell on it so that three separate men could each have three wishes from it.''

His manner was so impressive that his hearers were conscious that their light laughter jarred somewhat.

''Well, why don't you have three, sir?'' said Herbert White cleverly.

The soldier regarded him in the way that middle age is wont to regard presumptuous youth. ''I have,'' he said quietly, and his blotchy face whitened.

''And did you really have the three wishes granted?'' asked Mrs. White.

''I did,'' said the sergeant-major, and his glass tapped against his strong teeth.

''And has anybody else wished?'' inquired the old lady.

''The first man had his three wishes, yes,''

was the reply. "I don't know what the first two were, but the third was for death. That's how I got the paw."

His tones were so grave that a hush fell upon the group.

"If you've had your three wishes, it's no good to you now, then, Morris," said the old man at last. "What do you keep it for?"

The soldier shook his head. "Fancy, I suppose," he said slowly. "I did have some idea of selling it, but I don't think I will. It has caused enough mischief already. Besides, people won't buy. They think it's a fairy tale, some of them, and those who do think anything of it want to try it first and pay me afterward."

"If you could have another three wishes," said the old man, eyeing him keenly, "would you have them?"

"I don't know," said the other. "I don't know."

He took the paw, and dangling it between his front finger and thumb, suddenly threw it upon the fire. White, with a slight cry, stooped down and snatched it off.

"Better let it burn," said the soldier solemnly.

"If you don't want it, Morris," said the old man, "give it to me."

"I won't," said his friend doggedly. "I threw it on the fire. If you keep it, don't blame me for what happens. Pitch it on the fire again, like a sensible man."

The other shook his head and examined his new possession closely. "How do you do it?" he inquired.

"Hold it up in your right hand and wish aloud," said the sergeant-major, "but I warn you of the consequences."

"Sounds like the *Arabian Nights,*" said Mrs. White, as she rose and began to set the supper. "Don't you think you might wish for four pairs of hands for me?"

Her husband drew the talisman from his pocket and then all three burst into laughter as the sergeant-major, with a look of alarm on his face, caught him by the arm.

"If you must wish," he said gruffly, "wish for something sensible."

Mr. White dropped it back into his pocket, and placing chairs, motioned his friend to the table. In the business of supper the talisman was partly forgotten, and afterward the three sat listening in an enthralled fashion to a second installment of the soldier's adventures in India.

"If the tale about the monkey paw is not more truthful than those he has been telling us," said Herbert, as the door closed behind their guest, just in time for him to catch the last train, "we shan't make much out of it."

"Did you give him anything for it, father?" inquired Mrs. White, regarding her husband closely.

"A trifle," said he, coloring slightly. "He

didn't want it, but I made him take it. And he pressed me again to throw it away."

"Likely," said Herbert, with pretended horror. "Why, we're going to be rich, and famous, and happy. Wish to be an emperor, father, to begin with; then you can't be henpecked."

He darted round the table, pursued by the maligned Mrs. White armed with an antimacassar.

Mr. White took the paw from his pocket and eyed it dubiously. "I don't know what to wish for, and that's a fact," he said slowly. "It seems to me I've got all I want."

"If you only cleared the house, you'd be quite happy, wouldn't you?" said Herbert, with his hand on his shoulder. "Well, wish for two hundred pounds, then; that'll just do it."

His father, smiling shamefacedly at his own credulity, held up the talisman, as his son, with a solemn face somewhat marred by a wink at his mother, sat down at the piano and struck a few impressive chords.

"I wish for two hundred pounds," said the old man distinctly.

A fine crash from the piano greeted the words, interrupted by a shuddering cry from the old man. His wife and son ran toward him.

"It moved," he cried, with a glance of disgust at the object as it lay on the floor. "As I wished it twisted in my hands like a snake."

"Well, I don't see the money," said his son, as he picked it up and placed it on the table, "and I bet I never shall."

"It must have been your fancy, father," said his wife, regarding him anxiously.

He shook his head. "Never mind, though; there's no harm done, but it gave me a shock all the same."

They sat down by the fire again while the two men finished their pipes. Outside, the wind was higher than ever, and the old man started nervously at the sound of a door banging upstairs. A silence unusual and depressing settled upon all three, which lasted until the old couple rose to retire for the night.

"I expect you'll find the cash tied up in a big bag in the middle of your bed," said Herbert, as he bade them good night, "and something horrible squatting up on top of the wardrobe watching you as you pocket your ill-gotten gains."

II

In the brightness of the wintry sun next morning as it streamed over the breakfast table Herbert laughed at his fears. There was an air of prosaic wholesomeness about the room which it had lacked on the previous night, and the dirty, shriveled little paw was pitched on the sideboard with a carelessness which betokened no great belief in its virtues.

"I suppose all old soldiers are the same," said Mrs. White. "The idea of our listening to such nonsense! How could wishes be granted in these days? And if they could, how could two hundred pounds hurt you, father?"

"Might drop on his head from the sky," said the frivolous Herbert.

"Morris said the things happened so naturally," said his father, "that you might if you so wished attribute it to coincidence."

"Well, don't break into the money before I come back," said Herbert, as he rose from the table. "I'm afraid it'll turn you into a mean, avaricious man, and we shall have to disown you."

His mother laughed, and following him to the door, watched him down the road, and returning to the breakfast table, was very happy at the expense of her husband's credulity. All of which did not prevent her from scurrying to the door at the postman's knock, nor prevent her from referring somewhat shortly to retired sergeant-majors of bibulous habits when she found that the post brought a tailor's bill.

"Herbert will have some more of his funny remarks, I expect, when he comes home," said she, as they sat at dinner.

"I dare say," said Mr. White, pouring himself out some beer; "but for all that, the thing moved in my hand; that I'll swear to."

"You thought it did," said the old lady

soothingly.

"I say it did," replied the other. "There was no thought about it; I had just — What's the matter?"

His wife made no reply. She was watching the mysterious movements of a man outside, who, peering in an undecided fashion at the house, appeared to be trying to make up his mind to enter. In mental connection with the two hundred pounds, she noticed that the stranger was well dressed and wore a silk hat of glossy newness. Three times he paused at the gate, and then walked on again. The fourth time he stood with his hand upon it, and then with sudden resolution flung it open and walked up the path. Mrs. White at the same moment placed her hands behind her, and hurriedly unfastening the strings of her apron, put that useful article of apparel beneath the cushion of her chair.

She brought the stranger, who seemed ill at ease, into the room. He gazed furtively at Mrs. White, and listened in a preoccupied fashion as the old lady apologized for the appearance of the room, and her husband's coat, a garment which he usually reserved for the garden. She then waited as patiently as her sex would permit for him to broach his business, but he was at first strangely silent.

"I — was asked to call," he said at last, and stooped and picked a piece of cotton from his trousers. "I come from Maw and

Meggins.''

The old lady started. ''Is anything the matter?'' she asked breathlessly. ''Has anything happened to Herbert? What is it? What is it?''

Her husband interposed. ''There, there, mother,'' he said hastily. ''Sit down, and don't jump to conclusions. You've not brought bad news, I'm sure, sir,'' and he eyed the other wistfully.

''I'm sorry ——'' began the visitor.

''Is he hurt?'' demanded the mother.

The visitor bowed in assent. ''Badly hurt,'' he said quietly, ''but he is not in any pain.''

''Oh, thank God!'' said the old woman, clasping her hands. ''Thank God for that! Thank ——''

She broke off suddenly as the sinister meaning of the assurance dawned upon her and she saw the awful confirmation of her fears in the other's averted face. She caught her breath, and turning to her slower-witted husband, laid her trembling old hand upon his. There was a long silence.

''He was caught in the machinery,'' said the visitor at length, in a low voice.

''Caught in the machinery,'' repeated Mr. White, in a dazed fashion, ''yes.''

He sat staring blankly out at the window, and taking his wife's hand between his own, pressed it as he had been wont to do in their old courting days nearly forty years before.

''He was the only one left to us,'' he said,

turning gently to the visitor. "It is hard."

The other coughed, and rising, walked slowly to the window. "The firm wished me to convey their sincere sympathy with you in your great loss," he said, without looking round. "I beg that you will understand I am only their servant and merely obeying orders."

There was no reply; the old woman's face was white, her eyes staring, and her breath inaudible; on the husband's face was a look such as his friend the sergeant might have carried into his first action.

"I was to say that Maw and Meggins disclaim all responsibility," continued the other. "They admit no liability at all, but in consideration of your son's services they wish to present you with a certain sum as compensation."

Mr. White dropped his wife's hand, and rising to his feet, gazed with a look of horror at his visitor. His dry lips shaped the words, "How much?"

"Two hundred pounds," was the answer.

Unconscious of his wife's shriek, the old man smiled faintly, put out his hands like a sightless man, and dropped, a senseless heap, to the floor.

III

In the huge new cemetery, some two miles distant, the old people buried their dead, and came back to a house steeped in shadow and silence. It was all over so quickly that at first they could hardly realize it, and remained in a state of expectation as though of something else to happen — something else which was to lighten this load, too heavy for old hearts to bear. But the days passed, and expectation gave place to resignation — the hopeless resignation of the old, sometimes miscalled apathy. Sometimes they hardly exchanged a word, for now they had nothing to talk about, and their days were long to weariness.

It was about a week after that that the old man, waking suddenly in the night, stretched out his hand and found himself alone. The room was in darkness, and the sound of subdued weeping came from the window. He raised himself in bed and listened.

"Come back," he said tenderly. "You will be cold."

"It is colder for my son," said the old woman, and wept afresh.

The sound of her sobs died away on his ears. The bed was warm, and his eyes heavy with sleep. He dozed fitfully, and then slept until a sudden wild cry from his wife awoke him with a start.

"The monkey's paw!" she cried wildly. "The monkey's paw!"

He started up in alarm. "Where? Where is it? What's the matter?"

She came stumbling across the room toward

him. "I want it," she said quietly. "You've not destroyed it?"

"It's in the parlor, on the bracket," he replied, marveling. "Why?"

She cried and laughed together, and bending over, kissed his cheek.

"I only just thought of it," she said hysterically. "Why didn't I think of it before? Why didn't you think of it?"

"Think of what?" he questioned.

"The other two wishes," she replied rapidly. "We've only had one."

"Was not that enough?" he demanded fiercely.

"No," she cried triumphantly; "we'll have one more. Go down and get it quickly, and wish our boy alive again."

The man sat up in bed and flung the bedclothes from his quaking limbs. "Good God, you are mad!" he cried, aghast.

"Get it," she panted; "get it quickly, and wish — Oh, my boy, my boy!"

Her husband struck a match and lit the candle. "Get back to bed," he said unsteadily. "You don't know what you are saying."

"We had the first wish granted," said the old woman feverishly; "why not the second?"

"A coincidence," stammered the old man.

"Go and get it and wish," cried the old woman, and dragged him toward the door.

He went down in the darkness, and felt his way to the parlor, and then to the mantelpiece.

The talisman was in its place, and a horrible fear that the unspoken wish might bring his multilated son before him ere he could escape from the room seized upon him, and he caught his breath as he found that he had lost the direction of the door. His brow cold with sweat, he felt his way round the table, and groped along the wall until he found himself in the small passage with the unwholesome thing in his hand.

Even his wife's face seemed changed as he entered the room. It was white and expectant, and to his fears seemed to have an unnatural look upon it. He was afraid of her.

"Wish!" she cried, in a strong voice.

"It is foolish and wicked," he faltered.

"Wish!" repeated his wife.

He raised his hand. "I wish my son alive again."

The talisman fell to the floor, and he regarded it shudderingly. Then he sank trembling into a chair as the old woman, with burning eyes, walked to the window and raised the blind.

He sat until he was chilled with the cold, glancing occasionally at the figure of the old woman peering through the window. The candle end, which had burnt below the rim of the china candlestick, was throwing pulsating shadows on the ceiling and walls, until, with a flicker larger than the rest, it expired. The old man, with an unspeakable sense of relief at the failure of the talisman, crept back to his bed, and a minute or two afterward the old woman came silently and apathetically beside him.

Neither spoke, but both lay silently listening to the ticking of the clock. A stair creaked, and a squeaky mouse scurried noisily through the wall. The darkness was oppressive, and after lying for some time screwing up his courage, the husband took the box of matches, and striking one, went downstairs for a candle.

At the foot of the stairs the match went out, and he paused to strike another, and at the same moment a knock, so quiet and stealthy as to be scarcely audible, sounded on the front door.

The matches fell from his hand. He stood motionless, his breath suspended until the knock was repeated. Then he turned and fled swiftly back to his room, and closed the door behind him. A third knock sounded through the house.

"*What's that?*" cried the old woman, starting up.

"A rat," said the old man, in shaking tones — "a rat. It passed me on the stairs."

His wife sat up in bed listening. A loud knock resounded through the house.

"It's Herbert!" she screamed. "It's Herbert!"

She ran to the door, but her husband was before her, and catching her by the arm, held her tightly.

"What are you going to do?" he whispered hoarsely.

"It's my boy; it's Herbert!" she cried, struggling mechanically. "I forgot it was two miles away. What are you holding me for? Let go. I must open the door."

"For God's sake don't let it in," cried the old man, trembling.

"You're afraid of your own son," she cried, struggling. "Let me go. I'm coming, Herbert; I'm coming."

There was another knock, and another. The old woman with a sudden wrench broke free and ran from the room. Her husband followed to the landing, and called after her appealingly as she hurried downstairs. He heard the chain rattle back and the bottom bolt drawn slowly and stiffly from the socket. Then the old woman's voice, strained and panting.

"The bolt," she cried loudly. "Come down. I can't reach it."

But her husband was on his hands and knees groping wildly on the floor in search of the paw. If he could only find it before the thing outside got in. A perfect fusillade of knocks reverberated through the house, and he heard the scraping of a chair as his wife put it down in the passage against the door. He heard the creaking of the bolt as it came slowly back, and at the same moment he found the monkey's paw, and frantically breathed his third and last wish.

The knocking ceased suddenly, although the echoes of it were still in the house. He heard the chair drawn back and the door opened. A cold wind rushed up the staircase, and a long loud wail of disappointment and misery from his wife gave him courage to run down to her side, and then to the gate beyond. The street lamp flickering opposite shone on a quiet and deserted road.

The Gift of the Magi

O. Henry

ONE dollar and eighty-seven cents. That was all. And sixty cents of it was in pennies. Pennies saved one and two at a time by bulldozing the grocer and the vegetable man and the butcher until one's cheeks burned with the silent imputation of parsimony that such close dealing implied. Three times Della counted it. One dollar and eighty-seven cents. And the next day would be Christmas.

There was clearly nothing to do but flop down on the shabby little couch and howl. So Della did it. Which instigates the moral reflection that life is made up of sobs, sniffles, and smiles, with sniffles predominating.

While the mistress of the home is gradually subsiding from the first stage to the second, take a look at the home. A furnished flat at $8 per week. It did not exactly beggar description, but it certainly had that word on the lookout for the mendicancy squad.

In the vestibule below was a letter-box into which no letter would go, and an electric button from which no mortal finger could coax a ring. Also appertaining thereunto was a card bearing the name "Mr. James Dillingham Young."

The "Dillingham" had been flung to the breeze during a former period of prosperity when its possessor was being paid $30 per week. Now, when the income was shrunk to $20, the letters of "Dillingham" looked blurred, as though they were thinking seriously of contracting to a modest and unassuming D. But whenever Mr. James Dillingham Young came home and reached his flat above he was called "Jim" and greatly hugged by Mrs. James Dillingham Young, already introduced to you as Della. Which is all very good.

Della finished her cry and attended to her cheeks with the powder rag. She stood by the window and looked out dully at a gray cat walking a gray fence in a gray backyard. Tomorrow would be Christmas Day and she had only $1.87 with which to buy Jim a present. She had been saving every penny she could for months, with this result. Twenty dollars a week doesn't go far. Expenses had been greater than she had calculated. They always are. Only $1.87 to buy a present for Jim. Her Jim. Many a happy hour she had spent planning for something nice for him. Something fine and rare and sterling — something just a little bit near to being worthy of the honor of being owned by Jim.

There was a pier-glass between the windows of the room. Perhaps you have seen a pier-glass in an $8 flat. A very thin and very agile person may, by observing his reflection in a rapid sequence of longitudinal strips, obtain a fairly accurate conception of his looks. Della, being slender, had mastered the art.

Suddenly she whirled from the window and stood before the glass. Her eyes were shining brilliantly, but her face had lost its color within twenty seconds. Rapidly she pulled down her hair and let it fall to its full length.

Now, there were two possessions of the James Dillingham Youngs in which they both took a mighty pride. One was Jim's gold watch that had been his father's and his grandfather's. The other was Della's hair. Had the Queen of Sheba lived in the flat across the airshaft, Della would have let her hair hang out the window some day to dry just to depreciate Her Majesty's jewels and gifts. Had King Solomon been the janitor, with all his treasures piled up in the basement, Jim would have pulled out his watch every time he passed, just to see him pluck at his beard from envy.

So now Della's beautiful hair fell about her rippling and shining like a cascade of brown waters. It reached below her knee and made itself almost a garment for her. And then she did it up again nervously and quickly. Once she faltered for a minute and stood still while a tear or two splashed on the worn red carpet.

On went her old brown jacket; on went her old brown hat. With a whirl of skirts and with the brilliant sparkle still in her eyes, she fluttered out the door and down the stairs to the street.

Where she stopped the sign read: "Mme. Sofronie. Hair Goods of All Kinds." One flight up Della ran, and collected herself, panting. Madame, large, too white, chilly, hardly looked the "Sofronie."

"Will you buy my hair?" asked Della.

"I buy hair," said Madame. "Take yer hat off and let's have a sight at the looks of it."

Down rippled the brown cascade.

"Twenty dollars," said Madame, lifting the mass with a practised hand.

"Give it to me quick," said Della.

Oh, and the next two hours tripped by on rosy wings. Forget the hashed metaphor. She was ransacking the stores for Jim's present.

She found it at last. It surely had been made for Jim and no one else. There was no other like it in any of the stores, and she had turned all of them inside out. It was a platinum fob chain simple and chaste in design, properly proclaiming its value by substance alone and not by meretricious ornamentation — as all good things should do. It was even worthy of The Watch. As soon as she saw it she knew that it must be Jim's. It was like him. Quietness and value — the description applied to both. Twenty-one dollars they took from her for it, and she hurried home with the 87 cents. With that chain on his watch Jim might be properly anxious about the time in any company. Grand as the watch was, he sometimes looked at it on the sly on account of the old leather strap that he used in place of a chain.

When Della reached home her intoxication gave way a little to prudence and reason. She got out her curling irons and lighted the gas and went to work repairing the ravages made by generosity added to love. Which is always a tremendous task, dear friends — a mammoth task.

Within forty minutes her head was covered with tiny, close-lying curls that made her look wonderfully like a truant schoolboy. She looked at her reflection in the mirror long, carefully, and critically.

"If Jim doesn't kill me," she said to herself, "before he takes a second look at me, he'll say I look like a Coney Island chorus girl. But what could I do — oh! what could I do with a dollar and eighty-seven cents?"

At 7 o'clock the coffee was made and the frying-pan was on the back of the stove hot and ready to cook the chops.

Jim was never late. Della doubled the fob chain in her hand and sat on the corner of the table near the door that he always entered. Then she heard his step on the stair away down on the first flight, and she turned white for just a moment. She had a habit of saying little silent prayers about the simplest everyday things, and now she whispered: "Please God, make him think I am still pretty."

The door opened and Jim stepped in and closed it. He looked thin and very serious. Poor fellow, he was only twenty-two — and to be burdened with a family! He needed a new overcoat and he was without gloves.

Jim stepped inside the door, as immovable as a setter at the scent of quail. His eyes were fixed upon Della, and there was an expression in them that she could not read, and it terrified her. It was not anger, nor surprise, nor disapproval, nor horror, nor any of the sentiments that she had been prepared for. He simply stared at her fixedly with that peculiar expression on his face.

Della wriggled off the table and went for him.

"Jim, darling," she cried, "don't look at me that way. I had my hair cut off and sold it because I couldn't have lived through Christmas without giving you a present. It'll grow out again — you won't mind, will you? I just had to do it. My hair grows awfully fast. Say 'Merry Christmas!' Jim, and let's be happy. You don't know what a nice — what a beautiful, nice gift I've got for you."

"You've cut off your hair?" asked Jim, laboriously, as if he had not arrived at that patent fact yet even after the hardest mental labor.

"Cut it off and sold it," said Della. "Don't you like me just as well, anyhow? I'm me without my hair, ain't I?"

Jim looked about the room curiously.

"You say your hair is gone?" he said, with an air almost of idiocy.

"You needn't look for it," said Della. "It's sold, I tell you — sold and gone, too. It's Christmas Eve, boy. Be good to me, for it went for you. Maybe the hairs of my head were numbered," she went on with a sudden serious sweetness, "but nobody could ever count my love for you. Shall I put the chops on, Jim?"

Out of his trance Jim seemed quickly to wake. He enfolded his Della. For ten seconds let us regard with discreet scrutiny some inconsequential object in the other direction. Eight dollars a week or a million a year — what is the difference? A mathematician or a wit would give you the wrong answer. The magi brought valuable gifts, but that was not among them. This dark assertion will be illuminated later on.

Jim drew a package from his overcoat pocket and threw it upon the table.

"Don't make any mistake, Dell," he said, "about me. I don't think there's anything in the way of a haircut or a shave or a shampoo that could make me like my girl any less. But if you'll unwrap that package you may see why you had me going a while at first."

White fingers and nimble tore at the string

and paper. And then an ecstatic scream of joy; and then, alas! a quick feminine change to hysterical tears and wails, necessitating the immediate employment of all the comforting powers of the lord of the flat.

For there lay The Combs — the set of combs, side and back, that Della had worshipped for long in a Broadway window. Beautiful combs, pure tortoise shell, with jewelled rims — just the shade to wear in the beautiful vanished hair. They were expensive combs, she knew, and her heart had simply craved and yearned over them without the least hope of possession. And now, they were hers, but the tresses that should have adorned the coveted adornments were gone.

But she hugged them to her bosom, and at length she was able to look up with dim eyes and a smile and say: "My hair grows so fast, Jim!"

And then Della leaped up like a little singed cat and cried, "Oh, oh!"

Jim had not yet seen his beautiful present. She held it out to him eagerly upon her open palm. The dull precious metal seemed to flash with a reflection of her bright and ardent spirit.

"Isn't it a dandy, Jim? I hunted all over town to find it. You'll have to look at the time a hundred times a day now. Give me your watch. I want to see how it looks on it."

Instead of obeying, Jim tumbled down on the couch and put his hands under the back of his head and smiled.

"Dell," said he, "let's put our Christmas presents away and keep 'em a while. They're too nice to use just at present. I sold the watch to get the money to buy your combs. And now suppose you put the chops on."

The magi, as you know, were wise men — wonderfully wise men — who brought gifts to the Babe in the manger. They invented the art of giving Christmas presents. Being wise, their gifts were no doubt wise ones, possibly bearing the privilege of exchange in case of duplication. And here I have lamely related to you the uneventful chronicle of two foolish children in a flat who most unwisely sacrificed for each other the greatest treasures of their house. But in a last word to the wise of these days let it be said that of all who give gifts these two were the wisest. Of all who give and receive gifts, such as they are wisest. Everywhere they are wisest. They are the magi.

The Man Who Would Be King

Rudyard Kipling

Brother to a Prince and fellow to a beggar if he be found worthy.

THE law, as quoted, lays down a fair conduct of life, and one not easy to follow. I have been fellow to a beggar again and again under circumstances which prevented either of us finding out whether the other was worthy. I have still to be brother to a Prince, though I once came near to kinship with what might have been a veritable King and was promised the reversion of a Kingdom — army, law-courts, revenue and policy all complete. But, to-day, I greatly fear that my King is dead, and if I want a crown I must go hunt it for myself.

The beginning of everything was in a railway train upon the road to Mhow from Ajmir. There had been a Deficit in the Budget, which necessitated travelling, not Second-class, which is only half as dear as First-class, but by Intermediate, which is very awful indeed. There are no cushions in the Intermediate class, and the population are either Intermediate, which is Eurasian, or native, which for a long night journey is nasty, or Loafer, which is amusing though intoxicated. Intermediates do not buy from refreshment-rooms. They carry their food in bundles and pots, and buy sweets from the native sweetmeat-sellers, and drink the roadside water. That is why in hot weather Intermediates are taken out of the carriages dead, and in all weathers are most properly looked down upon.

My particular Intermediate happened to be empty till I reached Nasirabad, when a big black-browed gentleman in shirt-sleeves entered, and, following the custom of Intermediates, passed the time of day. He was a wanderer and a vagabond like myself, but with an educated taste for whiskey. He told tales of things he had seen and done, of out-of-the-way corners of the Empire into which he had penetrated, and of adventures in which he risked his life for a few days' food.

"If India was filled with men like you and me, not knowing more than the crows where they'd get their next day's rations, it isn't seventy millions of revenue the land would be paying — it's seven hundred millions," said he; and as I looked at his mouth and chin I was disposed to agree with him.

We talked politics — the politics of Loaferdom that sees things from the underside where the lath and plaster is not smoothed off

— and we talked postal arrangements because my friend wanted to send a telegram back from the next station to Ajmir, the turning-off place from the Bombay to the Mhow line as you travel westward. My friend had no money beyond eight annas which he wanted for dinner, and I had no money at all, owing to the hitch in the Budget before mentioned. Further, I was going into a wilderness where, though I should resume touch with the Treasury, there were no telegraph offices. I was, therefore, unable to help him in any way.

"We might threaten a Station-master, and make him send a wire on tick," said my friend, "but that'd mean enquiries for you and for me, and *I*'ve got my hands full these days. Did you say you were travelling back along this line, within any days?"

"Within ten," I said.

"Can't you make it eight?" said he. "Mine is rather urgent business."

"I can send your telegram within ten days if that will serve you," I said.

"I couldn't trust the wire to fetch him now I think of it. It's this way. He leaves Delhi on the 23rd for Bombay. That means he'll be running through Ajmir about the night of the 23rd."

"But I'm going into the Indian Desert," I explained.

"Well *and* good," said he. "You'll be changing at Marwar Junction to get into Jodhpore territory — you must do that — and he'll be coming through Marwar Junction in the early morning of the 24th by the Bombay Mail. Can you be at Marwar Junction on that time? 'Twon't be inconveniencing you because I know that there's precious few pickings to be got out of those Central India States — even though you pretend to be correspondent of the *Backwoodsman.*"

"Have you ever tried that trick?" I asked.

"Again and again, but the Residents find you out, and then you get escorted to the Border before you've time to get your knife into them. But about my friend here. I *must* give him a word o' mouth to tell him what's come to me or else he won't know where to go. I would take it more than kind of you if you was to come out of Central India in time to catch him at Marwar Junction, and say to him: 'He has gone South for the week.' He'll know what that means. He's a big man with a red beard, and a great swell he is. You'll find him sleeping like a gentleman with all his luggage round him in a Second-class apartment. But don't you be afraid. Slip down the window and say: 'He has gone South for the week,' and he'll tumble. It's only cutting your time of stay in those parts by two days. I ask you as a stranger — going to the West," he said with emphasis.

"Where have *you* come from?" said I.

"From the East," said he, "and I am hoping that you will give him the message on the

Square — for the sake of my Mother as well as your own.''

Englishmen are not usually softened by appeals to the memory of their mothers; but for certain reasons, which will be fully apparent, I saw fit to agree.

''It's more than a little matter,'' said he, ''and that's why I asked you to do it — and now I know that I can depend on you doing it. A Second-class carriage at Marwar Junction, and a red-haired man asleep in it. You'll be sure to remember. I get out at the next station, and I must hold on there till he comes or sends me what I want.''

''I'll give the message if I catch him,'' I said, ''and for the sake of your Mother as well as mine I'll give you a word of advice. Don't try to run the Central India States just now as the correspondent of the *Backwoodsman*. There's a real one knocking about here, and it might lead to trouble.''

''Thank you,'' said he simply, ''and when will the swine be gone? I can't starve because he's ruining my work. I wanted to get hold of the Degumber Rajah down here about his father's widow, and give him a jump.''

''What did he do to his father's widow, then?''

''Filled her up with red pepper and slippered her to death as she hung from a beam. I found that out myself and I'm the only man that would dare going into the State to get hush-money for it. They'll try to poison me, same as they did in Chortumna when I went on the loot there. But you'll give the man at Marwar Junction my message?''

''He got out at a little roadside station, and I reflected, I had heard, more than once, of men personating correspondents of newspapers and bleeding small Native States with threats of exposure, but I had never met any of the caste before. They lead a hard life, and generally die with great suddenness. The Native States have a wholesome horror of English newspapers, which may throw light on their peculiar methods of government, and do their best to choke correspondents with champagne, or drive them out of their mind with four-in-hand barouches. They do not understand that nobody cares a straw for the internal administration of Native States so long as oppression and crime are kept within decent limits, and the ruler is not drugged, drunk, or diseased from one end of the year to the other. They are the dark places of the earth, full of unimaginable cruelty, touching the Railway and the Telegraph on one side, and, on the other, the days of Harun-al-Raschid. When I left the train I did business with divers Kings, and in eight days passed through many changes of life. Sometimes I wore dress-clothes and consorted with Princes and Politicals, drinking from crystal and eating from silver. Sometimes I lay upon the ground and devoured what I could get, from a plate made of leaves, and drank the running water, and slept under the same rug as my servant. It was all in the day's work.

Then I headed for the Great Indian Desert upon the proper date, as I had promised, and the night Mail set me down at Marwar Junction, where a funny little, happy-go-lucky, native-managed railway runs to Jodhpore. The Bombay Mail from Delhi makes a short halt at Marwar. She arrived as I got in, and I had just time to hurry to her platform and go down the carriages. There was only one Second-class on the train. I slipped the window and looked down upon a flaming red beard, half covered by a railway rug. That was my man, fast asleep, and I dug him gently in the ribs. He woke with a grunt and I saw his face in the light of the lamps. It was a great and shining face.

"Tickets again?" said he.

"No," said I. "I am to tell you that he is gone South for the week. He has gone South for the week!"

The train had begun to move out. The red man rubbed his eyes. "He has gone South for the week," he repeated. "Now that's just like his impidence. Did he say that I was to give you anything? 'Cause I won't."

"He didn't," I said and dropped away, and watched the red lights die out in the dark. It was horribly cold because the wind was blowing off the sands. I climbed into my own train — not an Intermediate carriage this time — and went to sleep.

If the man with the beard had given me a rupee I should have kept it as a memento of a rather curious affair. But the consciousness of having done my duty was my only reward.

Later on I reflected that two gentlemen like my friends could not do any good if they foregathered and personated correspondents of newspapers, and might, if they black-mailed one of the little rat-trap states of Central India or Southern Rajputana, get themselves into serious difficulties. I therefore took some trouble to describe them as accurately as I could remember to people who would be interested in deporting them: and succeeded, so I was later informed, in having them headed back from the Degumber borders.

Then I became respectable, and returned to an Office where there were no Kings and no incidents outside the daily manufacture of a newspaper. A newspaper office seems to attract every conceivable sort of person, to the prejudice of discipline. Zenana-mission ladies arrive, and beg that the Editor will instantly abandon all his duties to describe a Christian prize-giving in a back-slum of a perfectly inaccessible village; Colonels who have been overpassed for command sit down and sketch the outline of a series of ten, twelve, or twenty-four leading articles on Seniority *versus*

Selection; missionaries wish to know why they have not been permitted to escape from their regular vehicles of abuse and swear at a brother-missionary under special patronage of the editorial We; stranded theatrical companies troop up to explain that they cannot pay for their advertisements, but on their return from New Zealand or Tahiti will do so with interest; inventors of patent punkah-pulling machines, carriage couplings and unbreakable swords and axle-trees call with specifications in their pockets and hours at their disposal; tea-companies enter and elaborate their prospectuses with the office pens; secretaries of ball-committees clamour to have the glories of their last dance more fully described; strange ladies rustle in and say: "I want a hundred lady's cards printed *at once,* please," which is manifestly part of an Editor's duty; and every dissolute ruffian that ever tramped the Grand Trunk Road makes it his business to ask for employment as a proofreader. And, all the time, the telephone-bell is ringing madly, and Kings are being killed on the Continent, and Empires are saying—"You're another," and Mister Gladstone is calling down brimstone upon the British Dominions, and the little black copy-boys are whining, *"kaa-pi chay-ha-yeh"* (copy wanted) like tired bees, and most of the paper is as blank as Modred's shield.

But that is the amusing part of the year. There are six other months when none ever come to call, and the thermometer walks inch by inch up to the top of the glass, and the office is darkened to just above reading-light, and the press-machines are red-hot to touch, and nobody writes anything but accounts of amusements in the Hill-stations or obituary notices. Then the telephone becomes a tinkling terror, because it tells you of the sudden deaths of men and women that you knew intimately, and the prickly heat covers you with a garment, and you sit down and write: "A slight increase of sickness is reported from the Khuda Janta Khan District. The outbreak is purely sporadic in its nature, and, thanks to the energetic efforts of the District authorities, is now almost at an end. It is, however, with deep regret we record the death," etc.

Then the sickness really breaks out, and the less recording and reporting the better for the peace of the subscribers. But the Empires and the Kings continue to divert themselves as selfishly as before, and the Foreman thinks that a daily paper really ought to come out once in twenty-four hours, and all the people at the Hill-stations in the middle of their amusements say: "Good gracious! Why can't the paper be sparkling? I'm sure there's plenty going on up here."

That is the dark half of the moon, and, as the advertisements say, "must be experienced to be appreciated."

It was in that season, and a remarkably evil

season, that the paper began running the last issue of the week on Saturday night, which is to say Sunday morning, after the custom of a London paper. This was a great convenience, for immediately after the paper was put to bed, the dawn would lower the thermometer from 96° to almost 84° for half an hour, and in that chill — you have no idea how cold is 84° on the grass until you begin to pray for it — a very tired man could get off to sleep ere the heat roused him.

One Saturday night it was my pleasant duty to put the paper to bed alone. A King or courtier or a courtesan or a Community was going to die or get a new Constitution, or do something that was important on the other side of the world, and the paper was to be held open till the latest possible minute in order to catch the telegram.

It was a pitchy black night, as stifling as a June night can be, and the *loo*, the red-hot wind from the westward, was booming among the tinder-dry trees and pretending that the rain was on its heels. Now and again a spot of almost boiling water would fall on the dust with the flop of a frog, but all our weary world knew that was only pretence. It was a shade cooler in the press-room than the office, so I sat there, while the type ticked and clicked, and the night-jars hooted at the windows, and the all but naked compositors wiped the sweat from their foreheads, and called for water. The thing that was keeping us back, whatever it was, would not come off, though the *loo* dropped and the last type was set, and the whole round earth stood still in the choking heat, with its fingers on its lip, to wait the event. I drowsed, and wondered whether the telegraph was a blessing, and whether this dying man, or struggling people, might be aware of the inconvenience the delay was causing. There was no special reason beyond the heat and worry to make tension, but, as the clock-hands crept up to three o'clock and the machines spun their fly-wheels two and three times to see that all was in order, before I said the word that would set them off, I could have shrieked aloud.

Then the roar and rattle of the wheels shivered the quiet into little bits. I rose to go away, but two men in white clothes stood in front of me. The first one said: "It's him!" The second said: "So it is!" And they both laughed almost as loudly as the machinery roared, and mopped their foreheads. "We seed there was a light burning across the road and we were sleeping in that ditch there for coolness, and I said to my friend here, The office is open. Let's come along and speak to him as turned us back from the Degumber State," said the smaller of the two. He was the man I had met in the Mhow train, and his fellow was the red-bearded man of Marwar Junction. There was no mistaking the eyebrows of the one or the beard of the other.

I was not pleased, because I wished to go to sleep, not to squabble with loafers. "What do you want?" I asked.

"Half an hour's talk with you, cool and comfortable, in the office," said the red-bearded man. "We'd *like* some drink — the Contrack doesn't begin yet, Peachey, so you needn't look — but what we really want is advice. We don't want money. We ask you as a favour, because we found out you did us a bad turn about Degumber State."

I led from the press-room to the stifling office with the maps on the walls, and the red-haired man rubbed his hands. "That's something like," said he. "This was the proper shop to come to. Now, Sir, let me introduce to you Brother Peachey Carnehan, that's him, and Brother Daniel Dravot, that is *me,* and the less said about our professions the better, for we have been most things in our time. Soldier, sailor, compositor, photographer, proofreader, street-preacher, and correspondents of the *Backwoodsman* when we thought the paper wanted one. Carnehan is sober, and so am I. Look at us first, and see that's sure. It will save you cutting into my talk. We'll take one of your cigars apiece, and you shall see us light up."

I watched the test. The men were absolutely sober, so I gave them each a tepid whiskey and soda.

"Well *and* good," said Carnehan of the eyebrows, wiping the froth from his moustache. "Let me talk now, Dan. We have been all over India, mostly on foot. We have been boiler-fitters, engine-drivers, petty contractors, and all that, and we have decided that India isn't big enough for such as us."

They certainly were too big for the office. Dravot's beard seemed to fill half the room and Carnehan's shoulders the other half, as they sat on the big table. Carnehan continued: "The country isn't half worked out because they that governs it won't let you touch it. They spend all their blessed time in governing it, and you can't lift a spade, nor chip a rock, nor look for oil, nor anything like that without all the Government saying — 'Leave it alone, and let us govern.' Therefore, such *as* it is, we will let it alone, and go away to some other place where a man isn't crowded and can come to his own. We are not little men, and there is nothing that we are afraid of except Drink, and we have signed a Contrack on that. *Therefore,* we are going away to be Kings."

"Kings in our own right," muttered Dravot.

"Yes, of course," I said. "You've been tramping in the sun, and it's a very warm night, and hadn't you better sleep over the notion? Come to-morrow."

"Neither drunk nor sunstruck," said Dravot. "We have slept over the notion half a year, and require to see Books and Atlases, and we have decided that there is only one place now in the world that two strong men can Sar-a-*whack*. They call it Kafiristan. By my reckoning it's the top right-hand corner of Afghanistan, not more than three hundred miles from Peshawar. They have two-and-thirty heathen idols there, and we'll be the thirty-third and fourth. It's a mountaineous country, and the women of those parts are very beautiful."

"But that is provided against in the Con-track," said Carnehan. "Neither Woman nor Liqu-or, Daniel."

"And that's all we know, except that no one has gone there, and they fight, and in any place where they fight a man who knows how to drill men can always be a King. We shall go to those parts and say to any King we find — 'D'you want to vanquish your foes?' and we will show him how to drill men; for that we know better than anything else. Then we will subvert that King and seize his Throne and establish a Dy-nasty."

"You'll be cut to pieces before you're fifty miles across the Border," I said. "You have to travel through Afghanistan to get to that country. It's one mass of mountains and peaks and glaciers, and no Englishman has been through it. The people are utter brutes, and even if you reached them you couldn't do anything."

"That's more like," said Carnehan. "If you

could think us a little more mad we would be more pleased. We have come to you to know about this country, to read a book about it, and to be shown maps. We want you to tell us that we are fools and to show us your books." He turned to the book-cases.

"Are you at all in earnest?" I said.

"A little," said Dravot sweetly. "As big a map as you have got, even if it's all blank where Kafiristan is, and any books you've got. We can read, though we aren't very educated."

I uncased the big thirty-two-miles-to-the-inch map of India, and two smaller Frontier maps, hauled down volume INF-KAN of the *Encyclopædia Britannica,* and the men consulted them.

"See here!" said Dravot, his thumb on the map. "Up to Jagdallak, Peachey and me know the road. We was there with Roberts' Army. We'll have to turn off to the right to Jagdallak through Laghmann territory. Then we get among the hills — fourteen thousand feet — fifteen thousand — it will be cold work there, but it don't look very far on the map."

I handed him Wood on the *Sources of the Oxus*. Carnehan was deep in the *Encyclopædia*.

"They're a mixed lot," said Dravot reflectively; "and it won't help us to know the names of their tribes. The more tribes the more they'll fight, and the better for us. From Jagdallak to

Ashang. H'mm!''

"But all the information about the country is as sketchy and inaccurate as can be," I protested. "No one knows anything about it really. Here's the file of the *United Services' Institute*. Read what Bellew says."

"Blow Bellew!" said Carnehan. "Dan, they're a stinkin' lot of heathens, but this book here says they think they're related to us English."

I smoked while the men pored over *Raverty*, *Wood*, the maps, and the *Encyclopædia*.

"There is no use your waiting," said Dravot politely. "It's about four o'clock now. We'll go before six o'clock if you want to sleep, and we won't steal any of the papers. Don't you sit up. We're two harmless lunatics, and if you come to-morrow evening down to the Serai we'll say good-bye to you."

"You *are* two fools," I answered. "You'll be turned back at the Frontier or cut up the minute you set foot in Afghanistan. Do you want any money or a recommendation down-country? I can help you to the chance of work next week."

"Next week we shall be hard at work ourselves, thank you," said Dravot. "It isn't so easy being a King as it looks. When we've got our Kingdom in going order we'll let you know, and you can come up and help us to govern it."

"Would two lunatics make a Contrack like

that?'' said Carnehan, with subdued pride, showing me a greasy half-sheet of notepaper on which was written the following. I copied it, then and there, as a curiosity —

This Contract between me and you persuing witnesseth in the name of God — Amen and so forth.

(One) That me and you will settle this matter together; ie., to be Kings of Kafiristan.

(Two) That you and me will not, while this matter is being settled, look at any Liquor, nor any Woman black, white, or brown, so as to get mixed up with one or the other harmful.

(Three) That we conduct ourselves with Dignity and Discretion, and if one of us gets into trouble the other will stay by him.

Signed by you and me this day.
Peachey Taliaferro Carnehan.
Daniel Dravot.
Both Gentlemen at Large.

''There was no need for the last article,'' said Carnehan, blushing modestly; ''but it looks regular. Now you know the sort of men that loafers are — we *are* loafers. Dan, until we get out of India — and *do* you think that we would sign a Contrack like that unless we was in earnest? We have kept away from the two things that make life worth having.''

"You won't enjoy your lives much longer if you are going to try this idiotic adventure. Don't set the office on fire," I said, "and go away before nine o'clock."

I left them still poring over the maps and making notes on the back of the "Contrack." "Be sure to come down to the Serai tomorrow," were their parting words.

The Kumharsen Serai is the great four-square sink of humanity where the strings of camels and horses from the North load and unload. All the nationalities of Central Asia may be found there, and most of the folk of India proper. Balkh and Bokhara there meet Bengal and Bombay, and try to draw eye-teeth. You can buy ponies, turquoises, Persian pussy-cats, saddle-bags, fat-tailed sheep and musk in the Kumharsen Serai, and get many strange things for nothing. In the afternoon I went down to see whether my friends intended to keep their word or were lying there drunk.

A priest attired in fragments of ribbons and rags stalked up to me, gravely twisting a child's paper whirligig. Behind him was his servant bending under the load of a crate of mud toys. The two were loading up two camels, and the inhabitants of the Serai watched them with shrieks of laughter.

"The priest is mad," said a horse-dealer to

me. "He is going up to Kabul to sell toys to the Amir. He will either be raised to honour or have his head cut off. He came in here this morning and has been behaving madly ever since."

"The witless are under the protection of God," stammered a flat-cheeked Usbeg in broken Hindi. "They foretell future events."

"Would they could have foretold that my caravan would have been cut up by the Shinwaris almost within shadow of the Pass!" grunted the Eusufzai agent of a Rajputana trading-house whose goods had been diverted into the hands of other robbers just across the Border, and whose misfortunes were the laughing-stock of the bazar. "Ohé, priest, whence come you and whither do you go?"

"From Roum have I come," shouted the priest, waving his whirligig; "from Roum, blown by the breath of a hundred devils across the sea! O thieves, robbers, liars, the blessing of Pir Khan on pigs, dogs, and perjurers! Who will take the Protected of God to the North to sell charms that are never still to the Amir? The camels shall not gall, the sons shall not fall sick, and the wives shall remain faithful while they are away, of the men who give me place in their caravan. Who will assist me to slipper the King of the Roos with a golden slipper with a silver heel? The protection of Pir Khan be upon his labours!" He spread out the skirts of his gaberdine and pirouetted between the lines of tethered horses.

"These starts a caravan from Peshawar to Kabul in twenty days, *Huzrut,*" said the Eusufzai trader. "My camels go therewith. Do thou also go and bring us good-luck."

"I will go even now!" shouted the priest. "I will depart upon my winged camels, and be at Peshawar in a day! Ho! Hazar Mir Khan," he yelled to his servant, "drive out the camels, but let me first mount my own."

He leaped on the back of his beast as it knelt, and, turning round to me, cried: "Come thou also, Sahib, a little along the road, and I will sell thee a charm — an amulet that shall make thee King of Kafiristan."

Then the light broke upon me, and I followed the two camels out of the Serai till we reached open road and the priest halted.

"What d'you think o' that?" said he in English. "Carnehan can't talk their patter, so I've made him my servant. He makes a handsome servant. 'Tisn't for nothing that I've been knocking about the country for fourteen years. Didn't I do that talk neat? We'll hitch on to a caravan at Peshawar till we get to Jagdallak, and then we'll see if we can get donkeys for our camels, and strike into Kafiristan. Whirligigs for the Amir, O Lor! Put your hand under the camel-bags and tell me what you feel."

I felt the butt of a Martini, and another and another.

"Twenty of 'em," said Dravot placidly.

"Twenty of 'em and ammunition to correspond, under the whirligigs and the mud dolls."

"Heaven help you if you are caught with those things!" I said. "A Martini is worth her weight in silver among the Pathans."

"Fifteen hundred rupees of capital — every rupee we could beg, borrow, or steal — are invested on these two camels," said Dravot. "We won't get caught. We're going through the Khaiber with a regular caravan. Who'd touch a poor mad priest?"

"Have you got everything you want?" I asked, overcome with astonishment.

"Not yet, but we shall soon. Give us a memento of your kindness, *Brother*, you did me a service, yesterday, and that time in Marwar. Half my Kingdom shall you have as the saying is." I slipped a small charm compass from my watch chain and handed it up to the priest.

"Good-bye," said Dravot, giving me hand cautiously. "It's the last time we'll shake hands with an Englishman these many days. Shake hands with him, Carnehan," he cried, as the second camel passed me.

Carnehan leaned down and shook hands. Then the camels passed away along the dusty road, and I was left alone to wonder. My eye could detect no failure in the disguises. The scene in the Serai proved that they were complete to the native mind. There was just the chance, therefore, that Carnehan and Dravot would be able to wander through Afghanistan without detection. But, beyond, they would find death — certain and awful death.

Ten days later a native correspondent giving me the news of the day from Peshawar, wound up his letter with: "There has been much laughter here on account of a certain mad priest who is going in his estimation to sell petty gauds and insignificant trinkets which he ascribes as great charms to H.H. the Amir of Bokhara. He passed through Peshawar and associated himself to the Second Summer caravan that goes to Kabul. The merchants are pleased because through superstition they imagine that such mad fellows bring good-fortune."

The two, then, were beyond the Border. I would have prayed for them, but, that night, a real King died in Europe, and demanded an obituary notice.

The wheel of the world swings through the same phases again and again. Summer passed and winter thereafter, and came and passed again. The daily paper continued and I with it, and upon the third summer there fell a hot night, a night-issue, and a strained waiting for something to be telegraphed from the other side of the world, exactly as had happened before. A few great men had died in the past two years, the machines worked with more clatter, and some of the trees in the Office garden were a few feet taller. But that was all the difference.

I passed over to the press-room, and went through just such a scene as I have already described. The nervous tension was stronger than it had been two years before, and I felt the heat more acutely. At three o'clock I cried, "Print off," and turned to go, when there crept to my chair what was left of a man. He was bent into a circle, his head was sunk between his shoulders, and he moved his feet one over the other like a bear. I could hardly see whether he walked or crawled — this rag-wrapped, whining cripple who addressed me by name, crying that he was come back. "Can you give me a drink?" he whimpered. "For the Lord's sake, give me a drink!"

I went back to the office, the man following with groans of pain, and I turned up the lamp.

"Don't you know me?" he gasped, dropping into a chair, and he turned his drawn face, surmounted by a shock of gray hair, to the light.

I looked at him intently. Once before had I seen eyebrows that met over the nose in an inch-broad black band, but for the life of me I could not tell where.

"I don't know you," I said, handing him the whiskey. "What can I do for you?"

He took a gulp of the spirit raw, and shivered in spite of the suffocating heat.

"I've come back," he repeated; "and I was

the King of Kafiristan — me and Dravot — crowned Kings we was! In this office we settled it — you setting there and giving us the books. I am Peachey — Peachey Taliaferro Carnehan, and you've been setting here ever since — O Lord!''

I was more than a little astonished, and expressed my feelings accordingly.

''It's true,'' said Carnehan, with a dry cackle, nursing his feet, which were wrapped in rags. ''True as gospel. Kings we were, with crowns upon our heads — me and Dravot — poor Dan — oh, poor, poor Dan, that would never take advice, not though I begged of him!''

''Take the whiskey,'' I said, ''and take your own time. Tell me all you can recollect of everything from beginning to end. You got across the border on your camels, Dravot dressed as a mad priest and you his servant. Do you remember that?''

''I ain't mad — yet, but I shall be that way soon. Of course I remember. Keep looking at me, or maybe my words will go all to pieces. Keep looking at me in my eyes and don't say anything.''

I leaned forward and looked into his face as steadily as I could. He dropped one hand upon the table and I grasped it by the wrist. It was twisted like a bird's claw, and upon the back was a ragged, red diamond-shaped scar.

''No, don't look there. Look at *me*,'' said

Carnehan. "That comes afterwards, but for the Lord's sake don't distrack me. We left with that caravan, me and Dravot playing all sorts of antics to amuse the people we were with. Dravot used to make us laugh in the evenings when all the people was cooking their dinners — cooking their dinners, and . . . what did they do then? They lit little fires with sparks that went into Dravot's beard, and we all laughed — fit to die. Little red fires they was, going into Dravot's big red beard — so funny." His eyes left mine and he smiled foolishly.

"You went as far as Jagdallak with that caravan," I said at a venture, "after you had lit those fires. To Jagdallak, where you turned off to try to get into Kafiristan."

"No, we didn't neither. What are you talking about? We turned off before Jagdallak, because we heard the roads were good. But they wasn't good enough for our two camels — mine and Dravot's. When we left the caravan, Dravot took off all his clothes and mine too, and said we would be heathen, because the Kafirs didn't allow Mohammedans to talk to them. So we dressed betwixt and between, and such a sight as Daniel Dravot I never saw yet nor expect to see again. He burned half his beard, and slung a sheep-skin over his shoulder, and shaved his head into patterns. He shaved mine, too, and made me wear outrageous things to look like a heathen. That was in a most mountaineous country, and our camels couldn't go along any more because of the mountains. They were tall and black, and coming home I saw them fight like wild goats — there are lots of goats in Kafiristan. And these mountains, they never keep still, no more than the goats. Always fighting they are, and don't let you sleep at night."

"Take some more whiskey," I said very slowly. "What did you and Daniel Dravot do when the camels could go no further because of the rough roads that led into Kafiristan?"

"What did which do? There was a party called Peachey Taliaferro Carnehan that was with Dravot. Shall I tell you about him? He died out there in the cold. Slap from the bridge fell old Peachey, turning and twisting in the air like a penny whirligig that you can sell to the Amir. — No; they was two for three ha'pence, those whirligigs, or I am much mistaken and woeful sore. . . . And then these camels were no use, and Peachey said to Dravot — 'For the Lord's sake let's get out of this before our heads are chopped off,' and with that they killed the camels all among the mountains, not having anything in particular to eat, but first they took off the boxes with the guns and the ammunition, till two men came along driving four mules. Dravot up and dances in front of them, singing — 'Sell me four mules.' Says the first man — 'If you are rich enough to buy, you are rich enough to rob'; but before ever he could put his hand to his knife, Dravot breaks his neck over his knee, and the other party runs away. so Carnehan loaded the mules with the rifles that was taken off the camels, and together we starts forward into those bitter cold mountaineous parts, and never a road broader than the back of your hand.''

He paused for a moment, while I asked him if he could remember the nature of the country through which he had journeyed.

``I am telling you as straight as I can, but my head isn't as good as it might be. They drove nails through it to make me hear better how Dravot died. The country was mountaineous and the mules were most contrary, and the inhabitants were dispersed and solitary. They went up and up, and down and down, and that other party, Carnehan, was imploring of Dravot not to sing and whistle so loud, for fear of bringing down the tremenjus avalanches. But Dravot says that if a King couldn't sing it wasn't worth being King, and whacked the mules over the rump, and never took no heed for ten cold days. We came to a big level valley all among the mountains, and the mules were near dead, so we killed them, not having anything in special for them or us to eat. We sat upon the boxes, and played odd and even with the cartridges that was jolted out.

``Then ten men with bows and arrows ran down that valley, chasing twenty men with bows and arrows, and the row was tremenjus. They was fair men — fairer than you or me — with yellow hair and remarkable well built. Says Dravot, unpacking the guns — 'This is the beginning of the business. We'll fight for the ten men,' and with that he fires two rifles at the twenty men, and drops one of them at two hundred yards from the rock where he was sitting. The other men began to run, but Carnehan and Dravot sits on the boxes picking them off at all ranges, up and down the valley. Then we goes up to the ten men that had run across the snow too, and they fires a footy little arrow at us. Dravot he shoots above their heads and they all falls down flat. Then he walks over them and kicks them, and then he lifts them up and shakes hands all round to make them friendly like. He calls them and gives them the boxes to carry, and waves his hand for all the world as though he was King already. They takes the boxes and him across the valley and up the hill into a pine wood on the top, where there was half a dozen big stone idols. Dravot he goes to the biggest — a fellow they call Imbra — and lays a rifle and a cartridge at his feet, rubbing his nose respectful with his own nose, patting him on the head, and saluting in front of it. He turns round to the men and nods his head, and says — 'That's all right. I'm in the know, too, and all these old jim-jams are my friends.' Then he opens his mouth and points down it, and when the first man brings him food, he says — 'No'; and when the second man brings him food he says — 'No'; but when one of the old priests and the boss of the village brings him food, he says — 'Yes'; very haughty, and eats it slow. That was how we came to our first village, without any trouble, just as though we had tumbled from the skies. But we tumbled from one of those damned rope-bridges, you see and — you couldn't expect a man to laugh much after that?''

''Take some more whiskey and go on,'' I said. ''That was the first village you came into. How did you get to be King?''

''I wasn't King,'' said Carnehan. ''Dravot he was the King, and a handsome man he looked with the gold crown on his head and all. Him and the other party stayed in that village, and every morning Dravot sat by the side of old Imbra, and the people came and worshipped. That was Dravot's order. Then a lot of men came into the valley, and Carnehan Dravot picks them off with the rifles before they knew where they was, and runs down into the valley and up again the other side and finds another village, same as the first one, and the people all falls down flat on their faces, and Dravot says — 'Now what is the trouble between you two villages?' and the people points to a woman, as fair as you or me, that was carried off, and Dravot takes her back to the first village and counts up the dead

— eight there was. For each dead man Dravot pours a little milk on the ground and waves his arms like a whirligig and 'That's all right,' says he. Then he and Carnehan takes the big boss of each village by the arm and walks them down into the valley, and shows them how to scratch a line with a spear right down the valley, and gives each a sod of turf from both sides of the line. Then all the people comes down and shouts like the devil and all, and Dravot says — 'Go and dig the land, and be fruitful and multiply,' which they did, though they didn't understand. Then we asks the names of things in their lingo — bread and water and fire and idols and such, and Dravot leads the priest of each village up to the idol, and says he must sit there and judge the people, and if anything goes wrong he is to be shot.

"'Next week they was all turning up the land in the valley as quiet as bees and much prettier, and the priests heard all the complaints and told Dravot in dumb show what it was about. 'That's just the beginning,' says Dravot. 'They think we're Gods.' He and Carnehan picks out twenty good men and shows them how to click off a rifle, and form fours, and advance in line, and they was very pleased to do so, and clever to see the hang of it. Then he takes out his pipe and his baccy-pouch and leaves one at one village, and one at the other, and off we two goes to see what was to be done in the next valley. That was all rock, and there was a little village there, and Carnehan says — 'Send 'em to the old valley to plant,' and takes 'em there and gives 'em some land that wasn't took before. They were a poor lot, and we blooded 'em with a kid before letting 'em into the new Kingdom. That was to impress the people, and then they settled down quiet, and Carnehan went back to Dravot who had got into another valley, all snow and ice and most mountaineous. There was no people there and the Army got afraid, so Dravot shoots one of them, and goes on till he finds some people in a village, and the Army explains that unless the people wants to be killed they had better not shoot their little matchlocks; for they had matchlocks. We made friends with the priest and I stays there alone with two of the Army, teaching the men how to drill, and a thundering big Chief comes across the snow with kettle-drums and horns twanging, because he heard there was a new God kicking about. Carnehan sights for the brown of the men half a mile across the snow and wings one of them. Then he sends a message to the Chief that, unless he wished to be killed, he must come and shake hands with me and leave his arms behind. The Chief comes alone first, and Carnehan shakes hands with him and whirls his arms about, same as Dravot used, and very much surprised that Chief was, and strokes my eyebrows. Then Carnehan goes alone to the Chief, and asks him in dumb show if he had an enemy he hated. 'I have,' says the Chief. So Carnehan weeds out the pick of the men, and sets the two of the Army to show them drill and at the end of two weeks the men can manœuvre about as well as Volunteers. So he marches with the Chief to a great big plain on the top of a mountain, and the Chief's men rushes into a village and takes it; we three Martinis firing into the brown of the enemy. So we took that village too, and I gives the Chief a rag from my coat and says 'Occupy till I come'; which was scriptural. By way of a reminder, when me and the Army was eighteen hundred yards away, I drops a bullet near him standing on the snow, and all the people falls flat on their faces. Then I sends a letter to Dravot wherever he be by land or by sea."

At the risk of throwing the creature out of train I interrupted — "How could you write a letter up yonder?"

"The letter? — Oh! — The letter! Keep looking at me between the eyes, please. It was a string-talk letter, that we'd learned the way of it from a blind beggar in the Punjab."

I remember that there had once come to the office a blind man with a knotted twig and a piece of string which he wound round the twig according to some cipher of his own. He could, after the lapse of days or hours, repeat the sentence which he had reeled up. He had reduced the alphabet to eleven primitive sounds; and tried to teach me his method, but I could not understand.

"I sent that letter to Dravot," said Carnehan; "and told him to come back because this Kingdom was growing too big for me to handle, and then I struck for the first valley, to see how the priests were working. They called the village we took along with the Chief, Bashkai, and the first village we took, Er-Heb. The priests at Er-Heb was doing all right, but they had a lot of pending cases about land to show me, and some men from another village had been firing arrows at night. I went out and looked for that village, and fired four rounds at it from a thousand yards. That used all the cartridges I cared to spend, and I waited for Dravot, who had been away two or three months, and I kept my people quiet.

"One morning I heard the devil's own noise of drums and horns, and Dan Dravot marches down the hill with his Army and a tail of hundreds of men, and, which was the most amazing, a great gold crown on his head. 'My Gord, Carnehan,' says Daniel, 'this is a tremenjus business, and we've got the whole country as far as it's worth having. I am the son of Alexander by Queen Semiramis, and you're my younger brother and a God too! It's the biggest thing we've ever seen. I've been marching and fighting for six weeks with the Army, and every footy little village for fifty miles has come in rejoiceful; and more than that, I've got the key of the whole show, as you'll see, and I've got a crown for you! I told 'em to make two of 'em at a place called Shu, where the gold lies in the rock like suet in mutton. Gold I've seen, and turquoise I've kicked out of the cliffs, and there's garnets in the sands of the river, and here's a chunk of amber that a man brought me. Call up all the priests and, here, take your crown.'

"'One of the men opens a black hair bag, and I slips the crown on. It was too small and too heavy, but I wore it for the glory. Hammered gold it was — five pound weight, like a hoop of a barrel.

"'Peachey,' says Dravot, 'we don't want to fight no more. The Craft's the trick so help me!' and he brings forward that same Chief that I left at Bashkai — Billy Fish we called him afterwards, because he was so like Billy Fish that drove the big tank-engine at Mach on the Bolan in the old days. 'Shake hands with him,' says Dravot, and I shook hands and nearly dropped, for Billy Fish gave me the Grip. I said nothing, but tried him with the Fellow Craft Grip. He answers, all right, and I tried the Master's Grip, but that was a slip. 'A Fellow Craft he is'; I says to Dan. 'Does he know the word?' — 'He does,' says Dan, 'and all the priests know. It's a miracle. The Chiefs and the priests can work a Fellow Craft Lodge in a way that's very like ours, and they've cut the marks on the rocks, but they don't know the Third Degree, and they've come to find out. It's Gord's Truth. I've known these long years that the Afghans knew up to the Fellow Craft Degree, but this is a miracle. A God and a Grand-Master of the Craft am I, and a Lodge in the Third Degree I will open, and we'll raise the head priests and the Chiefs of the villages.'

" 'It's against all the law,' I says, 'holding a Lodge without warrant from any one; and you know we never held office in any Lodge.'

" 'It's a master-stroke o' policy,' says Dravot. 'It means running the country as easy as a four-wheeled bogie on a down grade. We can't stop to enquire now, or they'll turn against us. I've forty Chiefs at my heel, and passed and raised according to their merit they shall be. Billet these men on his villages, and see that we run up a Lodge of some kind. The temple of Imbra will do for the Lodge-room. The women must make aprons as you show them. I'll hold a levee of Chiefs to-night and Lodge to-morrow.'

"I was fair run off my legs, but I wasn't such a fool as not to see what a pull this Craft business gave us. I showed the priests' families how to make aprons of the degrees, but for Dravot's apron the blue border and marks was made of turquoise lumps on white hide, not cloth. We took a great square stone in the temple for the Master's chair, and little stones for the officers' chairs, and painted the black pavement with white squares, and did what we could to make things regular.

"At the levee which was held that night on the hillside with big bonfires, Dravot gives out that him and me were Gods and sons of Alexander, and Past Grand Masters in the Craft, and was come to make Kafiristan a country where every man should eat in peace and drink in quiet, and specially obey us. Then the Chiefs come round to shake hands, and they were so hairy and white and fair it was just shaking hands with old friends. We gave them names according as they was like men we had known in India — Billy Fish, Holly Dilworth, Pikky Kergan, that was Bazar-master when I was at Mhow, and so on, and so on.

"*The* most amazing miracles was at Lodge next night. One of the old priests was watching us continuous, and I felt uneasy, for I knew we'd have to fudge the Ritual, and I didn't know what the men knew. The old priest was a stranger come in from beyond the village of Bashkai. The minute Dravot puts on the Master's apron that the girls had made for him, the priest fetches a whoop and a howl, and tries to overturn the stone that Dravot was sitting on. 'It's all up now,' I says. 'That comes of meddling with the Craft without warrant!' Dravot never winked an eye, not when ten priests took and tilted over the Grand-Master's chair — which was to say the stone of Imbra. The priest begins rubbing the bottom end of it to clear away the black dirt, and presently he shows all the other priests the Master's Mark, same as was on Dravot's apron, cut into the stone. Not even the priests of the temple of Imbra knew it was there. The old chap falls flat on his face at Dravot's feet and kisses 'em. 'Luck again,' says Dravot, across the Lodge to me, 'they say it's the missing Mark that no one could understand the why of. We're more than safe now.' Then he bangs the butt of his gun for a gavel and says: 'By virtue of the authority vested in me by my own right hand and the help of Peachey, I declare myself Grand-Master of all Freemasonry in Kafiristan in this the Mother Lodge o' the country, and King of Kafiristan equally with Peachey!' At that he puts on his crown and I puts on mine — I was doing Senior Warden — and we opens the Lodge in most ample form. It was a amazing miracle! The priests moved in Lodge through the first two degrees almost without telling, as if the memory was coming back to them. After that, Peachey and Dravot raised such as was worthy — high priests and Chiefs of far-off villages. Billy Fish was the first, and I can tell you we scared the soul out of him. It was not in any way according to Ritual, but it served our turn. We didn't raise more than ten of the biggest men, because we didn't want to make the Degree common. And they was clamouring to be raised.

" 'In another six months,' says Dravot, 'we'll hold another Communication, and see how you are working.' Then he asks them about their villages, and learns that they was fighting one against the other, and were sick and tired of it. And when they wasn't doing that they was fighting with the Mohammedans. 'You can fight those when they come into our country,' says Dravot. 'Tell off every tenth man of your tribes for a Frontier guard, and send two hundred at a time to this valley to be drilled. Nobody is going to be shot or speared any more so long as he does well, and I know that you won't cheat me, because you're white people — sons of Alexander — and not like common, black Mohammedans. You are *my* people, and by God,' says he, running off into English at the end — 'I'll make a damned fine Nation of you, or I'll die in the making!'

"I can't tell all we did for the next six months, because Dravot did a lot I couldn't see the hang of, and he learned their lingo in a way I never could. My work was to help the people plough, and now and again go out with some of the Army and see what the other villages were doing, and make 'em throw rope-bridges across the ravines which cut up the country horrid. Dravot was very kind to me, but when he walked up and down in the pine wood pulling that bloody red beard of his with both fists I knew he was thinking plans I could not advise about, and I just waited for orders.

"But Dravot never showed me disrespect

before the people. They were afraid of me and the Army, but they loved Dan. He was the best of friends with the priests and the Chiefs; but any one could come across the hills with a complaint, and Dravot would hear him out fair, and call four priests together and say what was to be done. He used to call in Billy Fish from Bashkai, and Pikky Kergan from Shu, and an old Chief we called Kafuzelum — it was like enough to his real name — and hold councils with 'em when there was any fighting to be done in small villages. That was his Council of War, and the four priests of Bashkai, Shu, Khawak, and Madora was his Privy Council. Between the lot of 'em they sent me, with forty men and twenty rifles, and sixty men carrying turquoises, into the Ghorband country to buy those hand-made Martini rifles, that come out of the Amir's workshops at Kabul, from one of the Amir's Herati regiments that would have sold the very teeth out of their mouths for turquoises.

"I stayed in Ghorband a month, and gave the governor there the pick of my baskets for hush-money, and bribed the Colonel of the regiment some more, and, between the two and the tribes-people, we got more than a hundred hand-made Martinis, a hundred good Kohat Jezails that'll throw to six hundred yards, and forty manloads of very bad ammunition for the rifles. I came back with what I had, and distributed 'em among the men that the Chiefs sent in to me to drill. Dravot was too busy to attend to those things, but the old Army that we first made helped me, and we turned out five hundred men that could drill, and two hundred that knew how to hold arms pretty straight. Even those cork-screwed, hand-made guns was a miracle to them. Dravot talked big about powder-shops and factories, walking up and down in the pine wood when the winter was coming on.

" 'I won't make a Nation,' says he. 'I'll make an Empire! These men aren't niggers; they're English! Look at their eyes — look at their mouths. Look at the way they stand up. They sit on chairs in their own houses. They're the Lost Tribes, or something like it, and they've grown to be English. I'll take a census in the spring if the priests don't get frightened. There must be a fair two million of 'em in these hills. The villages are full o' little children. Two million people — two hundred and fifty thousand fighting men — and all English! They only want the rifles and a little drilling. Two hundred and fifty thousand men, ready to cut in on Russia's right flank when she tries for India! Peachey, man,' he says, chewing his beard in great hunks, 'we shall be Emperors — Emperors of the Earth! Rajah Brooke will be a suckling to us. I'll treat with the Viceroy on equal terms. I'll ask him to send me twelve picked English — twelve that I know of — to help us govern a bit. There's Mackray,

Sergeant-pensioner at Segowli — many's the good dinner he's given me, and his wife a pair of trousers. There's Donkin, the Warder of Tounghoo Jail; there's hundreds that I could lay my hand on if I was in India. The Viceroy shall do it for me, I'll send a man through in the spring for those men, and I'll write for a dispensation from the Grand Lodge for what I've done as Grand-Master. That — and all the Sniders that'll be thrown out when the native troops in India take up the Martini. They'll be worn smooth, but they'll do for fighting in these hills. Twelve English, a hundred thousand Sniders run through the Amir's country in driblets — I'd be content with twenty thousand in one year — and we'd be an Empire. When everything was ship-shape, I'd hand over the crown — this crown I'm wearing now — to Queen Victoria on my knees, and she'd say: "Rise up, Sir Daniel Dravot." Oh, it's big! It's big, I tell you! But there's so much to be done in every place — Bashkai, Khawak, Shu, and everywhere else.'

" 'What is it?' I says. 'There are no more men coming in to be drilled this autumn. Look at those fat, black clouds, They're bringing the snow.'

" 'It isn't that,' says Daniel, putting his hand very hard on my shoulder; 'and I don't wish to say anything that's against you, for no other living man would have followed me and made me what I am as you have done. You're a first-class Commander-in-Chief, and the people know you; but — it's a big country, and somehow you can't help me, Peachey, in the way I want to be helped.'

" 'Go to your blasted priests, then!' I said, and I was sorry when I made that remark, but it did hurt me sore to find Daniel talking so superior when I'd drilled all the men, and done all he told me.

" 'Don't let's quarrel, Peachey,' says Daniel without cursing. 'You're a King too, and the half of this Kingdom is yours; but can't you see, Peachey, we want cleverer men than us now — three or four of 'em, that we can scatter about for our Deputies. It's a hugeous great State, and I can't always tell the right thing to do, and I haven't time for all I want to do, and here's the winter coming on and all.' He put half his beard into his mouth, all red like the gold of his crown.

" 'I'm sorry, Daniel,' says I. 'I've done all I could. I've drilled the men and shown the people how to stack their oats better; and I've brought in those tin-war rifles from Ghorband — but I know what you're driving at. I take it Kings always feel oppressed that way.'

" 'There's another thing too,' says Dravot, walking up and down. 'The winter's coming and these people won't be giving much trouble, and if they do we can't move about. I want a wife.'

" 'For Gord's sake leave the women alone!'

I says. 'We've both got all the work we can, though I *am* a fool. Remember the Contrack, and keep clear o' women.'

" 'The Contrack only lasted till such time as we was Kings; and Kings we have been these months past,' says Dravot, weighing his crown in his hand. 'You go get a wife too, Peachey — a nice, strappin', plump girl that'll keep you warm in the winter. They're prettier than English girls, and we can take the pick of 'em. Boil 'em once or twice in hot water, and they'll come out like chicken and ham.'

" 'Don't tempt me!' I says. 'I will not have any dealings with a woman not till we are a dam' side more settled than we are now. I've been doing the work o' two men, and you've been doing the work o' three. Let's lie off a bit, and see if we can get some better tobacco from Afghan country and run in some good liquor; but no women.'

" 'Who's talking o' *women?'* says Dravot. 'I said *wife* — a queen to breed a King's son for the King. A Queen out of the strongest tribe, that'll make them your blood-brothers, and that'll lie by your side and tell you all the people thinks about you and their own affairs. That's what I want.'

" 'Do you remember that Bengali woman I kept at Mogul Serai when I was a plate-layer?' says I. 'A fat lot o' good she was to me. She taught me the lingo and one or two other things; but what happened? She ran away with the Station Master's servant and half my month's pay. Then she turned up at Dadur Junction in tow of a half-caste, and had the impidence to say I was her husband — all among the drivers in the running-shed too!'

" 'We've done with that,' says Dravot, 'these women are whiter than you or me, and a Queen I will have for the winter months.'

" 'For the last time o' asking, Dan, do *not,*' I says. 'It'll only bring us harm. The Bible says that Kings ain't to waste their strength on women, 'specially when they've got a new raw Kingdom to work over.'

" 'For the last time of answering I will,' said Dravot, and he went away through the pine-trees looking like a big red devil, the sun being on his crown and beard and all.

"But getting a wife was not as easy as Dan thought. He put it before the Council, and there was no answer till Billy Fish said he'd better ask the girls. Dravot damned them all round. 'What's wrong with me?' he shouts, standing by the Idol Imbra. 'Am I a dog or am I not enough of a man for your wenches? Haven't I put the shadow of my hand over this country? Who stopped the last Afghan raid?' It was me really, but Dravot was too angry to remember. 'Who brought your guns? Who repaired the bridges? Who's the Grand-Master of the sign cut in the stone?' says he, and he thumped his hand on the block that he used to sit on in Lodge, and at Council, which opened like

Lodge always. Billy Fish said nothing and no more did the others. 'Keep your hair on, Dan,' said I; 'and ask the girls. That's how it's done at Home, and these people are quite English.'

" 'The marriage of the King is a matter of State,' says Dan, in a white-hot rage, for he could feel, I hope, that he was going against his better mind. He walked out of the Council-room, and the others sat still, looking at the ground.

" 'Billy Fish,' says I to the Chief of Bashkai, 'what's the difficulty here? A straight answer to a true friend.'

" 'You know,' says Billy Fish. 'How should a man tell you who knows everything? How can daughters of men marry Gods or Devils? It's not proper.'

"I remembered something like that in the Bible; but if, after seeing us as long as they had, they still believed we were Gods, it wasn't for me to undeceive them.

" 'A God can do anything,' says I. 'If the King is fond of a girl he'll not let her die.' — 'She'll have to,' said Billy Fish. 'There are all sorts of Gods and Devils in these mountains, and now and again a girl marries one of them and isn't seen any more. Besides, you two know the Mark cut in the stone. Only the Gods know that. We thought you were men till you showed the sign of the Master.'

"I wished then that we had explained about the loss of the genuine secrets of a Master-

Mason at the first go-off; but I said nothing. All that night there was a blowing of horns in a little dark temple half-way down the hill, and I heard a girl crying fit to die. One of the priests told us that she was being prepared to marry the King.

" 'I'll have no nonsense of that kind,' says Dan. 'I don't want to interfere with your customs, but I'll take my own wife.' — 'The girl's a little bit afraid,' says the priest. 'She thinks she's going to die, and they are a-heartening of her up down in the temple.'

" 'Hearten her very tender, then,' says Dravot, 'or I'll hearten you with the butt of a gun so you'll never want to be heartened again.' He licked his lips, did Dan, and stayed up walking about more than half the night, thinking of the wife that he was going to get in the morning. I wasn't by any means comfortable, for I knew that dealings with a woman in foreign parts, though you was a crowned King twenty times over, could not but be risky. I got up very early in the morning while Dravot was asleep, and I saw the priests talking together in whispers, and the Chiefs talking together too, and they looked at me out of the corners of their eyes.

" 'What is up, Fish?' I say to the Bashkai man, who was wrapped up in his furs and looking splendid to behold.

" 'I can't rightly say,' says he; 'but if you can make the King drop all this nonsense about marriage, you'll be doing him and me and yourself a great service.'

" 'That I do believe,' says I. 'But sure, you know, Billy, as well as me, having fought against and for us, that the King and me are nothing more than two of the finest men that God Almighty every made. Nothing more, I do assure you.'

" 'That may be,' says Billy Fish, 'and yet I should be sorry if it was.' He sinks his head upon his great fur cloak for a minute and thinks. 'King,' says he, 'be you man or God or Devil, I'll stick by you to-day. I have twenty of my men with me, and they will follow me. We'll go to Bashkai until the storm blows over.'

"A little snow had fallen in the night, and everything was white except the greasy fat clouds that blew down and down from the north. Dravot came out with his crown on his head, swinging his arms and stamping his feet, and looking more pleased than Punch.

" 'For the last time, drop it, Dan,' says I in a whisper, 'Billy Fish here says that there will be a row.'

" 'A row among my people!' says Dravot. 'Not much. Peachey, you're a fool not to get a wife too. Where's the girl?' says he with a voice as loud as the braying of a jackass. 'Call up all the Chiefs and priests, and let the Emperor see if his wife suits him.'

"There was no need to call any one. They

were all there leaning on their guns and spears round the clearing in the centre of the pine wood. A lot of priests went down to the little temple to bring up the girl, and the horns blew fit to wake the dead. Billy Fish saunters round and gets as close to Daniel as he could, and behind him stood his twenty men with matchlocks. Not a man of them under six feet. I was next to Dravot, and behind me was twenty men of the regular Army. Up comes the girl, and a strapping wench she was, covered with silver and turquoises but white as death, and looking back every minute at the priests.

" 'She'll do,' said Dan, looking her over. 'What's to be afraid of, lass? Come and kiss me.' He puts his arm round her. She shuts her eyes, gives a bit of a squeak, and down goes her face in the side of Dan's flaming red beard.

" 'The slut's bitten me!' says he, clapping his hand to his neck, and, sure enough, his hand was red with blood. Billy Fish and two of his matchlockmen catches hold of Dan by the shoulders and drags him into the Bashkai lot, while the priests howls in their lingo, — 'Neither God nor Devil but a man!' I was all taken aback, for a priest cut at me in front, and the Army began firing into the Bashkai men.

" 'God A'mighty!' says Dan. 'What is the meaning o' this?'

" 'Come back! Come away!' says Billy Fish. 'Ruin and Mutiny is the matter. We'll break for Bashkai if we can.'

"I tried to give some sort of orders to my men — the men o' the regular Army — but it was no use, so I fired into the brown of 'em with an English Martini and drilled three beggars in a line. The valley was full of shouting, howling creatures, and every soul was shrieking, 'Not a God nor a Devil but only a man!' The Bashkai troops stuck to Billy Fish all they were worth, but their matchlocks wasn't half as good as the Kabul breechloaders, and four of them dropped. Dan was bellowing like a bull, for he was very wrathy; and Billy Fish had a hard job to prevent him running out at the crowd.

" 'We can't stand,' says Billy Fish. 'Make a run for it down the valley! The whole place is against us.' The matchlock-men ran, and we went down the valley in spite of Dravot. He was swearing horrible and crying out he was a King. The priests rolled great stones on us, and the regular Army fired hard, and there wasn't more than six men, not counting Dan, Billy Fish, and Me, that came down to the bottom of the valley alive.

"Then they stopped firing and the horns in the temple blew again. 'Come away — for Gord's sake come away!' says Billy Fish. 'They'll send runners out to all the villages before ever we get to Bashkai. I can protect you there, but I can't do anything now.'

"My own notion is that Dan began to go

mad in his head from that hour. He stared up and down like a stuck pig. Then he was all for walking back alone and killing the priests with his bare hands; which he could have done. 'An Emperor am I,' says Daniel, 'and next year I shall be a Knight of the Queen.'

" 'All right, Dan,' says I; 'but come along now while there's time.'

" 'It's your fault,' says he, 'for not looking after your Army better. There was mutiny in the midst, and you didn't know — you damned engine-driving, plate-laying, missionary's-pass-hunting hound!'' He sat upon a rock and called me every foul name he could lay tongue to. I was too heart-sick to care, though it was all his foolishness that brought the smash.

" 'I'm sorry, Dan,' says I, 'but there's no accounting for natives. This business is our Fifty-seven. Maybe we'll make something out of it yet, when we've got to Bashkai.'

" 'Let's get to Bashkai, then,' says Dan, 'and, by God, when I come back here again I'll sweep the valley so there isn't a bug in a blanket left!'

"We walked all that day, and all that night Dan was stumping up and down on the snow, chewing his beard and muttering to himself.

" 'There's no hope o' getting clear,' said Billy Fish. 'The priests will have sent runners to the villages to say that you are only men. Why didn't you stick on as Gods till things was more settled? I'm a dead man,' says Billy

Fish, and he throws himself down on the snow and begins to pray to his Gods.

"Next morning we was in a cruel bad country — all up and down, no level ground at all, and no food either. The six Bashkai men looked at Billy Fish hungry-way as if they wanted to ask something, but they said never a word. At noon we came to the top of a flat mountain all covered with snow, and when we climbed up into it, behold, there was an Army in position waiting in the middle!

" 'The runners have been very quick,' says Billy Fish, with a little bit of a laugh. 'They are waiting for us.'

"Three or four men began to fire from the enemy's side, and a chance shot took Daniel in the calf of the leg. That brought him to his senses. He looks across the snow at the Army, and sees the rifles that we had brought into the country.

" 'We're done for,' says he. 'They are Englishmen, these people, — and it's my blasted nonsense that has brought you to this. Get back, Billy Fish, and take your men away; you've done what you could, and now cut for it. Carnehan,' says he, 'shake hands with me and go along with Billy. Maybe they won't kill you. I'll go and meet 'em alone. It's me that did it. Me, the King!'

" 'Go!' says I. 'Go to Hell, Dan. I'm with you here. Billy Fish, you clear out, and we two will meet those folk.'

" 'I'm a Chief,' says Billy Fish, quite quiet. 'I stay with you. My men can go.'

"The Bashkai fellows didn't wait for a second word but ran off, and Dan and Me and Billy Fish walked across to where the drums were drumming and the horns were horning. It was cold — awful cold. I've got that cold in the back of my head now. There's a lump of it there."

The punkah-coolies had gone to sleep. Two kerosene lamps were blazing in the office, and the perspiration poured down my face and splashed on the blotter as I leaned forward. Carnehan was shivering, and I feared that his mind might go. I wiped my face, took a fresh grip of the piteously mangled hands, and said, "What happened after that?"

The momentary shift of my eyes had broken the clear current.

"What was you pleased to say?" whined Carnehan. "They took them without any sound. Not a little whisper all along the snow, not though the King knocked down the first man that set hand on him — not though old Peachey fired his last cartridge into the brown of 'em. Not a single solitary sound did those swines make. They just closed up tight, and I tell you their furs stunk. There was a man called Billy Fish, a good friend of us all, and they cut his throat, Sir, then and there, like a pig; and the King kicks up the bloody snow and says: 'We've had a dashed fine run for our money. What's coming next?' But Peachey, Peachey Taliaferro, I tell you, Sir, in confidence as betwixt two friends, he lost his head, Sir. No, he didn't neither. The King lost his head, so he did, all along o' one of those cunning rope-bridges. Kindly let me have the paper-cutter, Sir. It tilted this way. They marched him a mile across that snow to a rope-bridge over a ravine with a river at the bottom. You may have seen such. They prodded him behind like an ox. 'Damn your eyes!' says the King. 'D'you suppose I can't die like a gentleman?' He turns to Peachey — Peachey that was crying like a child. 'I've brought you to this, Peachey,' says he. 'Brought you out of your happy life to be killed in Kafiristan where you was late Commander-in-Chief of the Emperor's forces. Say you forgive me, Peachey.' — 'I do,' says Peachey. 'Fully and freely do I forgive you, Dan.' — 'Shake hands, Peachey,' says he. 'I'm going now.' Out he goes, looking neither right nor left, and when he was plumb in the middle of those dizzy dancing ropes, — 'Cut, you beggars,' he shouts, and they cut, and old Dan fell, turning round and round and round, twenty thousand miles, for he took half an hour to fall till he struck the water, and I could see his body caught on a rock with the gold crown close beside.

"'But do you know what they did to Peachey between two pine-trees? They crucified him,

Sir, as Peachey's hands will show. They used wooden pegs for his hands and his feet; and he didn't die. He hung there and screamed, and they took him down next day, and said it was a miracle that he wasn't dead. They took him down — poor old Peachey that hadn't done them any harm — that hadn't done them any——"

He rocked to and fro and wept bitterly, wiping his eyes with the back of his scarred hands and moaning like a child for some ten minutes.

"They was cruel enough to feed him up in the temple, because they said he was more of a God than old Daniel that was a man. Then they turned him out on the snow, and told him to go home, and Peachey came home in about a year, begging along the roads quite safe; for Daniel Dravot he walked before and said: 'Come along, Peachey. It's a big thing we're doing.' The mountains they danced at night, and the mountains they tried to fall on Peachey's head, but Dan he held up his hand, and Peachey came along bent double. He never let go of Dan's hand, and he never let go of Dan's head. They gave it to him as a present in the temple, to remind him not to come again, and though the crown was pure gold, and Peachey was starving, never would Peachey sell the same. You knew Dravot, Sir! You knew Right Worshipful Brother Dravot! Look at him now!"

He fumbled in the mass of rags round his

bent waist; brought out a black horsehair bag embroidered with silver thread; and shook therefrom on to my table — the dried, withered head of Daniel Dravot! The morning sun that had long been paling the lamps struck the red beard and blind sunken eyes; struck, too, a heavy circlet of gold studded with raw turquoises, that Carnehan placed tenderly on the battered temples.

"You be'old now," said Carnehan, "the Emperor in his 'abit as he lived — the King of Kafiristan with his crown upon his head. Poor old Daniel that was a monarch once!"

I shuddered, for, in spite of defacements manifold, I recognized the head of the man of Marwar Junction. Carnehan rose to go. I attempted to stop him. He was not fit to walk abroad. "Let me take away the whiskey, and give me a little money," he gasped. "I was a King once. I'll go to the Deputy Commissioner and ask to set in the Poorhouse till I get my health. No, thank you, I can't wait till you get a carriage for me. I've urgent private affairs — in the South — at Marwar."

He shambled out of the office and departed in the direction of the Deputy Commissioner's house. That day at noon I had occasion to go down the blinding hot Mall, and I saw a crooked man crawling along the white dust of the roadside, his hat in his hand, quavering dolorously after the fashion of street-singers at Home. There was not a soul in sight, and he was out of all possible earshot of the houses. And he sang through his nose, turning his head from right to left: —

"The Son of Man goes forth to war,
A golden crown to gain;
His blood-red banner streams afar —
Who follows in his train?"

I waited to hear no more, but put the poor wretch into my carriage and drove him off to the nearest missionary for eventual transfer to the Asylum. He repeated the hymn twice while he was with me whom he did not in the least recognize, and I left him singing it to the missionary.

Two days later I enquired after his welfare of the Superintendent of the Asylum.

"He was admitted suffering from sunstroke. He died early yesterday morning," said the Superintendent. "Is it true that he was half an hour bareheaded in the sun at midday?"

"Yes," said I, "but do you happen to know if he had anything upon him by any chance when he died?"

"Not to my knowledge," said the Superintendent.

And there the matter rests.

The Open Window

Saki

"My aunt will be down presently, Mr. Nuttel," said a very self-possessed young lady of fifteen; "in the meantime you must try and put up with me."

Framton Nuttel endeavoured to say the correct something which should duly flatter the niece of the moment without unduly discounting the aunt that was to come. Privately he doubted more than ever whether these formal visits on a succession of total strangers would do much towards helping the nerve cure which he was supposed to be undergoing.

"I know how it will be," his sister had said when he was preparing to migrate to this rural retreat; "you will bury yourself down there and not speak to a living soul, and your nerves will be worse than ever from moping. I shall just give you letters of introduction to all the people I know there. Some of them, as far as I can remember, were quite nice."

Framton wondered whether Mrs. Sappleton, the lady to whom he was presenting one of the letters of introduction, came into the nice division.

"Do you know many of the people round here?" asked the niece, when she judged that they had had sufficient silent communion.

"Hardly a soul," said Framton. "My sister was staying here, at the rectory, you know, some four years ago, and she gave me letters of introduction to some of the people here."

He made the last statement in a tone of distinct regret.

"Then you know practically nothing about my aunt?" pursued the self-possessed young lady.

"Only her name and address," admitted the caller. He was wondering whether Mrs. Sappleton was in the married or widowed state. An undefinable something about the room seemed to suggest masculine habitation.

"Her great tragedy happened just three years ago," said the child; "that would be since your sister's time."

"Her tragedy?" asked Framton; somehow in this restful country spot tragedies seemed out of place.

"You may wonder why we keep that window wide open on an October afternoon," said the niece, indicating a large French window that opened on to a lawn.

"It is quite warm for the time of the year," said Framton; "but has that window got anything to do with the tragedy?"

"Out through that window, three years ago to a day, her husband and her two young brothers went off for their day's shooting. They never came back. In crossing the moor to their favourite snipe-shooting ground they were all three engulfed in a treacherous piece of bog. It had been that dreadful wet summer, you know, and places that were safe in other years gave way suddenly without warning. Their bodies were never recovered. That was the dreadful part of it." Here the child's voice lost its self-possessed note and became falteringly human. "Poor aunt always thinks that they will come back some day, they and the little brown spaniel that was lost with them, and walk in at that window just as they used to do. That is why the window is kept open every evening till it is quite dusk. Poor dear aunt, she has often told me how they went out, her husband with his white waterproof coat over his arm, and Ronnie, her youngest brother, singing, 'Bertie, why do you bound?' as he always did to tease her, because she said it got on her nerves. Do you know, sometimes on still, quiet evenings like this, I almost get a creepy feeling that they will all walk in through that window —"

She broke off with a little shudder. It was a relief to Framton when the aunt bustled into the room with a whirl of apologies for being late in making her appearance.

"I hope Vera has been amusing you?" she

said.

"She has been very interesting," said Framton.

"I hope you don't mind the open window," said Mrs. Sappleton briskly; "my husband and brothers will be home directly from shooting, and they always come in this way. They've been out for snipe in the marshes today, so they'll make a fine mess over my poor carpets. So like you men-folk, isn't it?"

She rattled on cheerfully about the shooting and the scarcity of birds, and the prospects for duck in the winter. To Framton, it was all purely horrible. He made a desperate but only partially successful effort to turn the talk on to a less ghastly topic; he was conscious that his hostess was giving him only a fragment of her attention, and her eyes were constantly straying past him to the open window and the lawn beyond. It was certainly an unfortunate coincidence that he should have paid his visit on this tragic anniversary.

"The doctors agree in ordering me complete rest, an absence of mental excitement, and avoidance of anything in the nature of violent physical exercise," announced Framton, who laboured under the tolerably wide-spread delusion that total strangers and chance acquaintances are hungry for the least detail of one's ailments and infirmities, their cause and cure. "On the matter of diet they are not so much in agreement," he continued.

"No?" said Mrs. Sappleton, in a voice which only replaced a yawn at the last moment. Then she suddenly brightened into alert attention — but not to what Framton was saying.

"Here they are at last!" she cried. "Just in time for tea, and don't they look as if they were muddy up to the eyes!"

Framton shivered slightly and turned towards the niece with a look intended to convey sympathetic comprehension. The child was staring out through the open window with dazed horror in her eyes. In a chill shock of nameless fear Framton swung round in his seat and looked in the same direction.

In the deepening twilight three figures were walking across the lawn towards the window; they all carried guns under their arms, and one of them was additionally burdened with a white coat hung over his shoulders. A tired brown spaniel kept close at their heels. Noiselessly they neared the house, and then a hoarse young voice chanted out of the dusk: "I said, Bertie, why do you bound?"

Framton grabbed wildly at his stick and hat; the hall-door, the gravel-drive, and the front gate were dimly noted stages in his headlong retreat. A cyclist coming along the road had to run into the hedge to avoid imminent collision.

"Here we are, my dear," said the bearer of the white mackintosh, coming in through the window; "fairly muddy, but most of it's dry. Who was that who bolted out as we came up?"

"A most extraordinary man, a Mr. Nuttel," said Mrs. Sappleton; "could only talk about his illnesses, and dashed off without a word of good-bye or apology when you arrived. One would think he had seen a ghost."

"I expect it was the spaniel," said the niece calmly; "he told me he had a horror of dogs. He was once hunted into a cemetery somewhere on the banks of the Ganges by a pack of pariah dogs, and had to spend the night in a newly dug grave with the creatures snarling and grinning and foaming just above him. Enough to make any one lose their nerve."

Romance at short notice was her speciality.

Tobermory

Saki

IT was a chill, rain-washed afternoon of a late August day, that indefinite season when partridges are still in security or cold storage, and there is nothing to hunt — unless one is bounded on the north by the Bristol Channel, in which case one may lawfully gallop after fat red stags. Lady Blemley's house-party was not bounded on the north by the Bristol Channel, hence there was a full gathering of her guests round the tea-table on this particular afternoon. And, in spite of the blankness of the season and the triteness of the occasion, there was no trace in the company of that fatigued restlessness which means a dread of the pianola and a subdued hankering for auction bridge. The undisguised open-mouthed attention of the entire party was fixed on the homely negative personality of Mr. Cornelius Appin. Of all her guests, he was the one who had come to Lady Blemley with the vaguest reputation. Some one had said he was "clever," and he had got his invitation in the moderate expectation, on the part of his hostess, that some portion at least of his cleverness would be contributed to the general entertainment. Until tea-time that day she had been unable to discover in what direction, if any, his cleverness lay. He was neither a wit nor a croquet champion, a hypnotic force nor a begetter of amateur theatricals. Neither did his exterior suggest the sort of man in whom women are willing to pardon a generous measure of mental deficiency. He had subsided into mere Mr. Appin, and the Cornelius seemed a piece of transparent baptismal bluff. And now he was claiming to have launched on the world a discovery beside which the invention of gunpowder, of the printing-press, and of steam locomotion were inconsiderable trifles. Science had made bewildering strides in many directions during recent decades, but this thing seemed to belong to the domain of miracle rather than to scientific achievement.

"And do you really ask us to believe," Sir Wilfrid was saying, "that you have discovered a means for instructing animals in the art of human speech, and that dear old Tobermory has proved your first successful pupil?"

"It is a problem at which I have worked for the last seventeen years," said Mr. Appin, "but only during the last eight or nine months have I been rewarded with glimmerings of success. Of course I have experimented with thousands of animals, but latterly only with cats, those wonderful creatures which have assimilated themselves so marvellously with our civilization while retaining all their highly developed feral instincts. Here and there among cats one comes across an outstanding superior intellect, just as one does among the ruck of human beings, and when I made the acquaintance of Tobermory a week ago I saw at once that I was in contact with a 'Beyond-cat' of extraordinary intelligence. I had gone far along the road to success in recent experiments; with Tobermory, as you call him, I have reached the goal."

Mr. Appin concluded his remarkable statement in a voice which he strove to divest of a triumphant inflection. No one said "Rats," though Clovis's lips moved in a monosyllabic contortion which probably invoked those rodents of disbelief.

"And do you mean to say," asked Miss Resker, after a slight pause, "that you have taught Tobermory to say and understand easy sentences of one syllable?"

"My dear Miss Resker," said the wonder-worker patiently, "one teaches little children and savages and backward adults in that piecemeal fashion; when one has once solved the problem of making a beginning with an animal of highly developed intelligence one has no need for those halting methods. Tobermory can speak our language with perfect correctness."

This time Clovis very distinctly said, "Beyond-rats!" Sir Wilfrid was more polite, but equally sceptical.

"Hadn't we better have the cat in and judge for ourselves?" suggested Lady Blemley.

Sir Wilfrid went in search of the animal, and the company settled themselves down to the languid expectation of witnessing some more or less adroit drawing-room ventriloquism.

In a minute Sir Wilfrid was back in the room, his face white beneath its tan and his eyes dilated with excitement.

"By Gad, it's true!"

His agitation was unmistakably genuine, and his hearers started forward in a thrill of awakened interest.

Collapsing into an armchair he continued breathlessly: "I found him dozing in the smoking-room, and called out to him to come for his tea. He blinked at me in his usual way, and I said, 'Come on, Toby; don't keep us waiting'; and, by Gad! he drawled out in a most horribly natural voice that he'd come when he dashed well pleased! I nearly jumped out of my skin!"

Appin had preached to absolutely incredulous hearers; Sir Wilfrid's statement carried instant conviction. A Babel-like chorus of startled exclamation arose, amid which the scientist sat mutely enjoying the first fruit of his stupendous discovery.

In the midst of the clamour Tobermory entered the room and made his way with velvet tread and studied unconcern across to the group seated round the tea-table.

A sudden hush of awkwardness and constraint fell on the company. Somehow there seemed an element of embarrassment in addressing on equal terms a domestic cat of acknowledged mental ability.

"Will you have some milk, Tobermory?" asked Lady Blemley in a rather strained voice.

"I don't mind if I do," was the response, couched in a tone of even indifference. A shiver of suppressed excitement went through the listeners, and Lady Blemley might be excused for pouring out the saucerful of milk rather unsteadily.

"I'm afraid I've spilt a good deal of it," she said apologetically.

"After all, it's not my Axminster," was Tobermory's rejoinder.

Another silence fell on the group, and then Miss Resker, in her best district-visitor manner, asked if the human language had been difficult to learn. Tobermory looked squarely at her for a moment and then fixed his gaze serenely on the middle distance. It was obvious that boring questions lay outside his scheme of life.

"What do you think of human intelligence?" asked Mavis Pellington lamely.

"Of whose intelligence in particular?" asked Tobermory coldly.

"'Oh, well, mine for instance,'' said Mavis, with a feeble laugh.

"You put me in an embarrassing position," said Tobermory, whose tone and attitude certainly did not suggest a shred of embarrassment. "When your inclusion in this house-party was suggested Sir Wilfrid protested that you were the most brainless woman of his acquaintance, and that there was a wide distinction between hospitality and the care of the feebleminded. Lady Blemley replied that your lack of brain-power was the precise quality which had earned you your invitation, as you were the only person she could think of who might be idiotic enough to buy their old car. You know, the one they call 'The Envy of Sisyphus,' because it goes quite nicely up-hill if you push it."

Lady Blemley's protestations would have had greater effect if she had not casually suggested to Mavis only that morning that the car in question would be just the thing for her down at her Devonshire home.

Major Barfield plunged in heavily to effect a diversion.

"How about your carryings-on with the tortoise-shell puss up at the stables, eh?"

The moment he had said it every one realized the blunder.

"One does not usually discuss these matters in public," said Tobermory frigidly. "From a slight observation of your ways since you've been in this house I should imagine you'd find it inconvenient if I were to shift the conversation on to your own little affairs."

The panic which ensued was not confined to the Major.

"Would you like to go and see if cook has got your dinner ready?" suggested Lady Blemley hurriedly, affecting to ignore the fact that it wanted at least two hours to Tobermory's dinner-time.

"Thanks," said Tobermory, "not quite so soon after my tea. I don't want to die of indigestion."

"Cats have nine lives, you know," said Sir Wilfrid heartily.

"Possibly," answered Tobermory; "but only one liver."

"Adelaide!" said Mrs. Cornett, "do you mean to encourage that cat to go out and gossip about us in the servants' hall?"

The panic had indeed become general. A narrow ornamental balustrade ran in front of most of the bedroom windows at the Towers, and it was recalled with dismay that this had formed a favourite promenade for Tobermory at all hours, whence he could watch the pigeons — and heaven knew what else besides. If he intended to become reminiscent in his present out-spoken strain the effect would be something more than disconcerting. Mrs. Cornett, who spent much time at her toilet table, and whose complexion was reputed to be of a nomadic though punctual disposition, looked as ill at ease as the Major. Miss Scrawen, who wrote fiercely sensuous poetry and led a blameless life, merely displayed irritation; if you are methodical and virtuous in private you don't necessarily want every one to know it. Bertie van Tahn, who was so depraved at seventeen that he had long ago given up trying to be any worse, turned a dull shade of gardenia white, but he did not commit the error of dashing out of the room like Odo Finsberry, a young gentleman who was understood to be reading for the Church and who was possibly disturbed at the thought of scandals he might hear concerning other people. Clovis had the presence of mind to maintain a composed exterior; privately he was calculating how long it would take to procure a box of fancy mice through the agency of the *Exchange and Mart* as a species of hush-money.

Even in a delicate situation like the present, Agnes Resker could not endure to remain too long in the background.

"Why did I ever come down here?" she asked dramatically.

Tobermory immediately accepted the opening.

"Judging by what you said to Mrs. Cornett on the croquet-lawn yesterday, you were out for food. You described the Blemleys as the dullest people to stay with that you knew, but said they were clever enough to employ a first-rate cook; otherwise they'd find it difficult to get any one to come down a second time."

"There's not a word of truth in it! I appeal to Mrs. Cornett——" exclaimed the discomfited Agnes.

"Mrs. Cornett repeated your remark afterwards to Bertie van Tahn," continued Tobermory, "and said, 'That woman is a regular Hunger Marcher; she'd go anywhere for four square meals a day,' and Bertie van Tahn said——"

At this point the chronicle mercifully ceased. Tobermory had caught a glimpse of the big yellow Tom from the Rectory working his way through the shrubbery toward the stable wing. In a flash he had vanished through the open French window.

With the disappearance of his too brilliant pupil Cornelius Appin found himself beset by a hurricane of bitter upbraiding, anxious inquiry, and frightened entreaty. The responsibility for the situation lay with him, and he must prevent matters from becoming worse. Could Tobermory impart his dangerous gift to other cats? was the first question he had to answer. It was possible, he replied, that he might have initiated his intimate friend the stable puss into his new accomplishment, but it was unlikely that his teaching could have taken a wider range as yet.

"Then," said Mrs. Cornett, "Tobermory may be a valuable cat and a great pet; but I'm sure you'll agree, Adelaide, that both he and the stable cat must be done away with without delay."

"You don't suppose I've enjoyed the last quarter of an hour, do you?" said Lady Blemley bitterly. "My husband and I are very fond of Tobermory — at least, we were before this horrible accomplishment was infused into him; but now, of course, the only thing is to have him destroyed as soon as possible."

"We can put some strychnine in the scraps he always gets at dinner-time," said Sir Wilfrid, "and I will go and drown the stable cat myself. The coachman will be very sore at losing his pet, but I'll say a very catching form of mange has broken out in both cats and we're afraid of it spreading to the kennels."

"But my great discovery!" expostulated Mr. Appin; "after all my years of research and experiment ——"

"You can go and experiment on the shorthorns at the farm, who are under proper control," said Mrs. Cornett, "or the elephants at the Zoological Gardens. They're said to be highly intelligent, and they have this recommendation, that they don't come creeping about our bedrooms and under chairs, and so forth."

An archangel ecstatically proclaiming the Millennium, and finding that it clashed unpardonably with Henley and would have to be indefinitely postponed, could hardly have felt more crestfallen than Cornelius Appin at the reception of his wonderful achievement. Public opinion, however, was against him — in fact, had the general voice been consulted on the subject it is probable that a strong minority vote would have been in favour of including him in the strychnine diet.

Defective train arrangements and a nervous desire to see matters brought to a finish prevented an immediate dispersal of the party, but dinner that evening was not a social success. Sir Wilfrid had had rather a trying time with the stable cat and subsequently with the coachman. Agnes Resker ostentatiously limited her repast to a morsel of dry toast, which she bit as though it were a personal enemy; while Mavis Pellington maintained a vindictive silence throughout the meal. Lady Blemley kept up a flow of what she hoped was conversation, but her attention was fixed on the doorway. A plateful of carefully dosed fish scraps was in readiness on the sideboard, but sweets and savoury and dessert went their way, and no Tobermory appeared either in the dining-room or kitchen.

The sepulchral dinner was cheerful compared with the subsequent vigil in the smoking-room. Eating and drinking had at least supplied a distraction and cloak to the prevailing embarrassment. Bridge was out of the question in the general tension of nerves and tempers, and after Odo Finsberry had given a lugubrious rendering of "Melisande in the Wood" to a frigid audience, music was tacitly avoided. At eleven the servants went to bed, announcing that the small window in the pantry had been left open as usual for Tobermory's private use. The guests read steadily through the current batch of magazines, and fell back gradually on the "Badminton Library" and bound volumes of *Punch*. Lady Blemley made periodic visits to the pantry, returning each time with an expression of listless depression which forestalled questioning.

At two o'clock Clovis broke the dominating silence.

"He won't turn up tonight. He's probably in the local newspaper office at the present moment, dictating the first instalment of his reminiscences. Lady What's-her-name's book won't be in it. It will be the event of the day."

Having made this contribution to the general cheerfulness, Clovis went to bed. At long intervals the various members of the house-party followed his example.

The servants taking round the early tea made a uniform announcement in reply to a uniform question. Tobermory had not returned.

Breakfast was, if anything, a more unpleasant function than dinner had been, but before its conclusion the situation was relieved. Tobermory's corpse was brought in from the shrubbery, where a gardener had just discovered it. From the bites on his throat and the yellow fur which coated his claws it was evident that he had fallen in unequal combat with the big Tom from the Rectory.

By midday most of the guests had quitted the Towers, and after lunch Lady Blemley had sufficiently recovered her spirits to write an extremely nasty letter to the Rectory about the loss of her valuable pet.

Tobermory had been Appin's one successful pupil, and he was destined to have no successor. A few weeks later an elephant in the Dresden Zoological Garden, which had shown no previous signs of irritability, broke loose and killed an Englishman who had apparently been teasing it. The victim's name was variously reported in the papers as Oppin and Eppelin, but his front name was faithfully rendered Cornelius.

"If he was trying German irregular verbs on the poor beast," said Clovis, "he deserved all he got."

The Bride Comes to Yellow Sky

Stephen Crane

THE great Pullman was whirling onward with such dignity of motion that a glance from the window seemed simply to prove that the plains of Texas were pouring eastward. Vast flats of green grass, dull-hued spaces of mesquit and cactus, little groups of frame houses, woods of light and tender trees, all were sweeping into the east, sweeping over the horizon, a precipice.

A newly married pair had boarded this coach at San Antonio. The man's face was reddened from many days in the wind and sun, and a direct result of his new black clothes was that his brick-coloured hands were constantly performing in a most conscious fashion. From time to time he looked down respectfully at his attire. He sat with a hand on each knee, like a man waiting in a barber's shop. The glances he devoted to other passengers were furtive and shy.

The bride was not pretty, nor was she very young. She wore a dress of blue cashmere, with small reservations of velvet here and there, and with steel buttons abounding. She continually twisted her head to regard her puff sleeves, very stiff, straight, and high. They embarrassed her. It was quite apparent that she had cooked, and that she expected to cook, dutifully. The blushes caused by the careless scrutiny of some passengers as she had entered the car were strange to see upon this plain, under-class countenance, which was drawn in placid, almost emotionless lines.

They were evidently very happy. "Ever been in a parlour-car before?" he asked, smiling with delight.

"No," she answered; "I never was. It's fine, ain't it?"

"Great! And then after a while we'll go forward to the diner, and get a big lay-out. Finest meal in the world. Charge a dollar."

"Oh, do they?" cried the bride. "Charge a dollar? Why, that's too much — for us — ain't it, Jack?"

"Not this trip, anyhow," he answered bravely. "We're going to go the whole thing."

Later he explained to her about the trains. "You see, it's a thousand miles from one end of Texas to the other; and this train runs right across it, and never stops but four times." He had the pride of an owner. He pointed out to her the dazzling fittings of the coach; and in truth her eyes opened wider as she contemplated the sea-green figured velvet, the shining brass, silver, and glass, the wood that gleamed as darkly brilliant as the surface of a pool of oil. At one end a bronze figure sturdily held a support for a separated chamber, and at convenient places on the ceiling were frescos in olive and silver.

To the minds of the pair, their surroundings reflected the glory of their marriage that morning in San Antonio; this was the environment of their new estate; and the man's face in particular beamed with an elation that made him appear ridiculous to the negro porter. This individual at times surveyed them from afar with an amused and superior grin. On other occasions he bullied them with skill in ways that did not make it exactly plain to them that they were being bullied. He subtly used all the manners of the most unconquerable kind of snobbery. He oppressed them; but of this oppression they had small knowledge, and they speedily forgot that infrequently a number of travellers covered them with stares of derisive enjoyment. Historically there was supposed to be something infinitely humorous in their situation.

"We are due in Yellow Sky at 3:42," he said, looking tenderly into her eyes.

"Oh, are we?" she said, as if she had not been aware of it. To evince surprise at her husband's statement was part of her wifely amiability. She took from a pocket a little silver watch; and as she held it before her, and stared at it with a frown of attention, the new husband's face shone.

"I bought it in San Anton' from a friend of mine," he told her gleefully.

"It's seventeen minutes past twelve," she said, looking up at him with a kind of shy and clumsy coquetry. A passenger, noting this play, grew excessively sardonic, and winked at himself in one of the numerous mirrors.

At last they went to the dining-car. Two rows of negro waiters, in glowing white suits, surveyed their entrance with the interest, and also the equanimity, of men who had been forewarned. The pair fell to the lot of a waiter who happened to feel pleasure in steering them through their meal. He viewed them with the manner of a fatherly pilot, his countenance radiant with benevolence. The patronage, entwined with the ordinary deference, was not plain to them. And yet, as they returned to their coach, they showed in their faces a sense of escape.

To the left, miles down a long purple slope, was a little ribbon of mist where moved the keening Rio Grande. The train was approaching it at an angle, and the apex was Yellow Sky. Presently it was apparent that, as the distance from Yellow Sky grew shorter, the husband became commensurately restless. His brick-red hands were more insistent in their prominence. Occasionally he was even rather absent-minded and far-away when the bride leaned forward and addressed him.

As a matter of truth, Jack Potter was beginning to find the shadow of a deed weigh upon him like a leaden slab. He, the town marshal of Yellow Sky, a man known, liked, and feared in his corner, a prominent person, had gone to San Antonio to meet a girl he believed he loved, and there, after the usual prayers, had actually induced her to marry him, without consulting Yellow Sky for any part of the transaction. He was now bringing his bride before an innocent and unsuspecting community.

Of course people in Yellow Sky married as it pleased them, in accordance with a general custom; but such was Potter's thought of his duty to his friends, or of their idea of his duty, or of an unspoken form which does not control men in these matters, that he felt he was heinous. He had committed an extraordinary crime. Face to face with this girl in San Antonio, and spurred by his sharp impulse, he had gone headlong over all the social hedges. At San Antonio he was like a man hidden in the dark. A knife to sever any friendly duty, any form, was easy to his hand in that remote city. But the hour of Yellow Sky — the hour of daylight — was approaching.

He knew full well that his marriage was an

important thing to his town. It could only be exceeded by the burning of the new hotel. His friends could not forgive him. Frequently he had reflected on the advisability of telling them by telegraph, but a new cowardice had been upon him. He feared to do it. And now the train was hurrying him toward a scene of amazement, glee, and reproach. He glanced out of the window at the line of haze swinging slowly in toward the train.

Yellow Sky had a kind of brass band, which played painfully, to the delight of the populace. He laughed without heart as he thought of it. If the citizens could dream of his prospective arrival with his bride, they would parade the band at the station and escort them, amid cheers and laughing congratulations, to his adobe home.

He resolved that he would use all the devices of speed and plainscraft in making the journey from the station to his house. Once within that safe citadel, he could issue some sort of vocal bulletin, and then not go among the citizens until they had time to wear off a little of their enthusiasm.

The bride looked anxiously at him. "What's worrying you, Jack?"

He laughed again. "I'm not worrying, girl; I'm only thinking of Yellow Sky."

She flushed in comprehension.

A sense of mutual guilt invaded their minds and developed a finer tenderness. They looked at each other with eyes softly aglow. But Potter often laughed the same nervous laugh; the flush upon the bride's face seemed quite permanent.

The traitor to the feelings of Yellow Sky narrowly watched the speeding landscape. "We're nearly there," he said.

Presently the porter came and announced the proximity of Potter's home. He held a brush in his hand, and, with all his airy superiority gone, he brushed Potter's new clothes as the latter slowly turned this way and that way. Potter fumbled out a coin and gave it to the porter, as he had seen others do. It was a heavy and muscle-bound business, as that of a man shoeing his first horse.

The porter took their bag, and as the train began to slow they moved forward to the hooded platform of the car. Presently the two engines and their long string of coaches rushed into the station of Yellow Sky.

"They have to take water here," said Potter, from a constricted throat and in mournful cadence, as one announcing death. Before the train stopped his eye had swept the length of the platform, and he was glad and astonished to see there was none upon it but the station-agent, who, with a slightly hurried and anxious air, was walking toward the water-tanks. When the train had halted, the porter alighted first, and placed in position a little temporary step.

"Come on, girl," said Potter, hoarsely. As he helped her down they each laughed on a false note. He took the bag from the negro, and bade his wife cling to his arm. As they slunk rapidly away, his hang-dog glance perceived that they were unloading the two trunks, and also that the station-agent, far ahead near the baggage-car, had turned and was running toward him, making gestures. He laughed, and groaned as he laughed, when he noted the first effect of his marital bliss upon Yellow Sky. He gripped his wife's arm firmly to his side, and they fled. Behind them the porter stood, chuckling fatuously.

II

The California express on the Southern Railway was due at Yellow Sky in twenty-one minutes. There were six men at the bar of the Weary Gentleman saloon. One was a drummer who talked a great deal and rapidly; three were Texans who did not care to talk at that time; and two were Mexican sheep-herders, who did not talk as a general practice in the Weary Gentleman saloon. The barkeeper's dog lay on the board walk that crossed in front of the door. His head was on his paws, and he glanced drowsily here and there with the constant vigilance of a dog that is kicked on occasion. Across the sandy street were some vivid green grass-plots, so wonderful in appearance, amid the sands that burned near them in a blazing sun, that they caused a doubt in the mind. They exactly resembled the grass mats used to represent lawns on the stage. At the cooler end of the railway station, a man without a coat sat in a tilted chair and smoked his pipe. The fresh-cut bank of the Rio Grande circled near the town, and there could be seen beyond it a great plum-coloured plain of mesquit.

Save for the busy drummer and his companions in the saloon, Yellow Sky was dozing. The new-comer leaned gracefully upon the bar, and recited many tales with the confidence of a bard who has come upon a new field.

"— and at the moment that the old man fell downstairs with the bureau in his arms, the old woman was coming up with two scuttles of coal, and of course —"

The drummer's tale was interrupted by a young man who suddenly appeared in the open door. He cried: "Scratchy Wilson's drunk, and has turned loose with both hands." The two Mexicans at once set down their glasses and faded out of the rear entrance of the saloon.

The drummer, innocent and jocular, answered: "All right, old man. S'pose he has? Come in and have a drink, anyhow."

But the information had made such an obvious cleft in every skull in the room that the drummer was obliged to see its importance. All had become instantly solemn. "Say," said he, mystified, "what is this?" His three companions made the introductory gesture of eloquent speech; but the young man at the door forestalled them.

"It means, my friend," he answered, as he came into the saloon, "that for the next two hours this town won't be a health resort."

The barkeeper went to the door, and locked and barred it; reaching out of the window, he pulled in heavy wooden shutters, and barred them. Immediately a solemn, chapel-like gloom was upon the place. The drummer was looking from one to another.

"But say," he cried, "what is this, anyhow? You don't mean there is going to be a gun-fight?"

"Don't know whether there'll be a fight or not," answered one man, grimly; "but there'll be some shootin' — some good shootin'."

The young man who had warned them waved his hand. "Oh, there'll be a fight fast enough, if any one wants it. Anybody can get a fight out there in the street. There's a fight just waiting."

The drummer seemed to be swayed between the interest of a foreigner and a perception of personal danger.

"What did you say his name was?" he asked.

"Scratchy Wilson," they answered in chorus.

"And will he kill anybody? What are you

going to do? Does this happen often? Does he rampage around like this once a week or so? Can he break in that door?''

''No; he can't break down that door,'' replied the barkeeper. ''He's tried it three times. But when he comes you'd better lay down on the floor, stranger. He's dead sure to shoot at it, and a bullet may come through.''

Thereafter the drummer kept a strict eye upon the door. The time had not yet been called for him to hug the floor, but, as a minor precaution, he sidled near to the wall. ''Will he kill anybody?'' he said again.

The men laughed low and scornfully at the question.

''He's out to shoot, and he's out for trouble. Don't see any good in experimentin' with him.''

''But what do you do in a case like this? What do you do?''

A man responded: ''Why, he and Jack Potter—''

''But,'' in chorus the other men interrupted, ''Jack Potter's in San Anton'.''

''Well, who is he? What's he got to do with it?''

''Oh, he's the town marshal. He goes out and fights Scratchy when he gets on one of these tears.''

''Wow!'' said the drummer, mopping his brow. ''Nice job he's got.''

The voices had toned away to mere whisperings. The drummer wished to ask further questions, which were born of an increasing anxiety and bewilderment; but when he attempted them, the men merely looked at him in irritation and motioned him to remain silent. A tense waiting hush was upon them. In the deep shadows of the room their eyes shone as they listened for sounds from the street. One man made three gestures at the barkeeper; and the latter, moving like a ghost, handed him a glass and a bottle. The man poured a full glass of whisky, and set down the bottle noiselessly. He gulped the whisky in a swallow, and turned again toward the door in immovable silence. The drummer saw that the barkeeper, without a sound, had taken a Winchester from beneath the bar. Later he saw this individual beckoning to him, so he tiptoed across the room.

"You better come with me back of the bar."

"No, thanks," said the drummer, perspiring; "I'd rather be where I can make a break for the back door."

Whereupon the man of bottles made a kindly but peremptory gesture. The drummer obeyed it, and, finding himself seated on a box with his head below the level of the bar, balm was laid upon his soul at sight of various zinc and copper fittings that bore a resemblance to armour-plate. The barkeeper took a seat comfortably upon an adjacent box.

"You see," he whispered, "this here Scratchy Wilson is a wonder with a gun — a perfect wonder; and when he goes on the war-trail, we hunt our holes — naturally. He's about the last one of the old gang that used to hang out along the river here. He's a terror when he's drunk. When he's sober he's all right — kind of simple — wouldn't hurt a fly — nicest fellow in town. But when he's drunk — whoo!"

There were periods of stillness. "I wish Jack Potter was back from San Anton'," said the barkeeper. "He shot Wilson up once — in the leg — and he would sail in and pull out the kinks in this thing."

Presently they heard from a distance the sound of a shot, followed by three wild yowls. It instantly removed a bond from the men in the darkened saloon. There was a shuffling of feet. They looked at each other. "Here he comes," they said.

III

A man in a maroon-coloured flannel shirt, which had been purchased for purposes of decoration, and made principally by some Jewish women on the East Side of New York, rounded a corner and walked into the middle of the main street of Yellow Sky. In either hand the man held a long, heavy, blue-black revolver. Often he yelled, and these cries rang through a semblance of a deserted village, shrilly flying over the roofs in a volume that seemed to have no relation to the ordinary vocal strength of a man. It was as if the surrounding stillness formed the arch of a tomb over him. These cries of ferocious challenge rang against walls of silence. And his boots had red tops with gilded imprints, of the kind beloved in winter by little sledding boys on the hillsides of New England.

The man's face flamed in a rage begot of whisky. His eyes, rolling, and yet keen for ambush, hunted the still doorways and windows. He walked with the creeping movement of the midnight cat. As it occurred to him, he roared menacing information. The long revolvers in his hands were as easy as straws; they were moved with an electric swiftness. The little fingers of each hand played sometimes in a musician's way. Plain from the low collar of the shirt, the cords of his neck straightened and sank, straightened and sank, as passion moved him. The only sounds were his terrible invitations. The calm adobes preserved their demeanour at the passing of this small thing in the middle of the street.

There was no offer of fight — no offer of fight. The man called to the sky. There were no attractions. He bellowed and fumed and swayed his revolvers here and everywhere.

The dog of the barkeeper of the Weary Gentleman saloon had not appreciated the advance of events. He yet lay dozing in front of his master's door. At sight of the dog, the man paused and raised his revolver humorously. At sight of the man, the dog sprang up and walked diagonally away, with a sullen head, and growling. The man yelled, and the dog broke into a gallop. As it was about to enter an alley, there was a loud noise, a whistling, and something spat the ground directly before it. The dog screamed, and, wheeling in terror, galloped headlong in a new direction. Again there was a noise, a whistling, and sand was kicked viciously before it. Fear-stricken, the dog turned and flurried like an animal in a pen. The man stood laughing, his weapons at his hips.

Ultimately the man was attracted by the closed door of the Weary Gentleman saloon. He went to it and, hammering with a revolver, demanded drink.

The door remaining imperturbable, he picked a bit of paper from the walk, and nailed it to the framework with a knife. He then turned his back contemptuously upon this popular resort and, walking to the opposite side of the street and spinning there on his heel quickly and lithely, fired at the bit of paper. He missed it by a half-inch. He swore at himself, and went away. Later he comfortably fusilladed the windows of his most intimate friend. The man was playing with this town; it was a toy for him.

But still there was no offer of fight. The name of Jack Potter, his ancient antagonist, entered his mind, and he concluded that it would be a glad thing if he should go to Potter's house, and by bombardment induce him to come out and fight. He moved in the direction of his desire, chanting Apache scalp-music.

When he arrived at it, Potter's house presented the same still front as had the other adobes. Taking up a strategic position, the man howled a challenge. But this house regarded him as might a great stone god. It gave no sign. After a decent wait, the man howled further challenges, mingling with them wonderful epithets.

Presently there came the spectacle of a man churning himself into deepest rage over the immobility of a house. He fumed at it as the winter wind attacks a prairie cabin in the North. To the distance there should have gone the sound of a tumult like the fighting of two hundred Mexicans. As necessity bade him, he paused for breath or to reload his revolvers.

IV

Potter and his bride walked sheepishly and with speed. Sometimes they laughed together shamefacedly and low.

"Next corner, dear," he said finally.

They put forth the efforts of a pair walking bowed against a strong wind. Potter was about to raise a finger to point the first appearance of the new home when, as they circled the corner, they came face to face with a man in a maroon-coloured shirt, who was feverishly pushing cartridges into a large revolver. Upon the instant the man dropped his revolver to the ground and, like lightning, whipped another from its holster. The second weapon was aimed at the bridegroom's chest.

There was a silence. Potter's mouth seemed to be merely a grave for his tongue. He exhibited an instinct to at once loosen his arm from the woman's grip, and he dropped the bag to the sand. As for the bride, her face had gone as yellow as old cloth. She was a slave to hideous rites, gazing at the apparitional snake.

The two men faced each other at a distance of three paces. He of the revolver smiled with a new and quiet ferocity.

"Tried to sneak up on me," he said. "Tried to sneak up on me!" His eyes grew more baleful. As Potter made a slight movement, the man thrust his revolver venomously forward "No; don't you do it, Jack Potter. Don't you move a finger toward a gun just yet. Don't you move an eyelash. The time has come for me to settle with you, and I'm goin' to do it my own way, and loaf along with no interferin'. So if you don't want a gun bent on you, just mind what I tell you."

Potter looked at his enemy. "I ain't got a gun on me Scratchy," he said. "Honest, I ain't." He was stiffening and steadying, but yet somewhere at the back of his mind a vision of the Pullman floated: the sea-green figured velvet, the shining brass, silver, and glass, the wood that gleamed as darkly brilliant as the surface of a pool of oil — all the glory of the marriage, the environment of the new estate. "You know I fight when it comes to fighting, Scratchy Wilson; but I ain't got a gun on me. You'll have to do all the shootin' yourself."

His enemy's face went livid. He stepped forward, and lashed his weapon to and fro before Potter's chest. "Don't you tell me you ain't got no gun on you, you whelp. Don't tell me no lie like that. There ain't a man in Texas ever seen you without no gun. Don't take me for no kid." His eyes blazed with light, and his throat worked like a pump.

"I ain't takin' you for no kid," answered Potter. His heels had not moved an inch backward. "I'm takin' you for a damn fool. I tell you I ain't got a gun, and I ain't. If you're goin' to shoot me up, you better begin now; you'll never get a chance like this again."

So much enforced reasoning had told on Wilson's rage; he was calmer. "If you ain't got a gun, why ain't you got a gun?" he sneered. "Been to Sunday-school?"

"I ain't got a gun because I've just come from San Anton' with my wife. I'm married," said Potter. "And if I'd thought there was going to be any galoots like you prowling around when I brought my wife home, I'd had a gun, and don't you forget it."

"Married!" said Scratchy, not at all comprehending.

"Yes, married. I'm married," said Potter, distinctly.

"Married?" said Scratchy. Seemingly for the first time, he saw the drooping, drowning woman at the other man's side. "No!" he said. He was like a creature allowed a glimpse of another world. He moved a pace backward, and his arm, with the revolver, dropped to his side. "Is this the lady?" he asked.

"Yes; this is the lady," answered Potter.

There was another period of silence.

"Well," said Wilson at last, slowly, "I s'pose it's all off now."

"It's all off if you say so, Scratchy. You know I didn't make the trouble." Potter lifted his valise.

"Well, I 'low it's off, Jack," said Wilson. He was looking at the ground. "Married!" He was not a student of chivalry; it was merely that in the presence of this foreign condition he was a simple child of the earlier plains. He picked up his starboard revolver, and, placing both weapons in their holsters, he went away. His feet made funnel-shaped tracks in the heavy sand.

The Horse Dealer's Daughter

D. H. Lawrence

"WELL, Mabel, and what are you going to do with yourself?" asked Joe, with foolish flippancy. He felt quite safe himself. Without listening for an answer, he turned aside, worked a grain of tobacco to the tip of his tongue, and spat it out. He did not care about anything, since he felt safe himself.

The three brothers and the sister sat round the desolate breakfast-table, attempting some sort of desultory consultation. The morning's post had given the final tap to the family fortunes, and all was over. The dreary dining-room itself, with its heavy mahogany furniture, looked as if it were waiting to be done away with.

But the consultation amounted to nothing. There was a strange air of ineffectuality about the three men, as they sprawled at table, smoking and reflecting vaguely on their own condition. The girl was alone, a rather short, sullen-looking young woman of twenty-seven. She did not share the same life as her brothers.

She would have been good-looking, save for the impressive fixity of her face, 'bull-dog', as her brothers called it.

There was a confused tramping of horses' feet outside. The three men all sprawled round in their chairs to watch. Beyond the dark holly bushes that separated the strip of lawn from the high-road, they could see a cavalcade of shire horses swinging out of their own yard, being taken for exercise. This was the last time. These were the last horses that would go through their hands. The young men watched with critical, callous look. They were all frightened at the collapse of their lives, and the sense of disaster in which they were involved left them no inner freedom.

Yet they were three fine, well-set fellows enough. Joe, the eldest, was a man of thirty-three, broad and handsome in a hot, flushed way. His face was red, he twisted his black moustache over a thick finger, his eyes were shallow and restless. He had a sensual way of uncovering his teeth when he laughed, and his bearing was stupid. Now he watched the horses with a glazed look of helplessness in his eyes, a certain stupor of downfall.

The great draught-horses swung past. They were tied head to tail, four of them, and they heaved along to where a lane branched off from the high-road, planting their great hoofs floutingly in the fine black mud, swinging their great rounded haunches sumptuously, and trotting a few sudden steps as they were led into the lane, round the corner. Every movement showed a massive, slumbrous strength, and a stupidity which held them in subjection. The groom at the head looked back, jerking the leading rope. And the cavalcade moved out of sight up the lane, the tail of the last horse, bobbed up tight and stiff, held out taut from the swinging great haunches as they rocked behind the hedges in a motion-like sleep.

Joe watched with glazed hopeless eyes. The horses were almost like his own body to him. He felt he was done for now. Luckily he was engaged to a woman as old as himself, and therefore her father, who was steward of a neighbouring estate, would provide him with a job. He would marry and go into harness. His life was over, he would be a subject animal now.

He turned uneasily aside, the retreating steps of the horses echoing in his ears. Then, with foolish restlessness, he reached for the scraps of bacon-rind from the plates, and making a faint whistling sound, flung them to the terrier that lay against the fender. He watched the dog swallow them, and waited till the creature looked into his eyes. Then a faint grin came on his face, and in a high, foolish voice he said:

"You won't get much more bacon, shall you, you little b——?"

The dog faintly and dismally wagged its tail,

then lowered its haunches, circled round, and lay down again.

There was another helpless silence at the table. Joe sprawled uneasily in his seat, not willing to go till the family conclave was dissolved. Fred Henry, the second brother, was erect, clean-limbed, alert. He had watched the passing of the horses with more *sang-froid*. If he was an animal, like Joe, he was an animal which controls, not one which is controlled. He was master of any horse, and he carried himself with a well-tempered air of mastery. But he was not master of the situations of life. He pushed his coarse brown moustache upwards, off his lip, and glanced irritably at his sister, who sat impassive and inscrutable.

"You'll go and stop with Lucy for a bit, shan't you?" he asked. The girl did not answer.

"I don't see what else you can do," persisted Fred Henry.

"Go as a skivvy," Joe interpolated laconically.

The girl did not move a muscle.

"If I was her, I should go in for training for a nurse," said Malcolm, the youngest of them all. He was the baby of the family, a young man of twenty-two, with a fresh, jaunty *museau*.

But Mabel did not take any notice of him. They had talked at her and round her for so many years, that she hardly heard them at all.

The marble clock on the mantelpiece softly chimed the half-hour, the dog rose uneasily from the hearth-rug and looked at the party at the breakfast-table. But still they sat on in ineffectual conclave.

"Oh, all right," said Joe suddenly, apropos of nothing. "I'll get a move on."

He pushed back his chair, straddled his knees with a downward jerk, to get them free, in horsey fashion, and went to the fire. Still he did not go out of the room; he was curious to know what the others would do or say. He began to charge his pipe, looking down at the dog and saying in a high, affected voice:

"Going wi' me? Going wi' me are ter? Tha'rt goin' further than tha counts on just now, dost hear?"

The dog faintly wagged its tail, the man stuck out his jaw and covered his pipe with his hands, and puffed intently, losing himself in the tobacco, looking down all the while at the dog with an absent brown eye. The dog looked up at him in mournful distrust. Joe stood with his knees stuck out, in real horsey fashion.

"Have you had a letter from Lucy?" Fred Henry asked of his sister.

"Last week," came the neutral reply.

"And what does she say?"

There was no answer.

"Does she *ask* you to go and stop there?" persisted Fred Henry.

"She says I can if I like."

"Well, then, you'd better. Tell her you'll come on Monday."

This was received in silence.

"That's what you'll do then, is it?" said Fred Henry, in some exasperation.

But she made no answer. There was a silence of futility and irritation in the room. Malcolm grinned fatuously.

"You'll have to make up your mind between now and next Wednesday," said Joe loudly, "or else find yourself lodgings on the kerbstone."

The face of the young woman darkened, but she sat on immutable.

"Here's Jack Fergusson!" exclaimed Malcolm, who was looking aimlessly out of the window.

"Where?" exclaimed Joe loudly.

"Just gone past."

"Coming in?"

Malcolm craned his neck to see the gate.

"Yes," he said.

There was a silence. Mabel sat on like one condemned, at the head of the table. Then a whistle was heard from the kitchen. The dog got up and barked sharply. Joe opened the door and shouted:

"Come on."

After a moment a young man entered. He was muffled up in overcoat and a purple woollen scarf, and his tweed cap, which he did not remove, was pulled down on his head. He was of medium height, his face was rather long and pale, his eyes looked tired.

"Hello, Jack! Well, Jack!" exclaimed Malcolm and Joe. Fred Henry merely said: "Jack."

"What's doing?" asked the newcomer, evidently addressing Fred Henry.

"Same. We've got to be out by Wednesday. Got a cold?"

"I have — got it bad, too."

"Why don't you stop in?"

"*Me* stop in? When I can't stand on my legs, perhaps I shall have a chance." The young man spoke huskily. He had a slight Scotch accent.

"It's a knock-out, isn't it," said Joe, boisterously, "if a doctor goes round croaking with a cold. Looks bad for the patients, doesn't it?"

The young doctor looked at him slowly.

"Anything the matter with *you*, then?" he asked sarcastically.

"Not as I know of. Damn your eyes, I hope not. Why?"

"I thought you were very concerned about the patients, wondered if you might be one yourself."

"Damn it, no, I've never been patient to no flaming doctor, and hope I never shall be," returned Joe.

At this point Mabel rose from the table, and they all seemed to become aware of her existence. She began putting the dishes together.

The young doctor looked at her, but did not address her. He had not greeted her. She went out of the room with the tray, her face impassive and unchanged.

"When are you off then, all of you?" asked the doctor.

"I'm catching the eleven-forty," replied Malcolm. "Are you goin' down wi' th' trap, Joe?"

"Yes, I've told you I'm going down wi' th' trap, haven't I?"

"We'd better be getting her in then. So long, Jack, if I don't see you before I go," said Malcolm, shaking hands.

He went out, followed by Joe, who seemed to have his tail between his legs.

"Well, this is the devil's own," exclaimed the doctor, when he was left alone with Fred Henry. "Going before Wednesday, are you?"

"That's the orders," replied the other.

"Where, to Northampton?"

"That's it."

"The devil!" exclaimed Ferguson, with quiet chagrin.

And there was silence between the two.

"All settled up, are you?" asked Ferguson.

"About."

There was another pause.

"Well, I shall miss yer, Freddy, boy," said the young doctor.

"And I shall miss thee, Jack," returned the other.

"Miss you like hell," mused the doctor.

Fred Henry turned aside. There was nothing to say. Mabel came in again, to finish clearing the table.

"What are *you* going to do, then, Miss Pervin?" asked Fergusson. "Going to your sister's, are you?"

Mabel looked at him with her steady, dangerous eyes, that always made him uncomfortable, unsettling his superficial ease.

"No," she said.

"Well, what in the name of fortune *are* you going to do? Say what you mean to do," cried Fred Henry, with futile intensity.

But she only averted her head, and continued her work. She folded the white table-cloth, and put on the chenille cloth.

"The sulkiest bitch that ever trod!" muttered her brother.

But she finished her task with perfectly impassive face, the young doctor watching her interestedly all the while. Then she went out.

Fred Henry stared after her, clenching his lips, his blue eyes fixing in sharp antagonism, as he made a grimace of sour exasperation.

"You could bray her into bits, and that's all you'd get out of her," he said, in a small, narrowed tone.

The doctor smiled faintly.

"What's she *going* to do, then?" he asked.

"Strike me if *I* know!" returned the other.

There was a pause. Then the doctor stirred.

"I'll be seeing you to-night, shall I?" he said to his friend.

"Ay — where's it to be? Are we going over to Jessdale?"

"I don't know. I've got such a cold on me. I'll come round to the 'Moon and Stars', anyway."

"Let Lizzie and May miss their night for once, eh?"

"That's it — if I feel as I do now."

"All's one ——"

The two young men went through the passage and down to the back door together. The house was large, but it was servantless now, and desolate. At the back was a small bricked houseyard and beyond that a big square, gravelled fine and red, and having stables on two sides. Sloping, dank, winter-dark fields stretched away on the open sides.

But the stables were empty. Joseph Pervin, the father of the family, had been a man of no education, who had become a fairly large horse dealer. The stables had been full of horses, there was a great turmoil and come-and-go of horses and of dealers and grooms. Then the kitchen was full of servants. But of late things had declined. The old man had married a second time, to retrieve his fortunes. Now he was dead and everything was gone to the dogs, there was nothing but debt and threatening.

For months, Mabel had been servantless in the big house, keeping the home together in penury for her ineffectual brothers. She had kept house for ten years. But previously it was with unstinted means. Then, however brutal and coarse everything was, the sense of money had kept her proud, confident. The men might be foul-mouthed, the women in the kitchen might have bad reputations, her brothers might have illegitimate children. But so long as there was money, the girl felt herself established, and brutally proud, reserved.

No company came to the house, save dealers and coarse men. Mabel had no associates of her own sex, after her sister went away. But she did not mind. She went regularly to church, she attended to her father. And she lived in the memory of her mother, who had died when she was fourteen, and whom she had loved. She had loved her father, too, in a different way, depending upon him, and feeling secure in him, until at the age of fifty-four he married again. And then she had set hard against him. Now he had died and left them all hopelessly in debt.

She had suffered badly during the period of poverty. Nothing, however, could shake the curious, sullen, animal pride that dominated each member of the family. Now, for Mabel, the end had come. Still she would not cast about her. She would follow her own way just the same. She would always hold the keys of her own situation. Mindless and persistent, she endured from day to day. Why should she think? Why should she answer anybody? It was enough that this was the end, and there was no way out. She need not pass any more darkly along the main street of the small town, avoiding every eye. She need not demean herself any more, going into the shops and buying the cheapest food. This was at an end. She thought of nobody, not even of herself. Mindless and persistent, she seemed in a sort of ecstasy to be coming nearer to her fulfilment, her own glorification, approaching her dead mother, who was glorified.

In the afternoon she took a little bag, with shears and sponge and a small scrubbing-brush, and went out. It was a grey, wintry day, with saddened, dark green fields and an atmosphere blackened by the smoke of foundries not far off. She went quickly, darkly along the causeway, heeding nobody, through the town to the churchyard.

There she always felt secure, as if no one could see her, although as a matter of fact she was exposed to the stare of everyone who passed along under the churchyard wall. Nevertheless, once under the shadow of the great looming church, among the graves, she felt immune from the world, reserved within the thick churchyard wall as in another country.

Carefully she clipped the grass from the grave, and arranged the pinky white, small chrysanthemums in the tin cross. When this was done, she took an empty jar from a neighbouring grave, brought water, and carefully, most scrupulously sponged the marble headstone and the coping-stone.

It gave her sincere satisfaction to do this. She felt in immediate contact with the world of her mother. She took minute pains, went through the park in a state bordering on pure happiness, as if in performing this task she came into a subtle, intimate connection with her mother. For the life she followed here in the world was far less real than the world of death she inherited from her mother.

The doctor's house was just by the church. Fergusson, being a mere hired assistant, was slave to the country-side. As he hurried now to attend to the out-patients in the surgery, glancing across the graveyard with his quick eye, he saw the girl at her task at the grave. She seemed so intent and remote, it was like looking into another world. Some mystical element was touched in him. He slowed down as he walked, watching her as if spellbound.

She lifted her eyes, feeling him looking. Their eyes met. And each looked again at once, each feeling, in some way, found out by the other. He lifted his cap and passed on down the road. There remained distinct in his consciousness, like a vision, the memory of her face, lifted from the tombstone in the churchyard, and looking at him with slow, large, portentous eyes. It *was* portentous, her face. It seemed to mesmerise him. There was a heavy power in her eyes which laid hold of his whole being, as if he had drunk some powerful drug. He had been feeling weak and done before. Now the life came back into him, he felt delivered from his own fretted, daily self.

He finished his duties at the surgery as quickly as might be, hastily filling up the bottles of the waiting people with cheap drugs. Then, in perpetual haste, he set off again to visit several cases in another part of his round, before tea-time. At all times he preferred to walk if he could, but particularly when he was not well. He fancied the motion restored him.

The afternoon was falling. It was grey, deadened, and wintry, with a slow, moist, heavy coldness sinking in and deadening all the faculties. But why should he think or notice? He hastily climbed the hill and turned across the dark green fields, following the black cinder-track. In the distance, across a shallow dip in the country, the small town was clustered like smouldering ash, a tower, a spire, a heap of low, raw, extinct houses. And on the nearest fringe of the town, sloping into the dip, was Oldmeadow, the Pervins' house. He could see the stables and the outbuildings distinctly, as they lay towards him on the slope. Well, he would not go there many more times! Another resource would be lost to him, another place gone: the only company he cared for in the alien, ugly little town he was losing.

Nothing but work, drudgery, constant hastening from dwelling to dwelling among the colliers and the iron-workers. It wore him out, but at the same time he had a craving for it. It was a stimulant to him to be in the homes of the working people, moving, as it were, through the innermost body of their life. His nerves were excited and gratified. He could come so near, into the very lives of the rough, inarticulate, powerfully emotional men and women. He grumbled, he said he hated the hellish hole. But as a matter of fact it excited him, the contact with the rough, strongly-feeling people was a stimulant applied direct to his nerves.

Below Oldmeadow, in the green, shallow, soddened hollow of fields, lay a square, deep pond. Roving across the landscape, the doctor's quick eye detected a figure in black passing through the gate of the field, down towards the pond. He looked again. It would be Mabel Pervin. His mind suddenly became alive and attentive.

Why was she going down there? He pulled up on the path on the slope above, and stood staring. He could just make sure of the small black figure moving in the hollow of the failing day. He seemed to see her in the midst of such obscurity, that he was like a clairvoyant, seeing rather with the mind's eye than with ordinary sight. Yet he could see her positively enough, whilst he kept his eye attentive. He felt, if he looked away from her, in the thick, ugly falling dusk, he would lose her altogether.

He followed her minutely as she moved, direct and intent, like something transmitted rather than stirring in voluntary activity, straight down the field towards the pond. There she stood on the bank for a moment. She never raised her head. Then she waded slowly into the water.

He stood motionless as the small black figure walked slowly and deliberately towards the centre of the pond, very slowly, gradually moving deeper into the motionless water, and still moving forward as the water got up to her breast. Then he could see her no more in the dusk of the dead afternoon.

"There!" he exclaimed. "Would you believe it?"

And he hastened straight down, running over the wet, soddened fields, pushing through the hedges, down into the depression of callous wintry obscurity. It took him several minutes to come to the pond. He stood on the bank, breathing heavily. He could see nothing. His eyes seemed to penetrate the dead water. Yes, perhaps that was the dark shadow of her black clothing beneath the surface of the water.

He slowly ventured into the pond. The bottom was deep, soft clay, he sank in, and the water clasped dead cold round his legs. As he stirred he could smell the cold, rotten clay that fouled up into the water. It was objectionable in his lungs. Still, repelled and yet not heeding, he moved deeper into the pond. The cold water rose over his thighs, over his loins, upon his abdomen. The lower part of his body was all sunk in the hideous cold element. And the bottom was so deeply soft and uncertain, he was afraid of pitching with his mouth underneath. He could not swim, and was afraid.

He crouched a little, spreading his hands under the water and moving them round, trying to feel for her. The dead cold pond swayed upon his chest. He moved again, a little deeper, and again, with his hands underneath, he felt all around under the water. And he touched her clothing. But it evaded his fingers. He made a desperate effort to grasp it.

And so doing he lost his balance and went under, horribly, suffocating in the foul earthy water, struggling madly for a few moments. At last, after what seemed an eternity, he got his footing, rose again into the air and looked around. He gasped, and knew he was in the world. Then he looked at the water. She had risen near him. He grasped her clothing, and drawing her nearer, turned to take his way to land again.

He went very slowly, carefully, absorbed in the slow progress. He rose higher, climbing out of the pond. The water was now only about his legs; he was thankful, full of relief to be out of the clutches of the pond. He lifted her and staggered on to the bank, out of the horror of wet, grey clay.

He laid her down on the bank. She was quite unconscious and running with water. He made the water come from her mouth, he worked to restore her. He did not have to work very long before he could feel the breathing begin again in her; she was breathing naturally. He worked a little longer. He could feel her live beneath his hands; she was coming back. He wiped her face, wrapped her in his overcoat, looked round into the dim, dark grey world, then lifted her and staggered down the bank and across the fields.

It seemed an unthinkably long way, and his burden so heavy he felt he would never get to the house. But at last he was in the stable-yard, and then in the house-yard. He opened the door and went into the house. In the kitchen he laid her down on the hearth-rug and called. The house was empty. But the fire was burning in the grate.

Then again he kneeled to attend to her. She was breathing regularly, her eyes were wide open and as if conscious, but there seemed something missing in her look. She was conscious in herself, but unconscious of her surroundings.

He ran upstairs, took blankets from a bed, and put them before the fire to warm. Then he removed her saturated, earthy-smelling clothing, rubbed her dry with a towel, and wrapped her naked in the blankets. Then he went into the dining-room, to look for spirits. There was a little whisky. He drank a gulp himself, and put some into her mouth.

The effect was instantaneous. She looked full into his face, as if she had been seeing him for some time, and yet had only just become conscious of him.

"Dr. Fergusson?" she said.

"What?" he answered.

He was divesting himself of his coat, intending to find some dry clothing upstairs. He could not bear the smell of the dead, clayey water, and he was mortally afraid for his own health.

"What did I do?" she asked.

"Walked into the pond," he replied. He had begun to shudder like one sick, and could hardly attend to her. Her eyes remained full on him, he seemed to be going dark in his mind, looking back at her helplessly. The shuddering became quieter in him, his life came back to him, dark and unknowing, but strong again.

"Was I out of my mind?" she asked, while her eyes were fixed on him all the time.

"Maybe, for a moment," he replied. He felt quiet, because his strength had come back. The strange fretful strain had left him.

"Am I out of my mind now?" she asked.

"Are you?" he reflected a moment. "No," he answered truthfully, "I don't see that you are." He turned his face aside. He was afraid now, because he felt dazed, and felt dimly that her power was stronger than his, in this issue. And she continued to look at him fixedly all the time. "Can you tell me where I shall find some dry things to put on?" he asked.

"Did you dive into the pond for me?" she asked.

"No," he answered. "I walked in. But I went in overhead as well."

There was silence for a moment. He hesitated. He very much wanted to go upstairs to get into dry clothing. But there was another desire in him. And she seemed to hold him. His will seemed to have gone to sleep, and left him, standing there slack before her. But he felt warm inside himself. He did not shudder at all, though his clothes were sodden on him.

"Why did you?" she asked.

"Because I didn't want you to do such a foolish thing," he said.

"It wasn't foolish," she said, still gazing at him as she lay on the floor, with a sofa cushion under her head. "It was the right thing to do. *I* knew best, then."

"I'll go and shift these wet things," he said. But still he had not the power to move out of her presence, until she sent him. It was as if she had the life of his body in her hands, and he could not extricate himself. Or perhaps he did not want to.

Suddenly she sat up. Then she became aware of her own immediate condition. She felt the blankets about her, she knew her own limbs. For a moment it seemed as if her reason were going. She looked round, with wild eye, as if seeking something. He stood still with fear. She saw her clothing lying scattered.

"Who undressed me?" she asked, her eyes resting full and inevitably on his face.

"I did," he replied, "to bring you round."

For some moments she sat and gazed at him awfully, her lips parted.

"Do you love me, then?" she asked.

He only stood and stared at her, fascinated. His soul seemed to melt.

She shuffled forward on her knees, and put her arms round him, round his legs, as he stood there, pressing her breasts against his knees and thighs, clutching him with strange, convulsive certainty, pressing his thighs against her, drawing him to her face, her throat, as she looked up at him with flaring, humble eyes of transfiguration, triumphant in first possession.

"You love me," she murmured, in strange transport, yearning and triumphant and confident. "You love me. I know you love me, I know."

And she was passionately kissing his knees, through the wet clothing, passionately and indiscriminately kissing his knees, his legs, as if unaware of everything.

He looked down at the tangled wet hair, the wild, bare, animal shoulders. He was amazed, bewildered, and afraid. He had never thought of loving her. He had never wanted to love her. When he rescued her and restored her, he was a doctor, and she was a patient. He had had no single personal thought of her. Nay, this introduction of the personal element was very distasteful to him, a violation of his professional honour. It was horrible to have her there embracing his knees. It was horrible. He revolted from it, violently. And yet — and yet — he had not the power to break away.

She looked at him again, with the same supplication of powerful love, and that same transcendent, frightening light of triumph. In view of the delicate flame which seemed to come from her face like a light, he was powerless. And yet he had never intended to love her. He had never intended. And something stubborn in him could not give way.

"You love me," she repeated, in a murmur of deep, rhapsodic assurance. "You love me."

Her hands were drawing him, drawing him down to her. He was afraid, even a little horrified. For he had, really, no intention of loving her. Yet her hands were drawing him towards her. He put out his hand quickly to steady himself, and grasped her bare shoulder. A flame seemed to burn the hand that grasped her soft shoulder. He had no intention of loving her: his whole will was against his yielding. It was horrible. And yet wonderful was the touch of her shoulders, beautiful the shining of her face. Was she perhaps mad? He had a horror of yielding to her. Yet something in him ached also.

He had been staring away at the door, away from her. But his hand remained on her shoulder. She had gone suddenly very still. He looked down at her. Her eyes were now wide with fear, with doubt, the light was dying from her face, a shadow of terrible greyness was returning. He could not bear the touch of her eyes' question upon him, and the look of death behind the question.

With an inward groan he gave way, and let his heart yield towards her. A sudden gentle smile came on his face. And her eyes, which never left his face, slowly, slowly filled with tears. He watched the strange water rise in her eyes, like some slow fountain coming up. And his heart seemed to burn and melt away in his breast.

He could not bear to look at her any more. He dropped on his knees and caught her head with his arms and pressed her face against his throat. She was very still. His heart, which seemed to have broken, was burning with a kind of agony in his breast. And he felt her slow, hot tears wetting his throat. But he could not move.

He felt the hot tears wet his neck and the hollows of his neck, and he remained motionless, suspended through one of man's eternities.

Only now it had become indispensable to him to have her face pressed close to him; he could never let her go again. He could never let her head go away from the close clutch of his arm. He wanted to remain like that for ever, with his heart hurting him in a pain that was also life to him. Without knowing, he was looking down on her damp, soft brown hair.

Then, as it were suddenly, he smelt the horrid stagnant smell of that water. And at the same moment she drew away from him and looked at him. Her eyes were wistful and unfathomable. He was afraid of them, and he fell to kissing her, not knowing what he was doing. He wanted her eyes not to have that terrible, wistful, unfathomable look.

When she turned her face to him again, a faint delicate flush was glowing, and there was again dawning that terrible shining of joy in her eyes, which really terrified him, and yet which he now wanted to see, because he feared the look of doubt still more.

"You love me?" she said, rather faltering.

"Yes." The word cost him a painful effort. Not because it wasn't true. But because it was too newly true, the *saying* seemed to tear open again his newly-torn heart. And he hardly wanted it to be true, even now.

She lifted her face to him, and he bent forward and kissed her on the mouth, gently, with the one kiss that is an eternal pledge. And as he kissed her his heart strained again in his breast. He never intended to love her. But now it was over. He had crossed over the gulf to her, and all that he had left behind had shrivelled and become void.

After the kiss, her eyes again slowly filled with tears. She sat still, away from him, with her face drooped aside, and her hands folded in her lap. The tears fell very slowly. There was complete silence. He too sat there motionless and silent on the hearth-rug. The strange pain of his heart that was broken seemed to consume him. That he should love her? That this was love! That he should be ripped open in this way! Him, a doctor! How they would all jeer if they knew! It was agony to him to think they might know.

In the curious naked pain of the thought he looked again to her. She was sitting there drooped into a muse. He saw a tear fall, and his heart flared hot. He saw for the first time that one of her shoulders was quite uncovered, one arm bare, he could see one of her small breasts; dimly, because it had become almost dark in the room.

"Why are you crying?" he asked, in an altered voice.

She looked up at him, and behind her tears the consciousness of her situation for the first time brought a dark look of shame to her eyes.

"I'm not crying, really," she said, watching him, half frightened.

He reached his hand, and softly closed it on

her bare arm.

"I love you! I love you!" he said in a soft, low vibrating voice, unlike himself.

She shrank, and dropped her head. The soft, penetrating grip of his hand on her arm distressed her. She looked up at him.

"I want to go," she said. "I want to go and get you some dry things."

"Why?" he said. "I'm all right."

"But I want to go," she said. "And I want you to change your things."

He released her arm, and she wrapped herself in the blanket, looking at him rather frightened. And still she did not rise.

"Kiss me," she said wistfully.

He kissed her, but briefly, half in anger.

Then, after a second, she rose nervously, all mixed up in the blanket. He watched her in her confusion as she tried to extricate herself and wrap herself up so that she could walk. He watched her relentlessly, as she knew. And as she went, the blanket trailing, and as he saw a glimpse of her feet and her white leg, he tried to remember her as she was when he had wrapped her in the blanket. But then he didn't want to remember, because she had been nothing to him then, and his nature revolted from remembering her as she was when she was nothing to him.

A tumbling, muffled noise from within the dark house startled him. Then he heard her voice: "There are clothes." He rose and went to the foot of the stairs, and gathered up the garments she had thrown down. Then he came back to the fire, to rub himself down and dress. He grinned at his own appearance when he had finished.

The fire was sinking, so he put on coal. The house was now quite dark, save for the light of a street-lamp that shone in faintly from beyond the holly trees. He lit the gas with matches he found on the mantelpiece. Then he emptied the pockets of his own clothes, and threw all his wet things in a heap into the scullery. After which he gathered up her sodden clothes, gently, and put them in a separate heap on the copper-top in the scullery.

It was six o'clock on the clock. His own watch had stopped. He ought to go back to the surgery. He waited, and still she did not come down. So he went to the foot of the stairs and called:

"I shall have to go."

Almost immediately he heard her coming down. She had on her best dress of black voile, and her hair was tidy, but still damp. She looked at him — and in spite of herself, smiled.

"I don't like you in those clothes," she said.

"Do I look a sight?" he answered.

They were shy of one another.

"I'll make you some tea," she said.

"No, I must go."

"Must you?" And she looked at him again

with the wide, strained, doubtful eyes. And again, from the pain of his breast, he knew how he loved her. He went and bent to kiss her, gently, passionately, with his heart's painful kiss.

"And my hair smells so horrible," she murmured in distraction. "And I'm so awful, I'm so awful! Oh no, I'm too awful." And she broke into bitter, heart-broken sobbing. "You can't want to love me, I'm horrible."

"Don't be silly, don't be silly," he said, trying to comfort her, kissing her, holding her in his arms. "I want you, I want to marry you, we're going to be married, quickly, quickly — to-morrow if I can."

But she only sobbed terribly, and cried:

"I feel awful. I feel awful. I feel I'm horrible to you."

"No, I want you, I want you," was all he answered, blindly, with that terrible intonation which frightened her almost more than her horror lest he should *not* want her.

Haircut

Ring Lardner

I GOT another barber that comes over from Carterville and helps me out Saturdays, but the rest of the time I can get along all right alone. You can see for yourself that this ain't no New York City and besides that, the most of the boys works all day and don't have no leisure to drop in here and get themselves prettied up.

You're a newcomer, ain't you? I thought I hadn't seen you round before. I hope you like it good enough to stay. As I say, we ain't no New York City or Chicago, but we have pretty good times. Not as good, though, since Jim Kendall got killed. When he was alive, him and Hod Meyers used to keep this town in an uproar. I bet they was more laughin' done here than any town its size in America.

Jim was comical, and Hod was pretty near a match for him. Since Jim's gone, Hod tries to hold his end up just the same as ever, but it's tough goin' when you ain't got nobody to kind of work with.

They used to be plenty fun in here Saturdays. This place is jam-packed Saturdays, from four o'clock on. Jim and Hod would show up right after their supper, round six o'clock. Jim would set himself down in that big chair, nearest the blue spittoon. Whoever had been settin' in that chair, why they'd get up when Jim come in and give it to him.

You'd of thought it was a reserved seat like they have sometimes in a theayter. Hod would generally always stand or walk up and down, or some Saturdays, of course, he'd be settin' in this chair part of the time, gettin' a haircut.

Well, Jim would set there a w'ile without openin' his mouth only to spit, and then finally he'd say to me, "Whitey," — my right name, that is, my right first name, is Dick, but everybody round here calls me Whitey — Jim would say, "Whitey, your nose looks like a rosebud tonight. You must of been drinkin' some of your aw de cologne."

So I'd say, "No, Jim, but you look like you'd been drinkin' somethin' of that kind or somethin' worse."

Jim would have to laugh at that, but then he'd speak up and say, "No, I ain't had nothin' to drink, but that ain't sayin' I wouldn't like somethin'. I wouldn't even mind if it was wood alcohol."

Then Hod Meyers would say, "Neither would your wife." That would set everybody to laughin' because Jim and his wife wasn't on very good terms. She'd of divorced him only they wasn't no chance to get alimony and she didn't have no way to take care of herself and the kids. She couldn't never understand Jim. He *was* kind of rough, but a good fella at heart.

Him and Hod had all kinds of sport with Milt Sheppard. I don't suppose you've seen Milt. Well, he's got an Adam's apple that looks more like a mushmelon. So I'd be shavin' Milt and when I'd start to shave down here on his neck, Hod would holler, "Hey, Whitey, wait a minute! Before you cut into it, let's make up a pool and see who can guess closest to the number of seeds."

And Jim would say, "If Milt hadn't of been so hoggish, he'd of ordered a half a cantaloupe instead of a whole one and it might not of stuck in his throat."

All the boys would roar at this and Milt himself would force a smile, though the joke was on him. Jim certainly was a card!

There's his shavin' mug, settin' on the shelf, right next to Charley Vail's. "Charles M. Vail." That's the druggist. He comes in regular for his shave, three times a week. And Jim's is the cup next to Charley's. "James H. Kendall." Jim won't need no shavin' mug no more, but I'll leave it there just the same for old time's sake. Jim certainly was a character!

Years ago, Jim used to travel for a canned goods concern over in Carterville. They sold canned goods. Jim had the whole northern half of the State and was on the road five days out of every week. He'd drop in here Saturdays and tell his experiences for that week. It was rich.

I guess he paid more attention to playin' jokes than makin' sales. Finally the concern let him out and he come right home here and told everybody he'd been fired instead of sayin' he'd resigned like most fellas would of.

It was a Saturday and the shop was full and Jim got up out of that chair and says, "Gentlemen, I got an important announcement to make. I been fired from my job."

Well, they asked him if he was in earnest and he said he was and nobody could think of nothin' to say till Jim finally broke the ice himself. He says, "I been sellin' canned goods and now I'm canned goods myself."

You see, the concern he'd been workin' for was a factory that made canned goods. Over in Carterville. And now Jim said he was canned himself. He was certainly a card!

Jim had a great trick that he used to play w'ile he was travelin'. For instance, he'd be ridin' on a train and they'd come to some little town like, well, like, we'll say, like Benton. Jim would look out the train window and read the signs on the stores.

For instance, they'd be a sign, "Henry Smith, Dry Goods." Well, Jim would write down the name and the name of the town and when he got to wherever he was goin' he'd mail back a postal card to Henry Smith at Benton and not sign no name to it, but he'd write on the card, well, somethin' like "Ask your wife about that book agent that spent the afternoon last week," or "Ask your Missus who kept her from gettin' lonesome the last time you was in Carterville." And he'd sign the card, "A Friend."

Of course, he never knew what really come of none of these jokes, but he could picture what *probably* happened and that was enough.

Jim didn't work very steady after he lost his position with the Carterville people. What he did earn, doin' odd jobs round town, why he spent pretty near all of it on gin and his family might of starved if the stores hadn't of carried them along. Jim's wife tried her hand at dressmakin', but they ain't nobody goin' to get rich makin' dresses in this town.

As I say, she'd of divorced Jim, only she seen that she couldn't support herself and the kids and she was always hopin' that some day Jim would cut out his habits and give her more than two or three dollars a week.

They was a time when she would go to whoever he was workin' for and ask them to give her his wages, but after she done this once or twice, he beat her to it by borrowin' most of his pay in advance. He told it all round town, how he had outfoxed his Missus. He certainly was a caution!

But he wasn't satisfied with just outwittin' her. He was sore the way she had acted, tryin' to grab off his pay. And he made up his mind he'd get even. Well, he waited till Evans's Circus was advertised to come to town. Then he told his wife and two kiddies that he was goin' to take them to the circus. The day of the circus, he told them he would get the tickets and meet them outside the entrance to the tent.

Well, he didn't have no intentions of bein' there or buyin' tickets or nothin'. He got full of gin and laid round Wright's poolroom all day. His wife and the kids waited and waited and of course he didn't show up. His wife didn't have a dime with her, or nowhere else, I guess. So she finally had to tell the kids it was all off and they cried like they wasn't never goin' to stop.

Well, it seems, w'ile they was cryin', Doc Stair came along and he asked what was the matter, but Mrs. Kendall was stubborn and wouldn't tell him, but the kids told him and he insisted on takin' them and their mother in the show. Jim found this out afterwards and it was one reason why he had it in for Doc Stair.

Doc Stair come here about a year and a half ago. He's a mighty handsome young fella and his clothes always look like he has them made to order. He goes to Detroit two or three times a year and w'ile he's there he must have a tailor take his measure and then make him a suit to order. They cost pretty near twice as much, but they fit a whole lot better than if you just bought them in a store.

For a w'ile everybody was wonderin' why a young doctor like Doc Stair should come to a town like this where we already got old Doc Gamble and Doc Foote that's both been here for years and all the practice in town was always divided between the two of them.

Then they was a story got round that Doc Stair's gal had throwed him over, a gal up in the Northern Peninsula somewheres, and the reason he come here was to hide himself away and forget it. He said himself that he thought they wasn't nothin' like general practice in a place like ours to fit a man to be a good all round doctor. And that's why he'd came.

Anyways, it wasn't long before he was makin' enough to live on, though they tell me that he never dunned nobody for what they owed him, and the folks here certainly has got the owin' habit, even in my business. If I had all that was comin' to me for just shaves alone, I could go to Carterville and put up at the Mercer for a week and see a different picture every night. For instance, they's old George Purdy — but I guess I shouldn't ought to be gossipin'.

Well, last year, our coroner died, died of the flu. Ken Beatty, that was his name. He was the coroner. So they had to choose another man to be coroner in his place and they picked Doc Stair. He laughed at first and said he didn't want it, but they made him take it. It ain't no job that anybody would fight for and what a man makes out of it in a year would just about buy seeds for their garden. Doc's the kind, though, that can't say no to nothin' if you keep at him long enough.

But I was goin' to tell you about a poor boy we got here in town — Paul Dickson. He fell out of a tree when he was about ten years old. Lit on his head and it done somethin' to him and he ain't never been right. No harm in him, but just silly. Jim Kendall used to call him cuckoo; that's a name Jim had for anybody that was off their head, only he called people's head their bean. That was another of his gags, callin' head bean and callin' crazy people cuckoo. Only poor Paul ain't crazy, but just silly.

You can imagine that Jim used to have all kinds of fun with Paul. He'd send him to the White Front Garage for a left-handed monkey wrench. Of course they ain't no such a thing as a left-handed monkey wrench.

And once we had a kind of a fair here and they was a baseball game between the fats and the leans and before the game started Jim called Paul over and sent him way down to Schrader's hardware store to get a key for the pitcher's box.

They wasn't nothin' in the way of gags that Jim couldn't think up, when he put his mind to it.

Poor Paul was always kind of suspicious of people, maybe on account of how Jim had kept foolin' him. Paul wouldn't have much to do with anybody only his own mother and Doc Stair and a girl here in town named Julie Gregg. That is, she ain't a girl no more, but pretty near thirty or over.

When Doc first come to town, Paul seemed to feel like here was a real friend and he hung round Doc's office most of the w'ile; the only time he wasn't there was when he'd go home to eat or sleep or when he seen Julie Gregg doin' her shoppin'.

When he looked out Doc's window and seen her, he'd run downstairs and join her and tag along with her to the different stores. The poor boy was crazy about Julie and she always treated him mighty nice and made him feel like he was welcome, though of course it wasn't nothin' but pity on her side.

Doc done all he could to improve Paul's mind and he told me once that he really thought the boy was gettin' better, that they was times when he was as bright and sensible as anybody else.

But I was goin' to tell you about Julie Gregg. Old Man Gregg was in the lumber business, but got to drinkin' and lost the most of his money and when he died, he didn't leave nothin' but the house and just enough insurance for the girl to skimp along on.

Her mother was a kind of a half invalid and didn't hardly ever leave the house. Julie wanted to sell the place and move somewheres else after the old man died, but the mother said she was born here and would die here. It was tough on Julie, as the young people round this town — well, she's too good for them.

She's been away to school and Chicago and New York and different places and they ain't no subject she can't talk on, where you take the rest of the young folks here and you mention anything to them outside of Gloria Swanson or Tommy Meighan and they think you're delirious. Did you see Gloria in Wages of Virtue? You missed somethin'!

Well, Doc Stair hadn't been here more than a week when he come in one day to get shaved and I recognized who he was as he had been pointed out to me, so I told him about my old lady. She's been ailin' for a couple years and either Doc Gamble or Doc Foote, neither one, seemed to be helpin' her. So he said he would come out and see her, but if she was able to get out herself, it would be better to bring her to his office where he could make a completer examination.

So I took her to his office and w'ile I was waitin' for her in the reception room, in come Julie Gregg. When somebody comes in Doc Stair's office, they's a bell that rings in his inside office so as he can tell they's somebody to see him.

So he left my old lady inside and come out to the front office and that's the first time him and Julie met and I guess it was what they call love at first sight. But it wasn't fifty-fifty. This young fella was the slickest lookin' fella she'd ever seen in this town and she went wild over him. To him she was just a young lady that wanted to see the doctor.

She'd come on about the same business I had. Her mother had been doctorin' for years with Doc Gamble and Doc Foote and without no results. So she'd heard they was a new doc in town and decided to give him a try. He promised to call and see her mother that same day.

I said a minute ago that it was love at first sight on her part. I'm not only judgin' by how she acted afterwards but how she looked at him that first day in his office. I ain't no mind reader, but it was wrote all over her face that she was gone.

Now Jim Kendall, besides bein' a jokesmith and a pretty good drinker, well, Jim was quite a lady-killer. I guess he run pretty wild durin' the time he was on the road for them Carterville people, and besides that, he'd had a couple little affairs of the heart right here in town. As I say, his wife could of divorced him, only she couldn't.

But Jim was like the majority of men, and women, too, I guess. He wanted what he couldn't get. He wanted Julie Gregg and worked his head off tryin' to land her. Only he'd of said bean instead of head.

Well, Jim's habits and his jokes didn't appeal to Julie and of course he was a married man, so he didn't have no more chance than, well, than a rabbit. That's an expression of Jim's himself. When somebody didn't have no chance to get elected or somethin', Jim would always say they didn't have no more chance than a rabbit.

He didn't make no bones about how he felt. Right in here, more than once, in front of the whole crowd, he said he was stuck on Julie and anybody that could get her for him was welcome to his house and his wife and kids included. But she wouldn't have nothin' to do with him; wouldn't even speak to him on the street. He finally seen he wasn't gettin' nowheres with his usual line so he decided to try the rough stuff. He went right up to her house one evenin' and when she opened the door he forced his way in and grabbed her. But she broke loose and before he could stop her, she run in the next room and locked the door and phoned to Joe Barnes. Joe's the marshal. Jim could hear who she was phonin' to and he beat it before Joe got there.

Joe was an old friend of Julie's pa. Joe went to Jim the next day and told him what would happen if he ever done it again.

I don't know how the news of this little affair leaked out. Chances is that Joe Barnes told his wife and she told somebody else's wife and they told their husband. Anyways, it did leak out and Hod Meyers had the nerve to kid Jim about it, right here in this shop. Jim didn't deny nothin' and kind of laughed it off and said for us all to wait; that lots of people had tried to make a monkey out of him, but he always got even.

Meanw'ile everybody in town was wise to Julie's bein' wild mad over the Doc. I don't suppose she had any idear how her face changed when him and her was together; of course she couldn't of, or she'd of kept away from him. And she didn't know that we was all noticin' how many times she made excuses to go up to his office or pass it on the other side of the street and look up in his window to see if he was there. I felt sorry for her and so did most other people.

Hod Meyers kept rubbin' it into Jim about how the Doc had cut him out. Jim didn't pay no attention to the kiddin' and you could see he was plannin' one of his jokes.

One trick Jim had was the knack of changin' his voice. He could make you think he was a girl talkin' and he could mimic any man's voice. To show you how good he was along this line, I'll tell you the joke he played on me once.

You know, in most towns of any size, when a man is dead and needs a shave, why the barber that shaves him soaks him five dollars for the job; that is, he don't soak *him,* but whoever ordered the shave. I just charge three dollars because personally I don't mind much shavin' a dead person. They lay a whole lot stiller than live customers. The only thing is that you don't feel like talkin' to them and you get kind of lonesome.

Well, about the coldest day we ever had here, two years ago last winter, the phone rung at the house w'ile I was home to dinner and I answered the phone and it was a woman's voice and she said she was Mrs. John Scott and her husband was dead and would I come out and shave him.

Old John had always been a good customer of mine. But they live seven miles out in the country, on the Streeter road. Still I didn't see how I could say no.

So I said I would be there, but would have to come in a jitney and it might cost three or four dollars besides the price of the shave. So she, or the voice, it said that was all right, so I got Frank Abbott to drive me out to the place and when I got there, who should open the door but old John himself! He wasn't no more dead than, well, than a rabbit.

It didn't take no private detective to figure out who had played me this little joke. Nobody could of thought it up but Jim Kendall. He certainly was a card!

I tell you this incident just to show you how he could disguise his voice and make you believe it was somebody else talkin'. I'd of swore it was Mrs. Scott had called me. Anyways, some woman.

Well, Jim waited till he had Doc Stair's voice down pat; then he went after revenge.

He called Julie up on a night when he knew Doc was over in Carterville. She never questioned but what it was Doc's voice. Jim said he must see her that night; he couldn't wait no longer to tell her somethin'. She was all excited and told him to come to the house. But he said he was expectin' an important long distance call and wouldn't she please forget her manners for once and come to his office. He said they couldn't nothin' hurt her and nobody would see her and he just *must* talk to her a little w'ile. Well, poor Julie fell for it.

Doc always keeps a night light in his office, so it looked to Julie like they was somebody there.

Meanw'ile Jim Kendall had went to Wright's poolroom, where they was a whole gang amusin' themselves. The most of them had drank plenty of gin, and they was a rough bunch even when sober. They was always strong for Jim's jokes and when he told them to come with him and see some fun they give up their card games and pool games and followed along.

Doc's office is on the second floor. Right outside his door they's a flight of stairs leadin' to the floor above. Jim and his gang hid in the dark behind these stairs.

Well, Julie come up to Doc's door and rung the bell and they was nothin' doin'. She rung it again and she rung it seven or eight times. Then she tried the door and found it locked. Then Jim made some kind of a noise and she heard it and waited a minute, and then she says, "Is that you, Ralph?" Ralph is Doc's first name.

They was no answer and it must of come to her all of a sudden that she'd been bunked. She pretty near fell downstairs and the whole gang after her. They chased her all the way home, hollerin', "Is that you, Ralph?" and "Oh, Ralphie, dear, is that you?" Jim says he couldn't holler it himself, as he was laughin' too hard.

Poor Julie! She didn't show up here on Main Street for a long, long time afterward.

And of course Jim and his gang told everybody in town, everybody but Doc Stair. They was scared to tell him, and he might of never knowed only for Paul Dickson. The poor cuckoo, as Jim called him, he was here in the shop one night when Jim was still gloatin' yet over what he'd done to Julie. And Paul took in as much of it as he could understand and he run to Doc with the story.

It's a cinch Doc went up in the air and swore he'd make Jim suffer. But it was a kind of a delicate thing, because if it got out that he had beat Jim up, Julie was bound to hear of it and then she'd know that Doc knew and of course knowin' that he knew would make it worse for her than ever. He was goin' to do somethin', but it took a lot of figurin'.

Well, it was a couple days later when Jim was here in the shop again, and so was the cuckoo. Jim was goin' duck-shootin' the next day and had come in lookin' for Hod Meyers to go with him. I happened to know that Hod had went over to Carterville and wouldn't be home till the end of the week. So Jim said he hated to go alone and he guessed he would call it off. Then poor Paul spoke up and said if Jim would take him he would go along. Jim thought a w'ile and then he said, well, he guessed a half-wit was better than nothin'.

I suppose he was plottin' to get Paul out in the boat and play some joke on him, like pushin' him in the water. Anyways, he said Paul could go. He asked him had he ever shot a duck and Paul said no, he'd never even had a gun in his hands. So Jim said he could set in the boat and watch him and if he behaved himself, he might lend him his gun for a couple of shots. They made a date to meet in the mornin' and that's the last I seen of Jim alive.

Next mornin', I hadn't been open more than ten minutes when Doc Stair come in. He looked kind of nervous. He asked me had I seen Paul Dickson. I said no, but I knew where he was, out duck-shootin' with Jim Kendall. So Doc says that's what he had heard, and he couldn't understand it because Paul had told him he wouldn't never have no more to do with Jim as long as he lived.

He said Paul had told him about the joke Jim had played on Julie. He said Paul had asked him what he thought of the joke and the Doc had told him that anybody that would do a thing like that ought not to be let live.

I said it had been a kind of a raw thing, but Jim just couldn't resist no kind of a joke, no matter how raw. I said I thought he was all right at heart, but just bubblin' over with mischief. Doc turned and walked out.

At noon he got a phone call from old John Scott. The lake where Jim and Paul had went shootin' is on John's place. Paul had came runnin' up to the house a few minutes before and said they'd been an accident. Jim had shot a few ducks and then give the gun to Paul and told him to try his luck. Paul hadn't never handled a gun and he was nervous. He was shakin' so hard that he couldn't control the gun. He let fire and Jim sunk back in the boat, dead.

Doc Stair, bein' the coroner, jumped in Frank Abbott's flivver and rushed out to Scott's farm. Paul and old John was down on the shore of the lake. Paul had rowed the boat to shore, but they'd left the body in it, waitin' for Doc to come.

Doc examined the body and said they might as well fetch it back to town. They was no use leavin' it there or callin' a jury, as it was a plain case of accidental shootin'.

Personally I wouldn't never leave a person shoot a gun in the same boat I was in unless I was sure they knew somethin' about guns. Jim was a sucker to leave a new beginner have his gun, let alone a half-wit. It probably served Jim right, what he got. But still we miss him round here. He certainly was a card!

Comb it wet or dry?

The Devil and Daniel Webster

Stephen Vincent Benét

It's a story they tell in the border country, where Massachusetts joins Vermont and New Hampshire.

Yes, Dan'l Webster's dead — or, at least, they buried him. But every time there's a thunderstorm around Marshfield, they say you can hear his rolling voice in the hollows of the sky. And they say that if you go to his grave and speak loud and clear, "Dan'l Webster — Dan'l Webster!" the ground'll begin to shiver and the trees begin to shake. And after a while you'll hear a deep voice saying, "Neighbor, how stands the Union?" Then you better answer the Union stands as she stood, rock bottomed and copper sheathed, one and indivisible, or he's liable to rear right out of the ground. At least, that's what I was told when I was a youngster.

You see, for a while, he was the biggest man in the country. He never got to be President, but he was the biggest man. There were thousands that trusted in him right next to God

Almighty, and they told stories about him and all the things that belonged to him that were like the stories of patriarchs and such. They said, when he stood up to speak, stars and stripes came right out in the sky, and once he spoke against a river and made it sink into the ground. They said, when he walked the woods with his fishing rod, Killhall, the trout would jump out of the streams right into his pockets, for they knew it was no use putting up a fight against him; and, when he argued a case, he could turn on the harps of the blessed and the shaking of the earth underground. That was the kind of man he was, and his big farm up at Marshfield was suitable to him. The chickens he raised were all white meat down through the drumsticks, the cows were tended like children, and the big ram he called Goliath had horns with a curl like a morning-glory vine and could butt through an iron door. But Dan'l wasn't one of your gentlemen farmers; he knew all the ways of the land, and he'd be up by candlelight to see that the chores got done. A man with a mouth like a mastiff, a brow like a mountain and eyes like burning anthracite — that was Dan'l Webster in his prime. And the biggest case he argued never got written down in the books, for he argued it against the devil, nip and tuck and no holds barred. And this is the way I used to hear it told.

There was a man named Jabez Stone, lived at Cross Corners, New Hampshire. He wasn't a bad man to start with, but he was an unlucky man. If he planted corn, he got borers; if he planted potatoes, he got blight. He had good-enough land, but it didn't prosper him; he had a decent wife and children, but the more children he had, the less there was to feed them. If stones cropped up in his neighbor's field, boulders boiled up in his; if he had a horse with the spavins, he'd trade it for one with the staggers and give something extra. There's some folks bound to be like that, apparently. But one day Jabez Stone got sick of the whole business.

He'd been plowing that morning and he'd just broke the plowshare on a rock that he could have sworn hadn't been there yesterday. And, as he stood looking at the plowshare, the off horse began to cough — that ropy kind of cough that means sickness and horse doctors. There were two children down with the measles, his wife was ailing, and he had a whitlow on his thumb. It was about the last straw for Jabez Stone. "I vow," he said, and he looked around him kind of desperate, "I vow it's enough to make a man want to sell his soul to the devil! And I would, too, for two cents!"

Then he felt a kind of queerness come over him at having said what he'd said; though, naturally, being a New Hampshireman, he wouldn't take it back. But, all the same, when it got to be evening and, as far as he could see, no notice had been taken, he felt relieved in his mind, for he was a religious man. But notice is always taken, sooner or later, just like the Good Book says. And, sure enough, next day, about suppertime, a soft-spoken, dark-dressed stranger drove up in a handsome buggy and asked for Jabez Stone.

Well, Jabez told his family it was a lawyer, come to see him about a legacy. But he knew who it was. He didn't like the looks of the stranger, nor the way he smiled with his teeth. They were white teeth, and plentiful — some say they were filed to a point, but I wouldn't vouch for that. And he didn't like it when the dog took one look at the stranger and ran away howling, with his tail between his legs. But having passed the word, more or less, he stuck to it, and they went out behind the barn and made their bargain. Jabez Stone had to prick his finger to sign, and the stranger lent him a silver pin. The wound healed clean, but it left a little white scar.

After that, all of a sudden, things began to pick up and prosper for Jabez Stone. His cows got fat and his horses sleek, his crops were the envy of the neighborhood, and lightning might strike all over the valley, but it wouldn't strike his barn. Pretty soon he was one of the prosperous people of the county; they asked him to stand for selectman, and he stood for it; there began to be talk of running him for state senate. All in all, you might say the Stone family was as happy and contented as cats in a dairy. And so they were, except for Jabez Stone.

He'd been contented enough the first few years. It's a great thing when bad luck turns; it drives most other things out of your head. True, every now and then, especially in rainy weather, the little white scar on his finger would give him a twinge. And once a year, punctual as clockwork, the stranger with the handsome buggy would come driving by. But the sixth year the stranger lighted, and, after that, his peace was over for Jabez Stone.

The stranger came up through the lower field, switching his boots with a cane — they were handsome black boots, but Jabez Stone never liked the look of them, particularly the toes. And, after he'd passed the time of day, he said, "Well, Mr. Stone, you're a hummer! It's a very pretty property you've got here, Mr. Stone."

"Well, some might favor it and others might not," said Jabez Stone, for he was a New Hampshireman.

"Oh, no need to decry your industry!" said the stranger, very easy, showing his teeth in a smile. "After all, we know what's been done, and it's been according to contract and specifications. So when — ahem — the mortgage falls due next year, you shouldn't have any regrets."

"Speaking of that mortgage, mister," said Jabez Stone, and he looked around for help to the earth and the sky, "I'm beginning to have one or two doubts about it."

"Doubts?" said the stranger not quite so pleasantly.

"Why, yes," said Jabez Stone. "This being the U.S.A. and me always having been a religious man." He cleared his throat and got bolder. "Yes, sir," he said, "I'm beginning to have considerable doubts as to that mortgage holding in court."

"There's courts and courts," said the stranger, clicking his teeth. "Still, we might as well have a look at the original document." And he hauled out a big black pocketbook, full of papers. "Sherwin, Slater, Stevens, Stone," he muttered. " 'I, Jabez Stone, for a term of seven years ——' Oh, it's quite in order, I think."

But Jabez Stone wasn't listening, for he saw something else flutter out of the black pocketbook. It was something that looked like a moth, but it wasn't a moth. And as Jabez Stone stared at it, it seemed to speak to him in a small sort of piping voice, terrible small and thin, but terrible human. "Neighbor Stone!" It squeaked. "Neighbor Stone! Help me! For God's sake, help me!"

But before Jabez Stone could stir hand or foot, the stranger whipped out a big bandanna handkerchief, caught the creature in it, just like a butterfly, and started tying up the ends of the bandanna.

"Sorry for the interruption," he said. "As I was saying ——"

But Jabez Stone was shaking all over like a scared horse.

"That's Miser Stevens' voice!" he said in a croak. "And you've got him in your handkerchief!"

The stranger looked a little embarrassed.

"Yes, I really should have transferred him to the collecting box," he said with a simper, "but there were some rather unusual specimens there and I don't want them crowded. Well, well, these little contretemps will occur."

"I don't know what you mean by contertan," said Jabez Stone, "but that was Miser Stevens' voice! And he ain't dead! You can't tell me he is! He was just as spry and mean as a woodchuck Tuesday!"

"In the midst of life . . ." said the stranger, kind of pious. "Listen!" Then a bell began to toll in the valley and Jabez Stone listened, with the sweat running down his face. For he knew it was tolled for Miser Stevens and that he was dead.

"These long-standing accounts," said the stranger with a sigh; "one really hates to close them. But business is business."

He still had the bandanna in his hand, and Jabez Stone felt sick as he saw the cloth struggle and flutter.

"Are they all as small as that?" he asked

hoarsely.

"Small?" said the stranger. "Oh, I see what you mean. Why, they vary." He measured Jabez Stone with his eyes, and his teeth showed. "Don't worry, Mr. Stone," he said. "You'll go with a very good grade. I wouldn't trust you outside the collecting box. Now, a man like Dan'l Webster, of course — well, we'd have to build a special box for him, and even at that, I imagine the wing spread would astonish you. He'd certainly be a prize. I wish we could see our way clear to him. But, in your case, as I was saying ——"

"Put that handkerchief away!" said Jabez Stone, and he began to beg and to pray. But the best he could get at the end was a three years' extension, with conditions.

But till you make a bargain like that, you've got no idea of how fast four years can run. By the last months of those years Jabez Stone's known all over the state and there's talk of running him for governor — and it's dust and ashes in his mouth. For every day, when he gets up, he thinks, "There's one more night gone," and every night, when he lies down, he thinks of the black pocketbook and the soul of Miser Stevens, and it makes him sick at heart. Till, finally, he can't bear it any longer, and, in the last days of the last year, he hitches up his horse and drives off to seek Dan'l Webster. For Dan'l was born in New Hampshire, only a few miles from Cross Corners, and it's well known that he has a particular soft spot for old neighbors.

It was early in the morning when he got to Marshfield, but Dan'l was up already, talking Latin to the farm hands and wrestling with the ram, Goliath, and trying out a new trotter and working up speeches to make against John C. Calhoun. But when he heard a New Hampshireman had come to see him, he dropped everything else he was doing, for that was Dan'l's way. He gave Jabez Stone a breakfast that five men couldn't eat, went into the living history of every man and woman in Cross Corners, and finally asked him how he could serve him.

Jabez Stone allowed that it was a kind of mortgage case.

"Well, I haven't pleaded a mortgage case in a long time, and I don't generally plead now, except before the Supreme Court," said Dan'l, "but if I can, I'll help you."

"Then I've got hope for the first time in ten years," said Jabez Stone and told him the details.

Dan'l walked up and down as he listened, hands behind his back, now and then asking a question, now and then plunging his eyes at the floor, as if they'd bore through it like gimlets. When Jabez Stone had finished, Dan'l puffed out his cheeks and blew. Then he turned to Jabez Stone and a smile broke over his face like the sunrise over Monadnock.

"You've certainly given yourself the devil's own row to hoe, Neighbor Stone," he said, "but I'll take your case."

"You'll take it?" said Jabez Stone, hardly daring to believe.

"Yes," said Dan'l Webster. "I've got about seventy-five other things to do and the Missouri Compromise to straighten out, but I'll take your case. For if two New Hampshiremen aren't a match for the devil, we might as well give the country back to the Indians."

Then he shook Jabez Stone by the hand and said, "Did you come down here in a hurry?"

"Well, I admit I made time," said Jabez Stone.

"You'll go back faster," said Dan'l Webster, and he told 'em to hitch up Constitution and Constellation to the carriage. They were matched grays with one white forefoot, and they stepped like greased lightning.

Well, I won't describe how excited and pleased the whole Stone family was to have the great Dan'l Webster for a guest, when they finally got there. Jabez Stone had lost his hat on the way, blown off when they overtook a wind, but he didn't take much account of that. But after supper he sent the family off to bed, for he had most particular business with Mr. Webster. Mrs. Stone wanted him to sit in the front parlor, but Dan'l Webster knew front parlors and said he preferred the kitchen. So it was there they sat, waiting for the stranger, with a jug on the table between them and a bright fire on the hearth — the stranger being scheduled to show up on the stroke of midnight, according to specification.

Well, most men wouldn't have asked for better company than Dan'l Webster and a jug. But with every tick of the clock Jabez Stone got sadder and sadder. His eyes roved round, and though he sampled the jug you could see he couldn't taste it. Finally, on the stroke of 11:30 he reached over and grabbed Dan'l Webster by the arm.

"Mr. Webster, Mr. Webster!" he said, and his voice was shaking with fear and a desperate courage. "For God's sake, Mr. Webster, harness your horses and get away from this place while you can!"

"You've brought me a long way, neighbor, to tell me you don't like my company," said Dan'l Webster, quite peaceable, pulling at the jug.

"Miserable wretch that I am!" groaned Jabez Stone. "I've brought you a devilish way, and now I see my folly. Let him take me if he wills. I don't hanker after it, I must say, but I can stand it. But you're the Union's stay and New Hampshire's pride! He mustn't get you, Mr. Webster! He mustn't get you!"

Dan'l Webster looked at the distracted man, all gray and shaking in the firelight, and laid a hand on his shoulder.

"I'm obliged to you, Neighbor Stone," he

said gently. "It's kindly thought of. But there's a jug on the table and a case in hand. And I never left a jug or a case half finished in my life."

And just at that moment there was a sharp rap on the door.

"Ah," said Dan'l Webster very coolly, "I thought your clock was a trifle slow, Neighbor Stone." He stepped to the door and opened it. "Come in!" he said.

The stranger came in — very dark and tall he looked in the firelight. He was carrying a box under his arm — a black japanned box with little air holes in the lid. At the sight of the box Jabez Stone gave a low cry and shrank into a corner of the room.

"Mr. Webster, I presume," said the stranger, very polite, but with his eyes glowing like a fox's deep in the woods.

"Attorney of record for Jabez Stone," said Dan'l Webster, but his eyes were glowing too. "Might I ask your name?"

"I've gone by a good many," said the stranger carelessly. "Perhaps Scratch will do for the evening. I'm often called that in these regions."

Then he sat down at the table and poured himself a drink from the jug. The liquor was cold in the jug, but it came steaming into the glass.

"And now," said the stranger, smiling and showing his teeth, "I shall call upon you, as a law-abiding citizen, to assist me in taking possession of my property.''

Well, with that the argument began — and it went hot and heavy. At first Jabez Stone had a flicker of hope, but when he saw Dan'l Webster being forced back at point after point, he just sat scrunched in his corner, with his eyes on that japanned box. For there wasn't any doubt as to the deed or the signature — that was the worst of it. Dan'l Webster twisted and turned and thumped his fist on the table, but he couldn't get away from that. He offered to compromise the case; the stranger wouldn't hear of it. He pointed out the property had increased in value, and state senators ought to be worth more; the stranger stuck to the letter of the law. He was a great lawyer, Dan'l Webster, but we know who's the King of Lawyers, as the Good Book tells us, and it seemed as if, for the first time, Dan'l Webster had met his match.

Finally, the stranger yawned a little. ''Your spirited efforts on behalf of your client do you credit, Mr. Webster,'' he said, ''but if you have no more arguments to adduce, I'm rather pressed for time . . .'' and Jabez Stone shuddered.

Dan'l Webster's brow looked dark as a thundercloud.

''Pressed or not, you shall not have this man!'' he thundered. ''Mr. Stone is an American citizen, and no American citizen may be forced into the service of a foreign prince. We fought England for that in '12 and we'll fight all hell for it again!"

"Foreign?" said the stranger. "And who calls me a foreigner?"

"Well, I never yet heard of the dev — of your claiming American citizenship," said Dan'l Webster with surprise.

"And who with better right?" said the stranger with one of his terrible smiles. "When the first wrong was done to the first Indian, I was there. When the first slaver put out for the Congo, I stood on her deck. Am I not in your books and stories and beliefs, from the first settlements on? Am I not spoken of still in every church in New England? 'Tis true the North claims me for a Southerner and the South for a Northerner, but I am neither. I am merely an honest American like yourself — and of the best descent — for, to tell the truth, Mr. Webster, though I don't like to boast of it, my name is older in this country than yours."

"Aha!" said Dan'l Webster with the veins standing out in his forehead. "Then I stand on the Constitution! I demand a trial for my client!"

"The case is hardly one for an ordinary court," said the stranger, his eyes flickering. "And, indeed, the lateness of the hour ——"

"Let it be any court you choose, so it is an

American judge and an American jury!'' said Dan'l Webster in his pride. ''Let it be the quick or the dead; I'll abide the issue!''

''You have said it,'' said the stranger, and pointed his finger at the door. And with that, and all of a sudden, there was a rushing of wind outside and a noise of footsteps. They came, clear and distinct, through the night. And yet they were not like the footsteps of living men.

''In God's name, who comes by so late?'' cried Jabez Stone in an ague of fear.

''The jury Mr. Webster demands,'' said the stranger, sipping at his boiling glass. ''You must pardon the rough appearance of one or two; they will have come a long way.''

And with that the fire burned blue and the door blew open and twelve men entered, one by one.

If Jabez Stone had been sick with terror before, he was blind with terror now. For there was Walter Butler, the loyalist, who spread fire and horror through the Mohawk Valley in the times of the Revolution; and there was Simon Girty, the renegade, who saw white men burned at the stake and whooped with the Indians to see them burn. His eyes were green, like a catamount's, and the stains on his hunting shirt did not come from the blood of the deer. King Philip was there, wild and proud as he had been in life, with the great gash in his head that gave him his death wound, and cruel Governor Dale, who broke men on the wheel. There was Morton of Merry Mount, who so vexed the Plymouth Colony, with his flushed, loose, handsome face and his hate of the godly. There was Teach, the bloody pirate, with his black beard curling on his breast. The Reverend John Smeet, with his strangler's hands and his Geneva gown, walked as daintily as he had to the gallows. The red print of the rope was still around his neck, but he carried a perfumed handkerchief in one hand. One and all, they came into the room with the fires of hell still upon them, and the stranger named their names and their deeds as they came, till the tale of twelve was told. Yet the stranger had told the truth — they had all played a part in America.

"Are you satisfied with the jury, Mr. Webster?" said the stranger mockingly, when they had taken their places.

The sweat stood upon Dan'l Webster's brow, but his voice was clear.

"Quite satisfied," he said. "Though I miss General Arnold from the company."

"Benedict Arnold is engaged upon other business," said the stranger with a glower. "Ah, you asked for a justice, I believe."

He pointed his finger once more, and a tall man, soberly clad in Puritan garb, with the burning gaze of the fanatic, stalked into the room and took his judge's place.

"Justice Hathorne is a jurist of experience,"

said the stranger. "He presided at certain witch trials once held in Salem. There were others who repented of the business later, but not he."

"Repent of such notable wonders and undertakings?" said the stern old justice. "Nay, hang them — hang them all!" And he muttered to himself in a way that struck ice into the soul of Jabez Stone.

Then the trial began, and, as you might expect, it didn't look anyways good for the defense. And Jabez Stone didn't make much of a witness in his own behalf. He took one look at Simon Girty and screeched, and they had to put him back in his corner in a kind of swoon.

It didn't halt the trial though; the trial went on, as trials do. Dan'l Webster had faced some hard juries and hanging judges in his time, but this was the hardest he'd ever faced, and he knew it. They sat there with a kind of glitter in their eyes, and the stranger's smooth voice went on and on. Every time he'd raise an objection, it'd be "Objection sustained," but whenever Dan'l objected, it'd be "Objection denied." Well, you couldn't expect fair play from a fellow like this Mr. Scratch.

It got to Dan'l in the end, and he began to heat, like iron in the forge. When he got up to speak he was going to flay that stranger with every trick known to the law, and the judge and jury too. He didn't care if it was contempt of court or what would happen to him for it. He didn't care any more what happened to Jabez Stone. He just got madder and madder, thinking of what he'd say. And yet, curiously enough, the more he thought about it, the less he was able to arrange his speech in his mind.

Till, finally, it was time for him to get up on his feet, and he did so, all ready to bust out with lightnings and denunciations. But before he started he looked over the judge and jury for a moment, such being his custom. And he noticed the glitter in their eyes was twice as strong as before, and they all leaned forward. Like hounds just before they get the fox, they looked, and the blue mist of evil in the room thickened as he watched them. Then he saw what he'd been about to do, and he wiped his forehead, as a man might who's just escaped falling into a pit in the dark.

For it was him they'd come for, not only Jabez Stone. He read it in the glitter of their eyes and in the way the stranger hid his mouth with one hand. And if he fought them with their own weapons, he'd fall into their power; he knew that, though he couldn't have told you how. It was his own anger and horror that burned in their eyes; and he'd have to wipe that out or the case was lost. He stood there for a moment, his black eyes burning like anthracite. And then he began to speak.

He started off in a low voice, though you could hear every word. They say he could call on the harps of the blessed when he chose. And this was just as simple and easy as a man could talk. But he didn't start out by condemning or reviling. He was talking about the things that make a country a country and a man a man.

And he began with the simple things that everybody's known and felt — the freshness of a fine morning when you're young, and the taste of food when you're hungry, and the new day that's every day when you're a child. He took them up and he turned them in his hands. They were good things for any man. But without freedom they sickened. And then he talked of those enslaved, and the sorrows of slavery, his voice got like a big bell. He talked of the early days of America and the men who had made those days. It wasn't a spread-eagle speech, but he made you see it. He admitted all the wrong that had ever been done. But he showed how, out of the wrong and the right, the suffering and the starvations; something new had come. And everybody had played a part in it, even the traitors.

Then he turned to Jabez Stone and showed him as he was — an ordinary man who'd had hard luck and wanted to change it. And, because he'd wanted to change it, now he was going to be punished for all eternity. And yet there was good in Jabez Stone, and he showed that good. He was hard and mean, in some ways, but he was a man. There was sadness in being a man, but it was a proud thing too. And he showed what the pride of it was till you couldn't help feeling it. Yes, even in hell, if a man was a man, you'd know it. And he wasn't pleading for any one person any more, though his voice rang like an organ. He was telling the story and the failures and the endless journey of mankind. They got tricked and trapped and bamboozled, but it was a great journey. And no demon that was ever foaled could know the inwardness of it — it took a man to do that.

The fire began to die on the hearth and the wind before morning to blow. The light was getting gray in the room when Dan'l Webster finished. And his words came back at the end to New Hampshire ground, and the one spot of land that each man loves and clings to. He painted a picture of that, and to each one of that jury he spoke of things long forgotten. For his voice could search the heart, and that was his gift and his strength. And to one his voice was like the forest and its secrecy, and to another like the sea and the storms of the sea; and one heard the cry of his lost nation in it, and another saw a little harmless scene he hadn't remembered for years. But each saw something. And when Dan'l Webster finished he didn't know whether or not he'd saved Jabez Stone. But he knew he'd done a miracle. For the glitter was gone from the eyes of judge and jury, and, for the moment, they were men again, and knew they were men.

"The defense rests," said Dan'l Webster and stood there like a mountain. His ears were still ringing with his speech, and he didn't hear anything else till he heard Judge Hathorne say, "The jury will retire to consider its verdict."

Walter Butler rose in his place and his face had a dark, gay pride on it.

"The jury has considered its verdict," he said and looked the stranger full in the eye. "We find for the defendant, Jabez Stone."

With that, the smile left the stranger's face, but Walter Butler did not flinch.

"Perhaps 'tis not strictly in accordance with the evidence," he said, "but even the damned may salute the eloquence of Mr. Webster."

With that, the long crow of a rooster split the gray morning sky, and judge and jury were gone from the room like a puff of smoke and as if they had never been there. The stranger returned to Dan'l Webster, smiling wryly.

"Major Butler was always a bold man," he said. "I had not thought him quite so bold. Nevertheless, my congratulations, as between two gentlemen."

"I'll have that paper first, if you please," said Dan'l Webster, and he took it and tore it into four pieces. It was queerly warm to the touch. "And now," he said, "I'll have you!" and his hand came down like a bear trap on the stranger's arm. For he knew that once you bested anybody like Mr. Scratch in fair fight, his power on you was gone. And he could see that Mr. Scratch knew it too.

The stranger twisted and wriggled, but he couldn't get out of that grip. "Come, come, Mr. Webster," he said, smiling palely. "This sort of thing is ridic — ouch! — is ridiculous. If you're worried about the costs of the case, naturally, I'd be glad to pay ——"

"And so you shall!" said Dan'l Webster, shaking him till his teeth rattled. "For you'll sit right down at that table and draw up a document, promising never to bother Jabez Stone nor his heirs or assigns nor any other New Hampshireman till doomsday! For any hades we want to raise in this state, we can raise ourselves, without assistance from strangers."

"Ouch!" said the stranger. "Ouch! Well, they never did run very big to the barrel, but — ouch! — I agree!"

So he sat down and drew up the document. But Dan'l Webster kept his hand on his coat collar all the time.

"And now may I go?" said the stranger, quite humble, when Dan'l'd seen the document's in proper and legal form.

"Go?" said Dan'l, giving him another shake. "I'm still trying to figure out what I'll do with you. For you've settled the costs of the case, but you haven't settled with me. I think I'll take you back to Marshfield," he said, kind of reflective.

"I've got a ram there named Goliath that

can butt through an iron door. I'd kind of like to turn you loose in his field and see what he'd do."

Well, with that the stranger began to beg and to plead. And he begged and he pled so humble that finally Dan'l, who was naturally kindhearted, agreed to let him go. The stranger seemed terrible grateful for that and said, just to show they were friends, he'd tell Dan'l's fortune before leaving. So Dan'l agreed to that, though he didn't take much stock in fortune-tellers ordinarily. But, naturally, the stranger was a little different.

Well, he pried and he peered at the lines in Dan'l's hands. And he told him one thing and another that was quite remarkable. But they were all in the past.

"Yes, all that's true, and it happened," said Dan'l Webster. "But what's to come in the future?"

The stranger grinned, kind of happily, and shook his head.

"The future's not as you think it," he said. "It's dark. You have a great ambition, Mr. Webster."

"I have," said Dan'l firmly, for everybody knew he wanted to be President.

"It seems almost within your grasp," said the stranger, "but you will not attain it. Lesser men will be made President and you will be passed over."

"And, if I am, I'll still be Daniel Webster,"

said Dan'l. "Say on."

"You have two strong sons," said the stranger, shaking his head. "You look to found a line. But each will die in war and neither reach greatness."

"Live or die, they are still my sons," said Dan'l Webster. "Say on."

"You have made great speeches," said the stranger. "You will make more."

"Ah," said Dan'l Webster.

"But the last great speech you make will turn many of your own against you," said the stranger. "They will call you Ichabod; they will call you by other names. Even in New England some will say you have turned your coat and sold your country, and their voices will be loud against you till you die."

"So it is an honest speech, it does not matter what men say," said Dan'l Webster. Then he looked at the stranger and their glances locked.

"One question," he said. "I have fought for the Union all my life. Will I see that fight won against those who would tear it apart?"

"Not while you live," said the stranger grimly, "but it will be won. And after you are dead, there are thousands who will fight for your cause, because of words that you spoke."

"Why, then, you long-barreled, slab-sided, lantern-jawed, fortune-telling note shaver," said Dan'l Webster with a great roar of laughter, "be off with you to your own place before I put my mark on you! For, by the thirteen original colonies, I'd go to the Pit itself to save the Union!''

And with that he drew back his foot for a kick that would have stunned a horse. It was only the tip of his shoe that caught the stranger, but he went flying out of the door with his collecting box under his arm.

''And now,'' said Dan'l Webster, seeing Jabez Stone beginning to rouse from his swoon, ''let's see what's left in the jug, for it's dry work talking all night. I hope there's pie for breakfast, Neighbor Stone.''

But they say that whenever the devil comes near Marshfield, even now, he gives it a wide berth. And he hasn't been seen in the state of New Hampshire from that day to this.

I'm not talking about Massachusetts or Vermont.

The Secret Life of Walter Mitty

James Thurber

WE'RE going through!'' The Commander's voice was like thin ice breaking. He wore his full-dress uniform, with the heavily braided white cap pulled down rakishly over one cold gray eye. ''We can't make it, sir. It's spoiling for a hurricane, if you ask me.'' ''I'm not asking you, Lieutenant Berg,'' said the Commander. ''Throw on the power lights! Rev her up to 8,500! We're going through!'' The pounding of the cylinders increased: ta-pocketa-pocketa-pocketa-*pocketa-pocketa*. The Commander stared at the ice forming on the pilot window. He walked over and twisted a row of complicated dials. ''Switch on No. 8 auxiliary!'' he shouted. ''Switch on No. 8 auxiliary!'' repeated Lieutenant Berg. ''Full strength in No. 3 turret!'' shouted the Commander. ''Full strength in No. 3 turret!'' The crew, bending to their various tasks in the huge, hurtling, eight-engined Navy hydroplane, looked at each other and grinned. ''The Old Man'll get us through,'' they said to one another. ''The Old Man ain't afraid of Hell!'' . . .

''Not so fast! You're driving too fast!'' said Mrs. Mitty. ''What are you driving so fast for?''

''Hmm?'' said Walter Mitty. He looked at his wife, in the seat beside him, with shocked astonishment. She seemed grossly unfamiliar, like a strange woman who had yelled at him in a crowd. ''You were up to fifty-five,'' she said. ''You know I don't like to go more than forty. You were up to fifty-five.'' Walter Mitty drove on toward Waterbury in silence, the roaring of the SN202 through the worst storm in twenty years of Navy flying fading in the remote, intimate airways of his mind. ''You're tensed up again,'' said Mrs. Mitty. ''It's one of your days. I wish you'd let Dr. Renshaw look you over.''

Walter Mitty stopped the car in front of the building where his wife went to have her hair done. ''Remember to get those overshoes while I'm having my hair done,'' she said. ''I don't need overshoes,'' said Mitty. She put her mirror back into her bag. ''We've been all through that,'' she said, getting out of the car. ''You're not a young man any longer.'' He raced the engine a little. ''Why don't you wear your gloves? Have you lost your gloves?'' Walter Mitty reached in a pocket and brought out the gloves. He put them on, but after she had turned and gone into the building and he had driven on to a red light, he took them off again. "Pick it up, brother!" snapped a cop as the light changed, and Mitty hastily pulled on his gloves and lurched ahead. He drove around the streets aimlessly for a time, and then he drove past the hospital on his way to the parking lot.

. . . "It's the millionaire banker, Wellington McMillan," said the pretty nurse. "Yes?" said Walter Mitty, removing his gloves slowly. "Who has the case?" "Dr. Renshaw and Dr. Benbow, but there are two specialists here, Dr. Remington from New York and Dr. Pritchard-Mitford from London. He flew over." A door opened down a long, cool corridor and Dr. Renshaw came out. He looked distraught and haggard. "Hello, Mitty," he said. "We're having the devil's own time with McMillan, the millionaire banker and close personal friend of Roosevelt. Obstreosis of the ductal tract. Tertiary. Wish you'd take a look at him." "Glad to," said Mitty.

In the operating room there were whispered introductions: "Dr. Remington, Dr. Mitty. Dr. Pritchard-Mitford, Dr. Mitty." "I've read your book on streptothricosis," said Pritchard-Mitford, shaking hands. "A brilliant performance, sir." "Thank you," said Walter Mitty. "Didn't know you were in the States, Mitty," grumbled Remington. "Coals to Newcastle, bringing Mitford and me up here for tertiary." "You are very kind," said Mitty. A huge, complicated machine, connected to the operating table, with many tubes and wires, began at this moment to go pocketa-pocketa-pocketa. "The new anaesthetizer is giving away!" shouted an interne. "There is no one in the East who knows how to fix it!" "Quiet, man!" said Mitty, in a low, cool voice. He sprang to the machine, which was now going pocketa-pocketa-queep-pocketa-queep. He began fingering delicately a row of glistening dials. "Give me a fountain pen!" he snapped. Someone handed him a fountain pen. He pulled a faulty piston out of the machine and inserted the pen in its place. "That will hold for ten minutes," he said. "Get on with the operation." A nurse hurried over and whispered to Renshaw, and Mitty saw the man turn pale. "Coreopsis has set in," said Renshaw nervously. "If you would take over, Mitty?" Mitty looked at him and at the craven figure of Benbow, who drank, and at the grave, uncertain faces of the two great specialists. "If you wish," he said. They slipped a white gown on him; he adjusted a mask and drew on thin gloves; nurses handed him shining . . .

"Back it up, Mac! Look out for that Buick!" Walter Mitty jammed on the brakes. "Wrong lane, Mac," said the parking-lot attendant, looking at Mitty closely. "Gee. Yeh," muttered Mitty. He began cautiously to back out of the lane marked "Exit Only." "Leave her sit there," said the attendant. "I'll put her away." Mitty got out of the car. "Hey, better leave the key." "Oh," said Mitty, handing the man the ignition key. The attendant vaulted into the car, backed it up with insolent skill, and put it where it belonged.

They're so damn cocky, thought Walter Mitty, walking along Main Street; they think they know everything. Once he had tried to take his chains off, outside New Milford, and he had got them wound around the axles. A man had had to come out in a wrecking car and unwind them, a young, grinning garage-man. Since then Mrs. Mitty always made him drive to a garage to have the chains taken off. The next time, he thought, I'll wear my right arm in a sling; they won't grin at me then. I'll have my right arm in a sling and they'll see I couldn't possibly take the chains off myself. He kicked at the slush on the sidewalk. "Overshoes," he said to himself, and he began looking for a shoe store.

When he came out into the street again, with the overshoes in a box under his arm, Walter Mitty began to wonder what the other thing was his wife had told him to get. She had told him, twice before they set out from their house for Waterbury. In a way he hated these weekly trips to town — he was always getting something wrong. Kleenex, he thought, Squibb's, razor blades? No. Toothpaste, toothbrush, bicarbonate, carborundum, initiative and referendum? He gave it up. But she would remember it. "Where's the what's-it's-name?" she would ask. "Don't tell me you forgot the what's-its-name." A newsboy went by shouting something about the Waterbury trial.

. . . "Perhaps this will refresh your memory." The District Attorney suddenly thrust a heavy automatic at the quiet figure on the witness stand. "Have you ever seen this before?" Walter Mitty took the gun and examined it expertly. "This is my Webley-Vickers 50.80," he said calmly. An excited buzz ran around the courtroom. The Judge rapped for order. "You are a crack shot with any sort of firearms, I believe?" said the District Attorney, insinuatingly. "Objection!" shouted Mitty's attorney. "We have shown that the defendant could not have fired the shot. We have shown that he wore his right arm in a sling on the night of the fourteenth of July." Walter Mitty raised his hand briefly and the bickering attorneys were stilled. "With any known make of gun," he said evenly, "I could have killed Gregory Fitzhurst at three hundred feet *with my left hand.*" Pandemonium broke loose in the courtroom. A woman's scream rose above the bedlam and suddenly a lovely, dark-haired girl was in Walter Mitty's arms. The District Attorney struck at her savagely. Without rising from his chair, Mitty let the man have it on the point of the chin. "You miserable cur!" . . .

"Puppy biscuit," said Walter Mitty. He

stopped walking and the buildings of Waterbury rose up out of the misty courtroom and surrounded him again. A woman who was passing laughed. "He said 'Puppy biscuit,'" she said to her companion. "That man said 'Puppy biscuit' to himself." Walter Mitty hurried on. He went into an A. & P., not the first one he came to but a smaller one farther up the street. "I want some biscuit for small, young dogs," he said to the clerk. "Any special brand, sir?" The greatest pistol shot in the world thought a moment. "It says 'Puppies Bark for It' on the box," said Walter Mitty.

His wife would be through at the hairdresser's in fifteen minutes, Mitty saw in looking at his watch, unless they had trouble drying it; sometimes they had trouble drying it. She didn't like to get to the hotel first; she would want him to be there waiting for her as usual. He found a big leather chair in the lobby, facing a window, and he put the overshoes and the puppy biscuit on the floor beside it. He picked up an old copy of *Liberty* and sank down into the chair. "Can Germany Conquer the World Through the Air?" Walter Mitty looked at the pictures of bombing planes and of ruined streets.

. . . "The cannonading has got the wind up in young Raleigh, sir," said the sergeant. Captain Mitty looked up at him through tousled hair. "Get him to bed," he said wearily, "with the others. I'll fly alone." "But you can't, sir,'' said the sergeant anxiously. ''It takes two men to handle that bomber and the Archies are pounding hell out of the air. Von Richtman's circus is between here and Saulier.'' ''Somebody's got to get that ammunition dump,'' said Mitty. ''I'm going over. Spot of brandy?'' He poured a drink for the sergeant and one for himself. War thundered and whined around the dugout and battered at the door. There was a rending of wood and splinters flew through the room. ''A bit of a near thing,'' said Captain Mitty carelessly. ''The box barrage is closing in,'' said the sergeant. ''We only live once, Sergeant,'' said Mitty, with his faint, fleeting smile. ''Or do we?'' He poured another brandy and tossed it off. ''I never see a man could hold his brandy like you, sir,'' said the sergeant. ''Begging your pardon, sir.'' Captain Mitty stood up and strapped on his huge Webley-Vickers automatic. ''It's forty kilometres through hell, sir,'' said the sergeant. Mitty finished one last brandy. ''After all,'' he said softly, ''what isn't?'' The pounding of the cannon increased; there was the rat-tat-tatting of machine guns, and from somewhere came the menacing pocketa-pocketa-pocketa of the new flamethrowers. Walter Mitty walked to the door of the dug-out humming ''Auprès de Ma Blonde.'' He turned and waved to the sergeant. ''Cheerio!'' he said. . . .

Something struck his shoulder. ''I've been

looking all over this hotel for you,'' said Mrs. Mitty. ''Why do you have to hide in this old chair? How did you expect me to find you?'' ''Things close in,'' said Walter Mitty vaguely. ''What?'' Mrs. Mitty said. ''Did you get the what's-its-name? The puppy biscuit? What's in that box?'' ''Overshoes,'' said Mitty. ''Couldn't you have put them on in the store?'' ''I was thinking,'' said Walter Mitty. ''Does it ever occur to you that I am sometimes thinking?'' She looked at him. ''I'm going to take your temperature when I get you home,'' she said.

They went out through the revolving doors that made a faintly derisive whistling sound when you pushed them. It was two blocks to the parking lot. At the drugstore on the corner she said, ''Wait here for me. I forgot something. I won't be a minute.'' She was more than a minute. Walter Mitty lighted a cigarette. It began to rain, rain with sleet in it. He stood up against the wall of the drugstore, smoking. . . . He put his shoulders back and his heels together. ''To hell with the handkerchief,'' said Walter Mitty scornfully. He took one last drag on his cigarette and snapped it away. Then, with that faint, fleeting smile playing about his lips, he faced the firing squad; erect and motionless, proud and disdainful, Walter Mitty the Undefeated, inscrutable to the last.

Life of Ma Parker

Katherine Mansfield

WHEN the literary gentleman, whose flat old Ma Parker cleaned every Tuesday, opened the door to her that morning, he asked after her grandson. Ma Parker stood on the doormat inside the dark little hall, and she stretched out her hand to help her gentleman shut the door before she replied. "We buried 'im yesterday, sir," she said quietly.

"Oh, dear me! I'm sorry to hear that," said the literary gentleman in a shocked tone. He was in the middle of his breakfast. He wore a very shabby dressing-gown and carried a crumpled newspaper in one hand. But he felt awkward. He could hardly go back to the warm sitting-room without saying something — something more. Then because these people set such store by funerals he said kindly, "I hope the funeral went off all right."

"Beg parding, sir?" said old Ma Parker huskily.

Poor old bird! She did look dashed. "I hope the funeral was a — a — success," said he.

Ma Parker gave no answer. She bent her head and hobbled off to the kitchen, clasping the old fish bag that held her cleaning things and an apron and a pair of felt shoes. The literary gentleman raised his eyebrows and went back to his breakfast.

"Overcome, I suppose," he said aloud, helping himself to the marmalade.

Ma Parker drew the two jetty spears out of her toque and hung it behind the door. She unhooked her worn jacket and hung that up too. Then she tied her apron and sat down to take off her boots. To take off her boots or to put them on was an agony to her, but it had been an agony for years. In fact, she was so accustomed to the pain that her face was drawn and screwed up ready for the twinge before she'd so much as untied the laces. That over, she sat back with a sigh and softly rubbed her knees. . . .

"Gran! Gran!" Her little grandson stood on her lap in his button boots. He'd just come in from playing in the street.

"Look what a state you've made your gran's skirt into — you wicked boy!"

But he put his arms round her neck and rubbed his cheek against hers.

"Gran, gi' us a penny!" he coaxed.

"Be off with you; Gran ain't got no pennies."

"Yes, you 'ave."

"No, I ain't."

"Yes, you 'ave. Gi' us one!"

Already she was feeling for the old, squashed, black leather purse.

"Well, what'll you give your gran?"

He gave a shy little laugh and pressed closer. She felt his eyelid quivering against her cheek. "I ain't got nothing," he murmured. . . .

The old woman sprang up, seized the iron kettle off the gas stove and took it over to the sink. The noise of the water drumming in the kettle deadened her pain, it seemed. She filled the pail, too, and the washing-up bowl.

It would take a whole book to describe the state of that kitchen. During the week the literary gentleman "did" for himself. That is to say, he emptied the tea leaves now and again into a jam jar set aside for that purpose, and if he ran out of clean forks he wiped over one or two on the roller towel. Otherwise, as he explained to his friends, his "system" was quite simple, and he couldn't understand why people make all this fuss about housekeeping.

"You simply dirty everything you've got, get a hag in once a week to clean up, and the thing's done."

The result looked like a gigantic dustbin. Even the floor was littered with toast crusts, envelopes, cigarette ends. But Ma Parker bore him no grudge. She pitied the poor young gentleman for having no one to look after him.

Out of the smudgy little window you could see an immense expanse of sad-looking sky, and whenever there were clouds they looked very worn, old clouds, frayed at the edges, with holes in them, or dark stains like tea.

While the water was heating, Ma Parker began sweeping the floor. "Yes," she thought, as the broom knocked, "what with one thing and another I've had my share. I've had a hard life."

Even the neighbours said that of her. Many a time, hobbling home with her fish bag she heard them, waiting at the corner, or leaning over the area railings, say among themselves, "She's had a hard life, has Ma Parker." And it was so true she wasn't in the least proud of it. It was just as if you were to say she lived in the basement-back at Number 27. A hard life . . .

At sixteen she'd left Stratford and come up to London as kitching-maid. Yes, she was born in Stratford-on-Avon. Shakespeare, sir? No, people were always arsking her about him. But she'd never heard his name until she saw it on the theatres.

Nothing remained of Stratford except that "sitting in the fireplace of a evening you could see the stars through the chimley," and "Mother always 'ad 'er side of bacon 'anging from the ceiling." And there was something — a bush, there was — at the front door, that smelt ever so nice. But the bush was very vague. She'd only remembered it once or twice in the hospital, when she'd been taken bad.

That was a dreadful place — her first place. She was never allowed out. She never went upstairs except for prayers morning and evening. It was a fair cellar. And the cook was a cruel woman. She used to snatch away her letters from home before she'd read them, and throw them in the range because they made her dreamy. . . . And the beedles! Would you believe it? — until she came to London she'd never seen a black beedle. Here Ma always gave a little laugh, as though — not to have seen a black beedle! Well! It was as if to say you'd never seen your own feet.

When that family was sold up she went as "help" to a doctor's house, and after two years there, on the run from morning till night, she married her husband. He was a baker.

"A baker, Mrs. Parker!" the literary gentleman would say. For occasionally he laid aside his tomes and lent an ear, at least, to this product called Life. "It must be rather nice to be married to a baker!"

Mrs. Parker didn't look so sure.

"Such a clean trade," said the gentleman.

Mrs. Parker didn't look convinced.

"And didn't you like handing the new loaves to the customers?"

"Well, sir," said Mrs. Parker, "I wasn't in the shop above a great deal. We had thirteen little ones and buried seven of them. If it wasn't the 'ospital it was the infirmary, you might say!"

"You might, *indeed,* Mrs. Parker!" said the gentleman, shuddering, and taking up his pen again.

Yes, seven had gone, and while the six were still small her husband was taken ill with consumption. It was flour on the lungs, the doctor told her at the time. . . . Her husband sat up in bed with his shirt pulled over his head, and the doctor's finger drew a circle on his back.

"Now, if we were to cut him open *here,* Mrs. Parker," said the doctor, "you'd find his lungs chock-a-block with white powder. Breathe, my good fellow!" And Mrs. Parker never knew for certain whether she saw or whether she fancied she saw a great fan of white dust come out of her poor dead husband's lips. . . .

But the struggle she'd had to bring up those six little children and keep herself to herself. Terrible it had been! Then, just when they were old enough to go to school her husband's sister came to stop with them to help things along, and she hadn't been there more than two months when she fell down a flight of steps and hurt her spine. And for five years Ma Parker had another baby — and such a one for crying! — to look after. Then young Maudie went wrong and took her sister Alice with her; the two boys emigrimated, and young Jim went to India with the army, and Ethel, the youngest, married a good-for-nothing little waiter who died of ulcers the year little Lennie was born. And now little Lennie — my grandson. . . .

The piles of dirty cups, dirty dishes, were washed and dried. The ink-black knives were cleaned with a piece of potato and finished off with a piece of cork. The table was scrubbed, and the dresser and the sink that had sardine tails swimming in it. . . .

He'd never been a strong child — never from the first. He'd been one of those fair babies that everybody took for a girl. Silvery fair curls he had, blue eyes, and a little freckle like a diamond on one side of his nose. The trouble she and Ethel had had to rear that child! The things out of the newspapers they tried him with! Every Sunday morning Ethel would read aloud while Ma Parker did her washing.

"Dear Sir, — Just a line to let you know my little Myrtil was laid out for dead. . . . After four bottils . . . gained 8 lbs. in 9 weeks, *and is still putting it on.*"

And then the egg-cup of ink would come off the dresser and the letter would be written, and Ma would buy a postal order on her way to work next morning. But it was no use. Nothing made little Lennie put it on. Taking him to the cemetery, even, never gave him a colour; a nice shake-up in the bus never improved his appetite.

But he was gran's boy from the first. . . .

"Whose boy are you?" said old Ma Parker, straightening up from the stove and going over to the smudgy window. And a little voice, so warm, so close, it half stifled her — it seemed to be in her breast under her heart — laughed out, and said, "I'm gran's boy!"

At that moment there was a sound of steps, and the literary gentleman appeared, dressed for walking.

"Oh, Mrs. Parker, I'm going out."

"Very good, sir."

"And you'll find your half-crown in the tray of the ink-stand."

"Thank you, sir."

"Oh, by the way, Mrs. Parker," said the literary gentleman quickly, "you didn't throw away any cocoa last time you were here — did you?"

"No, sir."

"*Very* strange. I could have sworn I left a teaspoonful of cocoa in the tin." He broke off. He said softly and firmly, "You'll always tell me when you throw things away — won't you, Mrs. Parker?" And he walked off very well pleased with himself, convinced, in fact, he'd shown Mrs. Parker that under his apparent carelessness he was as vigilant as a woman.

The door banged. She took her brushes and cloths into the bedroom. But when she began to make the bed, smoothing, tucking, patting, the thought of little Lennie was unbearable. Why did he have to suffer so? That's what she couldn't understand. Why should a little angel child have to arsk for his breath and fight for it? There was no sense in making a child suffer like that.

. . . From Lennie's little box of a chest there came a sound as though something was boiling. There was a great lump of something bubbling in his chest that he couldn't get rid of. When he coughed the sweat sprang out on his head; his eyes bulged, his hands waved, and the great lump bubbled as a potato knocks in a saucepan. But what was more awful than all was when he didn't cough he sat against the pillow and never spoke or answered, or even made as if he heard. Only he looked offended.

"It's not your poor old gran's doing it, my lovey," said old Ma Parker, patting back the damp hair from his little scarlet ears. But Lennie moved his head and edged away. Dreadfully offended with her he looked — and solemn. He bent his head and looked at her sideways as though he couln't have believed it of his gran.

But at the last . . . Ma Parker threw the counterpane over the bed. No, she simply couldn't think about it. It was too much — she'd had too much in her life to bear. She'd borne it up till now, she'd kept herself to herself, and never once had she been seen to cry.

Never by a living soul. Not even her own children had seen Ma break down. She'd kept a proud face always. But now! Lennie gone — what had she? She had nothing. He was all she'd got from life, and now he was took too. Why must it all have happened to me? she wondered. "What have I done?" said old Ma Parker. "What have I done?"

As she said those words she suddenly let fall her brush. She found herself in the kitchen. Her misery was so terrible that she pinned on her hat, put on her jacket and walked out of the flat like a person in a dream. She did not know what she was doing. She was like a person so dazed by the horror of what has happened that he walks away — anywhere, as though by walking away he could escape. . . .

It was cold in the street. There was a wind like ice. People went flitting by, very fast; the men walked like scissors; the women trod like cats. And nobody knew — nobody cared. Even if she broke down, if at last, after all these years, she were to cry, she'd find herself in the lock-up as like as not.

But at the thought of crying it was as though little Lennie leapt in his gran's arms. Ah, that's what she wants to do, my dove. Gran wants to cry. If she could only cry now, cry for a long time, over everything, beginning with her first place and the cruel cook, going on to the doctor's, and then the seven little ones, death of her husband, the children's leaving her, and all the years of misery that led up to Lennie. But to have a proper cry over all these things would take a long time. All the same, the time for it had come. She must do it. She couldn't put it off any longer; she couldn't wait any more. . . . Where could she go?

"She's had a hard life, has Ma Parker." Yes, a hard life, indeed! Her chin began to tremble; there was no time to lose. But where? Where?

She couldn't go home; Ethel was there. It would frighten Ethel out of her life. She couldn't sit on a bench anywhere; people would come arsking her questions. She couldn't possibly go back to the gentleman's flat; she had no right to cry in strangers' houses. If she sat on some steps a policeman would speak to her.

Oh, wasn't there anywhere where she could hide and keep herself to herself and stay as long as she liked, not disturbing anybody, and nobody worrying her? Wasn't there anywhere in the world where she could have her cry out — at last?

Ma Parker stood, looking up and down. The icy wind blew out her apron into a balloon. And now it began to rain. There was nowhere.

Winter Dreams

F. Scott Fitzgerald

SOME of the caddies were poor as sin and lived in one-room houses with a neurasthenic cow in the front yard, but Dexter Green's father owned the second best grocery-store in Black Bear — the best one was "The Hub," patronized by the wealthy people from Sherry Island — and Dexter caddied only for pocket-money.

In the fall when the days became crisp and gray, and the long Minnesota winter shut down like the white lid of a box, Dexter's skis moved over the snow that hid the fairways of the golf course. At these times the country gave him a feeling of profound melancholy — it offended him that the links should lie in enforced fallowness, haunted by ragged sparrows for the long season. It was dreary, too, that on the tees where the gay colors fluttered in summer there were now only the desolate sand-boxes knee-deep in crusted ice. When he crossed the hills the wind blew cold as misery, and if the sun was out he tramped with his eyes squinted up against the hard dimensionless glare.

In April the winter ceased abruptly. The snow ran down into Black Bear Lake scarcely tarrying for the early golfers to brave the season with red and black balls. Without elation, without an interval of moist glory, the cold was gone.

Dexter knew that there was something dismal about this Northern spring, just as he knew there was something gorgeous about the fall. Fall made him clinch his hands and tremble and repeat idiotic sentences to himself, and make brisk abrupt gestures of command to imaginary audiences and armies. October filled him with hope which November raised to a sort of ecstatic triumph, and in this mood the fleeting brilliant impressions of the summer at Sherry Island were ready grist to his mill. He became a golf champion and defeated Mr. T. A. Hedrick in a marvellous match played a hundred times over the fairways of his imagination, a match each detail of which he changed about untiringly — sometimes he won with almost laughable ease, sometimes he came up magnificently from behind. Again, stepping from a Pierce-Arrow automobile, like Mr. Mortimer Jones, he strolled frigidly into the lounge of the Sherry Island Golf Club — or perhaps, surrounded by an admiring crowd, he gave an exhibition of fancy diving from the spring-board of the club raft. . . . Among those who watched him in open-mouthed wonder was Mr. Mortimer Jones.

And one day it came to pass that Mr. Jones — himself and not his ghost — came up to Dexter with tears in his eyes and said that Dexter was the —— best caddy in the club, and wouldn't he decide not to quit if Mr. Jones made it worth his while, because every other —— caddy in the club lost one ball a hole for him — regularly ——

"No, sir," said Dexter decisively, "I don't want to caddy any more." Then, after a pause: "I'm too old."

"You're not more than fourteen. Why the devil did you decide just this morning that you wanted to quit? You promised that next week you'd go over to the state tournament with me."

"I decided I was too old."

Dexter handed in his "A Class" badge, collected what money was due him from the caddy master, and walked home to Black Bear Village.

"The best —— caddy I ever saw," shouted Mr. Mortimer Jones over a drink that afternoon. "Never lost a ball! Willing! Intelligent! Quiet! Honest! Grateful!"

The little girl who had done this was eleven — beautifully ugly as little girls are apt to be who are destined after a few years to be inexpressibly lovely and bring no end of misery to a great number of men. The spark, however, was perceptible. There was a general ungodliness in the way her lips twisted down at the corners when she smiled, and in the — Heaven help us! — in the almost passionate quality of her eyes. Vitality is born in such women. It was utterly in evidence now, shining through her thin frame in a sort of glow.

She had come eagerly out on to the course at nine o'clock with a white linen nurse and five small new golf-clubs in a white canvas bag which the nurse was carrying. When Dexter first saw her she was standing by the caddy house, rather ill at ease and trying to conceal the fact by engaging her nurse in an obviously unnatural conversation graced by startling and irrelevant grimaces from herself.

"Well, it's certainly a nice day, Hilda," Dexter heard her say. She drew down the corners of her mouth, smiled, and glanced furtively around, her eyes in transit falling for an instant on Dexter.

Then to the nurse:

"Well, I guess there aren't very many people out here this morning, are there?"

The smile again — radiant, blatantly artificial — convincing.

"I don't know what we're supposed to do now," said the nurse, looking nowhere in particular.

"Oh, that's all right. I'll fix it up."

Dexter stood perfectly still, his mouth slightly ajar. He knew that if he moved forward a step his stare would be in her line of vision

— if he moved backward he would lose his full view of her face. For a moment he had not realized how young she was. Now he remembered having seen her several times the year before — in bloomers.

Suddenly, involuntarily, he laughed, a short abrupt laugh — then, startled by himself, he turned and began to walk quickly away.

"Boy!"

Dexter stopped.

"Boy ——"

Beyond question he was addressed. Not only that, but he was treated to that absurd smile, that preposterous smile — the memory of which at least a dozen men were to carry into middle age.

"Boy, do you know where the golf teacher is?"

"He's giving a lesson."

"Well, do you know where the caddy-master is?"

"He isn't here yet this morning."

"Oh." For a moment this baffled her. She stood alternately on her right and left foot.

"We'd like to get a caddy," said the nurse. "Mrs. Mortimer Jones sent us out to play golf and we don't know how without we get a caddy."

Here she was stopped by an ominous glance from Miss Jones, followed immediately by the smile.

"There aren't any caddies here except me,"

said Dexter to the nurse, "and I got to stay here in charge until the caddy-master gets here."

"Oh."

Miss Jones and her retinue now withdrew, and at a proper distance from Dexter became involved in a heated conversation, which was concluded by Miss Jones taking one of the clubs and hitting it on the ground with violence. For further emphasis she raised it again and was about to bring it down smartly upon the nurse's bosom, when the nurse seized the club and twisted it from her hands.

"You damn little mean old *thing!*" cried Miss Jones wildly.

Another argument ensued. Realizing that the elements of the comedy were implied in the scene, Dexter several times began to laugh, but each time restrained the laugh before it reached audibility. He could not resist the monstrous conviction that the little girl was justified in beating the nurse.

The situation was resolved by the fortuitous appearance of the caddy-master, who was appealed to immediately by the nurse.

"Miss Jones is to have a little caddy, and this one says he can't go."

"Mr. McKenna said I was to wait here till you came," said Dexter quickly.

"Well, he's here now." Miss Jones smiled cheerfully at the caddy-master. Then she dropped her bag and set off at a haughty mince toward the first tee.

"Well?" The caddy-master turned to Dexter. "What you standing there like a dummy for? Go pick up the young lady's clubs."

"I don't think I'll go out to-day," said Dexter.

"You don't——"

"I think I'll quit."

The enormity of his decision frightened him. He was a favorite caddy, and the thirty dollars a month he earned through the summer were not to be made elsewhere around the lake. But he had received a strong emotional shock, and his perturbation required a violent and immediate outlet.

It is not so simple as that, either. As so frequently would be the case in the future, Dexter was unconsciously dictated to by his winter dreams.

II

Now, of course, the quality and the seasonability of these winter dreams varied, but the stuff of them remained. They persuaded Dexter several years later to pass up a business course at the State university — his father, prospering now, would have paid his way — for the precarious advantage of attending an older and more famous university in the East, where he was bothered by his scanty funds. But do not get the impression, because his winter dreams happened to be concerned at first with musings on the rich, that there was anything merely snobbish in the boy. He wanted not association with glittering things and glittering people — he wanted the glittering things themselves. Often he reached out for the best without knowing why he wanted it — and sometimes he ran up against the mysterious denials and prohibitions in which life indulges. It is with one of those denials and not with his career as a whole that this story deals.

He made money. It was rather amazing. After college he went to the city from which Black Bear Lake draws its wealthy patrons. When he was only twenty-three and had been there not quite two years, there were already people who liked to say: "Now *there's* a boy —" All about him rich men's sons were peddling bonds precariously, or investing patrimonies precariously, or plodding through the two dozen volumes of the "George Washington Commercial Course," but Dexter borrowed a thousand dollars on his college degree and his confident mouth, and bought a partnership in a laundry.

It was a small laundry when he went into it, but Dexter made a specialty of learning how the English washed fine woolen golf-stockings without shrinking them, and within a year he was catering to the trade that wore knickerbockers. Men were insisting that their Shetland hose and sweaters go to his laundry, just as they had insisted on a caddy who could find golf-balls. A little later he was doing their wives' lingerie as well — and running five branches in different parts of the city. Before he was twenty-seven he owned the largest string of laundries in his section of the country. It was then that he sold out and went to New York. But the part of his story that concerns us goes back to the days when he was making his first big success.

When he was twenty-three Mr. Hart — one of the gray-haired men who like to say "Now there's a boy" — gave him a guest card to the Sherry Island Golf Club for a week-end. So he signed his name one day on the register, and that afternoon played golf in a foursome with Mr. Hart and Mr. Sandwood and Mr. T. A. Hedrick. He did not consider it necessary to remark that he had once carried Mr. Hart's bag over these same links, and that he knew every trap and gully with his eyes shut — but he found himself glancing at the four caddies who trailed them, trying to catch a gleam or gesture that would remind him of himself, that would lessen the gap which lay between his present and his past.

It was a curious day, slashed abruptly with fleeting, familiar impressions. One minute he had the sense of being a trespasser — in the next he was impressed by the tremendous superiority he felt toward Mr. T. A. Hedrick, who was a bore and not even a good golfer any more.

Then, because of a ball Mr. Hart lost near the fifteenth green, an enormous thing happened. While they were searching the stiff grasses of the rough there was a clear call of "Fore!" from behind a hill in their rear. And as they all turned abruptly from their search a bright new ball sliced abruptly over the hill and caught Mr. T. A. Hedrick in the abdomen.

"By Gad!" cried Mr. T. A. Hedrick, "they ought to put some of these crazy women off the course. It's getting to be outrageous."

A head and a voice came up together over the hill:

"Do you mind if we go through?"

"You hit me in the stomach!" declared Mr. Hedrick wildly.

"Did I?" The girl approached the group of men. "I'm sorry. I yelled 'Fore!' "

Her glance fell casually on each of the men — then scanned the fairway for her ball.

"Did I bounce into the rough?"

It was impossible to determine whether this question was ingenuous or malicious. In a moment, however, she left no doubt, for as her partner came up over the hill she called cheerfully:

"Here I am! I'd have gone on the green except that I hit something."

As she took her stance for a short mashie shot, Dexter looked at her closely. She wore a blue gingham dress, rimmed at throat and shoulders with a white edging that accentuated her tan. The quality of exaggeration, of thinness, which had made her passionate eyes and down-turning mouth absurd at eleven, was gone now. She was arrestingly beautiful. The color in her cheeks was centered like the color in a picture — it was not a "high" color, but a sort of fluctuating and feverish warmth, so shaded that it seemed at any moment it would recede and disappear. This color and the mobility of her mouth gave a continual impression of flux, of intense life, of passionate vitality — balanced only partially by the sad luxury of her eyes.

She swung her mashie impatiently and without interest, pitching the ball into a sand-pit on the other side of the green. With a quick, insincere smile and a careless "Thank you!" she went on after it.

"That Judy Jones!" remarked Mr. Hedrick on the next tee, as they waited — some moments — for her to play on ahead. "All she needs is to be turned up and spanked for six months and then to be married off to an old-fashioned cavalry captain."

"My God, she's good-looking!" said Mr. Sandwood, who was just over thirty.

"Good-looking!" cried Mr. Hedrick contemptuously. "She always looks as if she wanted to be kissed! Turning those big cow-eyes on every calf in town!"

It was doubtful if Mr. Hedrick intended a reference to the maternal instinct.

"She'd play pretty good golf if she'd try," said Mr. Sandwood.

"She has no form," said Mr. Hedrick solemnly.

"She has a nice figure," said Mr. Sandwood.

"Better thank the Lord she doesn't drive a swifter ball," said Mr. Hart, winking at Dexter.

Later in the afternoon the sun went down with a riotous swirl of gold and varying blues and scarlets, and left the dry, rustling night of Western summer. Dexter watched from the veranda of the Golf Club, watched the even overlap of the waters in the little wind, silver molasses under the harvest-moon. Then the moon held a finger to her lips and the lake became a clear pool, pale and quiet. Dexter put on his bathing-suit and swam out to the farthest raft, where he stretched dripping on the wet canvas of the springboard.

There was a fish jumping and a star shining and the lights around the lake were gleaming. Over on a dark peninsula a piano was playing the songs of last summer and of summers before that — songs from "Chin-Chin" and "The Count of Luxemburg" and "The Chocolate Soldier" — and because the sound of a piano over a stretch of water had always seemed beautiful to Dexter he lay perfectly quiet and listened.

The tune the piano was playing at that moment had been gay and new five years before when Dexter was a sophomore at college. They had played it at a prom once when he could not afford the luxury of proms, and he had stood outside the gymnasium and listened. The sound of the tune precipitated in him a sort of ecstasy and it was with that ecstasy he viewed what happened to him now. It was a mood of intense appreciation, a sense that, for once, he was magnificently attune to life and that everything about him was radiating a brightness and a glamour he might never know again.

A low, pale oblong detached itself suddenly from the darkness of the Island, spitting forth the reverberate sound of a racing motorboat. Two white streamers of cleft water rolled themselves out behind it and almost immediately the boat was beside him, drowning out the hot tinkle of the piano in the drone of its spray. Dexter raising himself on his arms was aware of a figure standing at the wheel, of two dark eyes regarding him over the lengthening space of water — then the boat had gone by and was sweeping in an immense and purposeless circle of spray round and round in the middle of the lake. With equal eccentricity one of the circles flattened out and headed back toward the raft.

"Who's that?" she called, shutting off her motor. She was so near now that Dexter could see her bathing-suit, which consisted apparently of pink rompers.

The nose of the boat bumped the raft, and as the latter tilted rakishly he was precipitated toward her. With different degrees of interest they recognized each other.

"Aren't you one of those men we played through this afternoon?" she demanded.

He was.

"Well, do you know how to drive a motor-boat? Because if you do I wish you'd drive this one so I can ride on the surf-board behind. My name is Judy Jones" — she favored him with an absurd smirk — rather, what tried to be a smirk, for, twist her mouth as she might, it was not grotesque, it was merely beautiful — "and I live in a house over there on the Island, and in that house there is a man waiting for me. When he drove up at the door I drove out of the dock because he says I'm his ideal."

There was a fish jumping and a star shining and the lights around the lake were gleaming. Dexter sat beside Judy Jones and she explained how her boat was driven. Then she was in the water, swimming to the floating surf-board with sinuous crawl. Watching her was without effort to the eyes, watching a branch waving or a sea-gull flying. Her arms, burned to butternut, moved sinuously among the dull platinum ripples, elbow appearing first, casting the forearm back with a cadence of falling water, then reaching out and down, stabbing a path ahead.

They moved out into the lake; turning, Dexter saw that she was kneeling on the low rear of the now uptilted surf-board.

"Go faster," she called, "fast as it'll go."

Obediently he jammed the lever forward and the white spray mounted at the bow. When he looked around again the girl was standing up on the rushing board, her arms spread wide, her eyes lifted toward the moon.

"It's awful cold," she shouted. "What's your name?"

He told her.

"Well, why don't you come to dinner tomorrow night?"

His heart turned over like the fly-wheel of the boat, and, for the second time, her casual whim gave a new direction to his life.

III

Next evening while he waited for her to come down-stairs, Dexter peopled the soft deep summer room and the sun-porch that opened from it with the men who had already loved Judy Jones. He knew the sort of men they were — the men who when he first went to college had entered from the great prep schools with graceful clothes and the deep tan of healthy summers. He had seen that, in one sense, he was better than these men. He was newer and stronger. Yet in acknowledging to himself that he wished his children to be like them he was admitting that he was but the rough, strong stuff from which they eternally sprang.

When the time had come for him to wear good clothes, he had known who were the best tailors in America, and the best tailors in America had made him the suit he wore this evening. He had acquired that particular reserve peculiar to his university, that set it off from other universities. He recognized the value to him of such a mannerism and he had adopted it; he knew that to be careless in dress and manner required more confidence than to be careful. But carelessness was for his children. His mother's name had been Krimslich. She was a Bohemian of the peasant class and she had talked broken English to the end of her days. Her son must keep to the set patterns.

At a little after seven Judy Jones came downstairs. She wore a blue silk afternoon dress, and he was disappointed at first that she had not put on something more elaborate. This feeling was accentuated when, after a brief greeting, she went to the door of a butler's pantry and pushing it open called: "You can serve dinner, Martha." He had rather expected that a butler would announce dinner, that there would be a cocktail. Then he put these thoughts behind him as they sat down side by side on a lounge and looked at each other.

"Father and mother won't be here," she

said thoughtfully.

He remembered the last time he had seen her father, and he was glad the parents were not to be here to-night — they might wonder who he was. He had been born in Keeble, a Minnesota village fifty miles farther north, and he always gave Keeble as his home instead of Black Bear Village. Country towns were well enough to come from if they weren't inconveniently in sight and used as footstools by fashionable lakes.

They talked of his university, which she had visited frequently during the past two years, and of the near-by city which supplied Sherry Island with its patrons, and whither Dexter would return next day to his prospering laundries.

During dinner she slipped into a moody depression which gave Dexter a feeling of uneasiness. Whatever petulance she uttered in her throaty voice worried him. Whatever she smiled at — at him, at a chicken liver, at nothing — it disturbed him that her smile could have no root in mirth, or even in amusement. When the scarlet corners of her lips curved down, it was less a smile than an invitation to a kiss.

Then, after dinner, she led him out on the dark sun-porch and deliberately changed the atmosphere.

"Do you mind if I weep a little?" she said.

"I'm afraid I'm boring you," he responded

quickly.

"You're not. I like you. But I've just had a terrible afternoon. There was a man I cared about, and this afternoon he told me out of a clear sky that he was poor as a church-mouse. He'd never even hinted it before. Does this sound horribly mundane?"

"Perhaps he was afraid to tell you."

"Suppose he was," she answered. "He didn't start right. You see, if I'd thought of him as poor — well, I've been mad about loads of poor men, and fully intended to marry them all. But in this case, I hadn't thought of him that way, and my interest in him wasn't strong enough to survive the shock. As if a girl calmly informed her financé that she was a widow. He might not object to widows, but —

"Let's start right," she interrupted herself suddenly. "Who are you, anyhow?"

For a moment Dexter hesitated. Then:

"I'm nobody," he announced. "My career is largely a matter of futures."

"Are you poor?"

"No," he said frankly, "I'm probably making more money than any man my age in the Northwest. I know that's an obnoxious remark, but you advised me to start right."

There was a pause. Then she smiled and the corners of her mouth drooped and an almost imperceptible sway brought her closer to him, looking up into his eyes. A lump rose in Dexter's throat, and he waited breathless for the experiment, facing the unpredictable compound that would form mysteriously from the elements of their lips. Then he saw — she communicated her excitement to him, lavishly, deeply, with kisses that were not a promise but a fulfilment. They aroused in him not hunger demanding renewal but surfeit that would demand more surfeit . . . kisses that were like charity, creating want by holding back nothing at all.

It did not take him many hours to decide that he had wanted Judy Jones ever since he was a proud, desirous little boy.

IV

It began like that — and continued, with varying shades of intensity, on such a note right up to the dénouement. Dexter surrendered a part of himself to the most direct and unprincipled personality with which he had ever come in contact. Whatever Judy wanted, she went after with the full pressure of her charm. There was no divergence of method, no jockeying for position or premeditation of effects — there was a very little mental side to any of her affairs. She simply made men conscious to the highest degree of her physical loveliness. Dexter had no desire to change her. Her deficiencies were knit up with a passionate energy that transcended and justified them.

When, as Judy's head lay against his

shoulder that first night, she whispered, "I don't know what's the matter with me. Last night I thought I was in love with a man and to-night I think I'm in love with you——" — it seemed to him a beautiful and romantic thing to say. It was the exquisite excitability that for the moment he controlled and owned. But a week later he was compelled to view this same quality in a different light. She took him in her roadster to a picnic supper, and after supper she disappeared, likewise in her roadster, with another man. Dexter became enormously upset and was scarcely able to be decently civil to the other people present. When she assured him that she had not kissed the other man, he knew she was lying — yet he was glad that she had taken the trouble to lie to him.

He was, as he found before the summer ended, one of a varying dozen who circulated about her. Each of them had at one time been favored above all others — about half of them still basked in the solace of occasional sentimental revivals. Whenever one showed signs of dropping out through long neglect, she granted him a brief honeyed hour, which encouraged him to tag along for a year or so longer. Judy made these forays upon the helpless and defeated without malice, indeed half unconscious that there was anything mischievous in what she did.

When a new man came to town every one dropped out — dates were automatically cancelled.

The helpless part of trying to do anything about it was that she did it all herself. She was not a girl who could be "won" in the kinetic sense — she was proof against cleverness, she was proof against charm; if any of these assailed her too strongly she would immediately resolve the affair to a physical basis, and under the magic of her physical splendor the strong as well as the brilliant played her game and not their own. She was entertained only by the gratification of her desires and by the direct exercise of her own charm. Perhaps from so much youthful love, so many youthful lovers, she had come, in self-defense, to nourish herself wholly from within.

Succeeding Dexter's first exhilaration came restlessness and dissatisfaction. The helpless ecstasy of losing himself in her was opiate rather than tonic. It was fortunate for his work during the winter that those moments of ecstasy came infrequently. Early in their acquaintance it had seemed for a while that there was a deep and spontaneous mutual attraction — that first August, for example — three days of long evenings on her dusky veranda, of strange wan kisses through the late afternoon, in shadowy alcoves or behind the protecting trellises of the garden arbors, of mornings when she was fresh as a dream and almost shy at meeting him in the clarity of the rising day. There was all the ecstasy of an engagement about it, sharpened by his realization that there was no engagement. It was during those three days that, for the first time, he had asked her to marry him. She said "maybe some day," she said "kiss me," she said "I'd like to marry you," she said "I love you" — she said — nothing.

The three days were interrupted by the arrival of a New York man who visited at her house for half September. To Dexter's agony, rumor engaged them. The man was the son of the president of a great trust company. But at the end of a month it was reported that Judy was yawning. At a dance one night she sat all evening in a motor-boat with a local beau, while the New Yorker searched the club for her frantically. She told the local beau that she was bored with her visitor, and two days later he left. She was seen with him at the station, and it was reported that he looked very mournful indeed.

On this note the summer ended. Dexter was twenty-four, and he found himself increasingly in a position to do as he wished. He joined two clubs in the city and lived at one of them. Though he was by no means an integral part of the stag-lines at these clubs, he managed to be on hand at dances where Judy Jones was likely to appear. He could have gone out socially as much as he liked — he was an eligible young man, now, and popular with down-town fathers. His confessed devotion to

Judy Jones had rather solidified his position. But he had no social aspirations and rather despised the dancing men who were always on tap for the Thursday or Saturday parties and who filled in at dinners with the younger married set. Already he was playing with the idea of going East to New York. He wanted to take Judy Jones with him. No disillusion as to the world in which she had grown up could cure his illusion as to her desirability.

Remember that — for only in the light of it can what he did for her be understood.

Eighteen months after he first met Judy Jones he became engaged to another girl. Her name was Irene Scheerer, and her father was one of the men who had always believed in Dexter. Irene was light-haired and sweet and honorable, and a little stout, and she had two suitors whom she pleasantly relinquished when Dexter formally asked her to marry him.

Summer, fall, winter, spring, another summer, another fall — so much he had given of his active life to the incorrigible lips of Judy Jones. She had treated him with interest, with encouragement, with malice, with indifference, with contempt. She had inflicted on him the innumerable little slights and indignities possible in such a case — as if in revenge for having ever cared for him at all. She had beckoned him and yawned at him and beckoned him again and he had responded often with bitterness and narrowed eyes. She had brought him ecstatic happiness and intolerable agony of spirit. She had caused him untold inconvenience and not a little trouble. She had insulted him, and she had ridden over him, and she had played his interest in her against his interest in his work — for fun. She had done everything to him except to criticise him — this she had not done — it seemed to him only because it might have sullied the utter indifference she manifested and sincerely felt toward him.

When autumn had come and gone again it occurred to him that he could not have Judy Jones. He had to beat this into his mind but he convinced himself at last. He lay awake at night for a while and argued it over. He told himself the trouble and the pain she had caused him, he enumerated her glaring deficiencies as a wife. Then he said to himself that he loved her, and after a while he fell asleep. For a week, lest he imagined her husky voice over the telephone or her eyes opposite him at lunch, he worked hard and late, and at night he went to his office and plotted out his years.

At the end of a week he went to a dance and cut in on her once. For almost the first time since they had met he did not ask her to sit out with him or tell her that she was lovely. It hurt him that she did not miss these things — that was all. He was not jealous when he saw that there was a new man to-night. He had been hardened against jealousy long before.

He stayed late at the dance. He sat for an hour with Irene Scheerer and talked about books and about music. He knew very little about either. But he was beginning to be master of his own time now, and he had a rather priggish notion that he — the young and already fabulously successful Dexter Green — should know more about such things.

That was in October, when he was twenty-five. In January, Dexter and Irene became engaged. It was to be announced in June, and they were to be married three months later.

The Minnesota winter prolonged itself interminably, and it was almost May when the winds came soft and the snow ran down into Black Bear Lake at last. For the first time in over a year Dexter was enjoying a certain tranquillity of spirit. Judy Jones had been in Florida, and afterward in Hot Springs, and somewhere she had been engaged, and somewhere she had broken it off. At first, when Dexter had definitely given her up, it had made him sad that people still linked them together and asked for news of her, but when he began to be placed at dinner next to Irene Scheerer people didn't ask him about her any more — they told him about her. He ceased to be an authority on her.

May at last. Dexter walked the streets at night when the darkness was damp as rain, wondering that so soon, with so little done, so much of ecstasy had gone from him. May one year back had been marked by Judy's poignant, unforgivable, yet forgiven turbulence — it had been one of those rare times when he fancied she had grown to care for him. That old penny's worth of happiness he had spent for this bushel of content. He knew that Irene would be no more than a curtain spread behind him, a hand moving among gleaming teacups, a voice calling to children . . . fire and loveliness were gone, the magic of nights and the wonder of the varying hours and seasons . . . slender lips, down-turning, dropping to his lips and bearing him up into a heaven of eyes. . . . The thing was deep in him. He was too strong and alive for it to die lightly.

In the middle of May when the weather balanced for a few days on the thin bridge that led to deep summer he turned in one night at Irene's house. Their engagement was to be announced in a week now — no one would be surprised at it. And to-night they would sit together on the lounge at the University Club and look on for an hour at the dances. It gave him a sense of solidity to go with her — she was so sturdily popular, so intensely "great."

He mounted the steps of the brownstone house and stepped inside.

"Irene," he called.

Mrs. Scheerer came out of the living-room to meet him.

"Dexter," she said, "Irene's gone up-stairs

with a splitting headache. She wanted to go with you but I made her go to bed."

"Nothing serious, I ——"

"Oh, no. She's going to play golf with you in the morning. You can spare her for just one night, can't you, Dexter?"

Her smile was kind. She and Dexter liked each other. In the living-room he talked for a moment before he said good-night.

Returning to the University Club, where he had rooms, he stood in the doorway for a moment and watched the dancers. He leaned against the door-post, nodded at a man or two — yawned.

"Hello, darling."

The familiar voice at his elbow startled him. Judy Jones had left a man and crossed the room to him — Judy Jones, a slender enamelled doll in cloth of gold: gold in a band at her head, gold in two slipper points at her dress's hem. The fragile glow of her face seemed to blossom as she smiled at him. A breeze of warmth and light blew through the room. His hands in the pockets of his dinner-jacket tightened spasmodically. He was filled with a sudden excitement.

"When did you get back?" he asked casually.

"Come here and I'll tell you about it."

She turned and he followed her. She had been away — he could have wept at the wonder of her return. She had passed through enchanted streets, doing things that were like provocative music. All mysterious happenings, all fresh and quickening hopes, had gone away with her, come back with her now.

She turned in the doorway.

"Have you a car here? If you haven't, I have."

"I have a coupé."

In then, with a rustle of golden cloth. He slammed the door. Into so many cars she had stepped — like this — like that — her back against the leather, so — her elbow resting on the door — waiting. She would have been soiled long since had there been anything to soil her — except herself — but this was her own self outpouring.

With an effort he forced himself to start the car and back into the street. This was nothing, he must remember. She had done this before, and he had put her behind him, as he would have crossed a bad account from his books.

He drove slowly down-town and, affecting abstraction, traversed the deserted streets of the business section, peopled here and there where a movie was giving out its crowd or where consumptive or pugilistic youth lounged in front of pool halls. The clink of glasses and the slap of hands on the bars issued from saloons, cloisters of glazed glass and dirty yellow light.

She was watching him closely and the silence was embarrassing, yet in this crisis he could find no casual word with which to profane the hour. At a convenient turning he began to zigzag back toward the University Club.

"Have you missed me?" she asked suddenly.

"Everybody missed you."

He wondered if she knew of Irene Scheerer. She had been back only a day — her absence had been almost contemporaneous with his engagement.

"What a remark!" Judy laughed sadly — without sadness. She looked at him searchingly. He became absorbed in the dashboard.

"You're handsomer than you used to be," she said thoughtfully. "Dexter, you have the most rememberable eyes."

He could have laughed at this, but he did not laugh. It was the sort of thing that was said to sophomores. Yet it stabbed at him.

"I'm awfully tired of everything, darling." She called every one darling, endowing the endearment with careless, individual camaraderie. "I wish you'd marry me."

The directness of this confused him. He should have told her now that he was going to marry another girl, but he could not tell her. He could as easily have sworn that he had never loved her.

"I think we'd get along," she continued, on the same note, "unless probably you've forgotten me and fallen in love with another girl."

Her confidence was obviously enormous. She had said, in effect, that she found such a thing impossible to believe, that if it were true he had merely committed a childish indiscretion — and probably to show off. She would forgive him, because it was not a matter of any moment but rather something to be brushed aside lightly.

"Of course you could never love anybody but me," she continued, "I like the way you love me. Oh, Dexter, have you forgotten last year?"

"No, I haven't forgotten."

"Neither have I!"

Was she sincerely moved — or was she carried along by the wave of her own acting?

"I wish we could be like that again," she said, and he forced himself to answer:

"I don't think we can."

"I suppose not. . . . I hear you're giving Irene Scheerer a violent rush."

There was not the faintest emphasis on the name, yet Dexter was suddenly ashamed.

"Oh, take me home," cried Judy suddenly; "I don't want to go back to that idiotic dance — with those children."

Then, as he turned up the street that led to the residence district, Judy began to cry quietly to herself. He had never seen her cry before.

The dark street lightened, the dwellings of the rich loomed up around them, he stopped his coupé in front of the great white bulk of the Mortimer Joneses' house, somnolent, gorgeous, drenched with the splendor of the damp moonlight. Its solidity startled him. The strong walls, the steel of the girders, the breadth and beam and pomp of it were there only to bring out the contrast with the young beauty beside him. It was sturdy to accentuate her slightness — as if to show what a breeze could be generated by a butterfly's wing.

He sat perfectly quiet, his nerves in wild clamor, afraid that if he moved he would find her irresistibly in his arms. Two tears had rolled down her wet face and trembled on her upper lip.

"I'm more beautiful than anybody else," she said brokenly, "why can't I be happy?" Her moist eyes tore at his stability — her mouth turned slowly downward with an exquisite sadness: "I'd like to marry you if you'll have me, Dexter. I suppose you think I'm not worth having, but I'll be so beautiful for you, Dexter."

A million phrases of anger, pride, passion, hatred, tenderness fought on his lips. Then a perfect wave of emotion washed over him, carrying off with it a sediment of wisdom, of convention, of doubt, of honor. This was his girl who was speaking, his own, his beautiful, his pride.

"Won't you come in?" He heard her draw in her breath sharply.

Waiting.

"All right," his voice was trembling, "I'll come in."

V

It was strange that neither when it was over nor a long time afterward did he regret that night. Looking at it from the perspective of ten years, the fact that Judy's flare for him endured just one month seemed of little importance. Nor did it matter that by his yielding he subjected himself to a deeper agony in the end and gave serious hurt to Irene Scheerer and to Irene's parents, who had befriended him. There was nothing sufficiently pictorial about Irene's grief to stamp itself on his mind.

Dexter was at bottom hard-minded. The attitude of the city on his action was of no importance to him, not because he was going to leave the city, but because any outside attitude on the situation seemed superficial. He was completely indifferent to popular opinion. Nor, when he had seen that it was no use, that he did not possess in himself the power to move fundamentally or to hold Judy Jones, did he bear any malice toward her. He loved her, and he would love her until the day he was too old for loving — but he could not have her. So he tasted the deep pain that is reserved only for the strong, just as he had tasted for a little while the deep happiness.

Even the ultimate falsity of the grounds upon

which Judy terminated the engagement that she did not want to "take him away" from Irene — Judy who had wanted nothing else — did not revolt him. He was beyond any revulsion or any amusement.

He went East in February with the intention of selling out his laundries and settling in New York — but the war came to America in March and changed his plans. He returned to the West, handed over the management of the business to his partner, and went into the first officers' training-camp in late April. He was one of those young thousands who greeted the war with a certain amount of relief, welcoming the liberation from webs of tangled emotion.

VI

This story is not his biography, remember, although things creep into it which have nothing to do with those dreams he had when he was young. We are almost done with them and with him now. There is only one more incident to be related here, and it happens seven years farther on.

It took place in New York, where he had done well — so well that there were no barriers too high for him. He was thirty-two years old, and, except for one flying trip immediately after the war, he had not been West in seven years. A man named Devlin from Detroit came into his office to see him in a business way, and then and there this incident occurred, and closed out, so to speak, this particular side of his life.

"So you're from the Middle West," said the man Devlin with careless curiosity. "That's funny — I thought men like you were probably born and raised on Wall Street. You know — wife of one of my best friends in Detroit came from your city. I was an usher at the wedding."

Dexter waited with no apprehension of what was coming.

"Judy Simms," said Devlin with no particular interest; "Judy Jones she was once."

"Yes, I knew her." A dull impatience spread over him. He had heard, of course, that she was married — perhaps deliberately he had heard no more.

"Awfully nice girl," brooded Devlin meaninglessly, "I'm sort of sorry for her."

"Why?" Something in Dexter was alert, receptive, at once.

"Oh, Lud Simms has gone to pieces in a way. I don't mean he ill-uses her, but he drinks and runs around ——"

"Doesn't she run around?"

"No. Stays at home with her kids."

"Oh."

"She's a little too old for him," said Devlin.

"Too old!" cried Dexter. "Why, man, she's only twenty-seven."

He was possessed with a wild notion of rushing out into the streets and taking a train to Detroit. He rose to his feet spasmodically.

"I guess you're busy," Devlin apologized quickly. "I didn't realize ——"

"No, I'm not busy," said Dexter, steadying his voice. "I'm not busy at all. Not busy at all. Did you say she was — twenty-seven? No, I said she was twenty-seven."

"Yes, you did," agreed Devlin dryly.

"Go on, then. Go on."

"What do you mean?"

"About Judy Jones."

Devlin looked at him helplessly.

"Well, that's — I told you all there is to it. He treats her like the devil. Oh, they're not going to get divorced or anything. When he's particularly outrageous she forgives him. In fact, I'm inclined to think she loves him. She was a pretty girl when she first came to Detroit."

A pretty girl! The phrase struck Dexter as ludicrous.

"Isn't she — a pretty girl, any more?"

"Oh, she's all right."

"Look here," said Dexter, sitting down suddenly. "I don't understand. You say she was a 'pretty girl' and now you say she's 'all right.' I don't understand what you mean — Judy Jones wasn't a pretty girl, at all. She was a great beauty. Why, I knew her, I knew her. She was ——"

Devlin laughed pleasantly.

"I'm not trying to start a row," he said. "I think Judy's a nice girl and I like her. I can't understand how a man like Lud Simms could fall madly in love with her, but he did." Then he added: "Most of the women like her."

Dexter looked closely at Devlin, thinking wildly that there must be a reason for this, some insensitivity in the man or some private malice.

"Lots of women fade just like *that,"* Devlin snapped his fingers. "You must have seen it happen. Perhaps I've forgotten how pretty she was at her wedding. I've seen her so much since then, you see. She has nice eyes."

A sort of dullness settled down upon Dexter. For the first time in his life he felt like getting very drunk. He knew that he was laughing loudly at something Devlin had said, but he did not know what it was or why it was funny. When, in a few minutes, Devlin went he lay down on his lounge and looked out the window at the New York skyline into which the sun was sinking in dull lovely shades of pink and gold.

He had thought that having nothing else to lose he was invulnerable at last — but he knew that he had just lost something more, as surely as if he had married Judy Jones and seen her fade away before his eyes.

The dream was gone. Something had been taken from him. In a sort of panic he pushed the palms of his hands into his eyes and tried to bring up a picture of the waters lapping on Sherry Island and the moonlit veranda, and gingham on the golf-links and the dry sun and the gold color of her neck's soft down. And her mouth damp to his kisses and her eyes plaintive with melancholy and her freshness like new fine linen in the morning. Why, these things were no longer in the world! They had existed and they existed no longer.

For the first time in years the tears were streaming down his face. But they were for himself now. He did not care about mouth and eyes and moving hands. He wanted to care, and he could not care. For he had gone away and he could never go back any more. The gates were closed, the sun was gone down, and there was no beauty but the gray beauty of steel that withstands all time. Even the grief he could have borne was left behind in the country of illusion, of youth, of the richness of life, where his winter dreams had flourished.

"Long ago," he said, "long ago, there was something in me, but now that thing is gone. Now that thing is gone, that thing is gone. I cannot cry. I cannot care. That thing will come back no more."

The Killers

Ernest Hemingway

THE door of Henry's lunchroom opened and two men came in. They sat down at the counter.

"What's yours?" George asked them.

"I don't know," one of the men said. "What do you want to eat, Al?"

"I don't know," said Al. "I don't know what I want to eat."

Outside it was getting dark. The street-light came on outside the window. The two men at the counter read the menu. From the other end of the counter Nick Adams watched them. He had been talking to George when they came in.

"I'll have a roast pork tenderloin with apple sauce and mashed potatoes," the first man said.

"It isn't ready yet."

"What the hell do you put it on the card for?"

"That's the dinner," George explained. "You can get that at six o'clock."

George looked at the clock on the wall behind the counter.

"It's five o'clock."

"The clock says twenty minutes past five," the second man said.

"It's twenty minutes fast."

"Oh, to hell with the clock," the first man said. "What have you got to eat?"

"I can give you any kind of sandwiches," George said. "You can have ham and eggs, bacon and eggs, liver and bacon, or a steak."

"Give me chicken croquettes with green peas and cream sauce and mashed potatoes."

"That's the dinner."

"Everything we want's the dinner, eh? That's the way you work it."

"I can give you ham and eggs, bacon and eggs, liver —"

"I'll take ham and eggs," the man called Al said. He wore a derby hat and a black overcoat buttoned across the chest. His face was small and white and he had tight lips. He wore a silk muffler and gloves.

"Give me bacon and eggs," said the other man. He was about the same size as Al. Their faces were different, but they were dressed like twins. Both wore overcoats too tight for them. They sat leaning forward, their elbows on the counter.

"Got anything to drink?" Al asked.

"Silver beer, bevo, ginger-ale," George said.

"I mean you got anything to *drink?*"

"Just those I said."

"This is a hot town," said the other. "What do they call it?"

"Summit."

"Ever hear of it?" Al asked his friend.

"No," said the friend.

"What do you do here nights?" Al asked.

"They eat the dinner," his friend said. "They all come here and eat the big dinner."

"That's right," George said.

"So you think that's right?" Al asked George.

"Sure."

"You're a pretty bright boy, aren't you?"

"Sure," said George.

"Well, you're not," said the other little man. "Is he, Al?"

"He's dumb," said Al. He turned to Nick. "What's your name?"

"Adams."

"Another bright boy," Al said. "Ain't he a bright boy, Max?"

"The town's full of bright boys," Max said.

George put the two platters, one of ham and eggs, the other of bacon and eggs, on the counter. He set down two side-dishes of fried potatoes and closed the wicket into the kitchen.

"Which is yours?" he asked Al.

"Don't you remember?"

"Ham and eggs."

"Just a bright boy," Max said. He leaned

forward and took the ham and eggs. Both men ate with their gloves on. George watched them eat.

"What are *you* looking at?" Max looked at George.

"Nothing."

"The hell you were. You were looking at me."

"Maybe the boy meant it for a joke, Max," Al said.

George laughed.

"*You* don't have to laugh," Max said to him. "*You* don't have to laugh at all, see?"

"All right," said George.

"So he thinks it's all right." Max turned to Al. "He thinks it's all right. That's a good one."

"Oh, he's a thinker," Al said. They went on eating.

"What's the bright boy's name down the counter?" Al asked Max.

"Hey, bright boy," Max said to Nick. "You go around on the other side of the counter with your boy friend."

"What's the idea?" Nick asked.

"There isn't any idea."

"You better go around, bright boy," Al said. Nick went around behind the counter.

"What's the idea?" George asked.

"None of your damn business," Al said. "Who's out in the kitchen?"

"The nigger."

"What do you mean the nigger?"

"The nigger that cooks."

"Tell him to come in."

"What's the idea?"

"Tell him to come in."

"Where do you think you are?"

"We know damn well where we are," the man called Max said. "Do we look silly?"

"You talk silly," Al said to him. "What the hell do you argue with this kid for? Listen," he said to George, "tell the nigger to come out here."

"What are you going to do to him?"

"Nothing. Use your head, bright boy. What would we do to a nigger?"

George opened the slit that opened back into the kitchen. "Sam," he called. "Come in here a minute."

The door to the kitchen opened and the nigger came in. "What was it?" he asked. The two men at the counter took a look at him.

"All right, nigger. You stand right there," Al said.

Sam, the nigger, standing in his apron, looked at the two men sitting at the counter. "Yes, sir," he said. Al got down from his stool.

"I'm going back to the kitchen with the nigger and bright boy," he said. "Go on back to the kitchen, nigger. You go with him, bright boy." The little man walked after Nick and Sam, the cook, back into the kitchen. The door shut after them. The man called Max sat at the counter opposite George. He didn't look at George but looked in the mirror that ran along back of the counter. Henry's had been made over from a saloon into a lunch-counter.

"Well, bright boy," Max said, looking into the mirror, "why don't you say something?"

"What's it all about?"

"Hey, Al," Max called, "bright boy wants to know what it's all about."

"Why don't you tell him?" Al's voice came from the kitchen.

"What do you think it's all about?"

"I don't know."

"What do you think?"

Max looked into the mirror all the time he was talking.

"I wouldn't say."

"Hey, Al, bright boy says he wouldn't say what he thinks it's all about."

"I can hear you, all right," Al said from the kitchen. He had propped open the slit that dishes passed through into the kitchen with a catsup bottle. "Listen, bright boy," he said from the kitchen to George. "Stand a little further along the bar. You move a little to the left, Max." He was like a photographer arranging for a group picture.

"Talk to me, bright boy," Max said. "What do you think's going to happen?"

George did not say anything.

"I'll tell you," Max said. "We're going to

kill a Swede. Do you know a big Swede named Ole Andreson?"

"Yes."

"He comes here to eat every night, don't he?"

"Sometimes he comes here."

"He comes here at six o'clock, don't he?"

"If he comes."

"We know all that, bright boy," Max said. "Talk about something else. Ever go to the movies?"

"Once in a while."

"You ought to go to the movies more. The movies are fine for a bright boy like you."

"What are you going to kill Ole Andreson for? What did he ever do to you?"

"He never had a chance to do anything to us. He never even seen us."

"And he's only going to see us once," Al said from the kitchen.

"What are you going to kill him for, then?" George asked.

"We're killing him for a friend. Just to oblige a friend, bright boy."

"Shut up," said Al from the kitchen. "You talk too goddam much."

"Well, I got to keep bright boy amused. Don't I, bright boy?"

"You talk too damn much," Al said. "The nigger and my bright boy are amused by themselves. I got them tied up like a couple of girl friends in the convent."

"I suppose you were in a convent."

"You never know."

"You were in a kosher convent. That's where you were."

George looked up at the clock.

"If anybody comes in you tell them the cook is off, and if they keep after it, you tell them you'll go back and cook yourself. Do you get that, bright boy?"

"All right," George said. "What you going to do with us afterward?"

"That'll depend," Max said. "That's one of those things you never know at the time."

George looked up at the clock. It was a quarter past six. The door from the street opened. A street-car motorman came in.

"Hello, George," he said. "Can I get supper?"

"Sam's gone out," George said. "He'll be back in about half an hour."

"I'd better go up the street," the motorman said. George looked at the clock. It was twenty minutes past six.

"That was nice, bright boy," Max said. "You're a regular little gentleman."

"He knew I'd blow his head off," Al said from the kitchen.

"No," said Max. "It ain't that. Bright boy is nice. He's a nice boy. I like him."

At six-fifty-five George said: "He's not coming."

Two other people had been in the lunchroom. Once George had gone out to the kitchen and made a ham-and-egg sandwich "to go" that a man wanted to take with him. Inside the kitchen he saw Al, his derby hat tipped back, sitting on a stool beside the wicket with the muzzle of a sawed-off shotgun resting on the ledge. Nick and the cook were back to back in the corner, a towel tied in each of their mouths. George had cooked the sandwich, wrapped it up in oiled paper, put it in a bag, brought it in, and the man had paid for it and gone out.

"Bright boy can do everything," Max said. "He can cook and everything. You'd make some girl a nice wife, bright boy."

"Yes?" George said. "Your friend, Ole Andreson, isn't going to come."

"We'll give him ten minutes," Max said.

Max watched the mirror and the clock. The hands of the clock marked seven o'clock, and then five minutes past seven.

"Come on, Al," said Max. "We better go. He's not coming."

"Better give him five minutes," Al said from the kitchen.

In the five minutes a man came in, and George explained that the cook was sick.

"Why the hell don't you get another cook?" the man asked. "Aren't you running a lunch-counter?" He went out.

"Come on, Al," Max said.

"What about the two bright boys and the

nigger?"
"They're all right."
"You think so?"
"Sure. We're through with it."
"I don't like it," said Al. "It's sloppy. You talk too much."
"Oh, what the hell," said Max. "We got to keep amused, haven't we?"
"You talk too much, all the same," Al said. He came out from the kitchen. The cut-off barrels of the shotgun made a slight bulge under the waist of his too tight-fitting overcoat. He straightened his coat with his gloved hands.
"So long, bright boy," he said to George. "You got a lot of luck."
"That's the truth," Max said. "You ought to play the races, bright boy."
The two of them went out the door. George watched them, through the window, pass under the arc-light and cross the street. In their tight overcoats and derby hats they looked like a vaudeville team. George went back through the swinging-door into the kitchen and untied Nick and the cook.
"I don't want any more of that," said Sam, the cook. "I don't want any more of that."
Nick stood up. He had never had a towel in his mouth before.
"Say," he said. "What the hell?" He was trying to swagger it off.
"They were going to kill Ole Andreson," George said. "They were going to shoot him

when he came in to eat.''

''Ole Andreson?''

''Sure.''

The cook felt the corners of his mouth with his thumbs.

''They all gone?'' he asked.

''Yeah,'' said George. ''They're gone now.''

''I don't like it,'' said the cook. ''I don't like any of it at all.''

''Listen,'' George said to Nick. ''You better go see Ole Andreson.''

''All right.''

''You better not have anything to do with it at all,'' Sam, the cook said. ''You better stay way out of it.''

''Don't go if you don't want to,'' George said.

''Mixing up in this ain't going to get you anywhere,'' the cook said ''You stay out of it.''

''I'll go see him,'' Nick said to George. ''Where does he live?''

The cook turned away.

''Little boys always know what they want to do,'' he said.

''He lives up at Hirsch's rooming-house,'' George said to Nick.

''I'll go up there.''

Outside the arc-light shone through the bare branches of a tree. Nick walked up the street beside the car-tracks and turned at the next arc-light down a side-street. Three houses up the street was Hirsch's rooming house. Nick walked up the two steps and pushed the bell. A woman came to the door.

"Is Ole Andreson here?"

"Do you want to see him?"

"Yes, if he's in."

Nick followed the woman up a flight of stairs and back to the end of a corridor. She knocked on the door.

"Who is it?"

"It's somebody to see you, Mr. Andreson," the woman said.

"It's Nick Adams."

"Come in."

Nick opened the door and went into the room. Ole Andreson was lying on the bed with all his clothes on. He had been a heavyweight prizefighter and he was too long for the bed. He lay with his head on two pillows. He did not look at Nick.

"What was it?" he asked.

"I was up at Henry's," Nick said, "and two fellows came in and tied up me and the cook, and they said they were going to kill you."

It sounded silly when he said it. Ole Andreson said nothing.

"They put us out in the kitchen," Nick went on. "They were going to shoot you when you came in to supper."

Ole Andreson looked at the wall and did not

say anything.

"George thought I better come and tell you about it."

"There isn't anything I can do about it," Ole Andreson said.

"I'll tell you what they were like."

"I don't want to know what they were like," Ole Andreson said. He looked at the wall. "Thanks for coming to tell me about it."

"That's all right."

Nick looked at the big man lying on the bed.

"Don't you want me to go and see the police?"

"No," Ole Andreson said. "That wouldn't do any good."

"Isn't there something I could do?"

"No. There ain't anything to do."

"Maybe it was just a bluff."

"No. It ain't just a bluff."

Ole Andreson rolled over toward the wall.

"The only thing is," he said, talking toward the wall, "I just can't make up my mind to go out. I been in here all day."

"Couldn't you get out of town?"

"No," Ole Andreson said. "I'm through with all that running around."

He looked at the wall.

"There ain't anything to do now."

"Couldn't you fix it up some way?"

"No. I got in wrong." He talked in the same flat voice. "There ain't anything to do. After a while I'll make up my mind to go out."

"I better go back and see George," Nick said.

"So long," said Ole Andreson. He did not look toward Nick. "Thanks for coming around."

Nick went out. As he shut the door he saw Ole Andreson with all his clothes on, lying on the bed looking at the wall.

"He's been in his room all day," the landlady said downstairs. "I guess he don't feel well. I said to him: 'Mr. Andreson, you ought to go out and take a walk on a nice fall day like this,' but he didn't feel like it."

"He doesn't want to go out."

"I'm sorry he don't feel well," the woman said. "He's an awfully nice man. He was in the ring, you know."

"I know it."

"You'd never know it except from the way his face is," the woman said. They stood talking just inside the street door. "He's just as gentle."

"Well, good night, Mrs. Hirsch," Nick said.

"I'm not Mrs. Hirsch," the woman said. "She owns the place. I just look after it for her. I'm Mrs. Bell."

"Well, good night, Mrs. Bell," Nick said.

"Good night," the woman said.

Nick walked up the dark street to the corner under the arc-light, and then along the car-tracks to Henry's eating-house. George was inside, back of the counter.

"Did you see Ole?"

"Yes," said Nick. "He's in his room and he won't go out."

The cook opened the door from the kitchen when he heard Nick's voice.

"I don't even listen to it," he said and shut the door.

"Did you tell him about it?" George asked.

"Sure. I told him but he knows what it's all about."

"What's he going to do?"

"Nothing."

"They'll kill him."

"I guess they will."

"He must have got mixed up in something in Chicago."

"I guess so," said Nick.

"It's a hell of a thing."

"It's an awful thing," Nick said.

They did not say anything. George reached down for a towel and wiped the counter.

"I wonder what he did?" Nick said.

"Double-crossed somebody. That's what they kill them for."

"I'm going to get out of this town," Nick said.

"Yes," said George. "That's a good thing to do."

"I can't stand to think about him waiting in the room and knowing he's going to get it.

It's too damned awful."

"Well," said George, "you better not think about it."

Silent Snow, Secret Snow

Conrad Aiken

JUST why it should have happened, or why it should have happened just when it did, he could not, of course, possibly have said; nor perhaps would it even have occurred to him to ask. The thing was above all a secret, something to be preciously concealed from Mother and Father; and to that very fact it owed an enormous part of its deliciousness. It was like a peculiarly beautiful trinket to be carried unmentioned in one's trouser pocket — a rare stamp, an old coin, a few tiny gold links found trodden out of shape on the path in the park, a pebble of carnelian, a seashell distinguishable from all others by an unusual spot or stripe — and, as if it were any one of these, he carried around with him everywhere a warm and persistent and increasingly beautiful sense of possession. Nor was it only a sense of possession — it was also a sense of protection. It was as if, in some delightful way, his secret gave him a fortress, a wall behind which he could retreat into heavenly seclusion. This was almost the first thing he had noticed about it — apart from the oddness of the thing itself — and it was this that now again, for the fiftieth time, occurred to him, as he sat in the little schoolroom. It was the half-hour for geography. Miss Buell was revolving with one finger, slowly, a huge terrestrial globe which had been placed on her desk. The green and yellow continents passed and repassed, questions were asked and answered, and now the little girl in front of him, Deirdre, who had a funny little constellation of freckles on the back of her neck, exactly like the Big Dipper, was standing up and telling Miss Buell that the equator was the line that ran round the middle.

Miss Buell's face, which was old and grayish and kindly, with gray stiff curls beside the cheeks, and eyes that swam very brightly, like little minnows, behind thick glasses, wrinkled itself into a complication of amusements.

"Ah! I see. The earth is wearing a belt, or a sash. Or someone drew a line round it!"

"Oh no — not that — I mean ——"

In the general laughter, he did not share, or only a very little. He was thinking about the Arctic and Antarctic regions, which of course, on the globe, were white. Miss Buell was now telling them about the tropics, the jungles, the steamy heat of equatorial swamps, where the birds and butterflies, and even the snakes, were like living jewels. As he listened to these things, he was already, with a pleasant sense of half-effort, putting his secret between himself and the words. Was it really an effort at all? For effort implied something voluntary, and perhaps even something one did not especially want; whereas this was distinctly pleasant, and came almost of its own accord. All he needed to do was to think of that morning, the first one, and then of all the others ——

But it was all so absurdly simple! It had amounted to so little. It was nothing, just an idea — and just why it should have become so wonderful, so permanent, was a mystery — a very pleasant one, to be sure, but also, in an amusing way, foolish. However, without ceasing to listen to Miss Buell, who had now moved up to the north temperate zones, he deliberately invited his memory of the first morning. It was only a moment or two after he had waked up — or perhaps the moment itself. But was there, to be exact, an exact moment? Was one awake all at once? or was it gradual? Anyway, it was after he had stretched a lazy hand up toward the headrail, and yawned, and then relaxed again among his warm covers, all the more grateful on a December morning, that the thing had happened. Suddenly, for no reason, he had thought of the postman, he remembered the postman. Perhaps there was nothing so odd in that. After all, he heard the postman almost every morning in his life — his heavy boots could be heard clumping round the corner at the top of the little cobbled hill-street, and then, progressively nearer, progressively louder, the double knock at each door, the crossings and re-crossings of the street, till finally the clumsy steps came stumbling across to the very door, and the tremendous knock came which shook the house itself.

(Miss Buell was saying, "Vast wheat-growing areas in North America and Siberia."

Deirdre had for the moment placed her left hand across the back of her neck.)

But on this particular morning, the first morning, as he lay there with his eyes closed, he had for some reason *waited* for the postman. He wanted to hear him come round the corner. And that was precisely the joke — he never did. He never came. He never had come — *round the corner* — again. For when at last the steps *were* heard, they had already, he was quite sure, come a little down the hill, to the first house; and even so, the steps were curiously different — they were softer, they had a new secrecy about them, they were muffled and indistinct; and while the rhythm of them was the same, it now said a new thing — it said peace, it said remoteness, it said cold, it said sleep. And he had understood the situation at once — nothing could have seemed simpler — there had been snow in the night, such as all winter he had been longing for; and it was this which had rendered the postman's first footsteps inaudible, and the later ones faint. Of course! How lovely! And even now it must be snowing — it was going to be a snowy day — the long white ragged lines were drifting and sifting across the street, across the faces of the old houses, whispering and hushing, making little triangles of white in the corners between cobblestones, seething a little when the wind blew them over the ground to a drifted corner; and so it would be all day, getting deeper and deeper and silenter and silenter.

(Miss Buell was saying, "Land of perpetual snow.")

All this time, of course (while he lay in bed), he had kept his eyes closed, listening to the nearer progress of the postman, the muffled footsteps thumping and slipping on the snow-sheathed cobbles; and all the other sounds — the double knocks, a frosty far-off voice or two, a bell ringing thinly and softly as if under a sheet of ice — had the same slightly abstracted quality, as if removed by one degree from actuality — as if everything in the world had been insulated by snow. But when at last, pleased, he opened his eyes, and turned them toward the window, to see for himself this long-desired and now so clearly imagined miracle — what he saw instead was brilliant sunlight on a roof; and when, astonished, he jumped out of bed and stared down into the street, expecting to see the cobbles obliterated by the snow, he saw nothing but the bare bright cobbles themselves.

Queer, the effect this extraordinary surprise had had upon him — all the following morning he had kept with him a sense as of snow falling about him, a secret screen of new snow between himself and the world. If he had not dreamed such a thing — and how could he have dreamed it while awake? — how else could one explain it? In any case, the delusion had been so vivid as to affect his entire behavior. He could not now remember whether it was on the first or the second morning — or was it even the third? — that his mother had drawn attention to some oddness in his manner.

"But my darling" — she had said at the breakfast table — "what has come over you? You don't seem to be listening. . . ."

And how often that very thing had happened since!

(Miss Buell was now asking if anyone knew the difference between the North Pole and the Magnetic Pole. Deirdre was holding up her flickering brown hand, and he could see the four white dimples that marked the knuckles.)

Perhaps it hadn't been either the second or third morning — or even the fourth or fifth. How could he be sure? How could he be sure just when the delicious *progress* had become clear? Just when it had really *begun?* The intervals weren't very precise. . . . All he now knew was, that at some point or other —

perhaps the second day, perhaps the sixth — he had noticed that the presence of the snow was a little more insistent, the sound of it clearer; and, conversely, the sound of the postman's footsteps more indistinct. Not only could he not hear the steps come round the corner, he could not even hear them at the first house. It was below the first house that he heard them; and then, a few days later, it was below the second house that he heard them; and a few days later again, below the third. Gradually, gradually, the snow was becoming heavier, the sound of its seething louder, the cobblestones more and more muffled. When he found, each morning, on going to the window, after the ritual of listening, that the roofs and cobbles were as bare as ever, it made no difference. This was, after all, only what he had expected. It was even what pleased him, what rewarded him: the thing was his own, belonged to no one else. No one else knew about it, not even his mother and father. There, outside, were the bare cobbles; and here, inside, was the snow. Snow growing heavier each day, muffling the world, hiding the ugly, and deadening increasingly — above all — the steps of the postman.

"But, my darling" — she had said at the luncheon table — "what has come over you? You don't seem to listen when people speak to you. That's the third time I've asked you to pass your plate. . . ."

How was one to explain this to Mother? or to Father? There was, of course, nothing to be done about it: nothing. All one could do was to laugh embarrassedly, pretend to be a little ashamed, apologize, and take a sudden and somewhat disingenuous interest in what was being done or said. The cat had stayed out all night. He had a curious swelling on his left cheek — perhaps somebody had kicked him, or a stone had struck him. Mrs. Kempton was or was not coming to tea. The house was going to be housecleaned, or "turned out," on Wednesday instead of Friday. A new lamp was provided for his evening work — perhaps it was eyestrain which accounted for this new and so peculiar vagueness of his — Mother was looking at him with amusement as she said this, but with something else as well. A new lamp? A new lamp. Yes, Mother, No, Mother, Yes, Mother. School is going very well. The geometry is very easy. The history is very dull. The geography is very interesting — particularly when it takes one to the North Pole. Why the North Pole? Oh, well, it would be fun to be an explorer. Another Peary or Scott or Shackleton. And then abruptly he found his interest in the talk at an end, stared at the pudding on his plate, listened, waited, and began once more — ah, how heavenly, too, the first beginnings — to hear or feel — for could he actually hear it? — the silent snow, the secret snow.

(Miss Buell was telling them about the search for the Northwest Passage, about Hendrik Hudson, the *Half Moon*.)

This had been, indeed, the only distressing feature of the new experience; the fact that it so increasingly had brought him into a kind of mute misunderstanding, or even conflict, with his father and mother. It was as if he were trying to lead a double life. On the one hand, he had to be Paul Hasleman, and keep up the appearance of being that person — dress, wash, and answer intelligently when spoken to —; on the other, he had to explore this new world which had been opened to him. Nor could there be the slightest doubt — not the slightest — that the new world was the profounder and more wonderful of the two. It was irresistible. It was miraculous. Its beauty was simply beyond anything — beyond speech as beyond thought — utterly incommunicable. But how then, between the two worlds, of which he was thus constantly aware, was he to keep a balance? One must get up, one must go to breakfast, one must talk with Mother, go to school, do one's lessons — and, in all this, try not to appear too much of a fool. But if all the while one was also trying to extract the full deliciousness of another and quite separate existence, one which could not easily (if at all) be spoken of — how was one to manage? How was one to explain? Would it be safe to explain? Would it be absurd? Would it merely mean that he would get into some obscure kind of trouble?

These thoughts came and went, came and went, as softly and secretly as the snow; they were not precisely a disturbance, perhaps they were even a pleasure; he liked to have them; their presence was something almost palpable, something he could stroke with his hand, without closing his eyes, and without ceasing to see Miss Buell and the schoolroom and the globe and the freckles on Deirdre's neck; nevertheless he did in a sense cease to see, or to see the obvious external world, and substituted for this vision the vision of snow, the sound of snow, and the slow, almost soundless, approach of the postman. Yesterday, it had been only at the sixth house that the postman had become audible; the snow was much deeper now, it was falling more swiftly and heavily, the sound of its seething was more distinct, more soothing, more persistent. And this morning, it had been — as nearly as he could figure — just above the seventh house — perhaps only a step or two above; at most, he had heard two or three footsteps before the knock had sounded. . . . And with each such narrowing of the sphere, each nearer approach of the limit at which the postman was first audible, it was odd how sharply was increased the amount of illusion which had to be carried into the ordinary business of daily life. Each day, it was harder to get out of bed, to go to the window, to look out at the — as always — perfectly empty and snowless street. Each day it was more difficult to go through the perfunctory motions of greeting Mother and Father at breakfast, to reply to their questions, to put his books together and go to school. And at school, how extraordinarily hard to conduct with success simultaneously the public life and the life that was secret! There were times when he longed — positively ached — to tell everyone about it — to burst out with it — only to be checked almost at once by a far-off feeling as of some faint absurdity which was inherent in it — but *was* it absurd? — and more importantly by a sense of mysterious power in his very secrecy. Yes; it must be kept secret. That, more and more, became clear. At whatever cost to himself, whatever pain to others ——

(Miss Buell looked straight at him, smiling, and said, "Perhaps we'll ask Paul. I'm sure Paul will come out of his daydream long enough to be able to tell us. Won't you, Paul?" He rose slowly from his chair, resting one hand on the brightly varnished desk, and deliberately stared through the snow toward the blackboard. It was an effort, but it was amusing to make it. "Yes," he said slowly, "it was what we now call the Hudson River. This he thought to be the Northwest Passage. He was disappointed." He sat down again, and as he did so Deirdre half turned in her chair and gave him a shy smile, of approval and admiration.)

At whatever pain to others.

This part of it was very puzzling, very puzzling. Mother was very nice, and so was Father. Yes, that was all true enough. He wanted to be nice to them, to tell them everything — and yet, was it really wrong of him to want to have a secret place of his own?

At bed-time, the night before, Mother had said, "If this goes on, my lad, we'll have to see a doctor, we will! We can't have our boy —" But what was it she had said? "Live in another world"? "Live so far away"? The word "far" had been in it, he was sure, and then Mother had taken up a magazine again and laughed a little, but with an expression which wasn't mirthful. He had felt sorry for her. . . .

The bell rang for dismissal. The sound came to him through long curved parallels of falling snow. He saw Deirdre rise, and had himself risen almost as soon — but not quite as soon — as she.

II

On the walk homeward, which was timeless, it pleased him to see through the accompaniment, or counterpoint, of snow, the items of mere externality on his way. There were many kinds of brick in the sidewalks, and laid in many kinds of pattern. The garden walls, too, were various, some of wooden palings, some of plaster, some of stone. Twigs of bushes leaned over the walls: the little hard green winter-buds of lilac, on gray stems, sheathed and fat; other branches very thin and fine and black and desiccated. Dirty sparrows huddled in the bushes, as dull in color as dead fruit left in leafless trees. A single starling creaked on a weather vane. In the gutter, beside a drain, was a scrap of torn and dirty newspaper, caught in a little delta of filth; the word ECZEMA appeared in large capitals, and below it was a letter from Mrs. Amelia D. Cravath, 2100 Pine Street, Fort Worth, Texas, to the effect that after being a sufferer for years she had been cured by Caley's Ointment. In the little delta, beside the fan-shaped and deeply runneled continent of brown mud, were lost twigs, descended from their parent trees, dead matches, a rusty horse-chestnut burr, a small concentration of eggshell, a streak of yellow sawdust which had been wet and now was dry and congealed, a brown pebble, and a broken feather. Farther on was a cement sidewalk, ruled into geometrical parallelograms, with a brass inlay at one end commemorating the contractors who had laid it, and, halfway across, an irregular and random series of dog-tracks, immortalized in synthetic stone. He knew these well, and always stepped on them; to cover the little hollows with his own foot had always been a queer pleasure; today he did it once more, but perfunctorily and detachedly, all the while thinking of something else. That was a dog, a long time ago, who had made a mistake and walked on the cement while it was still wet. He had probably wagged his tail, but that hadn't been recorded. Now, Paul Hasleman, aged twelve, on his way home from school, crossed the same river, which in the meantime had frozen into rock. Homeward through the snow, the snow falling in bright sunshine. Homeward?

Then came the gateway with the two posts surmounted by egg-shaped stones which had been cunningly balanced on their ends, as if by Columbus, and mortared in the very act of balance; a source of perpetual wonder. On the brick wall just beyond, the letter H had been stenciled, presumably for some purpose. H? H.

The green hydrant, with a little green-painted chain attached to the brass screw-cap.

The elm tree, with the great gray wound in the bark, kidney-shaped, into which he always put his hand — to feel the cold but living wood. The injury, he had been sure, was due to the gnawings of a tethered horse. But now it deserved only a passing palm, a merely tolerant eye. There were more important things. Miracles. Beyond the thoughts of trees, mere elms. Beyond the thoughts of sidewalks, mere stone, mere brick, mere cement. Beyond the thoughts even of his own shoes, which trod these sidewalks obediently, bearing a burden — far above — of elaborate mystery. He watched them. They were not very well polished; he had neglected them, for a very good reason: they were one of the many parts of the increasing difficulty of the daily return to daily life, the morning struggle. To get up, having at last opened one's eyes, to go to the window, and discover no snow, to wash, to dress, to descend the curving stairs to breakfast ——

At whatever pain to others, nevertheless, one must persevere in severance, since the incommunicability of the experience demanded it. It was desirable, of course, to be kind to Mother and Father, especially as they seemed to be worried, but it was also desirable to be resolute. If they should decide — as appeared likely — to consult the doctor, Doctor Howells, and have Paul inspected, his heart listened to through a kind of dictaphone, his lungs, his stomach — well, that was all right. He would go through with it. He would give them answer for question, too — perhaps such answers as they hadn't expected? No. That would never do. For the secret world must, at all costs, be preserved.

The bird-house in the apple tree was empty — it was the wrong time of year for wrens. The little round black door had lost its pleasure. The wrens were enjoying other houses, other nests, remoter trees. But this too was a notion which he only vaguely and grazingly entertained — as if, for the moment, he merely touched an edge of it; there was something further on, which was already assuming a sharper importance; something which already teased at the corners of his eyes, teasing also at the corner of his mind. It was funny to think that he so wanted this, so awaited it — and yet found himself enjoying this momentary dalliance with the bird-house, as if for a quite deliberate postponement and enhancement of the approaching pleasure. He was aware of his delay, of his smiling and detached and now almost uncomprehending gaze at the little bird-house; he knew what he was going to look at next: it was his own little cobbled hill-street, his own house, the little river at the bottom of the hill, the grocer's shop with the cardboard man in the window — and now, thinking of all this, he turned his head, still smiling, and looking quickly right and left through the snow-laden sunlight.

And the mist of snow, as he had foreseen, was still on it — a ghost of snow falling in the bright sunlight, softly and steadily floating and turning and pausing, soundlessly meeting the snow that covered, as with a transparent mirage, the bare bright cobbles. He loved it — he stood still and loved it. Its beauty was paralyzing — beyond all words, all experience, all dream. No fairy story he had ever read could be compared with it — none had ever given him this extraordinary combination of ethereal loveliness with a something else, unnameable, which was just faintly and deliciously terrifying. What was this thing? As he thought of it, he looked upward toward his own bedroom window, which was open — and it was as if he looked straight into the room and saw himself lying half awake in his bed. There he was — at this very instant he was still perhaps actually there — more truly there than standing here at the edge of the cobbled hill-street, with one hand lifted to shade his eyes against the snow-sun. Had he indeed ever left his room, in all this time? since that very first morning? Was the whole progress still being enacted there, was it still the same morning, and himself not yet wholly awake? And even now, had the postman not yet come round the corner? . . .

This idea amused him, and automatically, as he thought of it, he turned his head and looked toward the top of the hill. There was, of course, nothing there — nothing and no one. The street was empty and quiet. And all the more because of its emptiness it occurred to him to count the houses — a thing which, oddly enough, he hadn't before thought of doing. Of course, he had known there weren't many — many, that is, on his own side of the street, which were the ones that figured in the postman's progress — but nevertheless it came as something of a shock to find that there were precisely *six*, above his own house — his own house was the seventh.

Six!

Astonished, he looked at his own house — looked at the door, on which was the number thirteen — and then realized that the whole thing was exactly and logically and absurdly what he ought to have known. Just the same, the realization gave him abruptly, and even a little frighteningly, a sense of hurry. He was being hurried — he was being rushed. For — he knit his brow — he couldn't be mistaken — it was just above the *seventh* house, his *own* house, that the postman had first been audible this very morning. But in that case — in that case — did it mean that tomorrow he would hear nothing? The knock he had heard must have been the knock of their own door. Did it mean — and this was an idea which gave him a really extraordinary feeling of surprise — that he would never hear the postman again? — that tomorrow morning the postman would already have passed the house, in a snow so deep as to render his footsteps completely inaudible? That he would have made his approach down the snow-filled street so soundlessly, so secretly, that he, Paul Hasleman, there lying in bed, would not have waked in time, or waking, would have heard nothing?

But how could that be? Unless even the knocker should be muffled in the snow — frozen tight, perhaps? . . . But in that case ——

A vague feeling of disappointment came

over him; a vague sadness as if he felt himself deprived of something which he had long looked forward to, something much prized. After all this, all this beautiful progress, the slow delicious advance of the postman through the silent and secret snow, the knock creeping closer each day, and the footsteps nearer, the audible compass of the world thus daily narrowed, narrowed, narrowed, as the snow soothingly and beautifully encroached and deepened, after all this, was he to be defrauded of the one thing he had so wanted — to be able to count, as it were, the last two or three solemn footsteps, as they finally approached his own door? Was it all going to happen, at the end, so suddenly? or indeed, had it already happened? with no slow and subtle gradations of menace, in which he could luxuriate?

He gazed upward again, toward his own window which flashed in the sun; and this time almost with a feeling that it would be better if he *were* still in bed, in that room; for in that case this must still be the first morning, and there would be six more mornings to come — or, for that matter, seven or eight or nine — how could he be sure? — or even more.

III

After supper, the inquisition began. He stood before the doctor, under the lamp, and submitted silently to the usual thumpings and tappings.

"Now will you please say 'Ah!'?"

"Ah!"

"Now again, please, if you don't mind."

"Ah."

"Say it slowly, and hold it if you can ——"

"Ah-h-h-h-h-h ——"

"Good."

How silly all this was. As if it had anything to do with his throat! Or his heart, or lungs!

Relaxing his mouth, of which the corners, after all this absurd stretching, felt uncomfortable, he avoided the doctor's eyes, and stared toward the fireplace, past his mother's feet (in gray slippers) which projected from the green chair, and his father's feet (in brown slippers) which stood neatly side by side on the hearth rug.

"Hm. There is certainly nothing wrong there . . . ?"

He felt the doctor's eyes fixed upon him, and, as if merely to be polite, returned the look, but with a feeling of justifiable evasiveness.

"Now, young man, tell me — do you feel all right?"

"Yes, sir, quite all right."

"No headaches? no dizziness?"

"No, I don't think so."

"Let me see. Let's get a book, if you don't mind — yes, thank you, that will do splendidly

— and now, Paul, if you'll just read it, holding it as you would normally hold it ——''

He took the book and read:

''And another praise have I to tell for this the city our mother, the gift of a great god, a glory of the land most high; the might of horses, the might of young horses, the might of the sea. . . . For thou, son of Cronus, our lord Poseidon, hath throned herein this pride, since in these roads first thou didst show forth the curb that cures the rage of steeds. And the shapely oar, apt to men's hands, hath a wondrous speed on the brine, following the hundred-footed Nereids. . . . O land that art praised above all lands, now is it for thee to make those bright praises seen in deeds.''

He stopped, tentatively, and lowered the heavy book.

''No — as I thought — there is certainly no superficial sign of eyestrain.''

Silence thronged the room, and he was aware of the focused scrutiny of the three people who confronted him. . . .

''We could have his eyes examined — but I believe it is something else.''

''What could it be?'' That was his father's voice.

''It's only this curious absent-mindedness —'' This was his mother's voice.

In the presence of the doctor, they both seemed irritatingly apologetic.

''I believe it is something else. Now Paul

— I would like very much to ask you a question or two. You will answer them, won't you — you know I'm an old, old friend of yours, eh? That's right! . . . ."

His back was thumped twice by the doctor's fat fist — then the doctor was grinning at him with false amiability, while with one fingernail he was scratching the top button of his waistcoat. Beyond the doctor's shoulder was the fire, the fingers of flame making light prestidigitation against the sooty fireback, the soft sound of their random flutter the only sound.

"I would like to know — is there anything that worries you?"

The doctor was again smiling, his eyelids low against the little black pupils, in each of which was a tiny white bead of light. Why answer him? why answer him at all? "At whatever pain to others" — but it was all a nuisance, this necessity for resistance, this necessity for attention; it was as if one had been stood up on a brilliantly lighted stage, under a great round blaze of spotlight; as if one were merely a trained seal, or a performing dog, or a fish, dipped out of an aquarium and held up by the tail. It would serve them right if he were merely to bark or growl. And meanwhile, to miss these last few precious hours, these hours of which each minute was more beautiful than the last, more menacing —! He still looked, as if from a great distance, at the beads of light in the doctor's eyes, at the fixed false smile, and then, beyond, once more at his mother's slippers, his father's slippers, the soft flutter of the fire. Even here, even amongst these hostile presences, and in this arranged light, he could see the snow, he could hear it — it was in the corners of the room, where the shadow was deepest, under the sofa, behind the half-opened door which led to the dining room. It was gentler here, softer, its seethe the quietest of whispers, as if, in deference to a drawing room, it had quite deliberately put on its "manners"; it kept itself out of sight, obliterated itself, but distinctly with an air of saying, "Ah, but just wait! Wait till we are alone together! Then I will begin to tell you something new! Something white! something cold! something sleepy! something of cease, and peace, and the long bright curve of space! Tell them to go away. Banish them. Refuse to speak. Leave them, go upstairs to your room, turn out the light and get into bed — I will go with you, I will be waiting for you, I will tell you a better story than Little Kay of the Skates, or The Snow Ghost — I will surround your bed, I will close the windows, pile a deep drift against the door, so that none will ever again be able to enter. Speak to them! . . ." It seemed as if the little hissing voice came from a slow white spiral of falling flakes in the corner by the front window — but he could not be sure. He felt himself smiling, then, and said to the doctor, but without looking at him, looking beyond him still ——

"Oh no, I think not ——"

"But are you sure, my boy?"

His father's voice came softly and coldly then — the familiar voice of silken warning.

"You needn't answer at once, Paul — remember we're trying to help you — think it over and be quite sure, won't you?"

He felt himself smiling again, at the notion of being quite sure. What a joke! As if he weren't so sure that reassurance was no longer necessary, and all this cross-examination a ridiculous farce, a grotesque parody! What could they know about it? these gross intelligences, these humdrum minds so bound to the usual, the ordinary? Impossible to tell them about it! Why, even now, even now, with the proof so abundant, so formidable, so imminent, so appallingly present here in this very room, could they believe it? — could even his mother believe it? No — it was only too plain that if anything were said about it, the merest hint given, they would be incredulous — they would laugh — they would say "Absurd!" — think things about him which weren't true. . . .

"Why no, I'm not worried — why should I be?"

He looked then straight at the doctor's low-lidded eyes, looked from one of them to the other, from one bead of light to the other, and gave a little laugh.

The doctor seemed to be disconcerted by this. He drew back in his chair, resting a fat white hand on either knee. The smile faded slowly from his face.

"Well, Paul!" he said, and paused gravely, "I'm afraid you don't take this quite seriously enough. I think you perhaps don't quite realize — don't quite realize —" He took a deep quick breath and turned, as if helplessly, at a loss for words, to the others. But Mother and Father were both silent — no help was forthcoming.

"You must surely know, be aware, that you have not been quite yourself, of late? Don't you know that? . . ."

It was amusing to watch the doctor's renewed attempt at a smile, a queer disorganized look, as of confidential embarrassment.

"I feel all right, sir," he said, and again gave the little laugh.

"And we're trying to help you." The doctor's tone sharpened.

"Yes, sir, I know. But why? I'm all right. I'm just *thinking,* that's all."

His mother made a quick movement forward, resting a hand on the back of the doctor's chair.

"Thinking?" she said. "But my dear, about what?"

This was a direct challenge — and would have to be directly met. But before he met it, he looked again into the corner by the door, as if for reassurance. He smiled again at what he saw, at what he heard. The little spiral was still there, still softly whirling, like the ghost of a white kitten chasing the ghost of a white tail, and making as it did so the faintest of whispers. It was all right! If only he could remain firm, everything was going to be all right.

"Oh, about anything, about nothing — *you* know the way you do!"

"You mean — daydreaming?"

"Oh, no — thinking!"

"But thinking about *what?*"

"Anything."

He laughed a third time — but this time, happening to glance upward toward his mother's face, he was appalled at the effect his laughter seemed to have upon her. Her mouth had opened in an expression of horror. . . . This was too bad! Unfortunate! He had known it would cause pain, of course — but he hadn't expected it to be quite so bad as this. Perhaps — perhaps if he just gave them a tiny gleaming hint ——?

"About the snow," he said.

"What on earth?" This was his father's voice. The brown slippers came a step nearer on the hearth-rug.

"But my dear, what do you mean?" This was his mother's voice.

The doctor merely stared.

"Just *snow,* that's all. I like to think about

it."

"Tell us about it, my boy."

"But that's all it is. There's nothing to tell. *You* know what snow is?"

This he said almost angrily, for he felt that they were trying to corner him. He turned sideways so as no longer to face the doctor, and the better to see the inch of blackness between the window-sill and the lowered curtain — the cold inch of beckoning and delicious night. At once he felt better, more assured.

"Mother — can I go to bed, now, please? I've got a headache."

"But I thought you said ——"

"It's just come. It's all these questions —! Can I, mother?"

"You can go as soon as the doctor has finished."

"Don't you think this thing ought to be gone into thoroughly, and *now?"* This was Father's voice. The brown slippers again came a step nearer, the voice was the well-known "punishment" voice, resonant and cruel.

"Oh, what's the use, Norman ——"

Quite suddenly, everyone was silent. And without precisely facing them, nevertheless he was aware that all three of them were watching him with an extraordinary intensity — staring hard at him — as if he had done something monstrous, or was himself some kind of monster. He could hear the soft irregular flutter of the flames; the cluck-click-cluck-click of the clock; far and faint, two sudden spurts of laughter from the kitchen, as quickly cut off as begun; a murmur of water in the pipes; and then, the silence seemed to deepen, to spread out, to become world-long and world-wide, to become timeless and shapeless, and to center inevitably and rightly, with a slow and sleepy but enormous concentration of all power, on the beginning of a new sound. What this new sound was going to be, he knew perfectly well. It might begin with a hiss, but it would end with a roar — there was no time to lose — he must escape. It mustn't happen here ——

Without another word, he turned and ran up the stairs.

IV

Not a moment too soon. The darkness was coming in long white waves. A prolonged sibilance filled the night — a great seamless seethe of wild influence went abruptly across it — a cold low humming shook the windows. He shut the door and flung off his clothes in the dark. The bare black floor was like a little raft tossed in waves of snow, almost overwhelmed, washed under whitely, up again, smothered in curled billows of feather. The snow was laughing; it spoke from all sides at once; it pressed closer to him as he ran and jumped exulting into his bed.

"Listen to us!" it said. "Listen! We have come to tell you the story we told you about. You remember? Lie down. Shut your eyes, now — you will no longer see much — in this white darkness who could see, or want to see? We will take the place of everything. . . . Listen ——"

A beautiful varying dance of snow began at the front of the room, came forward and then retreated, flattened out toward the floor, then rose fountain-like to the ceiling, swayed, recruited itself from a new stream of flakes which poured laughing in through the humming window, advanced again, lifted long white arms. It said peace, it said remoteness, it said cold — it said ——

But then a gash of horrible light fell brutally across the room from the opening door — the snow drew back hissing — something alien had come into the room — something hostile. This thing rushed at him, clutched at him, shook him — and he was not merely horrified, he was filled with such a loathing as he had never known. What was this? this cruel disturbance? this act of anger and hate? It was as if he had to reach up a hand toward another world for any understanding of it — an effort of which he was only barely capable. But of that other world he still remembered just enough to know the exorcising words. They tore themselves from his other life suddenly ——

"Mother! Mother! Go away! I hate you!"

And with that effort, everything was solved, everything became all right: the seamless hiss advanced once more, the long white wavering lines rose and fell like enormous whispering sea-waves, the whisper becoming louder, the laughter more numerous.

"Listen!" it said. "We'll tell you the last, the most beautiful and secret story — shut your eyes — it is a very small story — a story that gets smaller and smaller — it comes inward instead of opening like a flower — it is a flower becoming a seed — a little cold seed — do you hear? we are leaning closer to you ——"

The hiss was now becoming a roar — the whole world was a vast moving screen of snow — but even now it said peace, it said remoteness, it said cold, it said sleep.

The Jilting of Granny Weatherall

Katherine Anne Porter

SHE flicked her wrist neatly out of Doctor Harry's pudgy careful fingers and pulled the sheet up to her chin. The brat ought to be in knee breeches. Doctoring around the country with spectacles on his nose! "Get along now, take your schoolbooks and go. There's nothing wrong with me."

Doctor Harry spread a warm paw like a cushion on her forehead where the forked green vein danced and made her eyelids twitch. "Now, now, be a good girl, and we'll have you up in no time."

"That's no way to speak to a woman nearly eighty years old just because she's down. I'd have you respect your elders, young man."

"Well, Missy, excuse me." Doctor Harry patted her cheek. "But I've got to warn you, haven't I? You're a marvel, but you must be careful or you're going to be good and sorry."

"Don't tell me what I'm going to be. I'm on my feet now, morally speaking. It's Cornelia. I had to go to bed to get rid of her."

Her bones felt loose, and floated around in her skin, and Doctor Harry floated like a balloon around the foot of the bed. He floated and pulled down his waistcoat and swung his glasses on a cord. "Well, stay where you are, it certainly can't hurt you."

"Get along and doctor your sick," said Granny Weatherall. "Leave a well woman alone. I'll call for you when I want you. . . . Where were you forty years ago when I pulled through milk-leg and double pneumonia? You weren't even born. Don't let Cornelia lead you on," she shouted, because Doctor Harry appeared to float up to the ceiling and out. "I pay my own bills, and I don't throw my money away on nonsense!"

She meant to wave good-by, but it was too much trouble. Her eyes closed of themselves, it was like a dark curtain drawn around the bed. The pillow rose and floated under her, pleasant as a hammock in a light wind. She listened to the leaves rustling outside the window. No, somebody was swishing newspapers: no, Cornelia and Doctor Harry were whispering together. She leaped broad awake, thinking they whispered in her ear.

"She was never like this, *never* like this!" "Well, what can we expect?" "Yes, eighty years old. . . ."

Well, and what if she was? She still had ears. It was like Cornelia to whisper around doors. She always kept things secret in such a public way. She was always being tactful and kind. Cornelia was dutiful; that was the trouble with her. Dutiful and good: "So good and dutiful," said Granny, "that I'd like to spank her." She saw herself spanking Cornelia and making a fine job of it.

"What'd you say, Mother?"

Granny felt her face tying up in hard knots.

"Can't a body think, I'd like to know?"

"I thought you might want something."

"I do. I want a lot of things. First off, go away and don't whisper."

She lay and drowsed, hoping in her sleep that the children would keep out and let her rest a minute. It had been a long day. Not that she was tired. It was always pleasant to snatch a minute now and then. There was always so much to be done, let me see: tomorrow.

Tomorrow was far away and there was nothing to trouble about. Things were finished somehow when the time came; thank God there was always a little margin over for peace: then a person could spread out the plan of life and tuck in the edges orderly. It was good to have everything clean and folded away, with the hair brushes and tonic bottles sitting straight on the white embroidered linen: the day started without fuss and the pantry shelves laid out with rows of jelly glasses and brown jugs and white stone-china jars with blue whirligigs and words painted on them: coffee, tea, sugar, ginger, cinnamon, allspice: and the bronze clock with the lion on top nicely dusted off. The dust that lion could collect in twenty-four hours! The box in the attic with all those letters tied up, well, she'd have to go through that tomorrow. All those letters — George's letters and John's letters and her letters to them both — lying around for the children to find afterwards made her uneasy. Yes, that would be tomorrow's business. No use to let them know how silly she had been once.

While she was rummaging around she found death in her mind and it felt clammy and unfamiliar. She had spent so much time preparing for death there was no need for bringing it up again. Let it take care of itself now. When she was sixty she had felt very old, finished, and went around making farewell trips to see her children and grandchildren, with a secret in her mind: This is the very last of your mother, children! Then she made her will and came down with a long fever. That was all just a notion like a lot of other things, but it was lucky too, for she had once for all got over the idea of dying for a long time. Now she couldn't be worried. She hoped she had better sense now. Her father had lived to be one hundred and two years old and had drunk a noggin of strong hot toddy on his last birthday. He told the reporters it was his daily habit, and he owed his long life to that. He had made quite a scandal and was very pleased about it. She believed she'd just plague Cornelia a little.

"Cornelia! Cornelia!" No footsteps, but a sudden hand on her cheek. "Bless you, where have you been?"

"Here, mother."

"Well, Cornelia, I want a noggin of hot toddy."

"Are you cold, darling?"

"I'm chilly, Cornelia. Lying in bed stops the circulation. I must have told you that a thousand times."

Well, she could just hear Cornelia telling her husband that Mother was getting a little childish and they'd have to humor her. The thing that most annoyed her was that Cornelia thought she was deaf, dumb, and blind. Little hasty glances and tiny gestures tossed around her and over her head saying, "Don't cross her, let her have her way, she's eighty years old," and she sitting there as if she lived in a thin glass cage. Sometimes Granny almost made up her mind to pack up and move back to her own house where nobody could remind her every minute that she was old. Wait, wait, Cornelia, till your own children whisper behind your back!

In her day she had kept a better house and had got more work done. She wasn't too old yet for Lydia to be driving eighty miles for advice when one of the children jumped the track, and Jimmy still dropped in and talked things over: "Now, Mammy, you've a good business head, I want to know what you think of this? . . . .'' Old. Cornelia couldn't change the furniture around without asking. Little things, little things! They had been so sweet when they were little. Granny wished the old days were back again with the children young and everything to be done over. It had been a hard pull, but not too much for her. When she thought of all the food she had cooked, and all the clothes she had cut and sewed, and all the gardens she had made — well, the children showed it. There they were, made out of her, and they couldn't get away from that. Sometimes she wanted to see John again and point to them and say, Well, I didn't do so badly, did I? But that would have to wait. That was for tomorrow. She used to think of him as a man, but now all the children were older than their father, and he would be a child beside her if she saw him now. It seemed strange and there was something wrong in the idea. Why, he couldn't possibly recognize her. She had fenced in a hundred acres once, digging the post holes herself and clamping the wires with just a negro boy to help. That changed a woman. John would be looking for a young woman with the peaked Spanish comb in her hair and the painted fan. Digging post holes changed a woman. Riding country roads in the winter when women had their babies was another thing: sitting up nights with sick horses and sick negroes and sick children and hardly ever losing one. John, I hardly ever lost one of them! John would see that in a minute, that would be something he could understand, she wouldn't have to explain anything!

It made her feel like rolling up her sleeves and putting the whole place to rights again. No matter if Cornelia was determined to be everywhere at once, there were a great many things left undone on this place. She would start tomorrow and do them. It was good to be strong enough for everything, even if all you made melted and changed and slipped under your hands, so that by the time you finished you almost forgot what you were working for. What was it I set out to do? she asked herself intently, but she could not remember. A fog rose over the valley, she saw it marching across the creek swallowing the trees and moving up the hill like an army of ghosts. Soon it would be at the near edge of the orchard, and then it was time to go in and light the lamps. Come in, children, don't stay out in the night air.

Lighting the lamps had been beautiful. The children huddled up to her and breathed like little calves waiting at the bars in the twilight. Their eyes followed the match and watched the flame rise and settle in a blue curve, then they moved away from her. The lamp was lit, they didn't have to be scared and hang on to mother any more. Never, never, never more. God, for all my life I thank Thee. Without

Thee, my God, I could never have done it. Hail, Mary, full of grace.

I want you to pick all the fruit this year and see that nothing is wasted. There's always someone who can use it. Don't let good things rot for want of using. You waste life when you waste good food. Don't let things get lost. It's bitter to lose things. Now, don't let me get to thinking, not when I am tired and taking a little nap before supper. . . .

The pillow rose about her shoulders and pressed against her heart and the memory was being squeezed out of it: oh, push down the pillow, somebody: it would smother her if she tried to hold it. Such a fresh breeze blowing and such a green day with no threats in it. But he had not come, just the same. What does a woman do when she has put on the white veil and set out the white cake for a man and he doesn't come? She tried to remember. No, I swear he never harmed me but in that. He never harmed me but in that . . . and what if he did? There was the day, the day, but a whirl of dark smoke rose and covered it, crept up and over into the bright field where everything was planted so carefully in orderly rows. That was hell, she knew hell when she saw it. For sixty years she had prayed against remembering him and against losing her soul in the deep pit of hell, and now the two things were mingled in one and the thought of him was a smoky cloud from hell that moved and crept in her head when she had just got rid of Doctor Harry and was trying to rest a minute. Wounded vanity, Ellen, said a sharp voice in the top of her mind. Don't let your wounded vanity get the upper hand of you. Plenty of girls get jilted. You were jilted, weren't you? Then stand up to it. Her eyelids wavered and let in streamers of blue-gray light like tissue paper over her eyes. She must get up and pull the shades down or she'd never sleep. She was in bed again and the shades were not down. How could that happen? Better turn over, hide from the light, sleeping in the light gave you nightmares. "Mother, how do you feel now?" and a stinging wetness on her forehead. But I don't like having my face washed in cold water!

Hapsy? George? Lydia? Jimmy? No, Cornelia, and her features were swollen and full of little puddles. "They're coming, darling, they'll all be here soon." Go wash your face, child, you look funny.

Instead of obeying, Cornelia knelt down and put her head on the pillow. She seemed to be talking but there was no sound. "Well, are you tongue-tied? Whose birthday is it? Are you going to give a party?"

Cornelia's mouth moved urgently in strange shapes. "Don't do that, you bother me, daughter."

"Oh, no, Mother. Oh, no. . . ."

Nonsense. It was strange about children.

They disputed your every word. "No what, Cornelia?"

"Here's Doctor Harry."

"I won't see that boy again. He just left five minutes ago."

"That was this morning, Mother. It's night now. Here's the nurse."

"This is Doctor Harry, Mrs. Weatherall. I never saw you look so young and happy!"

"Ah, I'll never be young again — but I'd be happy if they'd let me lie in peace and get rested."

She thought she spoke up loudly, but no one answered. A warm weight on her forehead, a warm bracelet on her wrist, and a breeze went on whispering, trying to tell her something. A shuffle of leaves in the everlasting hand of God, He blew on them and they danced and rattled. "Mother, don't mind, we're going to give you a little hypodermic." "Look here, daughter, how do ants get in this bed? I saw sugar ants yesterday." Did you send for Hapsy too?

It was Hapsy she really wanted. She had to go a long way back through a great many rooms to find Hapsy standing with a baby on her arm. She seemed to herself to be Hapsy also, and the baby on Hapsy's arm was Hapsy and himself and herself, all at once, and there was no surprise in the meeting. Then Hapsy melted from within and turned flimsy as gray gauze and the baby was a gauzy shadow, and

Hapsy came up close and said, "I thought you'd never come," and looked at her very searchingly and said, "You haven't changed a bit!" They leaned forward to kiss, when Cornelia began whispering from a long way off, "Oh, is there anything you want to tell me? Is there anything I can do for you?"

Yes, she had changed her mind after sixty years and she would like to see George. I want you to find George. Find him and be sure to tell him I forgot him. I want him to know I had my husband just the same and my children and my house like any other woman. A good house too and a good husband that I loved and fine children out of him. Better than I hoped for even. Tell him I was given back everything he took away and more. Oh, no, oh, God, no, there was something else besides the house and the man and the children. Oh, surely they were not all? What was it? Something not given back. . . . Her breath crowded down under her ribs and grew into a monstrous frightening shape with cutting edges; it bored up into her head, and the agony was unbelievable: Yes, John, get the Doctor now, no more talk, my time has come.

When this one was born it should be the last. The last. It should have been born first, for it was the one she had truly wanted. Everything came in good time. Nothing left out, left over. She was strong, in three days she would be as well as ever. Better. A woman needed milk in her to have her full health.

"Mother, do you hear me?"

"I've been telling you —"

"Mother, Father Connolly's here."

"I went to Holy Communion only last week. Tell him I'm not so sinful as all that."

"Father just wants to speak to you."

He could speak as much as he pleased. It was like him to drop in and inquire about her soul as if it were a teething baby, and then stay on for a cup of tea and a round of cards and gossip. He always had a funny story of some sort, usually about an Irishman who made his little mistakes and confessed them, and the point lay in some absurd thing he would blurt out in the confessional showing his struggles between native piety and original sin. Granny felt easy about her soul. Cornelia, where are your manners? Give Father Connolly a chair. She had her secret comfortable understanding with a few favorite saints who cleared a straight road to God for her. All as surely signed and sealed as the papers for the new Forty Acres. Forever . . . heirs and assigns forever. Since the day the wedding cake was not cut, but thrown out and wasted. The whole bottom dropped out of the world, and there she was blind and sweating with nothing under her feet and the walls falling away. His hand had caught her under the breast, she had not fallen, there was the freshly polished floor with the green rug on it, just as before. He had cursed like a sailor's parrot and said, "I'll kill him for you." Don't lay a hand on him, for my sake leave something to God. "Now, Ellen, you must believe what I tell you. . . ."

So there was nothing, nothing to worry about any more, except sometimes in the night one of the children screamed in a nightmare, and they both hustled out shaking and hunting for the matches and calling, "There, wait a minute, here we are!" John, get the doctor now, Hapsy's time has come. But there was Hapsy standing by the bed in a white cap. "Cornelia, tell Hapsy to take off her cap. I can't see her plain."

Her eyes opened very wide and the room stood out like a picture she had seen somewhere. Dark colors with the shadows rising towards the ceiling in long angles. The tall black dresser gleamed with nothing on it but John's picture, enlarged from a little one, with John's eyes very black when they should have been blue. You never saw him, so how do you know how he looked? But the man insisted the copy was perfect, it was very rich and handsome. For a picture, yes, but it's not my husband. The table by the bed had a linen cover and a candle and a crucifix. The light was blue from Cornelia's silk lampshades. No sort of light at all, just frippery. You had to live forty years with kerosene lamps to appreciate honest electricity. She felt very strong and she saw Doctor Harry with a rosy nimbus around him.

"You look like a saint, Doctor Harry, and I vow that's as near as you'll ever come to it."

"She's saying something."

"I heard you, Cornelia. What's all this carrying-on?"

"Father Connolly's saying —"

Cornelia's voice staggered and bumped like a cart in a bad road. It rounded corners and turned back again and arrived nowhere. Granny stepped up in the cart very lightly and reached for the reins, but a man sat beside her and she knew him by his hands, driving the cart. She did not look in his face, for she knew without seeing, but looked instead down the road where the trees leaned over and bowed to each other and a thousand birds were singing a Mass. She felt like singing too, but she put her hand in the bosom of her dress and pulled out a rosary, and Father Connolly murmured Latin in a very solemn voice and tickled her feet. My God, will you stop that nonsense? I'm a married woman. What if he did run away and leave me to face the priest by myself? I found another a whole world better. I wouldn't have exchanged my husband for anybody except St. Michael himself, and you may tell him that for me with a thank you in the bargain.

Light flashed on her closed eyelids, and a deep roaring shook her. Cornelia, is that lightning? I hear thunder. There's going to be a storm. Close all the windows. Call the children in. . . . "Mother, here we are, all of us."

"Is that you Hapsy?" "Oh, no, I'm Lydia. We drove as fast as we could." Their faces drifted above her, drifted away. The rosary fell out of her hands and Lydia put it back. Jimmy tried to help, their hands fumbled together, and Granny closed two fingers around Jimmy's thumb. Beads wouldn't do, it must be something alive. She was so amazed her thoughts ran round and round. So, my dear Lord, this is my death and I wasn't even thinking about it. My children have come to see me die. But I can't, it's not time. Oh, I always hated surprises. I wanted to give Cornelia the amethyst set — Cornelia, you're to have the amethyst set, but Hapsy's to wear it when she wants, and, Doctor Harry, do shut up. Nobody sent for you. Oh, my dear Lord, do wait a minute. I meant to do something about the Forty Acres, Jimmy doesn't need it and Lydia will later on, with that worthless husband of hers. I meant to finish the altar cloth and send six bottles of wine to Sister Borgia for her dyspepsia. I want to send six bottles of wine to Sister Borgia, Father Connolly, now don't let me forget.

Cornelia's voice made short turns and tilted over and crashed. "Oh, Mother, oh, Mother, oh, Mother. . . ."

"I'm not going, Cornelia. I'm taken by surprise. I can't go."

You'll see Hapsy again. What about her? "I thought you'd never come." Granny made a long journey outward, looking for Hapsy. What if I don't find her? What then? Her heart sank down and down, there was no bottom to death, she couldn't come to the end of it. The blue light from Cornelia's lampshade drew into a tiny point in the center of her brain, it flickered and winked like an eye, quietly it fluttered and dwindled. Granny lay curled down within herself, amazed and watchful, staring at the point of light that was herself; her body was now only a deeper mass of shadow in an endless darkness and this darkness would curl around the light and swallow it up. God, give a sign!

For the second time there was no sign. Again no bridegroom and the priest in the house. She could not remember any other sorrow because this grief wiped them all away. Oh, no, there's nothing more cruel than this — I'll never forgive it. She stretched herself with a deep breath and blew out the light.

A Rose for Emily

William Faulkner

WHEN Miss Emily Grierson died, our whole town went to her funeral: the men through a sort of respectful affection for a fallen monument, the women mostly out of curiosity to see the inside of her house, which no one save an old man-servant — a combined gardener and cook — had seen in at least ten years.

It was a big, squarish frame house that had once been white, decorated with cupolas and spires and scrolled balconies in the heavily lightsome style of the Seventies, set on what had once been our most select street. But garages and cotton gins had encroached and obliterated even the august names of that neighborhood; only Miss Emily's house was left, lifting its stubborn and coquettish decay above the cotton wagons and the gasoline pumps — an eyesore among eyesores. And now Miss Emily had gone to join the representatives of those august names where they lay in the cedar-bemused cemetery among the ranked and anonymous graves of Union and

Confederate soldiers who fell at the battle of Jefferson.

Alive, Miss Emily had been a tradition, a duty, and a care; a sort of hereditary obligation upon the town, dating from that day in 1894 when Colonel Sartoris, the mayor — he who fathered the edict that no Negro woman should appear on the streets without an apron — remitted her taxes, the dispensation dating from the death of her father on into perpetuity. Not that Miss Emily would have accepted charity. Colonel Sartoris invented an involved tale to the effect that Miss Emily's father had loaned money to the town, which the town, as a matter of business, preferred this way of repaying. Only a man of Colonel Sartoris' generation and thought could have invented it, and only a woman could have believed it.

When the next generation, with its more modern ideas, became mayors and aldermen, this arrangement created some little dissatisfaction. On the first of the year they mailed her a tax notice. February came, and there was no reply. They wrote her a formal letter, asking her to call at the sheriff's office at her convenience. A week later the mayor wrote her himself, offering to call or to send his car for her, and received in reply a note on paper of an archaic shape, in a thin, flowing calligraphy in faded ink, to the effect that she no longer went out at all. The tax notice was also enclosed, without comment.

They called a special meeting of the Board of Aldermen. A deputation waited upon her, knocked at the door through which no visitor had passed since she ceased giving china-painting lessons eight or ten years earlier. They were admitted by the old Negro into a dim hall from which a stairway mounted into still more shadow. It smelled of dust and disuse — a close, dank smell. The Negro led them into the parlor. It was furnished in heavy, leather-covered furniture. When the Negro opened the blinds of one window, they could see that the leather was cracked; and when they sat down, a faint dust rose sluggishly about their thighs, spinning with slow motes in the single sun-ray. On a tarnished gilt easel before the fireplace stood a crayon portrait of Miss Emily's father.

They rose when she entered — a small, fat woman in black, with a thin gold chain descending to her waist and vanishing into her belt, leaning on an ebony cane with a tarnished gold head. Her skeleton was small and spare; perhaps that was why what would have been merely plumpness in another was obesity in her. She looked bloated, like a body long submerged in motionless water, and of that pallid hue. Her eyes, lost in the fatty ridges of her face, looked like two small pieces of coal pressed into a lump of dough as they moved from one face to another while the visitors stated their errand.

She did not ask them to sit. She just stood in the door and listened quietly until the spokesman came to a stumbling halt. Then they could hear the invisible watch ticking at the end of the gold chain.

Her voice was dry and cold. "I have no taxes in Jefferson. Colonel Sartoris explained it to me. Perhaps one of you can gain access to the city records and satisfy yourselves."

"But we have. We are the city authorities, Miss Emily. Didn't you get a notice from the sheriff, signed by him?"

"I received a paper, yes," Miss Emily said. "Perhaps he considers himself the sheriff . . . I have no taxes in Jefferson."

"But there is nothing on the books to show that, you see. We must go by the —"

"See Colonel Sartoris. I have no taxes in Jefferson."

"But, Miss Emily —"

"See Colonel Sartoris." (Colonel Sartoris had been dead almost ten years.) "I have no taxes in Jefferson. Tobe!" The Negro appeared. "Show these gentlemen out."

II

So she vanquished them, horse and foot, just as she had vanquished their fathers thirty years before about the smell. That was two years after her father's death and a short time after her sweetheart — the one we believed would marry her — had deserted her. After her father's death she went out very little; after her sweetheart went away, people hardly saw her at all. A few of the ladies had the temerity to call, but were not received, and the only sign of life about the place was the Negro man — a young man then — going in and out with a market basket.

"Just as if a man — any man — could keep a kitchen properly," the ladies said; so they were not surprised when the smell developed. It was another link between the gross, teeming world and the high and mighty Griersons.

A neighbor, a woman, complained to the mayor, Judge Stevens, eighty years old.

"But what will you have me do about it, madam?" he said.

"Why, send her word to stop it," the woman said. "Isn't there a law?"

"I'm sure that won't be necessary," Judge Stevens said. "It's probably just a snake or a rat that nigger of hers killed in the yard. I'll speak to him about it."

The next day he received two more complaints, one from a man who came in diffident deprecation. "We really must do something about it, Judge. I'd be the last one in the world to bother Miss Emily, but we've got to do something." That night the Board of Aldermen met — three gray-beards and one younger man, a member of the rising generation.

"It's simple enough," he said. "Send her

word to have her place cleaned up. Give her a certain time to do it in, and if she don't . . ."

"Dammit, sir," Judge Stevens said, "will you accuse a lady to her face of smelling bad?"

So the next night, after midnight, four men crossed Miss Emily's lawn and slunk about the house like burglars, sniffing along the base of the brickwork and at the cellar openings while one of them performed a regular sowing motion with his hand out of a sack slung from his shoulder. They broke open the cellar door and sprinkled lime there, and in all the outbuildings. As they recrossed the lawn, a window that had been dark was lighted and Miss Emily sat in it, the light behind her, and her upright torso motionless as that of an idol. They crept quietly across the lawn and into the shadow of the locusts that lined the street. After a week or two the smell went away.

That was when people had begun to feel really sorry for her. People in our town, remembering how Old Lady Wyatt, her great-aunt, had gone completely crazy at last, believed that the Griersons held themselves a little too high for what they really were. None of the young men was quite good enough to Miss Emily and such. We had long thought of them as a tableau: Miss Emily a slender figure in white in the background, her father a spraddled silhouette in the foreground, his back to her and clutching a horse-whip, the two of them framed by the back-flung front door. So when she got to be thirty and was still single, we were not pleased exactly, but vindicated; even with insanity in the family she wouldn't have turned down all of her chances if they had really materialized.

When her father died, it got about that the house was all that was left to her; and in a way, people were glad. At last they could pity Miss Emily. Being left alone, and a pauper, she had become humanized. Now she too would know the old thrill and the old despair of a penny more or less.

The day after his death all the ladies prepared to call at the house and offer condolence and aid, as is our custom. Miss Emily met them at the door, dressed as usual and with no trace of grief on her face. She told them that her father was not dead. She did that for three days, with the ministers calling on her, and the doctors, trying to persuade her to let them dispose of the body. Just as they were about to resort to law and force, she broke down, and they buried her father quickly.

We did not say she was crazy then. We believed she had to do that. We remembered all the young men her father had driven away, and we knew that with nothing left, she would have to cling to that which had robbed her, as people will.

III

She was sick for a long time. When we saw her again, her hair was cut short, making her look like a girl, with a vague resemblance to those angels in colored church windows — sort of tragic and serene.

The town had just let the contracts for paving the sidewalks, and in the summer after her father's death they began the work. The construction company came with niggers and mules and machinery, and a foreman named Homer Barron, a Yankee — a big, dark, ready man, with a big voice and eyes lighter than his face. The little boys would follow in groups to hear him cuss the niggers, and the niggers singing in time to the rise and fall of picks. Pretty soon he knew everybody in town. Whenever you heard a lot of laughing anywhere about the square, Homer Barron would be in the center of the group. Presently we began to see him and Miss Emily on Sunday afternoons driving in the yellow-wheeled buggy and the matched team of bays from the livery stable.

At first we were glad that Miss Emily would have an interest, because the ladies all said, "Of course a Grierson would not think seriously of a Northerner, a day laborer." But there were still others, older people, who said that even grief could not cause a real lady to forget *noblesse oblige* — without calling it *noblesse oblige*. They just said, "Poor Emily. Her kinsfolk should come to her." She had some kin in Alabama; but years ago her father had fallen out with them over the estate of Old Lady Wyatt, the crazy woman, and there was no communication between the two families. They had not even been represented at the funeral.

And as soon as the old people said, "Poor Emily," the whispering began. "Do you suppose it's really so?" they said to one another. "Of course it is. What else could . . ." This behind their hands; rustling of craned silk and satin behind jalousies closed upon the sun of Sunday afternoon as the thin, swift clop-clop-clop of the matched team passed: "Poor Emily."

She carried her head high enough — even when we believed that she was fallen. It was as if she demanded more than ever the recognition of her dignity as the last Grierson; as if it had wanted that touch of earthiness to reaffirm her imperviousness. Like when she bought the rat poison, the arsenic. That was over a year after they had begun to say "Poor Emily," and while the two female cousins were visiting her.

"I want some poison," she said to the druggist. She was over thirty then, still a slight woman, though thinner than usual, with cold, haughty black eyes in a face the flesh of which was strained across the temples and about the eye-sockets as you imagine a lighthouse-keeper's face ought to look. "I want some poison," she said.

"Yes, Miss Emily. What kind? For rats and such? I'd recom —"

"I want the best you have. I don't care what kind."

The druggist named several. "They'll kill anything up to an elephant. But what you want is —"

"Arsenic," Miss Emily said. "Is that a good one?"

"Is . . . arsenic? Yes, ma'am. But what you want —"

"I want arsenic."

The druggist looked down at her. She looked back at him, erect, her face like a strained flag. "Why, of course," the druggist said. "If that's what you want. But the law requires you to tell what you are going to use it for."

Miss Emily just stared at him, her head tilted back in order to look him eye for eye, until he looked away and went and got the arsenic and wrapped it up. The Negro delivery boy brought her the package; the druggist didn't come back. When she opened the package at home there was written on the box, under the skull and bones: "For rats."

IV

So the next day we all said, "She will kill herself"; and we said it would be the best thing. When she had first begun to be seen with Homer Barron, we had said, "She will marry him." Then we said, "She will persuade him yet," because Homer himself had remarked — he liked men, and it was known that he drank with the younger men in the Elks' Club — that he was not a marrying man. Later we said, "Poor Emily" behind the jalousies as they passed on Sunday afternoon in the glittering buggy, Miss Emily with her head high and Homer Barron with his hat cocked and a cigar in his teeth, reins and whip in a yellow glove.

Then some of the ladies began to say that it was a disgrace to the town and a bad example to the young people. The men did not want to interfere, but at last the ladies forced the Baptist minister — Miss Emily's people were Episcopal — to call upon her. He would never divulge what happened during that interview, but he refused to go back again. The next Sunday they again drove about the streets, and the following day the minister's wife wrote to Miss Emily's relations in Alabama.

So she had blood-kin under her roof again and we sat back to watch developments. At first nothing happened. Then we were sure that they were to be married. We learned that Miss

Emily had been to the jeweler's and ordered a man's toilet set in silver, with the letter H. B. on each piece. Two days later we learned that she had bought a complete outfit of men's clothing, including a nightshirt, and we said, "They are married." We were really glad. We were glad because the two female cousins were even more Grierson than Miss Emily had ever been.

So we were not surprised when Homer Barron — the streets had been finished some time since — was gone. We were a little disappointed that there was not a public blowing-off, but we believed that he had gone on to prepare for Miss Emily's coming, or to give her a chance to get rid of the cousins. (By that time it was a cabal, and we were all Miss Emily's allies to help circumvent the cousins.) Sure enough, after another week they departed. And, as we had expected all along, within three days Homer Barron was back in town. A neighbor saw the Negro man admit him at the kitchen door at dusk one evening.

And that was the last we saw of Homer Barron. And of Miss Emily for some time. The Negro man went in and out with the market basket, but the front door remained closed. Now and then we would see her at a window for a moment, as the men did that night when they sprinkled the lime, but for almost six months she did not appear on the streets. Then we knew that this was to be expected too; as if that quality of her father which had thwarted her woman's life so many times had been too virulent and too furious to die.

When we next saw Miss Emily, she had grown fat and her hair was turning gray. During the next few years it grew grayer and grayer until it attained an even pepper-and-salt iron-gray, when it ceased turning. Up to the day of her death at seventy-four it was still that vigorous iron-gray, like the hair of an active man.

From that time on her front door remained closed, save for a period of six or seven years, when she was about forty, during which she gave lessons in china-painting. She fitted up a studio in one of the downstairs rooms, where the daughters and granddaughters of Colonel Sartoris' contemporaries were sent to her with the same regularity and in the same spirit that they were sent to church on Sundays with a twenty-five-cent piece for the collection plate. Meanwhile her taxes had been remitted.

Then the newer generation became the backbone and the spirit of the town, and the painting pupils grew up and fell away and did not send their children to her with boxes of color and tedious brushes and pictures cut from the ladies' magazines. The front door closed upon the last one and remained closed for good. When the town got free postal delivery, Miss Emily alone refused to let them fasten the metal numbers above her door and attach a mailbox to it. She would not listen to them.

Daily, monthly, yearly we watched the Negro grow grayer and more stooped, going in and out with the market basket. Each December we sent her a tax notice, which would be returned by the post office a week later, unclaimed. Now and then we would see her in one of the downstairs windows — she had evidently shut up the top floor of the house — like the carven torso of an idol in a niche, looking or not looking at us, we could never tell which. Thus she passed from generation to generation — dear, inescapable, impervious, tranquil, and perverse.

And so she died. Fell ill in the house filled with dust and shadows, with only a doddering Negro man to wait on her. We did not even know she was sick; we had long since given up trying to get any information from the Negro. He talked to no one, probably not even to her, for his voice had grown harsh and rusty, as if from disuse.

She died in one of the downstairs rooms, in a heavy walnut bed with a curtain, her gray head propped on a pillow yellow and moldy with age and lack of sunlight.

V

The Negro met the first of the ladies at the front door and let them in, with their hushed, sibilant voices and their quick, curious glances, and then he disappeared. He walked right through the house and out the back and was not seen again.

The two female cousins came at once. They held the funeral on the second day, with the town coming to look at Miss Emily beneath a mass of bought flowers, with the crayon face of her father musing profoundly above the bier and the ladies sibilant and macabre; and the very old men — some in their brushed Confederate uniforms — on the porch and the lawn, talking of Miss Emily as if she had been a contemporary of theirs, believing that they had danced with her and courted her perhaps, confusing time with its mathematical progression, as the old do, to whom all the past is not a diminishing road but, instead, a huge meadow which no winter ever quite touches, divided from them now by the narrow bottleneck of the most recent decade of years.

Already we knew that there was one room in that region above stairs which no one had seen in forty years, and which would have to be forced. They waited until Miss Emily was decently in the ground before they opened it.

The violence of breaking down the door seemed to fill this room with pervading dust. A thin, acrid pall as of the tomb seemed to lie everywhere upon this room decked and furnished as for a bridal: upon the valence curtains of faded rose color, upon the rose-shaded lights, upon the dressing table, upon the delicate array of crystal and the man's toilet things backed with tarnished silver, silver so tarnished that the monogram was obscured. Among them lay a collar and tie, as if they had just been removed, which, lifted, left upon the surface a pale crescent in the dust. Upon a chair hung the suit, carefully folded; beneath it the two mute shoes and the discarded socks.

The man himself lay in the bed.

For a long while we just stood there, looking down at the profound and fleshless grin. The body had apparently once lain in the attitude of an embrace, but now the long sleep that outlasts love, that conquers even the grimace of love, had cuckolded him. What was left of him, rotted beneath what was left of the nightshirt, had become inextricable from the bed in which he lay; and upon him and upon the pillow beside him lay that even coating of the patient and biding dust.

Then we noticed that in the second pillow was the indentation of a head. One of us lifted something from it, and leaning forward, that faint and invisible dust dry and acrid in the nostrils, we saw a long strand of iron-gray hair.

The Lottery

Shirley Jackson

THE morning of June 27th was clear and sunny, with the fresh warmth of a full-summer day; the flowers were blossoming profusely and the grass was richly green. The people of the village began to gather in the square, between the post office and the bank, around ten o'clock; in some towns there were so many people that the lottery took two days and had to be started on June 26th, but in this village, where there were only about three hundred people, the whole lottery took less than two hours, so it could begin at ten o'clock in the morning and still be through in time to allow the villagers to get home for noon dinner.

The children assembled first, of course. School was recently over for the summer, and the feeling of liberty sat uneasily on most of them; they tended to gather together quietly for a while before they broke into boisterous play, and their talk was still of the classroom and the teacher, of books and reprimands. Bobby Martin had already stuffed his pockets full of stones, and the other boys soon followed his example, selecting the smoothest and roundest stones; Bobby and Harry Jones and Dickie Delacroix — the villagers pronounced this name "Dellacroy" — eventually made a great pile of stones in one corner of the square and guarded it against the raids of the other boys. The girls stood aside, talking among themselves, looking over their shoulders at the boys, and the very small children rolled in the dust or clung to the hands of their older brothers or sisters.

Soon the men began to gather, surveying their own children, speaking of planting and rain, tractors and taxes. They stood together, away from the pile of stones in the corner, and their jokes were quiet and they smiled rather than laughed. The women, wearing faded house dresses and sweaters, came shortly after their menfolk. They greeted one another and exchanged bits of gossip as they went to join their husbands. Soon the women, standing by their husbands, began to call to their children, and the children came reluctantly, having to be called four or five times. Bobby Martin ducked under his mother's grasping hand and ran, laughing, back to the pile of stones. His father spoke up sharply, and Bobby came quickly and took his place between his father and his oldest brother.

The lottery was conducted — as were the square dances, the teen-age club, the Halloween program — by Mr. Summers, who had time and energy to devote to civic activities. He was a round-faced, jovial man and he ran the coal business, and people were sorry for him, because he had no children and his wife was a scold. When he arrived in the square, carrying the black wooden box, there was a murmur of conversation among the villagers, and he waved and called, "Little late today, folks." The postmaster, Mr. Graves, followed him, carrying a three-legged stool, and the stool was put in the center of the square and Mr. Summers set the black box down on it. The villagers kept their distance, leaving a space between themselves and the stool, and when Mr. Summers said, "Some of you fellows want to give me a hand?" there was a hesitation before two men, Mr. Martin and his oldest son, Baxter, came forward to hold the box steady on the stool while Mr. Summers stirred up the papers inside it.

The original paraphernalia for the lottery had been lost long ago, and the black box now resting on the stool had been put into use even before Old Man Warner, the oldest man in town, was born. Mr. Summers spoke frequently to the villagers about making a new box, but no one liked to upset even as much tradition as was represented by the black box. There was a story that the present box had been made with some pieces of the box that had preceded it, the one that had been constructed when the first people settled down to make a village here. Every year, after the lottery, Mr. Summers began talking again about a new box, but every year the subject was allowed to fade off without anything's being done. The black box grew shabbier each year; by now it was no longer completely black but splintered badly along one side to show the original wood color, and in some places faded or stained.

Mr. Martin and his oldest son, Baxter, held the black box securely on the stool until Mr. Summers had stirred the papers thoroughly with his hand. Because so much of the ritual had been forgotten or discarded, Mr. Summers had been successful in having slips of paper substituted for the chips of wood that had been used for generations. Chips of wood, Mr. Summers had argued, had been all very well when the village was tiny, but now that the population was more than three hundred and likely to keep on growing, it was necessary to use something that would fit more easily into the black box. The night before the lottery, Mr. Summers and Mr. Graves made up the slips of paper and put them in the box, and it was then taken to the safe of Mr. Summers's coal company and locked up until Mr. Summers was ready to take it to the square next morning. The rest of the year the box was put away, sometimes one place, sometimes another; it had spent one year in Mr. Graves's barn and another year underfoot in the post office, and sometimes it was set on a shelf in the Martin grocery and left there.

There was a great deal of fussing to be done before Mr. Summers declared the lottery open. There were the lists to make up — of heads of families, heads of households in each family, members of each household in each family. There was the proper swearing-in of Mr. Summers by the postmaster, as the official of the lottery; at one time, some people remembered, there had been a recital of some sort, performed by the official of the lottery, a perfunctory, tuneless chant that had been rattled off duly each year; some people believed that the official of the lottery used to stand just so when he said or sang it, others believed that he was supposed to walk among the people, but years and years ago this part of the ritual had been allowed to lapse. There had been, also, a ritual salute, which the official of the lottery had had to use in addressing each person who came up to draw from the box, but this also had changed with time, until now it was felt necessary only for the official to speak to each person approaching. Mr. Summers was very good at all this; in his clean white shirt and blue jeans, with one hand resting carelessly on the black box, he seemed very proper and important as he talked interminably to Mr. Graves and the Martins.

Just as Mr. Summers finally left off talking and turned to the assembled villagers, Mrs.

Hutchinson came hurriedly along the path to the square, her sweater thrown over her shoulders, and slid into place in the back of the crowd. "Clean forgot what day it was," she said to Mrs. Delacroix, who stood next to her, and they both laughed softly. "Thought my old man was out back stacking wood," Mrs. Hutchinson went on, "and then I looked out the window and the kids was gone, and then I remembered it was the twenty-seventh and came a-running." She dried her hands on her apron, and Mrs. Delacroix said, "You're in time, though. They're still talking away up there."

Mrs. Hutchinson craned her neck to see through the crowd and found her husband and children standing near the front. She tapped Mrs. Delacroix on the arm as a farewell and began to make her way through the crowd. The people separated good-humoredly to let her through; two or three people said, in voices just loud enough to be heard across the crowd, "Here comes your Missus, Hutchinson," and "Bill, she made it after all." Mrs. Hutchinson reached her husband, and Mr. Summers, who had been waiting, said cheerfully, "Thought we were going to have to get on without you, Tessie." Mrs. Hutchinson said, grinning, "Wouldn't have me leave m'dishes in the sink, now, would you, Joe?" and soft laughter ran through the crowd as the people stirred back into position after Mrs. Hutchinson's arrival.

"Well, now," Mr. Summers said soberly, "guess we better get started, get this over with, so's we can go back to work. Anybody ain't here?"

"Dunbar," several people said. "Dunbar, Dunbar."

Mr. Summers consulted his list. "Clyde Dunbar," he said. "That's right. He's broke his leg, hasn't he? Who's drawing for him?"

"Me, I guess," a woman said, and Mr. Summers turned to look at her. "Wife draws for her husband," Mr. Summers said. "Don't you have a grown boy to do it for you, Janey?" Although Mr. Summers and everyone else in the village knew the answer perfectly well, it was the business of the official of the lottery to ask such questions formally. Mr. Summers waited with an expression of polite interest while Mrs. Dunbar answered.

"Horace's not but sixteen yet," Mrs. Dunbar said regretfully. "Guess I gotta fill in for the old man this year."

"Right," Mr. Summers said. He made a note on the list he was holding. Then he asked, "Watson boy drawing this year?"

A tall boy in the crowd raised his hand. "Here," he said. "I'm drawing for m'mother and me." He blinked his eyes nervously and ducked his head as several voices in the crowd said things like "Good fellow, Jack," and "Glad to see your mother's got a man to do it."

"Well," Mr. Summers said, "guess that's everyone. Old Man Warner make it?"

"Here," a voice said, and Mr. Summers nodded.

A sudden hush fell on the crowd as Mr. Summers cleared his throat and looked at the list. "All ready?" he called. "Now, I'll read the names — heads of families first — and the men come up and take a paper out of the box. Keep the paper folded in your hand without looking at it until everyone has had a turn. Everything clear?"

The people had done it so many times that they only half listened to the directions; most of them were quiet, wetting their lips, not looking around. Then Mr. Summers raised one hand high and said, "Adams." A man disengaged himself from the crowd and came forward. "Hi, Steve," Mr. Summers said, and Mr. Adams said, "Hi, Joe." They grinned at one another humorlessly and nervously. Then Mr. Adams reached into the black box and took out a folded paper. He held it firmly by one corner as he turned and went hastily back to his place in the crowd, where he stood a little apart from his family, not looking down at his hand.

"Allen," Mr. Summers said. "Anderson. . . . Bentham."

"Seems like there's no time at all between

lotteries any more,'' Mrs. Delacroix said to Mrs. Graves in the back row. ''Seems like we got through with the last one only last week.''

''Time sure goes fast,'' Mrs. Graves said.

''Clark. . . . Delacroix.''

''There goes my old man,'' Mrs. Delacroix said. She held her breath while her husband went forward.

''Dunbar,'' Mr. Summers said, and Mrs. Dunbar went steadily to the box while one of the women said, ''Go on, Janey,'' and another said, ''There she goes.''

''We're next,'' Mrs. Graves said. She watched while Mr. Graves came around from the side of the box, greeted Mr. Summers gravely, and selected a slip of paper from the box. By now, all through the crowd there were men holding the small folded papers in their large hands, turning them over and over nervously. Mrs. Dunbar and her two sons stood together, Mrs. Dunbar holding the slip of paper.

''Harburt. . . . Hutchinson.''

''Get up there, Bill,'' Mrs. Hutchinson said, and the people near her laughed.

''Jones.''

''They do say,'' Mr. Adams said to Old Man Warner, who stood next to him, ''that over in the north village they're talking of giving up the lottery.''

Old Man Warner snorted. ''Pack of crazy fools,'' he said. ''Listening to the young folks, nothing's good enough for *them*. Next thing you know, they'll be wanting to go back to living in caves, nobody work any more, live *that* way for a while. Used to be a saying about 'Lottery in June, corn be heavy soon.' First thing you know, we'd all be eating stewed chickweek and acorns. There's *always* been a lottery," he added petulantly. "Bad enough to see young Joe Summers up there joking with everybody."

"Some places have already quit lotteries," Mrs. Adams said.

"Nothing but trouble in *that,*" Old Man Warner said stoutly. "Pack of young fools."

"Martin." And Bobby Martin watched his father go forward. "Overdyke. . . . Percy."

"I wish they'd hurry," Mrs. Dunbar said to her older son. "I wish they'd hurry."

"They're almost through," her son said.

"You get ready to run tell Dad," Mrs. Dunbar said.

Mr. Summers called his own name and then stepped forward precisely and selected a slip from the box. Then he called, "Warner."

"Seventy-seventh year I been in the lottery," Old Man Warner said as he went through the crowd. "Seventy-seventh time."

"Watson." The tall boy came awkwardly through the crowd. Someone said, "Don't be nervous, Jack," and Mr. Summers said, "Take your time, son."

"Zanini."

After that, there was a long pause, a breathless pause, until Mr. Summers, holding his slip of paper in the air, said, "All right, fellows." For a minute, no one moved, and then all the slips of paper were opened. Suddenly, all the women began to speak at once, saying, "Who is it?" "Who's got it?" "Is it the Dunbars?" "Is it the Watsons?" Then the voices began to say, "It's Hutchinson. It's Bill," "Bill Hutchinson's got it."

"Go tell your father," Mrs. Dunbar said to her older son.

People began to look around to see the Hutchinsons. Bill Hutchinson was standing quiet, staring down at the paper in his hand. Suddenly, Tessie Hutchinson shouted to Mr. Summers, "You didn't give him time enough to take any paper he wanted. I saw you. It wasn't fair!"

"Be a good sport, Tessie," Mrs. Delacroix called, and Mrs. Graves said, "All of us took the same chance."

"Shut up, Tessie," Bill Hutchinson said.

"Well, everyone," Mr. Summers said, "that was done pretty fast, and now we've got to be hurrying a little more to get done in time." He consulted his next list. "Bill," he said, "you draw for the Hutchinson family. You got any other households in the Hutchinsons?"

"There's Don and Eva," Mrs. Hutchinson

yelled. "Make *them* take their chance!"

"Daughters draw with their husbands' families, Tessie," Mr. Summers said gently. "You know that as well as anyone else."

"It wasn't *fair,*" Tessie said.

"I guess not, Joe," Bill Hutchinson said regretfully. "My daughter draws with her husband's family, that's only fair. And I've got no other family except the kids."

"Then, as far as drawing for families is concerned, it's you," Mr. Summers said in explanation, "and as far as drawing for households is concerned, that's you, too. Right?"

"Right," Bill Hutchinson said.

"How many kids, Bill?" Mr. Summers asked formally.

"Three," Bill Hutchinson said. "There's Bill, Jr., and Nancy, and little Dave. And Tessie and me."

"All right, then," Mr. Summers said. "Harry, you got their tickets back?"

Mr. Graves nodded and held up the slips of paper. "Put them in the box, then," Mr. Summers directed. "Take Bill's and put it in."

"I think we ought to start over," Mrs. Hutchinson said, as quietly as she could. "I tell you it wasn't *fair*. You didn't give him time enough to choose. *Every*body saw that."

Mr. Graves had selected the five slips and put them in the box, and he dropped all the papers but those onto the ground, where the breeze caught them and lifted them off.

"Listen, everybody," Mrs. Hutchinson was saying to the people around her.

"Ready, Bill?" Mr. Summers asked, and Bill Hutchinson, with one quick glance around at his wife and children, nodded.

"Remember," Mr. Summers said, "take the slips and keep them folded until each person has taken one. Harry, you help little Dave." Mr. Graves took the hand of the little boy, who came willingly with him up to the box. "Take a paper out of the box, Davy," Mr. Summers said. Davy put his hand into the box and laughed. "Take just *one* paper," Mr. Summers said. "Harry, you hold it for him." Mr. Graves took the child's hand and removed the folded paper from the tight fist and held it while little Dave stood next to him and looked up at him wonderingly.

"Nancy next," Mr. Summers said. Nancy was twelve, and her school friends breathed heavily as she went forward, switching her skirt, and took a slip daintily from the box. "Bill, Jr.," Mr. Summers said, and Billy, his face red and his feet overlarge, nearly knocked the box over as he got a paper out. "Tessie," Mr. Summers said. She hesitated for a minute, looking around defiantly, and then set her lips and went up to the box. She snatched a paper out and held it behind her.

"Bill," Mr. Summers said, and Bill Hutchinson reached into the box and felt around, bringing his hand out at last with the slip of paper in it.

The crowd was quiet. A girl whispered, "I hope it's not Nancy," and the sound of the whisper reached the edges of the crowd.

"It's not the way it used to be," Old Man Warner said clearly. "People ain't the way they used to be."

"All right," Mr. Summers said. "Open the papers. Harry, you open little Dave's."

Mr. Graves opened the slip of paper and there was a general sigh through the crowd as he held it up and everyone could see that it was blank. Nancy and Bill, Jr., opened theirs at the same time, and both beamed and laughed, turning around to the crowd and holding their slips of paper above their heads.

"Tessie," Mr. Summers said. There was a pause, and then Mr. Summers looked at Bill Hutchinson, and Bill unfolded his paper and showed it. It was blank.

"It's Tessie," Mr. Summers said, and his voiced was hushed. "Show us her paper, Bill."

Bill Hutchinson went over to his wife and forced the slip of paper out of her hand. It had a black spot on it, the black spot Mr. Summers had made the night before with the heavy pencil in the coal-company office. Bill Hutchinson held it up, and there was a stir in the crowd.

"All right, folks," Mr. Summers said. "Let's finish quickly."

Although the villagers had forgotten the ritual and lost the original black box, they still remembered to use stones. The pile of stones the boys had made earlier was ready; there were stones on the ground with the blowing scraps of paper that had come out of the box. Mrs. Delacroix selected a stone so large she had to pick it up with both hands and turned to Mrs. Dunbar. "Come on," she said. "Hurry up."

Mrs. Dunbar had small stones in both hands, and she said, gasping for breath, "I can't run at all. You'll have to go ahead and I'll catch up with you."

The children had stones already, and someone gave little Davy Hutchinson a few pebbles.

Tessie Hutchinson was in the center of a cleared space by now, and she held her hands out desperately as the villagers moved in on her. "It isn't fair," she said. A stone hit her on the side of the head.

Old Man Warner was saying, "Come on, come on, everyone." Steve Adams was in the front of the crowd of villagers, with Mrs. Graves beside him.

"It isn't fair, it isn't right," Mrs. Hutchinson screamed, and then they were upon her.

Blackberry Winter

Robert Penn Warren

It was getting into June and past eight o'clock in the morning, but there was a fire — even if it wasn't a big fire, just a fire of chunks — on the hearth of the big stone fireplace in the living room. I was standing on the hearth, almost into the chimney, hunched over the fire, working my bare toes slowly on the warm stone. I relished the heat which made the skin of my bare legs warp and creep and tingle, even as I called to my mother, who was somewhere back in the dining room or kitchen, and said: "But it's June, I don't have to put them on!"

"You put them on if you are going out," she called.

I tried to assess the degree of authority and conviction in the tone, but at that distance it was hard to decide. I tried to analyze the tone, and then I thought what a fool I had been to start out the back door and let her see that I was barefoot. If I had gone out the front door or the side door she would never have known, not till dinner time anyway, and by then the day would have been half gone and I would have been all over the farm to see what the storm had done and down to the creek to see the flood. But it had never crossed my mind that they would try to stop you from going barefoot in June, no matter if there had been a gully-washer and a cold spell.

Nobody had ever tried to stop me in June as long as I could remember, and when you are nine years old, what you remember seems forever; for you remember everything and everything is important and stands big and full and fills up Time and is so solid that you can walk around and around it like a tree and look at it. You are aware that time passes, that there is a movement in time, but that is not what Time is. Time is not a movement, a flowing, a wind then, but is, rather, a kind of climate in which things are, and when a thing happens it begins to live and keeps on living and stands solid in Time like the tree that you can walk around. And if there is a movement, the movement is not Time itself, any more than a breeze is climate, and all the breeze does is to shake a little the leaves on the tree which is alive and solid. When you are nine, you know that there are things that you don't know, but you know that when you know something you know it. You know how a thing has been and you know that you can go barefoot in June. You do not understand that voice from back in the kitchen which says that you cannot go barefoot outdoors and run to see what has happened and rub your feet over the wet shivery grass and make the perfect mark of your foot in the smooth, creamy, red mud and then muse upon it as though you had suddenly come upon that single mark on the glistening auroral beach of the world. You have never seen a beach, but you have read the book and how the footprint was there.

The voice had said what it had said, and I looked savagely at the black stockings and the strong, scuffed brown shoes which I had brought from my closet as far as the hearth rug. I called once more, "But it's June," and waited.

"It's June," the voice replied from far away, "but it's blackberry winter."

I had lifted my head to reply to that, to make one more test of what was in that tone, when I happened to see the man.

The fireplace in the living room was at the end; for the stone chimney was built, as in so many of the farmhouses in Tennessee, at the end of a gable, and there was a window on each side of the chimney. Out of the window on the north side of the fireplace I could see the man. When I saw the man I did not call out what I had intended, but, engrossed by the strangeness of the sight, watched him, still far off, come along the path by the edge of the woods.

What was strange was that there should be a man there at all. That path went along the yard fence, between the fence and the woods which came right down to the yard, and then on back past the chicken runs and on by the woods until it was lost to sight where the woods bulged out and cut off the back field. There the path disappeared into the woods. It led on back, I knew, through the woods and to the swamp, skirted the swamp where the big trees gave way to sycamores and water oaks and willows and tangled cane, and then led on to the river. Nobody ever went back there except people who wanted to gig frogs in the swamp or to fish in the river or to hunt in the woods, and those people, if they didn't have a standing permission from my father, always stopped to ask permission to cross the farm. But the man whom I now saw wasn't, I could tell even at that distance, a sportsman. And what would a sportsman have been doing down there after a storm? Besides, he was coming from the river, and nobody had gone down there that morning. I knew that for a fact, because if anybody had passed, certainly if a stranger had passed, the dogs would have made a racket and would have been out on him. But this man was coming up from the river and had come up through the woods. I suddenly had a vision of him moving up the grassy path in the woods, in the green twilight under the big trees, not making any sound on the path, while now and then, like drops off the eaves, a big drop of water would fall from a leaf or bough and strike a stiff oak leaf lower down with a small, hollow sound like a drop of water hitting tin. That sound, in the silence of the woods, would be very significant.

When you are a boy and stand in the stillness of woods, which can be so still that your heart almost stops beating and makes you want to stand there in the green twilight until you feel your very feet sinking into and clutching the earth like roots and your body breathing slow through its pores like the leaves — when you stand there and wait for the next drop to drop with its small, flat sound to a lower leaf, that sound seems to measure out something, to put an end to something, to begin something, and you cannot wait for it to happen and are afraid it will not happen, and then when it has happened, you are waiting again, almost afraid.

But the man whom I saw coming through the woods in my mind's eye did not pause and wait, growing into the ground and breathing with the enormous, soundless breathing of the leaves. Instead, I saw him moving in the green twilight inside my head as he was moving at that very moment along the path by the edge of the woods, coming toward the house. He was moving steadily, but not fast, with his shoulders hunched a little and his head thrust forward, like a man who has come a long way and has a long way to go. I shut my eyes for a couple of seconds, thinking that when I opened them he would not be there at all. There was no place for him to have come from, and there was no reason for him to come where he was coming, toward our house. But I opened my eyes, and there he was, and he was coming steadily along the side of the woods. He was not yet even with the back chicken yard.

"Mama," I called.

"You put them on," the voice said.

"There's a man coming," I called, "out back."

She did not reply to that, and I guessed that she had gone to the kitchen window to look. She would be looking at the man and wondering who he was and what he wanted, the way you always do in the country, and if I went back there now she would not notice right off whether or not I was barefoot. So I went back to the kitchen.

She was standing by the window. "I don't recognize him," she said, not looking around at me.

"Where could he be coming from?" I asked.

"I don't know," she said.

"What would he be doing down at the river? At night? In the storm?"

She studied the figure out the window, then said, "Oh, I reckon maybe he cut across from the Dunbar place."

That was, I realized, a perfectly rational

explanation. He had not been down at the river in the storm, at night. He had come over this morning. You could cut across from the Dunbar place if you didn't mind breaking through a lot of elder and sassafras and blackberry bushes which had about taken over the old cross path, which nobody ever used any more. That satisfied me for a moment, but only for a moment. "Mama," I asked, "what would he be doing over at the Dunbar place last night?"

Then she looked at me, and I knew I had made a mistake, for she was looking at my bare feet. "You haven't got your shoes on," she said.

But I was saved by the dogs. That instant there was a bark which I recognized as Sam, the collie, and then a heavier, churning kind of bark which was Bully, and I saw a streak of white as Bully tore round the corner of the back porch and headed out for the man. Bully was a big, bone-white bull dog, the kind of dog that they used to call a farm bull dog but that you don't see any more, heavy chested and heavy headed, but with pretty long legs. He could take a fence as light as a hound. He had just cleared the white paling fence toward the woods when my mother ran out to the back porch and began calling, "Here you, Bully! Here you!"

Bully stopped in the path, waiting for the man, but he gave a few more of those deep, gargling, savage barks that reminded you of something down a stone-lined well. The red clay mud, I saw, was splashed up over his white chest and looked exciting, like blood.

The man, however, had not stopped walking even when Bully took the fence and started at him. He had kept right on coming. All he had done was to switch a little paper parcel which he carried from the right hand to the left, and then reach into his pants pocket to get something. Then I saw the glitter and knew that he had a knife in his hand, probably the kind of mean knife just made for devilment and nothing else, with a blade as long as the blade of a frog-sticker, which will snap out ready when you press a button in the handle. That knife must have had a button in the handle, or else how could he have had the blade out glittering so quick and with just one hand?

Pulling his knife against the dogs was a funny thing to do, for Bully was a big, powerful brute and fast, and Sam was all right. If those dogs had meant business, they might have knocked him down and ripped him before he got a stroke in. He ought to have picked up a heavy stick, something to take a swipe at them with and something which they could see and respect when they came at him. But he apparently did not know much about dogs. He just held the knife blade close against the right leg, low down, and kept on moving down the path.

Then my mother had called, and Bully had stopped. So the man let the blade of the knife snap back into the handle, and dropped it into his pocket, and kept on coming. Many women would have been afraid with the strange man who they knew had that knife in his pocket. That is, if they were alone in the house with nobody but a nine-year-old boy. And my mother was alone, for my father had gone off, and Dellie, the cook, was down at her cabin because she wasn't feeling well. But my mother wasn't afraid. She wasn't a big woman, but she was clear and brisk about everything she did and looked everybody and everything right in the eye from her own blue eyes in her tanned face. She had been the first woman in the county to ride a horse astride (that was back when she was a girl and long before I was born), and I have seen her snatch up a pump gun and go out and knock a chicken hawk out of the air like a busted skeet when he came over her chicken yard. She was a steady and self-reliant woman, and when I think of her now after all the years she has been dead, I think of her brown hands, not big, but somewhat square for a woman's hands, with square-cut nails. They looked, as a matter of fact, more like a young boy's hands than a grown woman's. But back then it never crossed my mind that she would ever be dead.

She stood on the back porch and watched the man enter the back gate, where the dogs

(Bully had leaped back into the yard) were dancing and muttering and giving sidelong glances back to my mother to see if she meant what she had said. The man walked right by the dogs, almost brushing them, and didn't pay them any attention. I could see now that he wore old khaki pants, and a dark wool coat with stripes in it, and a gray felt hat. He had on a gray shirt with blue stripes in it, and no tie. But I could see a tie, blue and reddish, sticking in his side coat-pocket. Everything was wrong about what he wore. He ought to have been wearing blue jeans or overalls, and a straw hat or an old black felt hat, and the coat, granting that he might have been wearing a wool coat and not a jumper, ought not to have had those stripes. Those clothes, despite the fact that they were old enough and dirty enough for any tramp, didn't belong there in our back yard, coming down the path, in Middle Tennessee, miles away from any big town, and even a mile off the pike.

When he got almost to the steps, without having said anything, my mother, very matter-of-factly, said, "Good morning."

"Good morning," he said, and stopped and looked her over. He did not take off his hat, and under the brim you could see the perfectly unmemorable face, which wasn't old and wasn't young, or thick or thin. It was grayish and covered with about three days of stubble. The eyes were a kind of nondescript, muddy hazel, or something like that, rather bloodshot. His teeth, when he opened his mouth, showed yellow and uneven. A couple of them had been knocked out. You knew that they had been knocked out, because there was a scar, not very old, there on the lower lip just beneath the gap.

"Are you hunting work?" my mother asked him.

"Yes," he said — not "yes, mam" — and still did not take off his hat.

"I don't know about my husband, for he isn't here," she said, and didn't mind a bit telling the tramp, or whoever he was, with the mean knife in his pocket, that no man was around, "but I can give you a few things to do. The storm has drowned a lot of my chicks. Three coops of them. You can gather them up and bury them. Bury them deep so the dogs won't get at them. In the woods. And fix the coops the wind blew over. And down yonder beyond that pen by the edge of the woods are some drowned poults. They got out and I couldn't get them in. Even after it started to rain hard. Poults haven't got any sense."

"What are them things — poults?" he demanded, and spat on the brick walk. He rubbed his foot over the spot, and I saw that he wore a black, pointed-toe low shoe, all cracked and broken. It was a crazy kind of shoe to be wearing in the country.

"Oh, they're young turkeys," my mother

was saying. "And they haven't got any sense. I oughtn't to try to raise them around here with so many chickens, anyway. They don't thrive near chickens, even in separate pens. And I won't give up my chickens." Then she stopped herself and resumed briskly on the note of business. "When you finish that, you can fix my flower beds. A lot of trash and mud and gravel has washed down. Maybe you can save some of my flowers if you are careful."

"Flowers," the man said, in a low, impersonal voice which seemed to have a wealth of meaning, but a meaning which I could not fathom. As I think back on it, it probably was not pure contempt. Rather, it was a kind of impersonal and distant marveling that he should be on the verge of grubbing in a flower bed. He said the word, and then looked off across the yard.

"Yes, flowers," my mother replied with some asperity, as though she would have nothing said or implied against flowers. "And they were very fine this year." Then she stopped and looked at the man. "Are you hungry?" she demanded.

"Yeah," he said.

"I'll fix you something," she said, "before you get started." She turned to me. "Show him where he can wash up," she commanded, and went into the house.

I took the man to the end of the porch where a pump was and where a couple of wash pans sat on a low shelf for people to use before they went into the house. I stood there while he laid down his little parcel wrapped in newspaper and took off his hat and looked around for a nail to hang it on. He poured the water and plunged his hands into it. They were big hands, and strong looking, but they did not have the creases and the earth-color of the hands of men who work outdoors. But they were dirty, with black dirt ground into the skin and under the nails. After he had washed his hands, he poured another basin of water and washed his face. He dried his face, and with the towel still dangling in his grasp, stepped over to the mirror on the house wall. He rubbed one hand over the stubble on his face. Then he carefully inspected his face, turning first one side and then the other, and stepped back and settled his striped coat down on his shoulders. He had the movements of a man who has just dressed up to go to church or a party — the way he settled his coat and smoothed it and scanned himself in the mirror.

Then he caught my glance on him. He glared at me for an instant out of the bloodshot eyes, then demanded in a low, harsh voice, "What you looking at?"

"Nothing," I managed to say, and stepped back a step from him.

He flung the towel down, crumpled, on the shelf, and went toward the kitchen door and entered without knocking.

My mother said something to him which I could not catch. I started to go in again, then thought about my bare feet, and decided to go back of the chicken yard, where the man would have to come to pick up the dead chicks. I hung around behind the chicken house until he came out.

He moved across the chicken yard with a fastidious, not quite finicking motion, looking down at the curdled mud flecked with bits of chicken-droppings. The mud curled up over the soles of his black shoes. I stood back from him some six feet and watched him pick up the first of the drowned chicks. He held it up by one foot and inspected it.

There is nothing deader looking than a drowned chick. The feet curl in that feeble, empty way which back when I was a boy, even if I was a country boy who did not mind hog-killing or frog-gigging, made me feel hollow in the stomach. Instead of looking plump and fluffy, the body is stringy and limp with the fluff plastered to it, and the neck is long and loose like a little string of rag. And the eyes have that bluish membrane over them which makes you think of a very old man who is sick about to die.

The man stood there and inspected the chick. Then he looked all around as though he didn't know what to do with it.

"There's a great big old basket in the shed," I said, and pointed to the shed attached to the chicken house.

He inspected me as though he had just discovered my presence, and moved toward the shed.

"There's a spade there, too," I added.

He got the basket and began to pick up the other chicks, picking each one up slowly by a foot and then flinging it into the basket with a nasty, snapping motion. Now and then he would look at me out of the bloodshot eyes. Every time he seemed on the verge of saying something, but he did not. Perhaps he was building up to say something to me, but I did not wait that long. His way of looking at me made me so uncomfortable that I left the chicken yard.

Besides, I had just remembered that the creek was in flood, over the bridge, and that people were down there watching it. So I cut across the farm toward the creek. When I got to the big tobacco field I saw that it had not suffered much. The land lay right and not many tobacco plants had washed out of the ground. But I knew that a lot of tobacco round the country had been washed right out. My father had said so at breakfast.

My father was down at the bridge. When I came out of the gap in the osage hedge into the road, I saw him sitting on his mare over the heads of the other men who were standing around, admiring the flood. The creek was big here, even in low water; for only a couple of miles away it ran into the river, and when a real flood came, the red water got over the pike where it dipped down to the bridge, which was an iron bridge, and high over the floor and even the side railings of the bridge. Only the upper iron work would show, with the water boiling and frothing red and white around it. That creek rose so fast and so heavy because a few miles back it came down out of the hills, where the gorges filled up with water in no time when a rain came. The creek ran in a deep bed with limestone bluffs along both sides until it got within three quarters of a mile of the bridge, and when it came out from between those bluffs in flood it was boiling and hissing and steaming like water from a fire hose.

Whenever there was a flood, people from half the county would come down to see the sight. After a gully-washer there would not be any work to do anyway. If it didn't ruin your crop, you couldn't plow and you felt like taking a holiday to celebrate. If it did ruin your crop, there wasn't anything to do except to try to take your mind off the mortgage, if you were rich enough to have a mortgage, and if you couldn't afford a mortgage you needed something to take your mind off how hungry you would be by Christmas. So people would come down to the bridge and look at the flood. It made something different from the run of days.

There would not be much talking after the

first few minutes of trying to guess how high the water was this time. The men and kids just stood around, or sat their horses or mules, as the case might be, or stood up in the wagon beds. They looked at the strangeness of the flood for an hour or two, and then somebody would say that he had better be getting on home to dinner and would start walking down the gray, puddled limestone pike, or would touch heel to his mount and start off. Everybody always knew what it would be like when he got down to the bridge, but people always came. It was like church or a funeral. They always came, that is, if it was summer and the flood unexpected. Nobody ever came down in winter to see high water.

When I came out of the gap in the bodock hedge, I saw the crowd, perhaps fifteen or twenty men and a lot of kids, and saw my father sitting his mare, Nellie Gray. He was a tall, limber man and carried himself well. I was always proud to see him sit a horse, he was so quiet and straight, and when I stepped through the gap of the hedge that morning, the first thing that happened was, I remember, the warm feeling I always had when I saw him up on a horse, just sitting. I did not go toward him, but skirted the crowd on the far side, to get a look at the creek. For one thing, I was not sure what he would say about the fact that I was barefoot. But the first thing I knew, I heard his voice calling, "Seth!"

I went toward him, moving apologetically past the men, who bent their large, red or thin, sallow faces above me. I knew some of the men, and knew their names, but because those I knew were there in a crowd, mixed with the strange faces, they seemed foreign to me, and not friendly. I did not look up at my father until I was almost within touching distance of his heel. Then I looked up and tried to read his face, to see if he was angry about my being barefoot. Before I could decide anything from that impassive, high-boned face, he had leaned over and reached a hand to me. "Grab on," he commanded.

I grabbed on and gave a little jump, and he said, "Up-see-daisy!" and whisked me, light as a feather, up to the pommel of his McClellan saddle.

"You can see better up here," he said, slid back on the cantle a little to make me more comfortable, and then, looking over my head at the swollen, tumbling water, seemed to forget all about me. But his right hand was laid on my side, just above my thigh, to steady me.

I was sitting there as quiet as I could, feeling the faint stir of my father's chest against my shoulders as it rose and fell with his breath, when I saw the cow. At first, looking up the creek, I thought it was just another big piece of driftwood steaming down the creek in the ruck of water, but all at once a pretty good-size boy who had climbed part way up a telephone pole by the pike so that he could see better yelled out, "Golly-damn, look at that-air cow!"

Everybody looked. It was a cow all right, but it might just as well have been driftwood; for it was dead as a chunk, rolling and roiling down the creek, appearing and disappearing, feet up or head up, it didn't matter which.

The cow started up the talk again. Somebody wondered whether it would hit one of the clear places under the top girder of the bridge and get through or whether it would get tangled in the drift and trash that had piled against the upright girders and braces. Somebody remembered how about ten years before so much driftwood had piled up on the bridge that it was knocked off its foundations. Then the cow hit. It hit the edge of the drift against one of the girders, and hung there. For a few seconds it seemed as though it might tear loose, but then we saw that it was really caught. It bobbed and heaved on its side there in a slow, grinding, uneasy fashion. It had a yoke around its neck, the kind made out of a forked limb to keep a jumper behind fence.

"She shore jumped one fence," one of the men said.

And another: "Well, she done jumped her last one, fer a fack."

Then they began to wonder about whose cow it might be. They decided it must belong to Milt Alley. They said that he had a cow that was a jumper, and kept her in a fenced-in piece of ground up the creek. I had never seen Milt Alley, but I knew who he was. He was a squatter and lived up the hills a way, on a shirt-tail patch of set-on-edge land, in a cabin. He was pore white trash. He had lots of children. I had seen the children at school, when they came. They were thin-faced, with straight, sticky-looking, dough-colored hair, and they smelled something like old sour buttermilk, not because they drank so much buttermilk but because that is the sort of smell which children out of those cabins tend to have. The big Alley boy drew dirty pictures and showed them to the little boys at school.

That was Milt Alley's cow. It looked like the kind of cow he would have, a scrawny, old, sway-backed cow, with a yoke around her neck. I wondered if Milt Alley had another cow.

"Poppa," I said, "do you think Milt Alley has got another cow?"

"You say 'Mr. Alley,' " my father said quietly.

"Do you think he has?"

"No telling," my father said.

Then a big gangly boy, about fifteen, who was sitting on a scraggly little old mule with a piece of croker sack thrown across the saw-tooth spine, and who had been staring at the cow, suddenly said to nobody in particular, "Reckin anybody ever et drownt cow?"

He was the kind of boy who might just as well as not have been the son of Milt Alley, with his faded and patched overalls ragged at the bottom of the pants and the mud-stiff brogans hanging off his skinny, bare ankles at the level of the mule's belly. He had said what he did, and then looked embarrassed and sullen when all the eyes swung at him. He hadn't meant to say it, I am pretty sure now. He would have been too proud to say it, just as Milt Alley would have been too proud. He had just been thinking out loud, and the words had popped out.

There was an old man standing there on the pike, an old man with a white beard. "Son," he said to the embarrassed and sullen boy on the mule, "you live long enough and you'll find a man will eat anything when the time comes."

"Time gonna come fer some folks this year," another man said.

"Son," the old man said, "in my time I et things a man don't like to think on. I was a sojer and I rode with Gin'l Forrest, and them things we et when the time come. I tell you. I et meat what got up and run when you taken out yore knife to cut a slice to put on the fire. You had to knock it down with a carbene butt, it was so active. That-air meat would jump like a bullfrog, it was so full of skippers."

But nobody was listening to the old man. The boy on the mule turned his sullen sharp face from him, dug a heel into the side of the mule and went off up the pike with a motion which made you think that any second you would hear mule bones clashing inside that lank and scrofulous hide.

"Cy Dundee's boy," a man said, and nodded toward the figure going up the pike on the mule.

"Reckin Cy Dundee's young-uns seen times they'd settle fer drownt cow," another man said.

The old man with the beard peered at them both from his weak, slow eyes, first at one and then at the other. "Live long enough," he said, "and a man will settle for what he kin git."

Then there was silence again, with the people looking at the red, foam-flecked water.

My father lifted the bridle rein in his left hand, and the mare turned and walked around the group and up the pike. We rode on up to our big gate, where my father dismounted to open it and let me myself ride Nellie Gray through. When he got to the lane that led off from the drive about two hundred yards from our house, my father said, "Grab on." I grabbed on, and he let me down to the ground. "I'm going to ride down and look at my corn," he said. "You go on." He took the lane, and I stood there on the drive and watched him ride off. He was wearing cowhide boots and an old hunting coat, and I thought that that made him look very military, like a picture. That and the way he rode.

I did not go to the house. Instead, I went by the vegetable garden and crossed behind the stables, and headed down for Dellie's cabin. I wanted to go down and play with Jebb, who was Dellie's little boy about two years older than I was. Besides, I was cold. I shivered as I walked, and I had gooseflesh. The mud which crawled up between my toes with every step I took was like ice. Dellie would have a fire, but she wouldn't make me put on shoes and stockings.

Dellie's cabin was of logs, with one side, because it was on a slope, set on limestone chunks, with a little porch attached to it, and had a little whitewashed fence around it and a gate with plow-points on a wire to clink when somebody came in, and had two big white oaks in the yard and some flowers and a nice privy in the back with some honeysuckle growing over it. Dellie and Old Jebb, who was Jebb's father and who lived with Dellie and had lived with her for twenty-five years even if they never had got married, were careful to keep everything nice around their cabin. They had the name all over the community for being clean and clever Negroes. Dellie and Jebb were what they used to call "white-folks' niggers." There was a big difference between their cabin and the other two cabins farther down where the other tenants lived. My father kept the other cabins weatherproof, but he couldn't undertake to go down and pick up after the litter they strewed. They didn't take the trouble to have a vegetable patch like Dellie and Jebb or to make preserves from wild plum, and jelly from crab apple the way Dellie did. They were shiftless, and my father was always threatening to get shed of them. But he never did. When they finally left, they just up and left on their own, for no reason, to go and be shiftless somewhere else. Then some more came. But meanwhile they lived down there, Matt Rawson and his family, and Sid Turner and his, and I played with their children all over the farm when they weren't working. But when I wasn't around they were mean sometimes to Little Jebb. That was because the other tenants down there were jealous of Dellie and Jebb.

I was so cold that I ran the last fifty yards to Dellie's gate. As soon as I had entered the yard, I saw that the storm had been hard on Dellie's flowers. The yard was, as I have said, on a slight slope, and the water running across had gutted the flower beds and washed out all the good black woods-earth which Dellie had brought in. What little grass there was in the yard was plastered sparsely down on the ground, the way the drainage water had left it. It reminded me of the way the fluff was plastered down on the skin of the drowned chicks that the strange man had been picking up, up in my mother's chicken yard.

I took a few steps up the path to the cabin, and then I saw that the drainage water had washed a lot of trash and filth out from under Dellie's house. Up toward the porch, the ground was not clean any more. Old pieces of rag, two or three rusted cans, pieces of rotten rope, some hunks of old dog dung, broken glass, old paper, and all sorts of things like that had washed out from under Dellie's house to foul her clean yard. It looked just as bad as the yards of the other cabins, or worse. It was worse, as a matter of fact, because it was a surprise. I had never thought of all that filth being under Dellie's house. It was not anything against Dellie that the stuff had been under the cabin. Trash will get under any house. But I did not think of that when I saw the foulness which had washed out on the ground which Dellie sometimes used to sweep with a twig broom to make nice and clean.

I picked my way past the filth, being careful not to get my bare feet on it, and mounted to Dellie's door. When I knocked, I heard her voice telling me to come in.

It was dark inside the cabin, after the daylight, but I could make out Dellie piled up in bed under a quilt, and Little Jebb crouched by the hearth, where a low fire simmered. "Howdy," I said to Dellie, "how you feeling?"

Her big eyes, the whites surprising and

glaring in the black face, fixed on me as I stood there, but she did not reply. It did not look like Dellie, or act like Dellie, who would grumble and bustle around our kitchen, talking to herself, scolding me or Little Jebb, clanking pans, making all sorts of unnecessary noises and mutterings like an old-fashioned black steam thrasher engine when it has got up an extra head of steam and keeps popping the governor and rumbling and shaking on its wheels. But now Dellie just lay up there on the bed, under the patch-work quilt, and turned the black face, which I scarcely recognized, and the glaring white eyes to me.

"How you feeling?" I repeated.

"I'se sick," the voice said croakingly out of the strange black face which was not attached to Dellie's big, squat body, but stuck out from under a pile of tangled bedclothes. Then the voice added: "Mighty sick."

"I'm sorry," I managed to say.

The eyes remained fixed on me for a moment, then they left me and the head rolled back on the pillow. "Sorry," the voice said, in a flat way which wasn't question or statement of anything. It was just the empty word put into the air with no meaning or expression, to float off like a feather or a puff of smoke, while the big eyes, with the whites like the peeled white of hard-boiled eggs, stared at the ceiling.

"Dellie," I said after a minute, "there's a

tramp up at the house. He's got a knife."

She was not listening. She closed her eyes.

I tiptoed over to the hearth where Jebb was and crouched beside him. We began to talk in low voices. I was asking him to get out his train and play train. Old Jebb had put spool wheels on three cigar boxes and put wire links between the boxes to make a train for Jebb. The box that was the locomotive had the top closed and a length of broom stick for a smoke stack. Jebb didn't want to get the train out, but I told him I would go home if he didn't. So he got out the train, and the colored rocks, and fossils of crinoid stems, and other junk he used for the load, and we began to push it around, talking the way we thought trainmen talked, making a chuck-chucking sound under the breath for the noise of the locomotive and now and then uttering low, cautious toots for the whistle. We got so interested in playing train that the toots got louder. Then, before he thought, Jebb gave a good, loud *toot-toot*, blowing for a crossing.

"Come here," the voice said from the bed.

Jebb got up slow from his hands and knees, giving me a sudden, naked, inimical look.

"Come here!" the voice said.

Jebb went to the bed. Dellie propped herself weakly up on one arm, muttering, "Come closer."

Jebb stood closer.

"Last thing I do, I'm gonna do it," Dellie

said. ''Done tole you to be quiet.''

Then she slapped him. It was an awful slap, more awful for the kind of weakness which it came from and brought to focus. I had seen her slap Jebb before, but the slapping had always been the kind of easy slap you would expect from a good-natured, grumbling Negro woman like Dellie. But this was different. It was awful. It was so awful that Jebb didn't make a sound. The tears just popped out and ran down his face, and his breath came sharp, like gasps.

Dellie fell back. ''Cain't even be sick,'' she said to the ceiling. ''Git sick and they won't even let you lay. They tromp all over you. Cain't even be sick.'' Then she closed her eyes.

I went out of the room. I almost ran getting to the door, and I did run across the porch and down the steps and across the yard, not caring whether or not I stepped on the filth which had washed out from under the cabin. I ran almost all the way home. Then I thought about my mother catching me with the bare feet. So I went down to the stables.

I heard a noise in the crib, and opened the door. There was Big Jebb, sitting on an old nail keg, shelling corn into a bushel basket. I went in, pulling the door shut behind me, and crouched on the floor near him. I crouched there for a couple of minutes before either of us spoke, and watched him shelling the corn.

He had very big hands, knotted and grayish at the joints, with calloused palms which seemed to be streaked with rust with the rust coming up between the fingers to show from the back. His hands were so strong and tough that he could take a big ear of corn and rip the grains right off the cob with the palm of his hand, all in one motion, like a machine. "Work long as me," he would say, "and the good Lawd'll give you a hand lak cass-ion won't nuthin' hurt." And his hands did look like cast iron, old cast iron streaked with rust.

He was an old man, up in his seventies, thirty years or more older than Dellie, but he was strong as a bull. He was a squat sort of man, heavy in the shoulders, with remarkably long arms, the kind of build they say the river natives have on the Congo from paddling so much in their boats. He had a round bullet-head, set on powerful shoulders. His skin was very black, and the thin hair on his head was now grizzled like tufts of old cotton batting. He had small eyes and a flat nose, not big, and the kindest and wisest old face in the world, the blunt, sad, wise face of an old animal peering tolerantly out on the goings-on of the merely human creatures before him. He was a good man, and I loved him next to my mother and father. I crouched there on the floor of the crib and watched him shell corn with the rusty cast-iron hands, while he looked down at me out of the little eyes set in the blunt face.

"Dellie says she's might sick," I said.

"Yeah," he said.

"What's she sick from?"

"Woman-mizry," he said.

"What's woman-mizry?"

"Hit comes on 'em," he said. "Hit just comes on 'em when the time comes."

"What is it?"

"Hit is the change," he said. "Hit is the change of life and time."

"What changes?"

"You too young to know."

"Tell me."

"Time come and you find out everything."

I knew that there was no use in asking him any more. When I asked him things and he said that, I always knew that he would not tell me. So I continued to crouch there and watch him. Now that I had sat there a little while, I was cold again.

"What you shiver fer?" he asked me.

"I'm cold. I'm cold because it's blackberry winter," I said.

"Maybe 'tis and maybe 'tain't," he said.

"My mother says it is."

"Ain't sayen Miss Sallie doan know and ain't sayen she do. But folks doan know everything."

"Why isn't it blackberry winter?"

"Too late fer blackberry winter. Blackberries done bloomed."

"She said it was."

"Blackberry winter just a leetle cold spell. Hit come and then hit go away, and hit is growed summer of a sudden lak a gunshot. Ain't no tellen hit will go way this time."

"It's June," I said.

"June," he replied with great contempt. "That what folks say. What June mean? Maybe hit is come cold to stay."

"Why?"

"Cause this-here old yearth is tahrd. Hit is tahrd and ain't gonna perduce. Lawd let hit come rain one time forty days and forty nights, 'cause He was tahrd of sinful folks. Maybe this-here old yearth say to the Lawd, Lawd, I done plum tahrd, Lawd, lemme rest. And Lawd say, Yearth, you done yore best, you give 'em cawn and you give 'em taters, and all they think on is they gut, and, Yearth, you kin take a rest."

"What will happen?"

"Folks will eat up everything. The yearth won't perduce no more. Folks cut down all the trees and burn 'em 'cause they cold, and the yearth won't grow no more. I been tellen 'em. I been tellen folks. Sayen, maybe this year, hit is the time. But they doan listen to me, how the yearth is tahrd. Maybe this year they find out."

"Will everything die?"

"Everything and everbody, hit will be so."

"This year?"

"Ain't no tellen. Maybe this year."

"My mother said it is blackberry winter," I said confidently, and got up.

"Ain't sayen nuthin' agin Miss Sallie," he said.

I went to the door of the crib. I was really cold now. Running, I had got up a sweat and now I was worse.

I hung on the door, looking at Jebb, who was shelling corn again.

"There's a tramp came to the house," I said. I had almost forgotten the tramp.

"Yeah."

"He came by the back way. What was he doing down there in the storm?"

"They comes and they goes," he said, "and ain't no tellen."

"He had a mean knife."

"The good ones and the bad ones, they comes and they goes. Storm or sun, light or dark. They is folks and they comes and they goes lak folks."

I hung on the door, shivering.

He studied me a moment, then said, "You git on to the house. You ketch yore death. Then what yore mammy say?"

I hesitated.

"You git," he said.

When I came to the back yard, I saw that my father was standing by the back porch and the tramp was walking toward him. They began talking before I reached them, but I got there just as my father was saying, "I'm sorry, but I haven't got any work. I got all the hands on the place I need now. I won't need any extra until wheat thrashing."

The stranger made no reply, just looked at my father.

My father took out his leather coin purse, and got out a half-dollar. He held it toward the man. "This is for half a day," he said.

The man looked at the coin, and then at my father, making no motion to take the money. But that was the right amount. A dollar a day was what you paid them back in 1910. And the man hadn't even worked half a day.

Then the man reached out and took the coin. He dropped it into the right side pocket of his coat. Then he said, very slowly and without feeling: "I didn't want to work on your — —farm."

He used the word which they would have frailed me to death for using.

I looked at my father's face and it was streaked white under the sunburn. Then he said, "Get off this place. Get off this place or I won't be responsible."

The man dropped his right hand into his pants pocket. It was the pocket where he kept the knife. I was just about to yell to my father about the knife when the hand came back out with nothing in it. The man gave a kind of twisted grin, showing where the teeth had been knocked out above the new scar. I thought that instant how maybe he had tried before to pull a knife on somebody else and had got his teeth knocked out.

So now he just gave that twisted, sickish grin out of the unmemorable, grayish face, and then spat on the brick path. The glob landed just about six inches from the toe of my father's right boot. My father looked down at it, and so did I. I thought that if the glob had hit my father's boot something would have happened. I looked down and saw the bright glob, and on one side of it my father's strong cowhide boots, with the brass eyelets and the leather thongs, heavy boots splashed with good red mud and set solid on the bricks, and on the other side the pointed-toe, broken, black shoes, on which the mud looked so sad and out of place. Then I saw one of the black shoes move a little, just a twitch first, then a real step backward.

The man moved in a quarter circle to the end of the porch, with my father's steady gaze upon him all the while. At the end of the porch, the man reached up to the shelf where the wash pans were to get his little newspaper-wrapped parcel. Then he disappeared around the corner of the house and my father mounted the porch and went into the kitchen without a word.

I followed around the house to see what the man would do. I wasn't afraid of him now, no matter if he did have the knife. When I got around in front, I saw him going out the yard gate and starting up the drive toward the pike.

So I ran to catch up with him. He was sixty yards or so up the drive before I caught up.

I did not walk right up even with him at first, but trailed him, the way a kid will, about seven or eight feet behind, now and then running two or three steps in order to hold my place against his longer stride. When I first came up behind him, he turned to give me a look, just a meaningless look, and then fixed his eyes up the drive and kept on walking.

When we had got around the bend in the drive which cut the house from sight, and were going along by the edge of the woods, I decided to come up even with him. I ran a few steps, and was by his side, or almost, but some feet off to the right. I walked along in this position for a while, and he never noticed me. I walked along until we got within sight of the big gate that let on the pike.

Then I said: "Where did you come from?"

He looked at me then with a look which seemed almost surprised that I was there. Then he said, "It ain't none of yore business."

We went on another fifty feet.

Then I said, "Where are you going?"

He stopped, studied me dispassionately for a moment, then suddenly took a step toward me and leaned his face down at me. The lips jerked back, but not in any grin, to show where the teeth were knocked out and to make the scar on the lower lip come white with the tension.

He said: "Stop following me. You don't stop following me and I cut yore throat, you little son-of-a-bitch."

Then he went on to the gate, and up the pike.

That was thirty-five years ago. Since that time my father and mother have died. I was still a boy, but a big boy, when my father got cut on the blade of a mowing machine and died of lockjaw. My mother sold the place and went to town to live with her sister. But she never took hold after my father's death, and she died within three years, right in middle life. My aunt always said, "Sallie just died of a broken heart, she was so devoted." Dellie is dead, too, but she died, I heard, quite a long time after we sold the farm.

As for Little Jebb, he grew up to be a mean and ficey Negro. He killed another Negro in a fight and got sent to the penitentiary, where he is yet, the last I heard tell. He probably grew up to be mean and ficey from just being picked on so much by the children of the other tenants, who were jealous of Jebb and Dellie for being thrifty and clever and being white-folks' niggers.

Old Jebb lived forever. I saw him ten years ago and he was about a hundred then, and not looking much different. He was living in town then, on relief — that was back in the Depression — when I went to see him. He said to me:

"Too strong to die. When I was a young feller just comen on and seen how things wuz, I prayed the Lawd. I said, O, Lawd, gimme strength and meke me strong fer to do and to in-dure. The Lawd hearkened to my prayer. He give me strength. I was in-duren proud fer being strong and me much man. The Lawd give me my prayer and my strength. But now He done gone off and fergot me and left me alone with my strength. A man doan know what to pray fer, and him mortal."

Jebb is probably living yet, as far as I know.

That is what has happened since the morning when the tramp leaned his face down at me and showed his teeth and said: "Stop following me. You don't stop following me and I cut yore throat, you little son-of-a-bitch." That was what he said, for me not to follow him. But I did follow him, all the years.

Index of Titles and Authors

The publishers hope that this Large Print Book has brought you pleasurable reading. Each title is designed to make the text as easy to see as possible. G. K. Hall Large Print Books are available from your library and your local bookstore. Or you can receive information on upcoming and current Large Print Books by mail and order directly from the publisher. Just send your name and address to:

G. K. Hall & Co.
70 Lincoln Street
Boston, Mass. 02111

A note on the text
Large print edition designed by Cindy Schrom.
Composed in 16 pt Times Roman on a Merganthaler Linotron 202 by Modern Graphics, Inc.